SIZZLING PRAISE FOR THE NOVELS OF
Jasmine Haynes

"Sexy."
—Sensual Romance Reviews

"More than a fast-paced erotic romance, this is a story of family, filled with memorable characters who will keep you engaged in the plot and the great sex. A good read to warm a winter's night."
—Romantic Times

"Bursting with sensuality and eroticism." *—In the Library Reviews*

"The passion is intense, hot, and purely erotic . . . recommended for any reader who likes their stories realistic, hot, captivating, and very, very well written." *—Road to Romance*

"Not your typical romance. This one's going to remain one of my favorites." *—The Romance Studio*

"Jasmine Haynes keeps the plot moving and the love scenes very hot."
—Just Erotic Romance Reviews

"A wonderful novel . . . Try this one—you won't be sorry."
—The Best Reviews

SHOW
AND
TELL

Jasmine Haynes

BERKLEY SENSATION, NEW YORK

THE BERKLEY PUBLISHING GROUP
Published by the Penguin Group
Penguin Group (USA) Inc.
375 Hudson Street, New York, New York 10014, USA
Penguin Group (Canada), 90 Eglinton Avenue East, Suite 700, Toronto, Ontario M4P 2Y3, Canada
(a division of Pearson Penguin Canada Inc.)
Penguin Books Ltd., 80 Strand, London WC2R 0RL, England
Penguin Group Ireland, 25 St. Stephen's Green, Dublin 2, Ireland (a division of Penguin Books Ltd.)
Penguin Group (Australia), 250 Camberwell Road, Camberwell, Victoria 3124, Australia
(a division of Pearson Australia Group Pty. Ltd.)
Penguin Books India Pvt. Ltd., 11 Community Centre, Panchsheel Park, New Delhi—110 017, India
Penguin Group (NZ), 67 Apollo Drive, Rosedale, North Shore 0632, New Zealand
(a division of Pearson New Zealand Ltd.)
Penguin Books (South Africa) (Pty.) Ltd., 24 Sturdee Avenue, Rosebank, Johannesburg 2196,
South Africa

Penguin Books Ltd., Registered Offices: 80 Strand, London WC2R 0RL, England

This book is an original publication of The Berkley Publishing Group.

This is a work of fiction. Names, characters, places, and incidents either are the product of the author's imagination or are used fictitiously, and any resemblance to actual persons, living or dead, business establishments, events, or locales is entirely coincidental. The publisher does not have any control over and does not assume any responsibility for author or third-party websites or their content.

First edition: July 2008

Library of Congress Cataloging-in-Publication Data

Haynes, Jasmine.
    Show and tell \ Jasmine Haynes.— 1st ed.
        p. cm
    ISBN 978-0-425-22158-7
    1. Divorced women—Fiction. I. Title.
    PS3608.A936S56 2008
    813'.6—dc22   2008004814

PRINTED IN THE UNITED STATES OF AMERICA

10 9 8 7 6 5

To my brother Michael
for looking up "persistence" in the dictionary
and seeing my name next to it

ACKNOWLEDGMENTS

Thanks to Jenn Cummings, Terri Schaefer, and Rose Lerma, for endless hours of reading. To Kathy Coatney, for checking up on me. To Christine Zika, for giving me the jumpstart. And to my agent, Lucienne Diver, and my editor, Wendy McCurdy, without whom none of this would be possible.

1

TRINITY Green sagged against the closed door of her condo and sighed. She was an extrovert. She loved people, *thrived* on their company. Yet for some reason, Faith's baby shower had totally exhausted her. She was happy for Faith, thrilled about the baby, a boy, and that Faith had fallen for Connor and he'd fallen for her. It made Trinity's matchmaking heart implode with happiness. Honest to God. That's why she'd planned the shower though Faith had three months to go. She wanted to make sure her best friend in all the world had plenty of time to get the baby things she absolutely must have but didn't receive at the party.

But with all that giddiness and the way Connor (who'd insisted on being there) kept touching Faith and looking at her with such an adoring gaze . . . Trinity didn't know why it gave her a headache, but it did. A migraine, which then gave her an upset stomach. As much as she loved, *loved* Faith, she had to get out.

Thank God Trinity had arranged for the party at a restaurant where all she had to do was pay the bill ahead of time and let the management clean up the banquet room. And Connor had said he'd make sure the truckload of presents got to their house.

Hence the reason she was home three hours earlier than she thought she'd be. Which would give her enough time to plan a perfect dinner for Harper. She'd get out Mama's china and the silver candlesticks, order up a delicious dinner from Vatovola's, and still have time to pamper herself with a soak in the bath. By the time Harper got home from his Sunday golf game at the country club, she'd be scented and perfect, and there was that new negligee she'd bought with him in mind.

Men liked the little gestures that made them feel they were kings of their castles. Their six-month anniversary wasn't until next week and Valentine's Day was almost three weeks away, so he wouldn't be expecting it.

Therefore it was, in a word, perfect. Her migraine was starting to go away.

Trinity hung her coat in the front closet. The entry hall was too small, but the condo was a starter home. At twenty-five hundred square feet, it wasn't conducive to entertaining, especially for Harper's business contacts. All his working capital was tied up in a deal, and her father had fronted them the money. With three bedrooms, two-and-a-half baths, living room, and dining room, they could survive for a while. The kitchen was a problem, however, when the caterers got in there. Like packed sardines. Trinity hadn't redecorated, though, and rented just the bare furniture essentials. It would only be until Harper's deal came through in a couple of months.

Kicking off her high heels, she carried them upstairs. As she stepped into the hall at the top, she realized the shower was running. So Harper was home. No long soak. But . . . there were other possibilities.

She could join him.

Harper was a fastidious lover. He didn't like to muss her hair. For the most part, she could keep her lipstick intact. Which was fine. Who wanted to wake up beside a woman who'd gotten all messy and sweaty with smudges of makeup all over her face? Trinity hated the "morning after" look. For her part, she always got up before Harper and made sure her hair and makeup were perfect by the time he joined her for breakfast.

Yet sometimes, she dreamed of unbridled lust and passion— when she didn't worry how she looked or if she perspired. Or even if her lipstick got all over his dipstick. She wanted something totally intense.

Like the fire she glimpsed between Connor and Faith.

Before she got married, Trinity made the occasional joke to Faith about having a passionate affair with a sexy man—which was pretty much as far as their sex discussions went—but Trinity had to admit she was all talk and no action. She'd never had hot, sweaty sex outside her fantasies. Even with Harper, everything was . . . controlled. But really, why was she thinking about all that now?

It was Faith's baby shower getting to her. The adoring look in Connor's eye.

Even after six months of marriage, she'd never engendered quite that expression in Harper. He was complimentary, of course, and he loved showing her off, squiring her around, and she knew he adored her. But . . .

Maybe tonight was the night for unbridled passion. They'd never taken a shower together, let alone made love under the steamy spray. Harper was a private sort when it came to bathroom activities.

But tonight . . .

Nipples already hard and panties damp, Trinity undid the top two buttons of her baby blue suit as she entered the bedroom.

Harper's shoes and his slacks lay in the middle of the bedroom carpet. His white polo shirt covered a corner of the flowered bedspread, and his Windbreaker listed off the side. This kind of disarray was unlike him. He must be tired.

The water pounded in the shower, and one of her black lace bras lay across the bathroom threshold. She couldn't remember leaving it there.

Except *that* wasn't one of her brassieres. It was too . . . big. The lace poked up proudly and . . . Trinity gulped . . . she wouldn't have filled even a quarter of a cup.

Steam puffed out the open bathroom door, carrying with it a sound barely discernible above the water's beat.

A moan. Or something.

Trinity's migraine came back full force. Vapor bathed her face as she put one hand on the bathroom doorjamb, perspiration covering her upper lip. She swallowed against a dry mouth, and it ached going down.

Please don't, please don't.

She thought the chant was in her mind, but then she realized her lips were moving. As much as she didn't want to, she couldn't *not* look.

The water ran in rivulets down the clear glass door, washing away the condensation. Supported by the shower wall, long, black wet hair spilled down the woman's face, shoulders, and large breasts. Her legs spread, one calf hooked over his shoulder, she fisted her fingers in his hair and held his face to her . . .

Harper's face. Harper's blond hair. Harper doing *that* with his mouth. A guttural male groan wafted on the steam vapors.

Harper never made a sound with her. Except when he came, and then it was merely a grunt before he rolled off.

Oh, oh, maybe it wasn't Harper at all. Maybe they'd broken into her house and were using her shower and . . . all right, that was ridiculous. And she needed to stop looking.

The woman's enormous breasts jiggled as she moaned and rolled her head against the marbled tile. She was not so much fat as voluptuous. *So* not like Trinity. Harper reached up and squeezed a nipple. The woman squealed. He lifted his head and put his hand between her legs. "That's it, baby."

Baby? He'd never called Trinity *baby*.

"Scream when you come. I want to hear you scream."

He hated it if Trinity made noise, so Trinity never made noise. It was . . . undignified.

Then Harper stood, water streaming down his back, his butt, his legs, and he grabbed the movable showerhead. "Hey, baby, let's say we blast you off."

He pinned his paramour to the wall with a hand on her breasts and shoved the showerhead between her spread legs. She squirmed and squealed and laughed, then started to moan.

The sounds assaulted Trinity's ears, the woman's cries mingling with her laughter as if she were actually having fun. Trinity wanted to have fun during sex, but she could never seem to let go. Not like her husband's . . . fuck buddy.

"Come on, baby, come for me, sing for me, baby." He crooned to her, chanted. And when she started to sing, as he called it, he took her mouth and kissed her long, hard, deep.

Trinity wanted to die.

She wanted someone to make her come the way Harper made his woman come. Oh God. She wanted a man to kiss her like *that*. As if she were the only woman that mattered in the world.

Obviously, Trinity wasn't *that* woman to her own husband.

That . . . that . . . that *asshole*.

How dare he? For a moment, seeing him in the shower, a completely different man from the one she thought she knew, Trinity had lost her sense of self. Who the hell did he think he was, screwing another woman in the shower Trinity's daddy had paid for, in the condo her father had given *her* the money to purchase, diddling his . . . his *whore* with the showerhead *Trinity* had bought?

She kicked the bra at her feet—that *woman* was still wailing—and gee, there were the matching panties on the bath mat. She marched right over and yanked open the shower door.

Harper stared at her, his facial muscles suddenly slack.

His lover squealed and tried to cover her breasts with her hands. It didn't work. And really, why bother at this point?

Trinity stepped aside, holding the door. "Get." She pointed at the open bathroom door. "Out."

"Honey." Harper still held the showerhead, water jetting against the side wall.

She noticed he didn't call *her* baby. How had she ever thought he was handsome? His penis was the size of a . . . pencil. And he was a girlie-man. She couldn't think of a worse word to call him. "Get out of my house. Or I'll call the police and report a break-in."

"We need to talk." He punched the shower knob off.

A drop of sweat trickled down her scalp to her nape. More droplets gathered along the line of her bra. She hated feeling sweaty. She hated that he'd made her sweaty.

"Do you remember Lorena Bobbitt?" she whispered.

He dropped the shower nozzle, banging the tile wall.

"Well, if you don't get out of here in five seconds"—she whipped a metal nail file off the bathroom counter and waved it at him— "I will Bobbittize you."

His shriveled penis went completely flaccid, and he grabbed his lover's hand and scrambled out of the shower, slipping on the tile. They ran, seizing pieces of clothing in their path, until she heard footsteps in the hall, then feet pounding down the stairs, and finally the slam of the front door. They couldn't have had time to dress.

"Whew, that felt good." She blew a few blond strands of hair out of her face and tossed the file back on the counter. Then she saw that pair of black lace panties on her pristine white bath mat.

And Trinity burst into tears.

Dammit. She couldn't stay. That was her shower. Oh God, they'd probably done it in *her* bed, too. Yanking her overnight bag out of the closet, she opened it on her vanity stool and threw in the necessities.

She'd go back to Daddy's.

Trinity stopped. No, she couldn't go home. If her mother was still alive . . . but she'd lost her mom the year after she graduated from high school. Cancer. That had been the worst eighteen months of Trinity's life, watching her mother waste away, helpless to stop it, not to mention how hard her mother's illness had been on Daddy. He'd never quite recovered. Which was another reason she couldn't run home with this. She'd caused enough havoc by marrying Harper up in Tahoe in a quickie wedding without telling Daddy first.

And as much as she wanted to, she wouldn't go to Faith's. Faith and Connor were getting ready for the baby. That was more important. Trinity couldn't dump on her friend now.

She'd go to a hotel for a night or two until she figured out what to do. Besides Bobbittizing that cheating bastard.

Before she left, she took off her rings and tossed them in the bathroom trashcan. She hadn't worn them long enough to leave a mark on her finger. God. That seemed so utterly wrong.

The five-star out by the airport had vacancies, and Trinity checked in less than half an hour later. She ordered room service, but couldn't eat. After tossing off her clothes in favor of her nightie, she watched old episodes of *CSI*, one of which featured a woman who'd fed her husband antifreeze for months before he died. It was a slow, painful death. She narrowed her eyes at the TV screen and smiled. Hmm, maybe antifreeze was better than Bobbittizing.

Yet beneath her jumble of emotions, she ached. She wanted to curl into the bedclothes, pull them over her head, and cry until the ache went away. Maybe she could call Faith and talk. She didn't have to say anything was wrong, but Faith knew how to listen. If Trinity *gave* her the chance to listen.

"I hurt," she whispered to the room.

She threw herself out of bed, marched into the bathroom, and stared in the mirror. "I hate self-pity," the reflection said. "It's pathetic."

The woman looking back at her was tall even in bare feet, though she had to admit she looked best in her three-inch heels, which put her at five eleven, or the five-inch ones, but they were a scooch difficult to walk in. Still, Trinity loved her high heels.

Her long blond hair curled softly over her shoulders, though the back did have a bedhead quality after watching hours of reruns. She had the requisite blue eyes to go with the blond look. But were those crow's feet? And lines between her brows? And by her mouth? Trinity leaned in. God. They *were*. She'd been thirty for four months. How could she have lines?

And how could Harper want that woman? Because that... *bitch* had breasts. In her mind's eye, Trinity could see his fingers squeezing a nipple. Trinity cupped her own breasts through her satin sleepshirt. At least she cupped what there was of them. Not even a handful. She undid two buttons and squished her breasts together, but she still couldn't find her cleavage. All right, so she didn't have breasts, but she had good legs. Sure, there were breast men, but there were also leg and butt men, too. Trinity stepped back and pulled her shirt to the small of her back and circled. Okay, not bad. Maybe her butt was a smidge big. Lose a couple of pounds?

A shower image battered her, almost bringing her to her knees until she dropped her shirt, covering herself, and grabbed the edge of the counter. Harper's hands caressing voluptuous hips as he tasted between full thighs. Trinity closed her eyes, and the tiniest of moans slipped past her lips.

All her life, she'd striven for perfection. Ate the right things, worked out endlessly, denied herself all her favorite foods. Like rack of lamb. With a baked potato and sour cream. Bread pudding. And *two* champagne cocktails.

And for what? So that Harper could go down on a woman at least three sizes larger than her? Fine, yippy-doodle, it was a bitchy thought, but she was feeling bitchy. She was feeling... she didn't know what she was feeling except wounded and yeah, a little murderous. If she knew where he'd gone, she might have run after him with the nail file and eviscerated him. It would have been oh-so-satisfyingly slow and painful.

Trinity always tried to look perfect for Harper.

Yet he'd done that woman in the shower, her hair wet and all over the place, mascara smudges beneath her eyes, her lipstick on her chin. How could he do that?

How. Could. He. Do. *That?*

Because Trinity herself didn't like to sweat or get her lipstick smudged or her hair askew. She liked to dream about it, but she never did it. Had Harper ever asked to get down and nasty with her? Or passionate?

The horrible, terrible truth was she couldn't remember. What did that say about how much effort she'd put into her marriage? How awful. How utterly pathetic. How . . .

"Will you stop?" The woman in the mirror blinked at her. "He cheated on you. You gave him your all, and he cheated."

She'd always denied herself anything that some man might disapprove of. She'd structured her whole existence around what she *thought* men wanted. What difference had it made? Harper had chosen someone completely different.

Maybe he'd been pissed that she'd kept her own name instead of taking his when they got married. It was easier than changing all her credit cards, that's how she'd thought of it. The truth was she didn't know what she'd done wrong. She'd tried to make everything perfect. *Why* had none of it been enough for Harper?

Suddenly Trinity wanted it all, rack of lamb and bread pudding with lots of brandy walnut sauce. She wanted passion. She wanted to get her hair mussed and her lipstick smudged. She wanted to get sweaty. She wanted the hot, screaming orgasms she'd always denied herself. Even if she had to give one to herself, dammit. She deserved it. Right now.

She wasn't going to deny herself one minute longer.

* * *

JUGGLING his briefcase, suit hanger, and PC, Scott Sinclair exited the elevator alone on the eighteenth floor. He had a hellaciously early Monday morning flight in order to make the nine o'clock investor meeting in Phoenix. Rather than drive over the hill from Santa Cruz, he'd opted to spend the night at a hotel and take their shuttle to the airport. Plus he could leave his car in the lot without the hassle of long-term parking.

The doors were set even and odd in small alcoves, and he found his room number halfway down the hall. Dropping his suit carrier to the carpet, he rummaged in his briefcase pocket where he'd stashed the card key.

From beneath the opposite door in his alcove, a woman's voice drifted up. Barely more than a whisper of sound. Or . . . Scott cocked his head . . . a moan? He chuckled, hoping to hell she wasn't a screamer. He had to get up at the crack of dawn.

Once inside, he tossed his bag on the bed and carried his briefcase and PC to the desk. He wanted to do a last-minute check on his presentation before he turned in.

A murmur wafted up from the socket above the bedside table. He moved closer, then sat down on the edge of the bed. Without a plug in the electrical socket, it was a pass-through from one room to the other. And that was definitely a woman's voice.

No, not a voice, just a gentle feminine moan. The couple next door was about to give him a show without the picture. Ha. Any minute now, he expected the wall to start banging. Yet there was only that low, breathy sound of pleasure. Damn, it was erotic in a kinky, voyeuristic way.

He couldn't help himself. What red-blooded male could? Scott laid back, moving closer to the wall socket to listen. Maybe it was because he hadn't been with a woman in a couple of months, but he could feel her voice like a stroke along his cock.

Lying on the bed, listening to her, his hands stacked beneath his head, he hardened in his jeans. The intensity of her moans rose. He no longer had to strain to hear. She panted, faster, the thread of her voice running through her breath. Yet the wall behind his head still didn't shake.

Jesus, her partner must be going down on her. And she was loving it.

So was Scott. He rubbed his cock through his pants. She had the most seductive moan he'd ever heard. Not a wail or screech or even a scream, but a soft, throaty pant that fed blood to his cock. He closed his eyes, her voice filling his head as his fingers worked open the button fly of his jeans, then he delved inside his briefs until he was stroking himself to her rhythm. Her voice rose in a crescendo. As she cried out, he felt the throes of her orgasm as if her body milked his erection.

He almost came with her.

It was like jerking off to a porn movie. Except that her voice spoke of balmy Caribbean nights, curtains blowing in a gentle breeze, and the scent of the ocean washing over him.

He figured the wall-banging would start pronto. Yet there was silence. Maybe her partner was getting his condom. He couldn't wait for their next act.

He had to laugh. He was such a freaking perv, but hell, he wouldn't deny how much he'd enjoyed listening. There was something indefinable about her voice that called to him. Maybe it was the circumstance, the unexpectedness, the fact she was a total stranger, faceless, just a voice.

He'd been married for twenty-two years. Since the divorce had become final a year ago, he'd had two brief relationships, both of which had skirted the edge of kinky, a few toys, a blindfold, scarves for ropes. But he'd felt no connection, and neither woman had fulfilled the craving in him. The passion he'd felt in his youth, the passion he'd showered on his wife, Katy.

The passion that had died through the job changes, raising children, climbing the corporate ladder, the fights about money, kids, sex, then the silences that drove him crazy. He'd thought when both the girls went off to college, he and Katy could start over, have time for each other, rekindle what they'd lost. He'd wanted that with every fiber of his being.

Instead, two weeks after Lexa, his youngest, went off for her freshman year, Katy asked for a divorce.

Scott swung his legs over the side of the bed and sat up. None of that mattered much now. His life had turned on a dime, but he wasn't one to wish for things he couldn't have. He had Lexa and Brooke, and he adored his girls.

He'd hoped, though, that he'd rediscover the passion of his youth, that he'd find a woman with whom he could share himself. That might be expecting too much at the age of forty-five. Maybe it came once in a lifetime, and all that was left was good sex.

Which is what the lady next door seemed to be getting tonight. He was envious of her partner. Yet they were taking their sweet time getting to the wall-banging. He was pervert enough to want to listen.

Finally, she started to moan again. His cock twitched as if her particular sweet pitch had a direct line to his libido. Oh man, he wouldn't make it through the next orgasm without coming.

He wasn't sure how you could want a voice, but he did. Christ, if he were next door, he'd have her screaming. The head of his cock rose out of his briefs, a drop of come leaking from the tip without even a touch.

"Fuck me, baby," he whispered.

She moaned louder. Higher. A touch more desperate.

He wrapped his thumb and forefinger around his crown and pumped, just that tight circle, as if he delved with short sharp bursts in her pussy.

On the other side of the wall, she went crazy. Panting again, moaning. He could almost feel her writhing beneath him on the mattress, and he pretended she was all his, imagining his cock sliding in her, her taste on his tongue. As if she could read his mind through the wall, she cried out with that same musical, breathy quality that made him a little nuts. He wanted that sound, he wanted his name on her lips.

She drove Scott to the edge with her voice, and still her lover was quiet as a mouse. Damn if he wasn't glad. He didn't think he'd enjoy hearing a man's grunts and groans anywhere near as much as listening to her by herself. Her voice enthralled him, made him actually feel she was there for him alone. *Alone.*

Scott started to get it. She *was* alone. The lover in her bed was her own hand. Or her vibrator. Christ, he almost exploded then. Perhaps because he couldn't see, the wall a solid barrier, her voice, her soft cries, evoked the most erotic images he'd ever known. Gorgeous legs spread, fingers buried, silky hair fanned across her pillow. His cock swelled, and he pumped faster. God, he wanted to do her. Worse, he simply wanted to watch her. A complete stranger. Learning who she was by the way she caressed herself. Her touch teaching him what she craved. His head back, he groaned deep in his gut.

And he knew if he didn't give in to this once-in-a-lifetime impulse, if he didn't beg her to let him watch, he'd regret it the rest of his days.

He made the move before he could actually contemplate that she might call the cops and get him arrested for being a pervert.

2

TRINITY rolled over and hugged the pillow. She could do better, she knew, because the two orgasms, though pleasant, had been a tad less than mind-blowing. She was left wanting . . . more.

It was sad, too, because the best orgasms she'd ever had were the ones she gave herself. It wasn't her lovers' fault, not even Harper's. She couldn't let go at the right moment. It seemed to take so long that she felt impatient. Then she'd fake it. Or the bliss didn't last. There were a million reasons, most of which centered around not looking ridiculous or sounding like a braying donkey or getting out of control or . . . show anything less than the perfect image she wanted to display.

She tugged her nightshirt over her butt and snuggled deeper beneath the cushy down comforter. She might have fallen asleep in two shakes if someone hadn't knocked on the door.

Who was it at this ungodly hour? Except the clock showed ten. It had to be room service wanting her tray. Trinity climbed out of bed. She'd forgotten a robe, and where had she thrown her undies? Whatever. The shirt covered her thighs.

Balancing the tray on her hand, she opened the door.

And almost dropped it. This was no hotel employee.

Oh my God. She didn't have on any makeup, and she hadn't even checked her hair in the bathroom mirror.

She had to look up, up, up, and she realized how Faith must feel all the time. Petite. It was kind of nice. The guy was at least six four, and he had the flat abs, muscled arms, and defined chest of a gym rat. His thighs in those tight black jeans were . . . yummy.

She shouldn't be looking at a man thinking "yum-yum" when she'd just kicked her husband of six months out of the house for cheating on her. She also shouldn't be searching for a wedding ring, either, yet she noted his hand was bare.

And he was looking at her as if he were doing the "yum-yum," too. It felt good, really good. Which it shouldn't, of course.

"Let me take that for you."

Lord. That voice. Deep, it started a thrum in her chest. He was older, but in a Kurt Russell/*Superdad* kind of way. In other words, more than sexy enough to turn heads, with short, dark brown hair and a strong, square chin. She let him take the tray without a peep, admiring his rearview as he bent to set her leftovers in the hall outside the alcove.

"I'm in the room next door." He pointed as if he thought she couldn't figure out where next door was.

She smiled politely. "That's nice." What did he want?

"I can hear you through the wall."

He could hear her? What, was the TV too loud? But she'd turned it off half an hour ago. Then a flush rose up her neck.

"Oh." What else was she supposed to say?

His chest expanded with a breath, then he raked both hands through his short hair before dropping them to his sides again.

"And it made me a little nuts," he finished as if he hadn't paused and she hadn't said "oh."

"I'll try to keep it down," she said in her most snooty voice while inside she was a mushy mess of embarrassment.

"I don't want you to keep it down." He breathed deeply again, his chest straining against his sky blue button-down, then held her with a penetrating pair of eyes a few shades richer than the brown of his hair. "I want to come in and watch."

If she'd still been holding the tray, it would have crashed to the floor and splattered the remains of runny fried eggs all over the carpet and his tennis shoes.

"You're joking, right?"

"No." He held up a hand. "But don't call hotel management. I promise not to touch you." He stopped, laughed softly, and shook his head almost absently. "I can't believe I'm over here asking for this anymore than you can believe I am." Tipping his head back, he contemplated the overhead spotlight before dropping back down to meet her gaze. "I heard your voice." Then he shrugged as if that said it all.

He'd heard her voice. Just her voice. "What if I'd turned out to be fifty pounds overweight with a face like a Gorgon?"

His lips flirted with a smile. "I'd still want to watch you and hear you make those sounds."

"This is the weirdest proposal I've ever had." But it made her sort of excited. Well, hell, there wasn't any "sort of" about it. Her body started clamoring, "More, more, more."

"It's the strangest proposal I've ever made."

"I'm—" She'd been about to say that she was married, but what difference did that make? Harper didn't want her. She had this horrible, terrible feeling that even if she took him back, he'd be sneaking off to his lover the first chance he got.

In six months, he'd never made her feel desired the way this man did with his utterly preposterous yet tantalizing request. But really, she couldn't.

"You might be an ax murderer."

He held up his hands. "No ax." He dug in his front and back pockets, the breast pocket of his shirt. "No weapons."

Her heart rate picked up. Letting a stranger into her room, wouldn't *that* show everyone, including herself, that Harper hadn't hurt her in the least? Yeah, it was better than having a good cry to get that bastard out of her system. Right? And she'd wanted something totally, utterly mind-blowing.

"Keep your cell phone on the bed right beside you so you can make an emergency call," he added.

"That means you can't get too close." Yet she thought about his gaze touching her body, and she heated inside, outside, the tips of her breasts, between her legs. Any minute, she'd go up in flames. And she wanted. God, no matter how crazy or preposterous or dangerous, she *wanted*.

"I won't even get on the bed with you."

"No touching," she said. Look but don't touch? Basically that could be a metaphor for her life. Good old look-but-don't-touch Trinity. It was too sad for words, because she *wanted* to be touched. Badly. She wanted a man's hand to make her explode into a million tiny little pieces.

He tipped his head slightly, and his voice dipped low. "I just want to watch."

Maybe having him watch was enough to detonate her. Oh yeah, *way* more than enough. She'd never felt quite so aroused. Or intrigued. She didn't have to impress him. She didn't have to worry about mussing her hair or smudging her makeup. All she had to do was close her eyes and make herself feel good. And let him watch. Her body tightened thinking about it.

"You'd have to leave as soon as I'm done." God. She wasn't *really* saying yes to this. It was a lark. She couldn't. She wouldn't. But God, she wanted to, badly. Her nerve endings screamed so loudly she was surprised he couldn't hear them.

"I won't get on the bed. I won't touch you. And I'll leave right after you come. I promise." His voice trickled like champagne down each and every one of her shrieking nerves. "Let me watch."

Harper had rejected her in the cruelest way possible. Yet here was a man who wanted her sight unseen after listening to her through a wall. Diddling herself for his pleasure, however, was a pathetic way to rebuild her trashed self-esteem. She'd regret it in the morning. She knew she would.

Yet she had the insane urge to touch herself for him even as she stood there, a death grip on the door.

One short hour ago, she'd gazed at her image in the mirror and swore she'd stop denying herself the pleasures she deserved. She'd craved something mind-blowing and hadn't quite achieved it.

Touching herself as he watched? *That* would be mind-blowing.

Trinity stepped back and opened the door all the way. She'd call herself crazy later. Tonight, she'd take what he offered.

IN his room, he hadn't questioned that she'd be a goddess. With that voice, Scott couldn't imagine her being anything less. The reality was she could have been any body shape, any size or age, not to mention bearing the face of a Gorgon. And he would have wanted her anyway.

Yet his mystery woman truly *was* a goddess. He wanted to kneel down and kiss the floor when she agreed to let him in instead of slamming the door and calling security.

The room was the mirror image of his, and neat despite her being a woman. After all, he'd lived with three of them, and he knew what it could be like. Yet not a single bit of clothing lay strewn on the floor. The only personal item was her purse on the desk. If she had a suitcase, she'd hidden it away. The light by the king-size bed was on, the covers rumpled, the pillow still bearing the imprint of her head, his favorite wall socket right beside it. No wonder he'd heard her as if she were in *his* bed.

She climbed on the mattress on all fours. The sight gave him heart palpitations despite the fact that her magnificent ass was covered by her green satin nightshirt. Looking over her shoulder at him, she tore back the covers and flopped down. He pulled out the desk chair, twirled it around to face the bed, and sat, gripping the wood armrests. Damn, he needed to do something with his hands since he couldn't touch her.

"Turn on the light." She pointed to his left, her nails polished in a muted shade. Scott figured her for a woman who would sometimes wear sizzling red and sometimes a prim pale pink.

Depending on whether she felt like being naughty or nice.

He flipped on the standing lamp between the desk and the entertainment center, its glow bathing her body in light and shadow when she shut off the bedside lamp.

Angling slightly toward him, she closed her eyes, turned her head on the pillow, and ran her hands down her thighs.

Christ, she had gorgeous legs. Long with firm feminine curves. Like a snake charmer, her hands forced his gaze to follow as they slid slowly over her hips, her abdomen, up to her breasts. Pinching both nipples through the nightshirt, she hissed in a breath, her hips arching off the bed. She moaned, and the sound sent his blood pressure skyrocketing.

That voice. He was hard. He wanted to come. Now. Instead he forced himself to relax into the chair, and he watched.

She unbuttoned three buttons and spread the satin to reveal two small pink-tipped breasts, her nipples distended from the pinch she'd applied. She cupped them, for his view he was sure, then moved down to the next buttons. Strips of tantalizing skin appeared, her belly, then she dipped to the bottom buttons and worked her way up to tease him.

When she undid the last one covering her mound, he realized she'd answered the door without panties. The idea got him all wound up. Like the thought of what a female exec might be wearing under her power suit. Lace and thigh highs. Or nothing at all. Yeah, he sometimes entertained brief flights of fancy at work during a particularly boring meeting.

This was a whole different caliber.

Then she spread the lapels of her nightshirt and let them fall to her sides.

Good God. Her perfection stole his breath.

Her hands began a slow, sinuous slide down her body once more. To the ridge of blond pubic hair several shades darker than her silky tresses. A real blonde, no less.

She spread her legs to reveal a beautiful pussy. Having been married for so long, he didn't have a lot of experience, but enough from his college days and after the divorce to know that women came in a variety. Some had slender lips and a barely there button. Some were fleshy. Or bushy. She was neatly trimmed. Her pink lips invited his mouth, and her clit, already engorged from her earlier play, begged for his tongue. And she was wet. He could see the moisture and hear the sexy slip-slide as she put a finger to her opening to coat herself with her own sweet cream.

She touched her clit and rewarded him with a moan. He was so hard, his jeans dug into his cock. She circled, arched into her fingers, and tossed her head on the pillow, her hair fanning across the cotton and down over her petite breasts. Then she relaxed into the bed once more.

She opened her eyes a moment to watch him watching her. He stroked the front of his pants, yet he didn't take his cock out for a whack. He wanted this to be purely about her. He needed to savor this without missing a single moment.

Yet not jerking off was the hardest thing he'd ever attempted to do. He undid the two top buttons of his fly to ease the pressure, but it didn't do much for the ache in his balls.

Her lashes drifted down once more, and her finger, the middle one, circled her clit, her pace building. She held her breath, bit her lip, then her hips arched off the bed slightly, and she let out one of her special, long sexy breaths, her pleasure threading through it with a gentle moan. She bucked and circled, going at herself, her breath coming in pants and moans and a myriad of pleasure sounds that wrapped around his erection like a luscious pair of lips.

When he was sure she'd come and blow the top off his world, she eased back against the mattress, breathing deeply. Then finally lifted her lids to look at him.

"Don't stop. Please." He was willing to beg.

The barest hint of a smile graced her sensual mouth, the mouth he wanted taking him to heaven and higher. She reveled in her feminine power, in the fact that she could make him beg. Her total lack of inhibition, even if for this one night alone, drew him like a drone to its queen.

"Please," he murmured again in the quiet of the room.

She cupped her breasts, held them out for him. She wanted him to watch. She loved it, he was sure. Then she pinched the pearled tips, sucking in her breath with the pleasure-pain of it, her body writhing on the bed. He felt the touch in his groin.

"Fuck yourself for me."

She did, sliding one hand down between her legs, while with the other she slowly caressed her throat, her breasts, her belly, then her hips and thighs. Her body rocked, her finger in constant motion. She used only the one, and beyond the first time she'd dipped down inside herself for her own cream, she played her button exclusively. Her body mesmerized him. If he ever got a chance to make her come, he knew exactly how. That button. Her ripe, hard clitoris. With her clit under his finger and her nipple between his teeth in a tender bite, he knew he could make her scream.

"Come for me, baby." He wanted a closer look, to drink in her heady sexual perfume. It filled the air, and he wanted her up close, to rub his finger in her juice and pass it over his lips so that he could catch her aroma for hours. What if he did crawl on the bed and put his hand between her legs? His body screamed, "Do it, do it, do it." The thought that she might stop and throw him out kept him glued to the chair.

He recognized the climb. Pink tinged her skin, and her sounds got louder. She had a sweet hum in her throat, then she opened her mouth, panted, sharp, fast exhalations laced with her sultry voice, until she broke into a low cry of mindlessness. Like the most erotic music, her voice wrapped around him, took him under, her cries rising as her body twitched and bucked beneath her finger. She rode out her orgasm, head thrown back, hair covering her face, breath hard and fast, until finally she clamped her legs together around her hand and rolled to her side. An orgasmic aftershock rolled through, and she shuddered, then lay still, a tiny hum of pleasure vibrating through her breath.

Jesus H. Christ. This was way up there as the hottest ten minutes he'd ever experienced. A wet spot stained his jeans, his balls ached with need, and his mind reeled. Yet it was such a damn good place to be.

Then he did what he promised. He rose from the chair and walked out of her room. Outside her door, he waited long moments until he heard the deadbolt close behind him.

He didn't know her name, and he didn't care. Tomorrow night, with the investor meeting long over, after twenty-four hours of re-playing every second of the encounter in his mind, when he'd savored the memory to the point of madness, he'd jerk off to the sound of her voice in his head.

HE'D called her *baby*. She hugged the word close to her still pounding heart. Take *that*, Harper. Oh God, oh God, that was so good. So perfect. Never, ever in her life had she come like that.

She'd let go, *really* let go. A deep lassitude spread through her limbs, and her lips flirted with a tiny smile.

Until she heard the snick of the door closing behind him. And suddenly, she remembered she didn't know him. He was a complete stranger.

Good Lord, what had she done?

Trinity plopped the pillow over her head.

What had possessed her to let a strange man into her room no matter how yummy he looked? Who had she become? It wasn't only tonight. It was running out on her best friend's baby shower. It was sneaking off to Tahoe—after knowing Harper a month—for a quickie wedding when all her life she'd wanted the white dress and a walk down the aisle on her father's arm. It was how badly she'd disappointed Daddy by cutting him out of that special day.

Finding Harper with that woman, she'd had the thought that she'd momentarily lost her sense of self. The truth was far worse. She'd never had a sense of self at all.

Will the real Trinity Green please stand up?

She came up for air, shoving the pillow aside, then rushed for the door to slam home the deadbolt.

She was her daddy's little girl, Harper's trophy wife, the country-club debutante, the elegant heiress. Yet she felt like the princess in *Shrek*. She wanted everyone to think she was the gorgeous Cameron Diaz when actually, beneath the enchantment, she was just a troll. Or was it the other way around, the troll was the enchantment and Cameron was real? Whatever. Trinity couldn't remember. The point was she didn't even know herself.

And she could now add to the list being an exhibitionist who masturbated for a complete and total stranger. And loved it.

What evil demon spirit had possessed her?

But, honest to God, it had been the hottest moment ever. Bar none. She hadn't cared how she sounded, braying donkey or not, or how she was splayed on the bed. It was the most liberating experience of her entire existence on planet Earth. Because he was so damn hot for her.

After her big moment, as she'd floated back down in a million little pieces like ash from Mount St. Helens, he'd white-knuckled the armrests. If she looked, she was sure she'd find little crescent moons in the wood.

He'd wanted her. Without makeup. Without her daddy's money. Sight unseen, he'd knocked on her door because her voice had driven him crazy with desire. Now *that* was a power trip.

Better than mind-blowing, she'd had the absolute best orgasm ever. With a total stranger. And he hadn't even touched her.

She wanted more of it.

Which was why it was a darn good thing that he didn't know her name and she didn't know his, much less have any way to contact him.

BY dawn's early light, Scott knew he couldn't walk away and leave it to the fates as to whether he saw her again. He'd fallen asleep to fantasies, half hoping she'd wake him in the night with the sound of her voice through the wall.

Instead, the call of the alarm had dragged him out of bed.

As he closed his door behind him, there wasn't a sound from beneath hers. Since it wasn't even five o'clock, he didn't expect there to be.

He couldn't pinpoint any one thing that made him want her with this intensity. Sure, there was the mystery element. Who was she? And yeah, she was goddess material, the way she looked, her moves, her sighs. She was also a lot younger than him, which brought to mind the midlife crisis issue. Except that he wasn't having a midlife crisis. He'd had that when Katy divorced him. Now he was moving on, doing well. He didn't have any desire to buy a fast sports car or marshal a younger woman around on his arm to show he was still virile.

His desire might have a helluva lot less to do with his mystery lady and far more to do with his state of mind at this time in his life. He needed connection, romance, passion; whatever the hell you called it, he wanted it. She captured his imagination with her voice. Her sexy, sultry bedroom sounds had wormed their way into his vitals, and he'd never get her out unless he followed through on this need. For him, she spelled excitement, and he wanted that feeling. He'd missed it during the last fifteen years of his marriage, started craving it the year before Lexa went off to college, before Katy had torn his world apart. He'd thought he and Katy could find each other again, recapture love, yet she'd checked out of the relationship long before she actually told him.

Now, he didn't care how he got that passion back. He didn't care how long the thrill lasted. He wanted a taste of it for any length of time he could grab hold of. It was probably ridiculous to hope he could get what he needed from a stranger, but then fantasy was all about believing the impossible could be possible. He wanted a woman in his life. He wanted *this* woman. Days, weeks, months, he'd take whatever she'd give him.

Scribbling a couple of lines on a piece of hotel notepaper, he shoved that and his business card under her door before he gave himself time to debate the wisdom of giving his name, his company, and his work number to a stranger he'd gotten kinky with. He was the picture of conservative, the suit, the tie, the dress shirt, serious when required, responsible, all that. He'd be the executive voted least likely to pick up a woman at a hotel bar while away on a business trip. It was also true that while he'd experimented a bit after his divorce, his sex life prior to that had been pretty vanilla.

Yet he'd knocked on a woman's door and asked to watch her masturbate.

She'd made him feel completely alive for the first time in years. And he wanted to feel it again. The thought of acting out a few of his fantasies with her was titillating. No, too mild a word. The possibilities were downright exhilarating.

Now he just had to hope she didn't tear up the card.

3

SHE should have torn up the card. Oh my Lord. Her friends would host an intervention if they knew. He could have been a serial killer. Not that he looked like any serial killer she'd ever seen on TV, and she didn't believe it when the neighbors all said, "But he was such a nice guy." A serial killer had to *look* like a serial killer.

Still, this morning Trinity had slipped the card into her purse instead of throwing it out, and she'd thought about him all day. Scott Sinclair. He worked at some Silicon Valley firm. Chief financial officer. He'd folded a note around the card. "Back from a trip tomorrow, Tuesday. Call me. Since you'll go through our phone system, there's no caller ID so you have no worries about me tracking the number back."

Would a serial killer bother to write a note like that? She knew his name, not the other way around. She could meet him, then disappear again, and he'd never know who she was.

It had such delicious possibilities.

Total control.

Lord, that thought felt good after the morning she'd had. Returning to the condo, she found Harper had been and gone, taking one suitcase. She'd promptly had the locks changed, then called the security company and altered the alarm code. Thankfully her father hadn't let her put Harper on the account. His reasoning: *When Harper pays back the down payment, we'll put him on the paperwork.* Until then, the condo would stay in her father's name. Thank God. Otherwise, Harper could have claimed half ownership. The last thing she'd done was to leave a note for Edith, her twice-weekly housekeeper, to wash all the sheets, towels, and bath mats. She didn't want a trace of Harper left.

Trinity heaved a great sigh.

Her father's secretary Verna Underwood misinterpreted the sound. "He'll be done in a minute."

"That's all right. I'll wait." What could he be talking about that he didn't want her to overhear?

Seated in one of the armchairs, Trinity sifted through the magazines, but neither *Money* nor *Popular Mechanics* grabbed her interest. She sometimes slipped in through Daddy's second office doorway, which exited directly onto the executive row hallway at Green Industries. This morning, however, that door had been locked, a fact which Verna explained away as a "very important *private* conference call."

So here she was in the outer office with too much time to think about how she'd break the news. She hated to hurt Daddy or worry him. Since her mother died, she'd tried to spare him as much trauma as possible. She must have had a momentary brain malfunction marrying Harper the way she did. How could she have done that without a thought for how badly her father would feel? It was an unconscionable act. Another sigh puffed out.

"You all right, hon?"

Verna had been around forever, though she didn't look older

than fifty-five. Her hair had long since turned from black to blue gray, and her skirts had inched down from above the knee to below. She was now the closest thing Trinity had to a mother.

Still, she couldn't say to Verna, "Yesterday, I caught my husband screwing another woman in our shower, I masturbated for a total stranger last night, and today I'm filing for divorce."

The thought did not make her feel sick or scared. It did *not*. She'd made up her mind. As if her subconscious had made plans in her sleep, she'd woken this morning knowing that's what she'd do.

She shuddered with the thought of how upset Daddy would be. Still, she smiled for Verna, though it felt a little brittle. "I'm fine. Honestly. But thanks for asking."

Verna gave her a look that said she didn't believe a word, then her phone beeped. "Oh, there he is. You can go in."

When Trinity walked through the door, her father was shoving a file folder in his middle drawer.

"Hey, Daddy." She rounded the desk and kissed his cheek.

He worried her. As had happened while her mother was ill, he'd lost weight in the last few months since the merger with Castle Heavy Mining. Until last year, Green Industries had been an independent supplier of Castle. Her father was on Castle's board, and he still ran Green as a subsidiary, but . . . he'd changed. The weight loss wasn't bad on its own, but instead of looking healthier and more fit, he appeared haggard and gaunt. He wouldn't give up his cigars, either, as the ubiquitous ashes on his blotter attested. His favorite saying was, "I'm sixty-eight and too old to give up the one last thing I enjoy in life."

Now Trinity had to add to his burden.

"To what do I owe the honor of your visit, sweetie?"

Brushing aside ashes, she perched on the edge of his desk. There was no appropriate lead-in. "I'm getting a divorce."

He sat back in his leather chair. He'd had that chair so long that his bottom left a permanent imprint. Everything else in the office was relatively new, and definitely luxurious, but he wouldn't give up his favorite chair. Now, he sank into the soft leather, closed his eyes, and sighed.

"Praise the Lord," he murmured, though he'd never been a religious man.

Trinity flopped down in the chair opposite his massive desk. Thank *God* he wasn't upset. "Didn't you like Harper?"

Her father leaned forward once again, both elbows on the desk. "No man is good enough for my little girl." He reached into his middle drawer and drew out the folder she'd seen him stash when she walked in. "But Harper Harrington the Third"—he gave the title a derisive slur—"wasn't worthy of washing the underside of your Mustang."

He opened the folder, and Trinity got a bad feeling. She noticed he hadn't asked why she was divorcing Harper. He didn't care. Or maybe he already knew why. "What's that?" she asked.

"Background check."

Her mouth was suddenly dry and swallowing hurt. "When did you do that?"

"I had it done when you came back from Tahoe." He tapped the top page in the file. "I have the private investigator update me monthly on Harper's activities."

"You were talking to your investigator, weren't you?" That supposed conference call.

He nodded.

Trinity stared at him. Her heart beat faster, and the blood rushed in her ears, the sound like a million ants going to town on a picnic table. Her breath felt harsh, like the first time she'd smoked a cigarette when she was thirteen and knew she was never going to smoke another.

She remembered a time with Faith when she'd claimed Daddy could do a background check on Harper *if* she decided to marry him. She'd never given her father the chance, and now she didn't want to know what was in the report. She'd already seen enough.

Her father didn't let her say no. "He's a liar and possibly an embezzler." His lip curled as he spoke. "That so-called business deal is a fabrication, and the last deal he was involved with, a quarter of a million dollars disappeared. They couldn't prove how he stole it, but"—Daddy shrugged—"you're well rid of him. I'm so glad you've seen the light."

Thank God he didn't ask how she'd come to see the light on her own. What he'd revealed about Harper was humiliation enough. It was obvious she'd been married for her money.

She toyed with a tiny prick in the leather arm of her chair. "Why didn't you tell me this right after I married him?"

"You wouldn't have believed me."

"I might have."

"Then you'd have hated me for telling you. And I'd already lost Lance."

Lance. Her brother. Another reason Trinity hated to add to her father's burdens right now. Lance had never forgiven Daddy for "selling out" to Castle. Daddy had never forgiven Lance for his lies. There was more to the story, a lot more, but Trinity and her father never talked about it. She'd learned the details from Faith. She hated the rift between them, hated not knowing how to fix it, but Lance had broken Daddy's heart, and her father had gone so far as to forbid Trinity to speak her brother's name in front of him. Now, it seemed, Daddy had feared *she'd* break his heart if he'd told her the truth about Harper.

Still. "I had a right to know."

He stroked his double chin. He'd lost so much weight that the flesh hung loosely. "Maybe. Then again, just because he'd screwed up in the past, didn't mean he'd make you a bad husband. I didn't think it fair to judge the boy before giving him a chance." He ran a fingernail along the edge of the blue manila.

Trinity wondered why he hadn't given Lance the same kind of second chance, though she didn't dare ask the question. "But you kept on checking up on Harper."

"I wanted to make sure you were adequately protected." Daddy shrugged tired shoulders. "Just in case."

"That's why you put the condo in your name."

"Yes."

It wasn't only Harper. Daddy didn't trust her, either. She had to grant he was right. She'd demonstrated appallingly poor judgment. And she felt like a gullible fool. Harper had probably seen her as a ditzy blond heiress he could bamboozle, and he'd been right. She remembered the first day she'd met him at her salon. She'd been having her nails done, and he'd claimed he'd gotten the time of his appointment mixed up with hers.

She should have known any man having his nails done in the middle of the day was suspect.

Her father pushed the folder halfway across the desk. "Do you want to read it?"

Would it mention Harper's cheating? She didn't want to know if last night was the first time or if it had been going on their entire marriage. All those months ago, Faith had been right when she claimed she didn't want to know if Connor was cheating on her. She wanted to believe in him. She'd made the right choice.

Trinity would have chosen the same. If her father had given her the folder six months ago, she wouldn't have believed. She might even have resented Daddy. She certainly would have given Harper a chance to prove the background check wrong.

But there were no second chances now. Her husband had brought that woman into their home. He'd made love to her in their shower. He'd called her *baby*.

"I'll make sure he doesn't get one thin dime, sweetie."

Not even a thick one. "Thank you, Daddy."

She was free. Her marriage could be swept under the rug as if it had never happened. As if she'd never made a bad choice. She could go back to being . . . what, Daddy's little girl?

"Don't think about him another second. He isn't worth it."

No. He wasn't. But how much was *she* worth now?

Will the real Trinity Green please stand up?

She didn't know who she was anymore. She didn't know what to do with herself. She certainly couldn't go back to her lackadaisical debutante days.

She thought of Scott Sinclair's card still in her purse. He wasn't an answer, either.

She needed to do something big. She needed purpose.

"Daddy, have you got a job opening I can fill?"

"SO I want to say I'm sorry for running out early from your baby shower, but my headache is totally gone. Completely."

At least it would be as soon as Trinity had the divorce papers. Daddy's lawyer had started drawing them up right after she talked to her father this afternoon. It did have the flavor of her being a little girl who needed to be taken care of instead of a grown woman who could take care of herself. But Daddy had the contacts. It made sense to let his people handle it. This would be the last time, though. Starting next Monday, a week away, she'd have a job. She'd do everything for herself. She'd make her father proud of her.

"Don't be silly, Trin." Faith closed the blinds over her big kitchen window, shutting out the late-January night, then reached for the boiling kettle. "You don't need to apologize for having a headache." She poured three cups of tea. "Josie, I forget, do you like sugar and milk?"

Josie was Faith's cousin, second or third or something. A year or so younger than Faith, they'd never been close until she got married. They were as different as night and day, too. Faith was on the short side with gorgeous hair the perfect shade of red, while Josie was at least as tall as Trinity, with dark brown hair cut fairly short, though in the last couple of months she'd been letting it grow a bit. Faith had been Trinity's best friend almost their whole lives, most especially since they were in the seventh grade. Josie was a new friend, but fast becoming a close one. She was funny and cool and easy to be around. She never got worked up, or at least it took a lot to get her miffed. Being around Faith and Josie was . . . relaxing. Although today, with what Trinity had to reveal, it might not be so restful.

"Can I have a soda?" Josie made a face. "You know, I never told you I hate tea."

"Gosh, I have water, milk, or juice. That's it." Faith had stopped drinking soda almost right after she got pregnant. She didn't want the baby hooked on sugar in the womb.

Josie chose milk, and they all settled around Faith's kitchen table. Three months ago Faith and Connor had moved into the cutest house in a nice suburb not too far from the private school they'd already picked out. The large kitchen was attached to a great room in an L-shape, and beyond the back patio was a good-sized yard with grass, a sandbox, and a swing set. Four bedrooms for more children, too. Faith wanted a big family. And Connor, well, talk about a proud papa, Connor Kingston took the prize. Funny, Trinity never would have thought it of him.

Speaking of which. "Where's Connor anyway?"

Faith stirred her tea and got that dreamy, goofy smile she always had for the man. "He's working late."

Trinity's heart lurched. Faith had no doubt her husband was working late rather than playing hanky-panky. Trinity didn't doubt it, either. When they'd first gotten married, Trinity had some misgivings, but she'd learned pretty quickly that Connor wasn't a cheat and liar.

Connor was nothing like Harper Harrington the Third. The third what, she wondered. The third asshole in his family? Or was it the terrible triad—cheat, liar, and embezzler? God.

"I'm getting a divorce."

Faith gagged on her cookie, and Josie almost snorted her milk out her nose.

"Oh man." Josie made another face, this one suggesting disgust. "Men are dickheads. You're better off without him."

Had Josie had a bad experience, or was she commiserating? Whatever the reason, Trinity appreciated the support.

"Why?" Faith asked.

Trinity felt a knife right through her chest. "He cheated."

"Well, that sucks the big one." Josie slapped her milk glass down in punctuation.

Faith put her hand over Trinity's. "Oh Trin, I'm so sorry."

That was the thing about Faith and Josie. They didn't ask for dirty details they could spread around the country club. Whatever she said would stay at this table. She'd even get a little sympathy, too. "I found him in the shower doing some floozy, but I'm so over it now. It doesn't hurt a bit."

She'd convinced herself it didn't. Honest.

"When did this happen?" Josie wanted to know.

"Last night."

"And you're *so* over it?" Josie scoffed, yet not in a bitchy I'm-getting-a-kick-out-of-your-misery way.

Trinity toyed with her mug. She wasn't fond of tea, either. Then she sighed. "There's nothing to be done. I can't go back and change it, and I'm not going to forgive him." She twisted her hands and looked at Faith. "I mean, *should* I forgive him?"

"Do you think it was a onetime thing, and he's sorry and it'll never happen again?"

It wasn't that he'd called the woman *baby*. It was the *way* he said it. As if he'd always used the word for her alone. The fact that Trinity could still hear the endearment ringing in her ears cut deep enough to draw blood. "I don't think this was the first time," she whispered. "I don't think he'll stop even if he says he's going to."

"Oh, Trin." Faith gave her hand a heartfelt squeeze.

"I *am* going to be over it, *so* over it."

"I'm still not sure why you married him." Faith didn't phrase it as a question. Which was good, because Trinity didn't have an answer.

Had she loved him? She'd convinced herself she did. But if she had, why wasn't she *completely* devastated? She was angry more than anything else. It hurt that he'd chosen someone over her, that he'd used her house for his assignation, that he'd probably married her for nothing more than her money.

But she couldn't say she hurt because *he* was gone. God, she was a shallow person. She didn't say that aloud. Faith would tell her she wasn't, yet Trinity had to admit, if to no one else, that she lived on surface emotions. She wasn't a deep thinker. She didn't like self-analysis, in general, though she'd been doing exactly that last night . . . among other things. The memory of Scott Sinclair watching her almost made her blush. Almost.

"Now that I look back on it, I'm not sure why I married Harper, either," she said, because it was the least innocuous and invited the fewest questions.

"Want us to whoop his ass for you?" Josie offered.

"We'll hang his entrails from the Golden Gate," Faith added.

Trinity had once threatened to drape Connor's entrails over the bridge if he *ever* hurt Faith.

She laughed despite how it made her throat ache. Her friends were the best ever. "Harper isn't worth you two getting arrested for the deed. But thanks." And that was all she'd say. She couldn't quite define her own feelings other than being messed up. If her emotions hadn't been topsy-turvy, she never would have let a stranger into her room last night.

Not that she'd tell her friends about *that* insane interlude. First of all, they'd freak that she took such a risk. But it was also a private, titillating experience that once shared would lose some of the specialness. It was *hers*.

"And I got a job working at Daddy's company."

Faith's jaw dropped.

"What the hell are you going to do there?" Josie burst out, almost as if she didn't believe Trinity was capable of doing anything useful.

"I did graduate from college, you know."

"I didn't mean that the way it sounded."

"I know." Trinity wasn't so sure, though. Josie was a career woman, like Faith, for whom being a kindergarten teacher was a calling. Some sort of program manager for Castle Heavy Mining, Josie had just returned from managing a two-month project down in South America. Castle wasn't a mining company itself, but they manufactured massive mining equipment. Monetarily, neither Faith nor Josie had to work. Faith's daddy, Jarvis, was the largest shareholder in Castle Heavy Mining, the family business, and Connor was CEO. Josie's father also had a big share as well as a board position. Yet both her friends had chosen to do something useful, while Trinity had merely drifted.

Gee, the best thing she could say she'd ever done was introduce Connor to Faith. Other than that . . . she was useless.

Well, no more. She could handle this job, do it well. In fact, she might prove herself worthy of taking over from her father. Why not? She wouldn't let herself be offended by Josie's words. Her feelings were simply tender after the trashing Harper had given them.

"I'm going to be the Accounts Receivable and Payables supervisor." Before the merger, Green Industries had one major customer, Castle, for whom Green plated and machined component parts, but under the Castle umbrella, her father began courting new customers. "Daddy thinks that as I excel at charity fund-raising, I'll be great in collections." She spread her hands and beamed at her audience. "It's a win-win situation."

Yet it was one thing to guilt her friends at the country club into donating for a good cause and quite another hassling customers to pay up. But she could make her father proud.

"You do have a way with people," Faith agreed.

"A job is going to be a lot of fun." If she didn't slash her wrists from sheer terror before she started. When she thought about it too hard, the prospect of having a job and people working for her was a tad frightening.

Josie raised one brow as if she could read Trinity's mind.

"Honest." Trinity punctuated with a vigorous head nod. "I want something to do. I *need* something to do. And this is it."

"You shouldn't let a man make you change your whole life. Men just aren't that important."

Ooh, Josie'd definitely had a bad experience in the past.

"Maybe it's time to change my life." Maybe it was time to figure out what she truly wanted. Honestly, Trinity didn't know. "I mean, Faith wants to be a teacher and a mother. You want to be the head of Program Management."

"Excuse me, I want to be head of the whole company, not just Program Management." Josie grabbed Faith's hand. "I told Connor I wanted his job when he becomes chairman. The first female Castle CEO, what do you think?"

Faith smiled indulgently. "I'm sure that's what you'll be."

"See?" Trinity huffed. "You both know what *you* want."

Faith turned her way. "*You* wanted to be first lady."

Trinity shrugged. "That was a pipe dream. I wasn't serious." She was never serious about anything.

Maybe that's why Harper had found it so easy to use her.

Oops, that was a maudlin thought creeping in. She beat it back with details. "I start work next Monday." A week away.

"We've got to celebrate," Faith said, standing slowly and massaging her huge tummy. "Let's have a glass of champagne."

Trinity gaped. "But you don't drink with the baby."

"I've got some sparkling cider as well."

"I've got a better idea." A brilliant idea. It was growing on Trinity. "Let's have some ice cream."

"I don't have anything fat free."

"I don't want fat free." She had a quick flash of Harper and his *voluptuous* woman, and her migraine stabbed right through her temple. Damn him anyway. "I want the full-fatted stuff, and pregnant women always have ice cream in the freezer." Not that Trinity had spent a lot of time around pregnant women before.

Faith stared at her as if antennae suddenly sprouted out of her head, but Trinity wouldn't say that Harper's *woman* looked as if she ate *all* her favorite flavors of ice cream.

And Harper had still wanted her.

Josie popped up to open the freezer door. "Look at this." She pointed. "She's got tons."

"Connor bought all that," Faith jumped in. "He didn't want to run out in the middle of the night when I had cravings."

Josie tipped her head. "I thought cravings were an old wives' tale."

Faith blushed for no apparent reason.

"Ooh, I know what she's craving in the middle of the night." Trinity laughed.

"Ooh," Josie seconded.

"I'll admit the butter pecan is mine," Faith said primly.

"I want rocky road." Trinity's mouth watered. God, she hadn't had real chocolate ice cream in . . . well, not since she'd started wearing makeup in junior high.

There were so many things she hadn't indulged in, yet what had been the point in denying herself? Harper cheated anyway.

From now on, she wasn't going to deny herself a thing. Not one single thing.

"Do you have any caramel sauce?" she asked.

Ice cream. Champagne cocktails. Baked potatoes with sour cream. And passionate sex with a virtual stranger? She remembered how good Scott made her feel. Why deny herself *that*?

She could call him when she wanted to, and he couldn't call her back. She could meet him anywhere, then take off in a cab. A quickie, all night, or just a naughty phone conversation. She could control when, where, what, and how, every detail. Control had never seemed important to her before, yet now it was almost a need, like water or food. Their meetings would be about sex and nothing more. Total pleasure. Total control. After finding Harper, pleasure and control now seemed to go hand in hand. She couldn't achieve one without the other.

In her whole life, Trinity had never been the one in charge. She *told* people she was, she liked to make other women *think* she was, but the truth? She molded herself into what she thought a man wanted.

Well, no more. She was going to indulge.

And the next thing she'd indulge in would be Scott Sinclair.

THE investors' dinner went on and on. Scott took a five-minute break to check his work messages. Ah hell, why not admit it? He wanted to see if she'd called. His presentation that morning had gone off without a hitch, adequately explaining the issues causing Millennium Robotics' downward financial trend in the last three reported quarters while at the same time keeping the company's outlook upbeat, though that was a difficult line to walk. His part done, he'd sat through the other presenters, the questions, the discussion, yet he'd had to force his mind to stay on track. It wanted to wander to his mystery lady.

He had to smile to himself, because damn if he wasn't hooked. Until halfway through the day, he hadn't bothered to consider whether she even lived in the San Francisco Bay Area. After all, she'd been staying at a hotel, yet he hadn't allowed it as a possibility that she was from out of town.

Outside the restaurant door, the cool evening washing over him, he punched in his voice mail. His heart started to beat faster the moment he heard her voice on the message, and he felt almost giddy, like a dorky teenager the first time he was absolutely sure he'd caught the head cheerleader's eye.

"We're going to have a hot, passionate, anything-goes affair. I'll call you tomorrow and tell you how it'll work."

She was a tease. His cock was damn near combustible. He'd forgotten how good it felt to want a woman this badly. With his blood rushing in his veins, he was completely jacked, totally alive. He loved the mystery, the tension of waiting, the fear she might not call again. She was his drug. He was her addict.

He had one major problem. She'd used the word *affair*. Somewhere along the way, he'd forgotten to wonder whether she was married. In his mind, she couldn't belong to anyone else.

But what if she did?

4

SCOTT Sinclair had *the* hottest voice. In fact, Trinity had called his number a second time last night to listen to his voice mail recording all over again.

Letting his voice play in her head was better than allowing the sound of Harper's harpy to ring in her ears. Heh. Harper's harpy. She liked the sound of *that*. It didn't make her a bitter bitch. Well, yes, it did, but she couldn't help herself.

After returning from Faith's, she'd moved her stuff into the guest room. It might be pathetic, but she couldn't stay in the master bedroom. And this morning, she was not one darn bit maudlin. Honest.

In the kitchen, the coffee was already dripping, scenting the condo with a rich aroma. She popped her usual half piece of bread into the toaster, and when it was done, she had it halfway to her mouth before she realized what she was doing.

"A real woman doesn't have to live on half a piece of dry toast." Throwing it in the sink, she turned on the garbage disposal and ground it up with malice aforethought.

A real woman didn't need a man to give her great orgasms either. But having Scott Sinclair listen in on a few would certainly be extra stimulating. And if he watched again? Ooh.

Granola streamed out of the package, clattering into her bowl. She used the rest of Harper's fresh blueberries and covered them in whole, honest-to-goodness vitamin D milk without measuring a half-cup serving. Regardless of calories, calcium was good for a woman's bones.

God, she felt free as she carried her cereal and the phone into the family room. The berries and milk-soaked granola were damn near . . . orgasmic. Trinity closed her eyes and savored every single delicious bite.

Now, she had to take a bite out of life. For today, that meant a phone call to her favorite CFO, Scott Sinclair. That definitely had an *ooh* factor involved. Slipping in her Bluetooth—she wanted to be totally hands free for whatever naughty thing she felt compelled to do— she couldn't wait to hear his voice, for real instead of a recording.

Life without Harper was going to be grand.

"ARE you married?" It wasn't a statement on her morals, but a need to know. Scott wouldn't share, even if she was just a voice on his office phone.

She waited a beat too long to answer, and his gut tensed.

"No."

His tension didn't ease. "Are you sure?"

She puffed out a little breath. "I'm divorced." Then she sighed. "Recently," and before he could ask, she followed up with, "Satisfied now that I've bared my soul?"

He liked that she was snarky. He didn't like that he was probably a rebound thing, but beggars couldn't be choosers. He'd been hooked from the moment he heard her voice through the wall.

"What about you?" she asked.

"I'm divorced, not so recently. Tell me your name."

She laughed. It was musical. It made him hard.

"I'm not telling you my name. That's my secret."

As was her number. The company phone system went through a PBX, and there was no direct line, only his extension, and no caller ID. She was safe. That was his intention. And she enjoyed playing it.

"What should I call you, then?"

"Well, Scott"—she said his name with a definite emphasis on the *T*—"maybe you should call me . . . Vixen."

His turn to laugh, and it came from deep in his belly. "I don't think so. Doesn't suit you at all."

Passing the office door, his controller glanced inside, brow raised as if she'd heard something different in his voice.

"Hold on a minute."

He rose to shut the door, but left the blinds open. His office was fronted by half windows that looked over the bullpen of accounting activity. Closed blinds meant someone was getting his or her ass chewed. Closed door, however, merely indicated he was discussing proprietary business.

"I almost hung up," she said when he once again had the receiver to his ear.

"No, you didn't. You called for phone sex, and you haven't had an orgasm." He expected her to balk or get snarky again.

"I've never had phone sex."

"Never?" He'd tried it a time or two after the divorce.

She hummed a second. "What's it like? Tell me."

The invitation in those two words was a stroke along his cock. He had a meeting at nine with his CEO and VPs to discuss the investor meeting. Fifteen minutes. Could he get her to come? Could he at least get her to touch herself for him?

"What are you wearing?"

She snorted. "That sounds like what some skanky guy would say when he calls one of those 900 numbers."

Scott laughed. She wasn't going to make it easy. "Are you going to do what I tell you or argue?" He allowed his authoritative side to sift through.

"Yes, sir," she said with the sweetest sassy edge. "I'm wearing silk pajamas."

"Unbutton the top."

"There, it's unbuttoned."

"Now pinch your nipples."

She huffed. "But that will hurt."

"It'll feel good." He remembered the shape and texture, the dusky rose tint, small but pert, eminently suckable. He also remembered that she'd pinched her nipples for him that night. Now she was just being feisty. "Do it."

She gasped, and his cock jerked inside his pants. His controller passed his now closed door again, same raised eyebrow. She was a matronly type, perhaps a couple of years older than he was, with knee-length skirts and a sharp accounting mind.

"Told you it would be good," he said to his mystery lady, dropping his voice. "Say, 'Yes, Scott, it felt so damn good.'"

"Yes, Scott," she whispered, "it felt really good."

"Wrong," he snapped. "Say it the way I told you."

"Yes, Scott," she murmured, "it felt so damn good."

In fact, Trinity was close to panting for the man. Phone sex had always seemed so . . . undignified, yet Scott had the best voice for it.

"Are you wet?"

"Yes, Scott." She was so darn wet. Her skin was flushed. She lay sprawled across the sofa, her pajama top unbuttoned and askew, her hair in her face. She puffed it away with a breath.

"Touch yourself and tell me how wet you are."

"Yes, Scott." The flesh between her legs seemed to vibrate. Trinity slipped her hand beneath the elastic of her pajama shorts. Closing her eyes, she imagined she was spreading her legs for him the way she had in the hotel room. Her center was creamy, warm, and her whole body shivered as she rolled her finger over her clitoris. "Oh Scott, I am *so* wet for you."

He made a noise, a soft groan. "Do you like that I can't touch myself, that I can only listen while I sit in my office and everyone can see me talking through the windows?"

"Yes, I like it." She loved it. Even as he told her what to do, she knew she held him in thrall, and it was so powerful. She could get used to it. She could come to hunger for it.

"Pinch your nipple again," he demanded.

Gliding the tip of one wet finger around her nipple, she pinched. Oh. Oh, that was perfect. A moan slipped out.

"How does it feel?" His voice was huskier, deeper.

"Electrifying." She sighed. Her body buzzed. Her clitoris ached for more.

"Do it harder this time."

She let out a long, low sound of pleasure as tiny jolts zipped from her nipple to her extremities. God, sex could be good. She'd never imagined how good. And he wasn't even with her in the room. It was amazing. "That felt sooo hot."

"Pinch it again, but hold it."

"Yes, sir," she whispered, playing with first one nipple, then the other. "Is this like dominance and submission?"

"It's about directing your play. It makes me a part of it rather than simply a voyeur." He lowered his voice. "It makes me fucking hot."

She'd never been into dirty talk, but the way he said that word was almost as good as the feel of her hand between her legs. "I liked it when you were a voyeur." *Like* was far too mild.

"I noticed. But I also notice you aren't making any noises like you're pinching your nipple." He gave a little *tsk*.

"Sorry." Trinity dipped her head to watch herself, and this time she took both nipples. "Now I'm doing it."

"Hold it, hold it, hold it."

His voice mesmerized her. Her nipples shrieked, yet it wasn't pain but the height of pleasure. She seemed to spin off into another place. On their own, her hips bucked and writhed on the sofa. She closed her eyes, moaning, riding the wave, imagining his hands on her, his lips, tongue driving her crazy.

"Now let go."

Air rushed over her swollen nipples. "Oh, oh, that was so good." She sucked in a breath. A second more, and she would have come just from the ache and his voice pushing her. She'd never felt anything like it in her life. And she wanted more. "Scott, I wanna touch myself. Please." She'd die if he didn't let her.

"Rub your clit for me."

She shoved her hand into her shorts. "Oh God."

She moaned, groaned, tossed her head on a sofa cushion. She didn't sound like Miss Perfect Trinity Green. She sounded like the perfect naughty lover. Scott made sounds, spoke words, urged her on, told her how good, how perfect, how hot, how wonderful she was. And Trinity soared beyond any peak she'd ever achieved.

"Do you want to come?" He toyed with her. It made her crazy, just as she'd been the other night while he watched her.

"Yes, please." She'd beg, plead, anything he wanted.

"You can come on the count of ten. But don't come until then, or I won't let you come at all. Do it exactly when I say."

Making her wait for his command brought him right into the room with her. With her eyes closed, she could almost feel him kneeling on the floor beside the sofa, sweet warm breath on her, the light touch of a finger along her arm. He was *there*.

He counted. She moaned. He hit number five. She thought she'd die. Crazy little noises welled up in her throat. Colors swirled behind her closed lids.

"Nine . . . ten . . . now. Come now or I won't let you at all."

She cried out, long, wild, everything inside bursting free, careening off. She cried out for him, for herself, the sound of her voice in

total abandon almost as good as the deepness of his in her ear.
Nothing. Ever. Never. Not like this.

Then she hiccupped, laughed with the slightest edge of hysteria,
and murmured, "Oh my God."

And the Bluetooth went dead.

HIS cock surged in his pants, and if he'd been alone, he'd have cli-
maxed in two seconds flat with one pass of his hand.

Sitting in his office, the door closed, talking a gorgeous woman
through an orgasm, it was the hottest damn thing he'd ever done.
Telling her what to do was so immediate, making him a part of her
action. His cock was an aching rock in his pants, but he hadn't felt
this damn exhilarated, this *alive* in so many years, it was frightening to count them.

He knew without a doubt that she'd call back. He had something
she wanted. Perhaps because she was "recently" divorced, or because
she'd never stepped out of her safe, secure vanilla world. He had the
sense to realize she'd never done anything remotely like opening her
door to a stranger who wanted to watch her. Yet now that she'd had
a taste of the wild side, she'd have to have more. So did he. He
wanted to unearth every naughty desire, taste it, touch it, explore it,
feel alive with it. This would be so damn good for both of them.

He was still hard as a metal spike, even a bit dazed. Outside his
office window, Ron Rudd raised his arm and tapped his wrist-
watch, reminding him of the meeting. A second later his CEO
opened the office door without knocking.

Well, hell, there went a pleasant buzz. Scott straightened, slid
closer to the desk and rested on his elbows. "I'll be there in a couple, Ron." As soon as he got control of his cock.

"I was taking a look at the prelims." Rudd stroked the top of
his bald head.

The man never should have shaved off the rest of his hair. A year younger than Scott, he'd had a large bald spot. Now, his head resembled an egg. "Egghead" was not a reputable nickname for the CEO of Millennium Robotics, yet Scott had heard it bandied about in the halls.

"They aren't preliminary numbers. They're close to final." They had to go through audit, and these days all bets were off on what could change, but in Scott's mind, they were solid.

Rudd's lips twitched, and he drew in a deep breath of air. "You realize our jobs are on the line with numbers like that."

Rudd's very well could be. His decision making in the two years since he'd become CEO had, in a word, sucked.

Leaning both fists on the desk, Rudd homed in, his chin jutting. "You've got to find something, Scott. In my opinion, we're way over-reserved."

"The reserves analysis proved out." There wasn't much room for pickup there considering last year's disastrous product release. "We haven't paid the piper on the Millennium 4 yet."

"The M4 is done." Rudd knocked the desk. "Get rid of the reserve. Do whatever you have to, I want some improvement."

Scott rose. He didn't use his height to intimidate, but he'd make damn sure Rudd understood he wasn't compromising his own ethics to shore up a shitty bottom line. At six four, he towered over his boss's five ten with a very good view of the top of the egg. "There isn't anything that's going to get this year out of the hole."

Rudd narrowed his eyes. "I suggest you find a way."

"Or what?" Scott murmured. The man was an ass.

"Or heads will roll."

And the first one would be the egghead.

"OH my God." Trinity must have whispered that aloud at least four times since she hung up.

Her nipples were tender, sensitive nubs. They ached so *good*. She could see why men paid beaucoup bucks for phone sex.

Over the years, she'd had five lovers, including Harper, yet none of them had ever made her feel like this. Scott wasn't even in the room, yet he'd left her boneless, satisfied, languorous, and sleepy, all rolled into one delicious package. He'd told her to come on the count of ten, and she'd actually held off until he gave her the word. If he'd told her to stop in the middle and began his count all over again, she still would have waited until he'd granted her permission.

Why had it gotten her so excited?

Because . . . well, heck, it was fun. Sex had never been just plain old fun, especially with someone who actually seemed to care about her orgasm. And he wasn't even getting any since he was sitting in his office. He hadn't interjected his own fantasies, he'd simply directed hers. It had all been about *her*. On second thought, it seemed a bit selfish, but she could swear he'd enjoyed it as much as she had, so where was the harm in that? It had been good for *both* of them.

Trinity climbed the stairs. It was after nine, and she hadn't even dressed yet. Not that she had much to do today. She'd done most of her running around yesterday. She could even call Scott again, right now, or later. If she wanted to. She was in total control of the next move.

In the guest room, which was now *her* room, she tapped a key on her computer and the screen came to life. Logging on, she brought up her Internet e-mail. To avoid getting a bunch of spam to her real address, she always kept an anonymous e-mail account for shopping online.

Typing in Scott's address—okay, yes, she'd memorized it off his card—she gave him a one-line message. "Thank you."

Thank you for the orgasm and thank you for setting her free.

When she'd finished drying off after her shower, she checked. Nothing. Mild disappointment circled in her belly.

She moisturized and lotioned, put on her makeup, and blow-dried her hair, then checked. Still nothing. Okay, the disappointment was a tad more than mild—it had moved from her belly to her chest.

She chose the peach Evan-Picone and color-matched Manolo Blahniks.

Her screen bleeped. Her heart gave a little kick.

"That, my dear, was incredibly hot." The address was different, a personal account instead of work, but it was Scott. And his words made her pulse do a little happy dance.

She couldn't resist typing back. "And you have an incredibly hot voice." She chewed her lip a second. "Okay, I promise not to call you every day begging to hear it again."

He came back in less than a minute. "You can call me any time you want."

Ooh. She typed quickly. "I might do that." Then she signed out with no good-bye. The key to power was to leave when *you* were ready. Besides, she had this overwhelming need to continuing flirting with him all day long.

Of course, when she got back from a quick errand, she was back in e-mail before she'd even removed her Manolos.

And there he was. Her heart beat faster as she read.

"I went to the gym for a good long workout, forty-five minutes of StairMaster to sweat you out. Needless to say, all I did was play back the whole conversation in my head. Damn. You are naughty and fun."

It was oh-so-thrilling that he was some bigwig executive eating out of her hand. For anyone watching him, he had to look all circumspect when he was talking on the phone with her, yet she brought out the bad boy in him. Trinity loved the power trip. "I hope you weren't able to sweat me out that easily."

He must have had his e-mail open right there on his screen at work because he came back in what seemed like seconds. "You definitely are a rare breed. Open, sexual, and very tempting. I haven't gotten nearly enough of you yet."

His words turned her mushy inside. To him, she was special. Open and sexual. Trinity had never thought herself capable of that before. He'd opened up a whole new world to her. She *would* call again. Once or twice. Oh, hell, face it, the e-mails and phone calls were fun and flirty, and concentrating on *that* drowned out the echo of Harper's harpy in the master bathroom shower.

"I need to call you *something*. Give me a name, any name."

Scott lounged in his leather desk chair, the phone glued to his ear, his office door closed for the second time on Wednesday. They'd had their first call yesterday, and she'd stepped up to twice today. The woman was insatiable. He loved it. He'd never thought he'd be into phone sex, but he couldn't get enough of her. Hell, what he really wanted was to see her again, but he was biding his time until he had her as hooked as he was.

"I'm whoever you want me to be." She hummed lightly through the connection. He felt it in his cock. "Maybe a girlfriend's name, one that got away, a girl you still think about?"

"No one like that." He'd dated in high school and college, but the relationships had always ended fairly amicably. Then he met Katy in his senior year. Katy was the only one that got away, but he sure as hell wasn't going to call his mystery lady by his ex-wife's name. "I think I'll call you Jezebel."

"Jezebel? Wasn't she a prostitute."

"No." He wasn't actually sure. "She wrapped every man she met around her gorgeous little finger."

"Ooh, I like that."

He loved the way she said *ooh*.

"Start my countdown again, Scott," she whispered.

And he did. Yeah, his Jezebel had him hook, line, and sinker. He was madly in lust with a woman he didn't even know.

COULD a woman have *too* many orgasms? By Friday, Trinity lost count. Her breasts had grown from all the hormones.

She hoped it wasn't all the ice cream she'd eaten.

"My daughter's coming home from college this weekend," Scott said while she was drifting in orgasmic aftermath.

"Your daughter?" She didn't mean to let it slip out of her mouth, but it did.

"Yeah, Lexa. She's my youngest. She's a sophomore at—"

"Wait." She held up her hand as if he could see her. "Don't tell me." She didn't want to know about his daughter. Jeez, a daughter in college. She'd figured he was in his midforties, but a college-age kid made Trinity feel young. And so not together. She was thirty and *just* getting her first job.

She blew out a breath. "New rule. We don't get personal."

"We're having sex on the phone. That's personal." A slight edge ran through his voice.

"Yes, well." She bit her lip. Next week she started work. "I can't call so much after this." She thought up a good lie. "I was on vacation this week, and I'm back to work on Monday."

"Call my cell in the evenings, then."

"But you'd know my number."

"You can block it."

"I like calling you at the office." The whole bigwig thing.

"But at home, I can come with you."

He was pushing. She was losing control. "No. We can only talk when you're at work. If you want to stay late so I can call, that's fine. But those are the rules." That felt better. Setting rules gave her a sense of control.

"So you're not going to call me this weekend?"

"You'll have your daughter with you." A reasonable explanation. "Monday. I'll call when I get home. Hopefully you can stay late at work." Said as if it didn't matter one way or the other.

Scott laughed. "You really are a Jezebel, aren't you?"

This time he hung up first.

Was he angry? God, even allowing the question in her mind was frightening, as if she were letting her former self, the woman who *lived* to please a man, sneak back inside her. She couldn't let that happen.

"YOU look pretty chipper, Dad." Lexa chewed on a carrot stick as he put the artichokes on to boil. She'd driven up from San Luis Obispo, arriving late last night. They'd spent Saturday morning running errands, then hanging out around the house. "Got a new hottie?" she added before another carrot crunch.

Scott's heart gave an odd jump. Lexa had had a much harder time with the divorce than Brooke. A couple of years older, Brooke had been going into her junior year at college, and though she'd been sad, it hadn't affected her in the same way. Then suddenly, Lexa, after spending last summer bouncing between his place and Katy's, had gone back to school with a new attitude. She'd started treating him like her buddy, looking for dates, pointing out "hotties" when they went to the movies or out to dinner.

But no freaking way was he telling Lexa about Jezebel.

"I'm just glad to have you for the weekend, honey."

She popped him on the arm. "You're a fibber." Dumping the bottle of spaghetti sauce into a pot, she set it on the glass-top stove. "Seriously, Dad, Brooke and I want you to find a woman."

She caught him off guard once again. She would always be his little girl, and there was something about her picking out women for him that felt . . . queasy. Yet she thought of herself as grown-up, no matter how much he'd always see her as his baby, and she was doing her best to have him treat her as an adult.

Still, some things were going too far even for him.

Scott put his hands over his ears. "I'm not listening." Then he reached for the linguine noodles in the cupboard over the stove. He hadn't cooked a day in his life when Katy walked out. The last year had been a crash course since he didn't want to subsist on fast food. When he bought this house, he'd upgraded the kitchen, and at least learned to boil noodles.

"Tell your sister my sex life is off-limits."

"Da-ad." Lexa put her hands on her hips and pouted.

Despite being two years apart, she and Brooke were as alike as twins. Five foot ten, they got their height, brown hair, and brown eyes from him while their beauty and slender build came from their mother. They even said *Da-ad* identically. God, they were so beautiful his heart ached looking at them.

"We weren't talking about your sex life." Lexa flipped her long hair over her shoulder. "We're talking about your love life. And we think you're lonely."

After salting the water, Scott put the pan on to boil. "You used the term *hottie*. That doesn't refer to a love life." He opened the can of clams to add to the sauce.

Hottie did, however, refer to Jezebel. She'd cut him off until Monday. Even then, he'd have to stay late if he wanted to talk to her. He recognized a woman's need to assert control, but it made him nuts. He was deep in withdrawal. Yet that was part of her lure. She kept him on edge, and he couldn't wait to hear her voice, her musical laugh, the heady sound of her orgasm.

If he wasn't careful, he'd be embarrassed in front of his daughter. He needed to corral his thoughts. "I'm not lonely. I've got a busy life with work"—he held up a finger when Lexa opened her mouth—"but I promise that when I do meet a wonderful woman, I will give the whole love life thing a chance again."

"Good. 'Cause, well, you know, after Mom and everything, we were afraid that you might be gun-shy."

He'd painted Katy's actions in the best light possible for his daughters. He never blamed her, never voiced the thought that she might be seriously depressed. Though he had to Katy. She'd refused to seek treatment. Instead, she'd moved into a condo and lived her days the same as she had when they were married, sewing, arts and crafts, volunteering at her church.

She simply did it without him in the house.

"I'm not gun-shy." He dumped the linguine into the now boiling water. "There's just no one I wanted to introduce."

Lexa set the colander in the sink. "You will let us meet her if you do, though, right? Brooke and I, we *want* you to find someone." She tucked her hair behind her ear. "I said the same thing to Mom, too, but I don't think . . . ," she trailed off.

Scott tipped her chin with a finger. "I promise, sweetie, that as soon as I meet someone I like, I'll introduce you." He smoothed the hair away from her forehead. "And don't worry about your mom. She'll find what she's looking for when she's ready."

All Katy had been ready for was getting him out of the house. He'd moved on. Now, he felt sorry for her. He was sure she'd never find that elusive "thing" she was looking for, be it love or happiness, but at least she seemed content.

His monotone relationship with his ex-wife was a far cry from the volatile emotions Jezebel evoked. She made him feel alive. Aware. Passionate. Damn. He wasn't sure how he'd make it through to Monday night.

5

TRINITY wasn't nervous Monday morning. She was terrified. She'd always entered Green Industries with a song in her heart and a bounce to her high heels clicking across the lobby's terra-cotta tile floor. That was an exaggeration, yet this morning she'd felt second class when her father trundled her off to Human Resources to fill out an application and give them her Social Security number. Not that she expected special treatment.

For the first day on the job, she'd worn her best red power suit, the one she saved for fund-raising committees and asking her father's associates to donate large sums of money or their son's two-year-old BMW to breast cancer research. Despite the red, Trinity wasn't feeling particularly powerful.

Instead, she gathered her portfolio of important papers about company policy, e-mail etiquette, and 401(k) information, and headed upstairs. The employees she greeted were all familiar, at least for the most part. What wasn't familiar was the wary glances and the pinched-lip assessments.

At the entryway to the Accounting Department, she stopped a young woman in crisp blue jeans. "Could you tell me where Anthony's office is?" Anthony, her new boss.

She'd met him at the company Christmas parties and summer barbecues. He was a nice sort, in his midforties, married, two kids. His wife was pretty and blond and her name was . . . darn, Trinity couldn't remember. It wasn't good not to remember her boss's wife's name.

For her question, she received a surly glare and a curt answer. "*Mr.* Ackerman's office is in the corner." The girl pointed over a maze of cubicles.

Mr. Ackerman? Trinity started to get it. Green employees tolerated her bouncing through as the boss's daughter. But working with them? They hated it.

Is this the way her brother had felt? Like an outsider?

"Thank you," Trinity said, and the girl shrugged, then headed out into the hall for the ladies' room.

The Accounting area was a din of voices and phones with the cubicles haphazardly thrown together, some facing each other, others back to back, and a center area filled with four-drawer filing cabinets. Rather than finding her way through the cubicle aisles, she skirted the dividers past the offices built along the outside walls. In one cube she passed, a youngish guy slumped over his ten-key adding machine, fingers flying. She'd thought everyone used the computer these days. In another cubicle, a girl chattered on the phone in what Trinity believed was Chinese.

Anthony's door was closed, but through the glass side panel, a buxom blonde was visible occupying one of the two chairs in front of his desk. Her thick hair, pulled back in a knot, perched at the back of her neck as she drummed her fingers on an armrest.

Trinity tapped on the door.

Anthony stood and signaled her in. Tall and skinny, he had receding hair, with just a tuft sticking up where once he might have had a widow's peak.

"Perfect timing," he said, a grin stretched across his face like a rubber band pulled too tight.

"I was down in HR filling out paperwork," Trinity said as if she needed to explain to the teacher why she was late.

"Yes, yes, of course." Anthony waved her in, the flat of his hand landing on the chair next to the blonde. "Well, it's so perfect because I've got Inga right here."

Something told Trinity it wasn't at all perfect in Anthony's opinion. Then Inga stood. Good God, she was an Amazon. Or Brunhilda. Trinity had chosen the three-inch Manolos, but Inga had chosen *her* heels well, too, and she towered over Trinity.

"Inga Rice, Trinity Green," Anthony did the introductions.

A simple green sheath made of some soft jersey material clung to Inga Rice's curves. She had bosoms and hips, and Trinity noted a slight sheen of sweat along Anthony's upper lip just from being trapped behind closed doors with her.

Inga Rice was the type to make men sweat. Anthony dabbed a handkerchief to the top of his head. "Inga is our lead Accounts Payable clerk. She knows everything there is to know and can walk you through the whole system."

"It's so nice to meet you." She put out her hand.

And Inga crushed it, her blue eyes sparkling. "It's such a pleasure." *Not.*

Her voice had a breathy quality that had Anthony dabbing the tuft on his head once again.

"Inga, why don't you introduce Trinity around?"

Trinity had the feeling he wanted them gone from his office before the claws came out.

"Thanks. I'd appreciate that." She'd give Inga the benefit of the doubt. The woman probably didn't know her own strength.

And Inga led her around the department. The Asian girl in the first cubicle was Christina Lee, Accounts Receivable clerk and relatively new. She shrank when Inga stepped into her cube.

"This is Trinity The-Boss's-Daughter." Said with hyphens and capitals as if that were Trinity's last name.

The young man with fast fingers was Boyd Osterlot, general ledger accountant. Whatever the general ledger was. Trinity had some things to learn.

"He doesn't work for you," Inga said as Boyd drooled, his gaze fixed on Inga's upper body curves.

In the end, Trinity met three Accounts Payable clerks (including the girl in blue jeans), two general ledger accountants, one cost accountant, and a partridge in a pear tree. Okay, sorry, but she couldn't keep the names straight, or the titles or the jobs. She'd thought she'd have an office—not because she was Daddy's little girl, but because she was a supervisor—yet her twelve-by-twelve cubicle was three cubes down from Inga's ten-by-ten. At least Trinity had four extra square feet, but that was about all.

Trinity had never felt so out of her depth in her whole life. Especially with big, blonde, knock-'em-dead gorgeous Inga Rice standing three inches taller that she did.

TRINITY gave herself a pep talk all the way home. She'd left on the dot of five. Her head was about to explode like those of the little aliens in *Mars Attacks!*

"*I can do this.*"

Except that Inga hated her.

"*I can make her my friend.*"

Except that Inga had wanted Trinity's job. Had believed she *deserved* the job.

Trinity was nice, she was personable, she went out of her way to make people feel comfortable. Even old ladies liked her! Trinity liked to be liked. She'd never dealt with such animosity, at least not right in her face. Sure, at the country club there was a bit of vindictive backstabbing, but this was . . . different. She couldn't quite comprehend it, except to liken it to junior high when that nasty gang of girls had picked on Faith mercilessly until Trinity stepped in and gave them what for.

It was just that Inga was so . . . pretty? No. In all honesty, Trinity was pretty. She wasn't stuck-up, but she knew she was pretty. Good bone structure from her mother. Her mama had been absolutely gorgeous. Trinity always strove to be perfect like she'd been. *Everyone* loved her mother.

A light turned red before she even saw it turn yellow, and Trinity slammed on the brakes. At least no one rear-ended her.

Back to Inga. It wasn't jealousy or anything like that. It didn't bother her that men's eyes followed Inga's swaying backside while they were still shaking Trinity's hand.

The light turned. She told herself to pay attention, but all she could see was Anthony dabbing the sweat off his head and Boyd all googly-eyed over Inga . . . or rather Inga's breasts.

It was Inga's bosom. That's what bothered Trinity. Inga had bosoms. Like Harper's harpy.

After thirty years of feeling fine with her body, suddenly, Trinity wasn't sure she was good enough. It was demoralizing. She felt oodles of empathy for Faith, who'd *always* felt inadequate. Not that Faith *was* inadequate. She was gorgeous and perfect. Certainly Connor thought so and adored her.

She punched the Mustang's accelerator and buzzed around a slow-moving minivan full of soccer moms and kids. She had to wonder when Connor would switch out Faith's Lexus for a minivan. He was such a dad. Trinity's heart ached a little bit thinking about the two of them. She'd dreamed about that with Harper, not the minivan or even the pregnancy itself, but the way Connor touched Faith, the expression on his face, an indescribable look of pure joy that actually brought a tear to Trinity's eye.

She would *not* get maudlin. She would not be demoralized. She wasn't the mothering type like Faith anyway. Climbing out of the car and heading into the small courtyard, she flipped through her jumble of keys for the alarm remote, which she'd also had reprogrammed. The rhododendrons were about to bud, and soon after would be the camellias and azaleas. The flowering bushes in the courtyard were one of the reasons she'd picked the condo.

"Trinity."

She shrieked and dropped everything, finally catching her breath to say, "What are you doing here, Harper?" She would have liked her voice to be more assertive, but she sounded like a scared little mouse.

He was seated in one of the black wrought iron chairs at the little café table. "Honey, we need to talk."

"Don't"—she sucked in a breath—"call me *honey*."

"I'm sorry."

Harper was a golden child, fair hair styled in a short cut, blue eyes, and pale, barely there eyebrows. With the few extra inches he had over her height, she could always wear her best high heels with him.

Now *that* was a recommendation for marrying a man. What had gone wrong with her over the last few months?

"Can I at least come in so we can talk?" His eyes begged.

"No." Instead, she sat on the chair opposite him. "I'm getting a divorce." She didn't feel a single emotion. Honest. All right, she was trying not to feel anything, especially anger, which was such a wasted, useless emotion.

He put a long-fingered hand on the table as if he were actually thinking about touching her. "Before you do that, I want to explain—"

"There's nothing to explain."

His Adam's apple slid up and down. "I'm sorry. I know how that must have hurt you."

"She had breasts, Harper." Trinity slapped her hand over her mouth in horror, then gathered herself. "Not that I cared." Yet his *harpy* was everything she wasn't. Just as Inga Rice was. Next to the two of them, Trinity felt downright androgynous.

See, that was the problem. Harper showed up at the end of an Inga-infested day. Trinity wouldn't have been so weak if it weren't for that.

"You're so much more perfect than her." He passed a hand over his hair without actually mussing it. "I don't know what came over me. It was a momentary blip."

Except that he'd had time to bring the woman to their *house,* for God's sake. That took more than a momentary *blip.* She itched to slap his face, but that would be undignified. Instead she went for his egotistical jugular. "I married you because I was trying to give myself what Faith had."

She felt a flush rush straight up her body to her face. Good Lord. That *wasn't* true. She wasn't *jealous* of her best friend. Yet some needy part of her wanted a man to look at her the way Connor gazed at Faith, as if no other woman existed. But no, no, she *couldn't* have married Harper out of envy.

Trinity jumped to her feet, and her heel slipped sideways, throwing her off balance. "You have to leave right now."

He stood with her, then went down on his knees, looking up. "Please. I made a mistake. A huge mistake, I know."

Oh God. This couldn't be happening. She could barely manage a whisper. "I don't care about your mistakes, Harper."

"I want to come home."

"This *isn't* your home. It belongs to my father." *Please get up, just get up.* She couldn't stand him down on his knees, and she backed toward the front door. She didn't want to feel sorry for him.

She didn't even want to find him pathetic. She didn't want any emotions about Harper at all. "You have to go."

He held out a hand. "Will you at least think about it?"

One question burned in her mind. Did Harper want her for herself? Or was it her father's money he was going to miss? She could ask him. He'd swear it wasn't the money, yet she'd never ever believe him again.

She'd forever see him in the shower with his head between that woman's legs.

Maybe she needed to find a new condo. Except that she would *not* let Harper run her out of her home.

"Have some dignity, Harper. Get up and get out." Trinity was surprised at how strong and assertive she sounded. It was in direct opposition to how she felt.

He was still on his knees when she locked the front door. Right now, she could think of only one way to feel better.

She wanted Scott to tell her she was gorgeous and perfect for him. She needed it badly.

"I'M in the bathtub sipping a glass of wine and eating chocolate. Dark chocolate. And it's sooo good."

Scott pulled up a pant leg, crossed a foot over his knee, and leaned back in his leather office chair. It was seven o'clock on Monday. The office was empty, his last accountant having gone home half an hour ago. Which was lucky for him. He wanted to come *with* her this time, instead of merely listening.

"Are you touching yourself?" He had to know what she was doing beneath the steaming water.

"No. I told you, I'm eating chocolate," she answered, her tone a hint sassy, as if she thought he'd lost his mind.

"I want to hear you come."

She moaned, a sweet, delicious sound that wrapped around his cock and wound up inside his guts. "Chocolate," she said with emphasis, "*is* orgasmic." Then she punctuated with another long hum of pleasure.

"You know you're killing me with those sounds."

"Of course I do. I want you to be very hard." She paused a beat. "Are you?"

Oh, hell yeah. "Very."

She sighed, and he could see her slipping further into the water, bubbles trifling with her nipples. "Good. Now we're going to play." She splashed the water for emphasis.

"I'm ready." Before, he'd been the one to play her. This time, she wanted the lead, and he was happy to give it to her. He'd closed his office blinds, locked the door in case an unaccounted-for employee wandered by, and plugged in his hands-free receiver. "Tell me what to do."

She made a sound he identified as the clink of her wineglass on the porcelain tub. "Pretend we're on a train in . . . France," she mused. "Can you hear the clickety-clack on the tracks?"

So she wanted a little role-play. "Yeah, I can hear it." He switched position, leaned back, and crossed his ankles on top of his desk. "Do I know you?"

"No. We're strangers. I'm reading a book, sitting across from you. You're looking over a folded newspaper, and I can't help myself, I keep glancing up at you."

"What are you wearing?"

"A skirt. And a low-cut shirt. Nothing tasteless."

"Of course not." A bit of naughty and nice, perhaps, but he considered her incapable of being tasteless. "You're sitting with your legs crossed."

He actually heard her smile as she said, "I can *feel* you looking at my legs. I wriggle my foot, and my pump slips off my heel. I lean forward and slide it back on, *very* slowly."

"And when you sit back, you glide your hand all the way up,

your ankle, your calf, the side of your knee." Damn, he could see her, smell her hot scent.

"I never look at you beyond one or two flirty glances."

He'd kill for one of her flirty glances. "You look just enough to know that I'm checking you out and loving what I see."

"Then I uncross my legs, slowly cross them the other way."

Holy hell. A Sharon Stone move from *Basic Instinct*. His cock was so damn hard, he had to stroke it through his pants. Yet he wasn't ready to unzip. If he did, everything would be over far too soon.

"You're wearing stockings, not panty hose. I can see a flash of gorgeous thigh above the black lace."

"Am I wearing panties?"

"I can't tell. Do it again," he whispered.

"No." She sighed. "That would be obvious. I'm not easy."

She was so far from easy and so fucking hot. His cock was painful. "You haven't turned a page in five minutes."

She laughed. "And you've been reading the same newspaper article for at least ten minutes."

The sultry sound made the tip of his cock tingle. His briefs were wet with pre-come. "Your stop must be coming because you stand up."

"Oh, something's coming up all right." Her husky chuckle was almost his undoing.

"I stand, too. I'm close enough to breathe you in." He scented her from that night in the hotel, the musky delicate aroma of feminine arousal.

She moaned for him. He knew she was touching herself. It ratcheted Scott higher as he wove the fantasy around her. "I don't even see the tunnel ahead until we're plunged into darkness, then all I can think about is touching you."

She hummed again, half moan, half cry, soft, sweet, making his cock pulse.

He took her deeper. "I run my hands down your sides, to your hips, and pull you close enough to feel my cock."

"You are so hard. And so big."

With his eyes closed and her voice in his ear, it was all so fucking real. God, she smelled good, her skin silky smooth. "I slip a finger down the crease of your ass, and you're warm."

"Mmm." Her little noise went on forever, and he was sure she didn't even hear herself.

"I can't resist tracing up the inside of your thigh and pushing between your legs. Christ, you're wet, so warm and so wet. I can feel it. I can hear it in your breathing. I want it. I want you. You arch into my hand, taking me deeper. Just a little longer, but I can see the damn light at the end of the tunnel. I raise my hand to my nose, and I smell you, and God, I wanna make you come, I want to hear you scream . . ."

She cried out, long and low, and he knew she was coming hard. If he wanted to come with her, he had only a moment, and he didn't know which to savor. Her come, or his? In the end, he held off stroking himself, instead letting her sounds ride through him and drag him under.

When he finally came with her, he wanted to orgasm all over her, face-to-face, no phone, no fantasy, no promises that he wouldn't touch her. She had a mind as delicious as her body, and somehow, some way, he would talk her into meeting him. He wanted more than just a voice on the phone.

6

WOW. Tuesday was a whole new day, and Trinity was a whole new woman.

That fantasy. She couldn't get over it. Scott made it so real, she could feel his hands all over her in the dark. She *wanted* his hands all over her. In the dark. In the light. Anywhere. For real. Her desire was sort of scary while at that same time exciting. She almost wished she'd let him touch her that night in the hotel.

Altogether, she felt much better about Harper and Inga and the job and all that stuff. Because of good phone sex? Well . . . yeah! For work, she'd chosen a nice sweater—okay, it showed her breasts to advantage—paired with a short, flared skirt and black stockings. She'd gotten the stocking idea from Scott last night. Not that anyone at Green would know what was under her skirt, but *she* knew. And she'd brought a philodendron for her office cubicle. The drab gray blue needed some greenery.

An office would have been better. She could close her door and call Scott. Instead, Christina Lee's voice melted through the partition wall on her left, as did the AP girl's sitting on the other side of the divider right in front of Trinity, all of which meant that Trinity's voice melted right back to them. She couldn't check e-mail because while working at her computer, her back was to the cubicle opening. What if someone soft-shoed up behind her and saw a naughty Scotty e-mail? Good Lord.

A shadow flickered over her computer monitor.

Bam! The whole cubicle rattled, and two fifty-pound binders almost crushed Trinity's fingers.

"Excuse me?" She knew the scowl looked terrible on her forehead, but really.

"Read that." Today Inga had outfitted herself in jeans so tight the rivets along the seams were in danger of blowing out. In a sweater more form-fitting than Trinity's, her breasts were coneshaped, like those old brassieres the women wore in classic movies from the 1940s.

Inga hadn't *guessed* Trinity's insecurity, had she? Trinity's face flamed at the thought that perhaps yesterday she'd accidentally *stared* at Inga's breasts. No, no, she hadn't.

Rather than show fear, Trinity attacked. "What is *that*?" She slapped a binder.

"That one"—Inga pointed at the smaller of the two books with a red-tipped nail—"is the wire transfer book." Then she singsonged, "Your job now. Instructions are in the front flap. And this"—she tapped the fatter binder—"is everything you need to know about the system." Inga grinned. It wasn't pretty.

"It was my understanding that you were assigned to show me."

"I don't have *time* to show you." *You idiot.* Yes, that comment was tacked on even if Inga didn't say it.

"It shouldn't take very long," Trinity said patiently, "I'm a fast learner."

Inga covered her mouth, but Trinity recognized the snort of laughter.

She would *not* let this woman get the better of her. Rising from her secretarial chair, Trinity pushed it toward Inga. "Please"—one should always be polite with subordinates—"have a seat and sign us onto the system." She might never have had a *real* job but she had oodles of organizational experience working on charity funds.

"You better take quick notes," the snide *b-i-t-c-h* said.

Trinity pulled over the guest chair. She *would* manage this woman. Even if it killed her. Crossing her legs, she propped a yellow pad on her knee, pencil poised. "Fire away."

And Inga fired.

"It's a Web-based enterprise system, and our sign-on is your last and first name," Inga rattled off, "so is your password, until you change it." The blonde's fingers flew over the keys, and screens flickered across the monitor so fast Trinity couldn't follow. She hadn't gotten past first and last name. Or was that last and first name?

"We have to change it right now. What do you want?" Inga sat, hands poised.

Trinity couldn't think beyond not wanting Inga to know her password. "Faith." She'd change it as soon as she got a chance.

Inga tipped her head and punctuated a look with a puff of breath.

Trinity wasn't about to explain her choice had nothing to do with religion and everything to do with her best friend.

Inga typed that in. "Now we've got your AP and AR screens." She tapped the monitor with her nail. "This icon is a shortcut to all the past-due receivables." She flashed Trinity a raised-brow glance. "You'll have to call all the deadbeats and get them to pay up." She hit a key and pointed once more. "And here's your shortcut to the past-due payables. You have to call them all, make nice, bend over and take it—" Inga stopped, gave Trinity that little smile akin to a Nazi concentration camp commandant. "Got all that?"

Trinity wasn't even sure how they'd gotten to the main accounts receivable and payable screens. She wasn't about to admit it, though. "Why are there so many past-due payables? I thought you were lead and taking care of all that." Trinity emphasized her retort with her own commandant smile.

Inga growled low in her throat like an angry feline. "Every single one of my accounts is in order. I might be lead, but I'm not a babysitter." Then she fluttered her eyelashes. "I've been here the longest, have the most knowledge, and everyone comes to *me*"—she tapped her chest—"with all their questions."

Well, whoop-de-doo. Trinity thought perhaps Inga had a habit of calling attention to her breasts, reminding all the men in their sphere that they were there.

"Inga?" The cry flew through the divider right by the computer monitor. Trinity couldn't put the name and the voice with the right AP clerk face.

"Yes?" Inga ever so sweetly answered.

"I can't figure out this metals consignment thingie for Handle and Harbin. Will you help me?"

"Of course, sweetie, I'll be right there."

Sweetie?

Inga stood, dwarfing Trinity in her chair. "That's enough to get you started." She smirked. "I've got *other*"—*much more important*—"things to do." She waltzed out of Trinity's cube.

Men liked a woman that sashayed, but one had to have nice hips with which to do it. Trinity realized she didn't have hips anymore than she had breasts. *Ooh, would you stop?*

She sat in the vacated chair in front of her computer. Her fingers itched to check her e-mail, not the company stuff but her special Scott address. He was beginning to become an addiction, as in, when she was feeling out of sorts, she needed a Scott fix. She decided caffeine was healthier and retrieved a fresh cup from the break room. It was funny how the sounds, voices, computer keys, an air-conditioning hum, the *chunk-chunk* of the copy machine, a printer *whir* as it spat out pages, all seemed to fade into background noise. She passed hard-at-work Boyd in his cube, then Christina Lee, who was once again speaking a foreign language—foreign customers, hopefully, whittling down that past-due receivable amount.

In her own cubicle once again, she tingled all over to check for a Scott mail. Too much stress. But she was *working*. After a deep breath, she sipped her coffee. All right. She had a system to learn. She surfed the Web all the time, making her way through a maze of screens to buy what she needed. Maybe if she applied the same logic to a Web-based enterprise system . . . it couldn't hurt, and she might avoid having to ask Inga for help.

She logged off so that she could write down all the steps to get back in. By following the Internet history, she was able to see the process Inga had used to get to the system sign-on. Typing her user ID, she followed that with *faith*. Reject. She snorted out a breath. Okay, so maybe she'd typed too fast and messed up a key. She tried two more times, then got a message that the system had locked her out for ten minutes due to a password violation. Shoving the keyboard aside, she laid her head on the desk and did a little more deep breathing. At this rate, she'd get light-headed.

She narrowed her eyes. Her nemesis had done it on purpose. Another deep breath, then Trinity stared at the divider as if she could see right through it, and sucked it up. "Inga?"

"Yes," said through the cloth partition with a note of glee.

Oh yeah, Inga had messed with her password on purpose. Trinity was used to encountering a backstabber. You didn't survive in her social set without knowing how to deal with it.

What she didn't have a lot of experience with was how to keep the backstabber on your side once you slammed them down. It was a fine line to walk. She needed Inga to show her the ropes, to back her up, be a team. Inga could make or break her.

"When you have a moment," Trinity said, sweet as apple pie à la mode, "if you could help me sign on to the enterprise system again, I'd appreciate the help." Barf-barf. Yet she would not let Inga get her down.

A long-suffering sigh, then, "Fine, let me finish over here," followed by whispers and tittering. Trinity had been whispered about before, she would be again.

She keyed into her e-mail, she couldn't help it. Yes, yes, yes! An unopened message in her inbox. Her finger poised over her mouse, she was one click away from . . .

Stomp-stomp. High-heeled shoes around the cubicle perimeter announced Inga's route. Trinity wondered how she could possibly have missed the woman's imminent arrival with the binders.

Dammit. Emailus interruptus. She shut down immediately. No way was she giving Inga any*more* ammunition.

Jamming her hands on her hips, Inga hung over Trinity's shoulder. "*What* did you do?"

"I typed in the password I told *you* and it didn't work."

"You typed it *wrong* three times, and now you're locked out."

"I typed in *faith*, which was *not* wrong."

"That's five letters. The password has to be six, so there's a number one on the end."

"You didn't tell me that."

"You saw me type it in."

Between checking e-mail and arguing, the ten-minute lockout period ended. Trinity typed, the system worked, and the opening screen flowed across her monitor. "Thank you so much for your help. I'll play around with the menus you showed me earlier."

She wanted to scream, "Get out." Which made her think of Harper on his knees in her perfect little courtyard last night.

Inga backed away. "Don't mess anything up."

"I'm only going to look." With the binder open. Following its instructions carefully. Maybe there was a class she could go to instead of dealing with Inga. She was a good student. She'd graduated from college. She'd raised over a million dollars for charity. She could *do* this.

Maybe she should have swatted Inga down for insubordination, but that would put them at war before she'd even started.

The rest of the day went downhill from there.

SCOTT held up a hand as he picked up the receiver. "I need to take this call."

Elton, his lead general accountant, stopped, his mouth still open, his words trapped.

"Here's what you're going to do." Her voice, low, musical yet dominant over the phone, stroked Scott's cock. She loved the dominant role, but he played it better.

In his gut, he'd known it was her, and he couldn't chance letting her go to voice mail. "Can you hold a moment?"

"I'll hold, but I'm not happy about it." Her snarky replies never failed to amuse him.

He dispatched Elton, assuring him they'd take up the discussion on the returns analysis as soon as his call was complete. "Close the door on your way out."

Elton pushed his wire rims back up his nose and gazed at Scott a full two seconds before doing just that.

Scott had to admit his behavior was atypical. He didn't interrupt conversations for phone calls. He didn't close his door several times a day. He didn't do phone sex in his office.

She made him do a lot of things out of the norm.

"Now what can I do for you? Another train ride?" A few minutes after five, she couldn't have gotten home yet.

"Seven thirty. Same hotel as before. I'll call you with the room number." Then the connection went dead.

He held the phone out and stared at it. She couldn't mean that.

It was too damn easy. And *she* wasn't easy. Why now? Without even a hint of coaxing?

Something was wrong. Or something was very, very right. And Scott would sure as hell be there to find out what she had planned for him.

TRINITY knew she was crazy, but she needed a sexual boost. And wasn't that the craziest thing of all? She of the perfect sexual tryst, makeup just so, not a hair out of place, nor a trace of perspiration, was planning a down and dirty session in an anonymous hotel room with a virtual stranger. Again.

The second time she called Scott, she'd gotten his voice mail. Citing the room number, she gave specific instructions on what he was to do when he arrived. Then she ran a bath in the oversized tub, dumping the contents of the little shampoo bottle in the water to foam.

It had been an awful day. Why was she letting Inga get to her? She knew perfectly well how to slam someone down when they needed it. But Inga Rice seemed to . . .

Trinity unbuttoned and folded her sweater on the counter. Steam began to cloud the mirror. She unsnapped her bra.

Though mortifying to admit, Inga made her feel inadequate. She had Catherine Zeta-Jones breasts, Angelina Jolie lips, and Marilyn Monroe hips. And she knew the job better than Trinity.

Still, Trinity wouldn't have called Scott and gotten a hotel room if Harper's car wasn't parked opposite the condo when she turned onto her street. As pathetic as it might be, she hadn't wanted another confrontation. Instead, she'd flipped a U-ie, pulled over, and punched in Scott's number.

Slipping out of her skirt, she stood for a moment. Steam misted the top half of the mirror. Black lace thong, stockinged legs, and high heels were all that was visible. She had good legs. *Damn* good.

"You are hot," she whispered. It had nothing to do with the steamy bathroom and everything to do with the look in Scott's eyes that first night. "You deserve this. You will have it."

She'd be bold and unabashed. She'd step out of her comfort zone and demand what she wanted. The affirmation made her feel powerful, in control. Just what she needed after an arduous day. Trinity stripped down and climbed into the tub to lounge.

An hour later, she was ready for him. At precisely seven thirty, there was a rap on the door. Peeping out the hole, she smiled, unlatched the door, leaving it slightly ajar.

As she'd instructed him, he didn't come in right away. Counting to ten, the length of time he was to wait, she skipped to the bed. Flopping down on her stomach, she propped her face on her crossed arms.

Like a bowl of chocolate ice cream, she wanted to savor the look in his eye the moment he saw her.

HOLY Hell. The room was a duplicate of that other night, white down comforter, soft lighting, the scent of soap and steam lingering in the air. But the woman laying belly down across the bed wasn't at all the same. His Jezebel exuded raw sexuality, definitely the naughty incarnation tonight. Mile-high heels, long legs in black stockings, the squeezable globes of her ass framed by a lace thong, and a gorgeous expanse of naked back.

Scott wanted to eat her up.

"Strip," she said, her take-charge attitude a new facet.

He tugged off his suit jacket and yanked on his tie, throwing both across a chair, twin to the one he'd sat in watching as she made herself come. In his haste to undo his shirt, he tore a button loose.

She propped herself on an elbow to watch him, her other arm tucked against her, a delicious breast playing peekaboo.

Naked from the waist up, he stopped with his hand on his belt. "Everything?"

She gave him a sexy, seductive half smile. "Nervous about exposing yourself?"

"Not in the least." He got that she was turning the tables. Last time she'd been the one exposed. He hadn't been able to get the picture out of his mind, her legs open, inviting, her skin flushed with orgasm. Now, though she was virtually naked, she still hid all the essential parts from him.

"I was more worried about your delicate sensibilities," he finished, allowing himself a slight smile.

Jezebel laughed, a sound as sexy as the name he'd given her. "Delicate sensibilities? What are you? Mr. Darcy?"

Scott tipped his head.

"From the movie? *Pride and Prejudice*." She laughed again. "Or maybe it was *Clueless*." Then she shook her head. "You don't get it anyway, so forget it. Take off your pants."

"Yes, ma'am." He toed off his dress shoes, then shucked his slacks, only his underwear left.

"Ooh," she cooed, "I figured you for a briefs kind of guy."

Under the white cotton, his cock was already hard. "What *is* a briefs kind of guy?"

She bent both legs at the knee, waving her feet in the air, twining her ankles. "Someone who is controlled," she said while his gaze was riveted on her gorgeous ass, "but waiting to burst free."

His cock wanted to burst free, all right.

She nodded with her chin. "Take them off," she whispered. It was the hottest damn sound he'd ever heard.

When he was naked before her, next to the bed, she took in every line of his body from chest to thigh. His erection grew under her scrutiny.

"Very nice." She licked her lips. "Stroke it."

He wondered if it was payback. Whacking off for a woman

wasn't part of his normal routine. He'd stroked while a lady sucked, but he'd never stood in front of her and performed. He had an inkling of how she'd felt that first night, but for him it was so damn good to have her watch that he risked coming with one pass of his hand.

"Whatever you want." Wrapping his fist around himself, he slowly pumped, his eyes never leaving her. He drank in the flush riding up her skin, the sexual sheen in her blue irises, her tongue darting out to wet her lips. She might be one-upping him, but she was into watching as much as he'd been.

A drop of pre-come dribbled from his crown. Coating his palm, he used it for lubrication. He wanted to go down on his knees for her. Needed her to touch him, suck him, more. For now, all he had was her avid gaze.

She pulled her lower lip between her teeth and inhaled deeply. "How long does it take you to come?"

He snorted out a breath. "With you watching, two seconds."

Glancing up to his face, she said, "Then you better slow down. We don't want this to be over too soon." Then she dropped her gaze once more to his cock. "I like watching," she murmured.

He loved that she did. He felt his orgasm build in his balls and backed off, slowing his stroke and easing his grip. "That better?"

She wriggled across the bed, closer, somehow miraculously keeping her breasts from his hungry eyes. Propped on her elbows, her arms folded in front of her, she settled in for a bird's-eye view. He wanted her touch, but he'd take what he could get right now, even if it was only her total fascination.

"Much better," she murmured. "I've always wondered how a man did it when he was on his own. You kind of twist your hand, not just straight up and down. And you don't do it as fast as I'd thought you'd have to."

He laughed, a deep sound straight from the gut. "And I've never had a woman analyze the technique."

Trinity had never analyzed anything about sex before. But he was beautiful, thick, big, hard. He was perfect, with strong thighs she wanted to hold onto as she watched every single moment of his rise to orgasm. She'd always been remote, never doing a man with her hand. It wasn't dignified, and what did you do with . . . the mess? Nor had she taken anyone all the way with her mouth. What if she hated the man's taste? What bothered her was all the cleanup, the aftermath, fixing her lipstick, making herself presentable again. How could you make a man think you were perfect when you had to take care of the unpleasant details?

Yet she'd missed so many delicious sensations.

Watching Scott was . . . earthy. Like Tarzan and Jane doing it deep in the jungle with fresh rain falling and the scent of green growing things all around them. As he slowly stroked, another bead of juice seeped from the tip. The emotions rolling through her mind and body weren't remotely like her, certainly not the person she'd been for thirty years. But a little over a week ago, her world, everything she'd thought she believed, wanted, and trusted in had turned upside down. Now, more than anything, Trinity needed to know how Scott would taste on her tongue.

Close enough to touch, she ran her finger across his crown. Sucking in his breath, his penis surged, and he pumped faster.

Trinity licked her finger, Scott groaned, and her taste buds went into overload. Closing her eyes, she held his flavor on her tongue, savored him. Salty and sweet combined for a slight zest.

Then she raised her eyes to meet his gaze. "You taste good," she whispered.

His lids half closed, a muscle rippled in his jaw. "That," he murmured, "made me crazy." His look ate her up like an expensive chocolate truffle. Then he went down on his knees in front of her. "Do it again."

Gathering another luscious bead, she locked gazes with him and brought her finger to her mouth, rubbing his come all over, then flicking her tongue out to lick her lips clean. Finally, she drew her finger all the way in, sucked it, and moaned, nothing more than a little hum in her throat. His pupils widened, his nostrils flared. It was better than anything she'd ever experienced before in her life.

"Suck me." His strain rippled through his voice.

"No." As much as she wanted to, she liked keeping the power to say no.

He swore.

"I can't watch if I'm sucking"—she waited a beat—"your cock." It wasn't one of her usual words, but she adored the sound of it on her tongue as much as she'd loved his taste. "And I do need to see you come. Every moment of it."

She wanted to feel things she'd never felt, sexual, naughty, undignified things. Like watching a man bring himself to orgasm. Scott had awakened her sexuality, and she wanted to taste it all. How could she ever thank him or repay him for that?

"Come for me, Scott," she whispered.

He growled, cursed again, and threw his head back. His thighs tensed, his hand twisted, pumped, his stomach went taut, and he came. Hard. His warmth splashed her neck, bathed her throat, trickled down between her breasts. Her nipples peaked with the luxurious sensation. And when he finally looked at her again, Trinity did something she could never have dreamed of. She smoothed all that sweet come over her breasts, around her nipples, rubbed it in. It was so damn hot, so good, so decadent. Raising her hand to her mouth, she licked her palm, and relished the sweet, unique taste of him.

"You're killing me, you know that?" Harsh, low, gut-deep, his voice didn't even sound like him. His pupils almost obscured his brown eyes, and his breath came in a harsh rasp.

"Did you like that?" Trinity allowed herself a sexy smile.

"Fuck yes."

She liked the word. No, she loved it. It wasn't polite, it was elemental. It was need, desire, heat, and passion all rolled into one and all for her. The high was so good she didn't even need her own orgasm. God, what she'd missed all these years. It was a crime against nature, a crime against herself.

"You know what I want?" she whispered.

"No. But whatever it is, it's yours."

"Chocolate ice cream."

He sat back on his haunches, still large, still semihard, his hands on his thighs. "Plain chocolate? What about nuts or marshmallows."

"Just chocolate." She glanced down pointedly at his lovely cock— oh yes, she did like that word, too. "There are some things that don't need any special adornment." Even as she made the double entendre, she couldn't quite believe herself.

She'd invited a man to a hotel room, made him strip, told him to masturbate, let him come on her. Then she'd rubbed it in. And licked it off.

She loved it all. The naughtiness, the freedom, the power. In those few moments, Scott would have done anything for her. The knowledge was heady. A drug. It erased the day's tension, work, coming home. It erased the last week and a half, right from the second she'd heard the shower in the master bathroom.

She would have that drug again. And again.

7

THE woman had him head over heels. Scott was mad for her. His cock got hard merely watching her lick an ice-cream cone. She savored it as she'd savored his come, closing her eyes, letting it melt in her mouth. He wanted to suck the chocolate off her tongue, kiss it from her lips. He wanted to smear it all over her, melt it with her body heat, then lick her clean like an animal. She was excitement, mystery, and kink all rolled into a delicious blonde package.

Damn, he had it bad.

Jezebel lounged on a white wrought iron chair on the walk outside the ice-cream parlor. Though the rains would start soon, January had moved into February, carrying with it the cool, but sunny days. Twilight had settled into a cold evening, and she wore a tight sweater to ward off the chill.

"You ever done that before?" She licked her single scoop.

Scott glanced at the nearby table of giggling teenage girls. They were too busy reading each other's text messages to pay attention to the "old folks." He leaned closer anyway, an excuse to inhale her scent. "Masturbate?" he murmured for her ears alone. "Yeah, I've done that before."

"You know what I mean." She bit off a tiny chunk of cone.

He knew exactly what she meant. She wore the sweater over a black skirt, circumspect enough for work, but he knew what lay beneath. Stockings and lace panties and a hot, hot body. Despite having revealed herself to him that first night, tonight she'd grabbed a pillow and covered her breasts on her way to the bathroom to dress. She'd allowed him to put his clothes on once she was fully dressed, and she'd watched the reverse strip show.

She was a tease, and she'd enjoyed telling him what to do. Because he told her what to do on the phone? Why didn't matter. He loved it. Her zest for life, for sex, for *him* was fast becoming irresistible.

"You're not answering me," she singsonged at him, bouncing her crossed leg until the back of her shoe dropped off her heel. Like his train fantasy.

"No, I haven't done anything like that." Never like *that*.

Leaning down, she popped her high heel back on her foot, trailing her hand up her calf as she sat back. His pulse picked up. Then she smiled. She remembered the train fantasy, too.

He captured her pinkie. "But you didn't get anything."

She lowered her lids to give him a sexy, bedroom perusal. "Oh, I got exactly what I wanted."

The gaggle of girls, laughing, talking, rose from the table to wander off in huddle formation down the sidewalk.

With no further potential eavesdroppers, Scott pinned her down. "You didn't have an orgasm."

"I didn't need one."

"But you deserved one."

She nibbled her cone. "You're right, I did. But I can wait until next time." Finally, she licked a dab of ice cream from her upper lip. "I wonder what I should make you do." She smiled, and his cock filled out his pants.

He anticipated with pleasure what she'd want next time. The thought would keep him jacked up and hard tonight. "So, I take it you want me to be your plaything."

She laughed, leaned forward so that he could see down her sweater to the soft swell of her breasts. "That would be awesome. I've never had a boy toy before."

Aside from being gorgeous, she was pretty damn amusing. "I'm a little old to be a boy toy, especially when you're a lot younger than me."

"But that's why it's perfect."

"That doesn't compute for me."

"Said by Mr. Big CFO," she scoffed. "It's perfect because it's the opposite of what people expect, an older woman with a younger boy toy." She leaned close enough to run a hand through his hair. "That little bit of gray is attractive, and I like being able to tell some company bigwig what to do."

He'd wondered earlier what her game was. She loved it when he told her how to touch herself for him over the phone, yet turned it all around tonight and made him do what *she* wanted. In the final analysis, though, her last statement said it all. She liked the power play.

Yet he wanted more than what she offered. He wanted entire nights with her. Even as her anonymity excited the hell out of him, it made him nuts that she could walk away and he'd never find her. She had something special—she *was* special. He feared that if she left him now, he'd be forever comparing every other woman and relationship to her and find them wanting.

"Tell me your name, and I'll consider being your boy toy."

Without dropping her gaze, she shook her head.

"Then we're at a stalemate, aren't we?" It was a calculated risk that rumbled in his gut. If he lost . . .

Reaching into her purse, she pulled out her car keys. He'd followed her little red Mustang over from the hotel. "Guess we are," she said, "but I'm not giving you my name."

"Not fair. You know everything about me."

She laughed as she rose. "That was your mistake, not mine." Backing up two steps, she stopped before making it to the curb. "So is this good-bye?"

He'd seen her license plate number. Was that a way to track her? He could also let her get to her car, then follow wherever she went. Both those things were tantamount to stalking her. He wasn't a stalker. Her anonymity had to remain her choice. Then again, she'd escalated tonight, asked to meet him. *She* had to see him again. He couldn't allow himself to think any other way.

"You still have my number." He rose, too, and pulled his keys from his pocket. "If you call it, I'll answer." Yet he felt a hitch in his gut that he'd overplayed his hand.

"So true." She waved her fingers at him. "Nightie-night, Scott. And thanks for"—she shot him one of her sexy half smiles—"that very delicious show."

"It was my pleasure."

Her Mustang was on the other side of the street. She waited as a car passed, then ran across. The remote beeped, and she glanced back at him for a long moment.

Scott stood beneath a streetlamp in a pool of light. Behind him, a couple, laughing, swung through the ice-cream parlor door.

Trinity knew she'd see him again. There was no question about that. He thrilled her, gave her power. Yet he'd remain her secret. She wouldn't even tell Faith. How could she explain that after finding Harper in the shower with another woman, less than two weeks later she was playing sex games with a new man? There *was* no reasonable explanation, and she couldn't bear it if anyone passed negative judgment on her. All right, she *knew* Faith would never do that, yet she couldn't tell her anyway.

Nor would she tell Scott her name. If she did, she risked becoming *that* Trinity, the one who worried about her hair, her makeup, her figure, her clothes. She'd be afraid to do those sweet, naughty things, afraid of what he'd think of her if she was less than perfect. All the freshness, the excitement would be lost. She couldn't lose what he gave her now she'd found it.

Across the street, Scott backed away and headed to his car two parking spots up. A couple of suit-clad thirtyish career women passed him, one of them turning to admire his butt before poking her friend to make sure she got a look, too.

A tall, imposing, handsome, well-dressed figure, Scott Sinclair was hot. He wore his authority like a second skin. One look and a woman knew he had power.

Trinity was hooked on playing with that power.

TWO very long days later, Trinity sat in her father's office, tapping her fingernails on the arm of her chair. "Daddy, I need an office."

With his reading glasses perched on his nose, her father continued perusing a competitor's annual report on his blotter in front of him. "Sweetheart, we don't have any extra offices right now." He glanced over the rims. "Besides, managers and above get offices. No one else."

Yes, yes, she already knew that. *Inga* had informed her. So had Anthony Ackerman. "Then make me a manager."

Her father smiled benevolently. "That would be showing favoritism."

Hadn't he already shown favoritism by giving her the job in the first place? Whatever. "Here's the problem, Daddy. I have to make phone calls to customers and vendors, and it isn't appropriate to have everyone overhear what I'm saying to them. This is confidential stuff."

Besides, she couldn't call Scott for a quickie. Not that she'd actually have real phone sex with him while she was at work, but she did want to get a bit sexy and tease him a little. If she didn't get an office, she'd have to relent and start calling him at night on his cell phone. She'd figured out how to do onetime blocks on her number, but somehow, contacting him outside of his office felt dangerous. It sent the message that she needed him. While she was honest enough to admit she needed the way he made her feel, letting *him* know shifted the power.

As it was, she hadn't gotten hold of him since their Tuesday rendezvous. And she didn't want her next call to be a hurried few minutes between the time she got home and when he left work.

Trinity sagged in her chair as her father transcribed a few numbers from the annual report onto a pad.

Okay, there was another reason. Without an office, she was virtually on the same rung of the ladder as Inga. She needed to show the woman she was one rung higher. But how to explain *that*? "I think my job will garner more respect if I'm a manager."

Her father removed his glasses and set them aside. "Honey, I don't want this to be harsh, but you're supervising clerks, not fully degreed accountants. And *you* aren't a degreed accountant."

Yet she did have a college degree, even if it wasn't in accounting. "I have to work deals with deadbeat customers."

He shook his head, smiling indulgently. "It's not as if we have a huge customer base as this point, dear. It can't take too much time."

Since the merger with Castle Heavy Mining, Daddy had been seriously expanding his customer list. With her brother Lance's actions, they could have been out of business altogether if Castle's management had decided to cut off Green Industries and do the work in-house. Connor and Faith's father, Jarvis, however, had worked the merger deal and saved Green, though they had both insisted that Lance was out. Since then, her father had courted new customers, swearing he'd never allow the company to get into the same state of dependency on one customer.

Still, he was right, calling customers took up less than 10 percent of her day. What she needed was some credibility. But how to get it?

Somehow Inga came out smelling like Christian Dior after every battle, while Trinity was merely cheap cologne from a drugstore shelf.

If she could get rid of Inga. There had to be a way. She tipped her head. "Daddy, do you think—" She stopped the horrific words before they came out of her mouth.

"Do I think what, honey?" Thank goodness his attention was still on the numbers.

"Nothing. I'll be fine with a cubicle." She rose and sidled toward his outside door, avoiding his main door so she wouldn't have to face Verna in the outer office. Verna always knew when something was wrong. Turning the handle, she backed out into the hallway, then blew her father a kiss.

With the door closed, Trinity sagged against the wall. Good Lord. She'd actually been about to ask her father to fire Inga. When had she become such a weakling? Worse, she sounded like a spoiled brat whining because things weren't going her way. What was *wrong* with her? To even *think* about firing someone simply because she didn't know how to handle her was . . . unthinkable.

Her mother would be ashamed of her. Her mother would have figured out the secret to making Inga like her. Hah, her mother never would have had the problem in the first place.

What Trinity needed was some good old-fashioned girl talk to help her devise a plan of attack. Back at her desk, she sent an immediate distress text message to Faith and Josie inviting them to dinner. Then she e-mailed Scott because she couldn't stand getting his voice mail one more time. Hearing his recorded voice was no longer enough.

Short and sweet. "If you want me to call you tonight, then you better send me your cell number."

Now all she had to do was get through an Inga-infested afternoon.

*　*　*

HIS heart beat faster when he saw her e-mail in his in-box. Getting ready for audit, too many numbers fogging his brain, and Ron Rudd going on about the bottom line had drained him and kept him in meetings. He'd missed her. Badly. For two straight nights, he'd dreamed of making kinky love to her. He hadn't gotten enough of her. He hadn't even touched her yet.

"Scott, have you got a few minutes?"

Damn. He almost said no. Grace Bunnell was his controller and exceptionally capable. If she wanted a few minutes, it was something important. Despite his instant hard-on at nothing more than a virtual address, he shut down his personal e-mail.

Pulling the chair back opposite his desk, Grace settled and crossed her legs. If he wasn't mistaken, she was wearing a shorter skirt. He couldn't remember seeing her knees before. Or that much thigh. She'd been the picture of prim and proper, yet there'd been her recent nasty divorce. She'd told him because she wanted to assure him it wouldn't interfere with her work. Interesting, perhaps she'd started dating. Good for her. It wasn't his business, though, and he certainly wouldn't ask.

"What can I do for you, Grace?"

She swung her leg, reminding him instantly of Jezebel's high heel slipping off, the way she'd leaned down, slid it on, then trailed her fingers all the way back up her leg, forcing his eyes to follow. Damn. He could not stop thinking about the woman.

"It's about this prototype we're buying from Green Industries. They want half the cost of the gold up front. According to their CEO, they buy their metal on consignment, but they have to fund the first shipment, and they don't have any gold reserves at this time."

"How much cash are we talking about?" Green did plating, bonding, and machining. They'd come in with a good bid on some components for the Millennium 5 wet-environment prealigner for robotic wafer manufacturing. The new machine would launch in six months.

Grace recrossed her legs, and the skirt rode higher. He could almost swear something flickered in her eyes, as if she were watching for his reaction. Then she named a dollar figure. It was reasonable.

"That's fine." He tapped a couple of keys and brought up the cash forecast. "We've got it covered." Why was she asking? "You don't have to check with me on something at that level."

She blinked. "I know, I just . . ."

A good-looking woman, pretty brown hair, in decent shape, she tended toward pastel colors, blouses, and knee-length skirts. But yeah, if he wasn't mistaken, she had changed her wardrobe to shorter skirts, and today, a sweater that molded to her chest. He hadn't noticed when she'd made the change.

"Is something bothering you about Green?" he asked.

"Uh, no." She stood, straightened her skirt.

He got the oddest feeling she was trying to draw attention to it. Was she expecting a compliment on the new attire? He never made personal comments. When she'd started crying in his office the day she'd told him she wouldn't let the divorce get in the way, he'd awkwardly handed her a tissue. He hadn't been good with a woman's tears since the girls were over ten. And when they cried about boys, damn, he'd wanted to come out swinging.

"Well"—Grace backed toward the door—"I'll authorize the wire transfer then."

Once she was gone, he cocked his head at the open office door. Weird. Something else was going on. He wondered if someone had sexually harassed her, and she didn't quite know how to speak up. Nah. Grace wouldn't let anyone pull any crap.

He opened his e-mail and typed in his cell number.

Glancing at his watch, he had hours to go. Hell, knowing Jezebel, she'd call him at midnight just to keep him on his toes.

* * *

"HOW long has she worked there?" Josie dipped her bread in the balsamic vinegar, then gave a to-die-for moan of pleasure. "God, I love this stuff. Don't let me have any more or I won't eat my dinner."

Trinity had ordered the pine nut salad because she wanted to save room for every last crumb of brandy-soaked bread pudding. They'd commandeered a quiet booth tucked in the back corner of Vatovola's, her very favorite restaurant. She usually shared the bread pudding with Faith—or whomever she was dining with—but she'd never allowed herself more than one mind-blowing bite. All afternoon, except when she was fantasizing about Scott, she'd dreamed about feasting on the whole dessert.

"I have no idea how long she's been there." She tipped her head, visualizing Daddy's Christmas parties and company picnics. "You know, I think it might be five years or so."

"And you didn't even know her name until your boss introduced you?" Josie let her jaw drop for emphasis.

Faith didn't say a word, concentrating instead on her own balsamic-dipped bread. That was the difference between the two cousins. Josie came out with whatever was on her mind while Faith always thought through every nuance of what she wanted to say. Then again, maybe she was feeling the baby.

Sitting in the booth across from her, Trinity patted her hand. "You okay?"

Faith smiled. "I don't want to get in the middle of the argument I see coming."

"We don't argue," Josie said. She tucked locks of her unruly dark hair behind her ear. "We discuss vociferously."

Trinity liked Josie's forthright manner. She said it like it was. Trinity needed to hear it that way, because Faith's toned-down-to-protect-her-best-friend's-feelings method didn't always get through Trinity's thick skull. Trinity readily admitted she had one.

She went back to the *vociferous* discussion with Josie. "I bet you don't know everyone's name down at Castle."

Josie waved her bread. "Of course, I do."

"Every single one?" Trinity held up her finger when Josie opened her mouth. "Think about it a second."

"I don't need to think about it. I know them all."

"But," Faith interjected, "you've worked at Daddy's company since you got out of college, Josie."

"Trinity went practically every day to the plant for one reason or another even before she started this new job. It's the same thing."

Josie was right. Trinity often popped down to say hello to her father or Lance or have a daughterly chat with Verna. Or if there was a particularly cute guy. Not that Daddy would ever have approved of her dating an employee, but Trinity did like to look. In fact, that's how she'd met Connor, when he worked for Daddy, and she'd known right away that he'd be right for Faith. Look how perfect that had turned out.

But she was getting off topic here. "All right, so I totally blew it." She threw up both hands in surrender. "But that's water under the bridge now. How do I fix it?"

"Well . . ." Josie was saved from having to answer by their waiter's timely arrival.

"Salad for you." He placed Trinity's pine nut extravaganza in front of her, beaming at her with pearly whites from within a nicely trimmed mustache. "And salad for the little momma." He gave an equally sweet smile to Faith. "And the teriyaki skirt steak for you." Hmm, was that an extra heavy-duty smile for Josie? "Anything else I can get you lovely ladies?"

Faith held up her glass. "More water with lemon, please?"

A moment later he sent over a busboy with the water pitcher and a plate of lemon quarters.

The salad, pine nuts with vinegar dressing over tart greens, was yummy. Before she'd always picked off the pine nuts. What a waste. "I've been comparing the whole problem to fund-raising."

"Huh?" Josie followed up the inelegant sound with a grimace.

Trinity savored another bite of salad even as she found herself eyeing Josie's skirt steak and garlic mashed potatoes. They smelled divine. "Fund-raising is like being a supervisor. You've got all these worker bees that you have to organize and somehow make sure they do what needs to be done."

Trinity was an expert. She beguiled, soft-shoed, bribed, sweetened the pot. And if that didn't work, she stopped giving the helper any tasks. Hence the problem. In order to be successful, she needed Inga's help.

Why couldn't she get Inga to like her? *That* was the problem. "I don't know what that woman wants," she concluded.

"You mean besides *your* job." Faith hit the nail on the head.

"She's not getting that. I am not giving up." It came down to a matter of pride. She would make this job work and her father proud of her. Not that he thought she was a dilettante, but maybe he did see her as more decorative than useful.

She polished off her salad, finding the last of her greens almost as bitter as that thought.

"Get to know her better." Josie pushed her plate away, the meat devoured, but she'd hardly touched the garlic potatoes.

No. Trinity would *not* ask to finish them. She had to save room for bread pudding. "She won't let me. Every time I attempt a friendly personal comment, like whether she has family or whatnot, she tells me it's none of my business."

"What a bitch," Josie said. Ah, finally, they agreed on something. "Have you taken her out to lunch yet?"

Trinity felt her chest seize up in horror. "Why on earth would I subject myself to *that*? It's the only time I can get away from her." She'd go crazy.

"Josie's right, Trinity."

"But Faith, she'll think I'm doing a snow job on her."

Then she smelled the brandy sauce wafting on the air. Her

tummy rumbled in anticipation. She'd have the bread pudding now, and Scott on the phone later. What could be better than her two most favorite desserts?

Their waiter set down the two bowls and smiling, took away the dirty plates. Josie picked up her fork. "You two have gone on and on about this so much, I have to try."

Trinity held her own fork poised to stab. "I didn't ask for your skirt steak."

Faith looked at her as if her lipstick was smeared on her teeth. "You're not going to eat all that, Trinity."

"Oh yes, I am."

"You've *never* eaten a whole dessert." Faith put down her own fork and touched the back of Trinity's hand. "Are you sick?"

"I'm tired of denial."

"I think she's having a nervous breakdown," Josie added. "I mean, last week you had *ice cream*."

"I even bought a gallon and put it in the freezer." Yet truly, tasting Scott was far more exquisite.

They stared at her.

"What?"

"We didn't think you meant all that stuff." Josie spoke for both of them.

Trinity looked to Faith. "You didn't think I'd stick with the job?"

"It wasn't that," Faith argued. "I was afraid you were jumping in before you were ready to make too many decisions about anything." She rolled her lips between her teeth, then puffed them back out. "I mean, after Harper and everything."

That could very well be how her changes came across. "This is more than Harper. This is about my life and why I did all the things I did and how I'm going to make sure I start doing the things I really want to do." And make her father proud. He needed *something* after his disappointment in Lance.

Faith gazed at her a long moment. "And is this job what you *really* want?"

Trinity gave her the grace of mulling over the question. She wanted to feel in control, but she also wanted to be useful, have a purpose, accomplish *something* in her life that she could look back on with a good feeling. Something more than having brought Faith and Connor together or cajoling millionaires into donating money. Not that it wasn't worthy, but it wasn't enough. At this point, she didn't think her mother would have beamed with pride over her daughter's accomplishments. Then again, if her mother was alive, Trinity wondered if she'd ever have fallen for Harper in the first place. She'd have been a different person.

She wanted to be a different person now. "Yes, this is something I want."

"Then take Inga out to lunch," Faith concluded. "Take *all* your employees out for a get-to-know-you lunch. It can't hurt."

Trinity stared at Faith. She'd gotten prettier with pregnancy, and her hair shone like a red gold halo. Or maybe it was loving and being loved in return. Whatever the reason, Faith was absolutely beautiful. And smart. "You know, that's why you two are my very best friends in all the world."

Josie snorted. "Right." But her dark eyes sparkled, and a smile she tried to hide lifted her mouth.

"It's true. I love you both. You have all the right answers." She'd ask all her girls out to lunch tomorrow and start her campaign to win over Inga.

"Hear, hear." Faith raised her water, and both Josie and Trinity tapped it with their wineglasses.

"And what's the toast to?" Appearing virtually out of nowhere, Connor leaned down to kiss the top of Faith's head.

"To best friends," Trinity quickly said. She didn't want to talk about her job. Faith would already have told Connor, of course, but she didn't want to discuss it with him. What if he said something disparaging? Of course, that wasn't doing him justice, because Connor was a big old sweetie, but . . . she didn't want to talk about it.

"And you"—Josie stabbed a finger at him—"are only here to make sure we aren't corrupting your wife."

Trailing his finger down Faith's arm, he gazed at her. It was so sweet, Trinity got that same ache she'd had the day of the baby shower. Tall, dark-haired, dark-eyed, and handsome, he'd let Faith capture him utterly.

Trinity almost closed her eyes against the sudden shard of pain that wedged up under her ribs. She wasn't jealous. She was oh so happy for Faith and Connor and the baby.

She just . . . wanted. Something. Anything. That all-powerful, all-consuming feeling Scott gave her when he moaned for her, came for her.

"You ready to go, sweetheart?" Connor was totally overprotective. He didn't want Faith driving in the dark, as if being pregnant somehow impaired her night vision. Trinity had picked her up, but Connor insisted on taking her home.

Or maybe he wanted to take a night drive in the mountains. She and Faith didn't talk explicitly about sex, especially as it pertained to Connor, but they had shared a smile or two about Connor's love of driving, with a hint of the things he liked to do in some of those little pull-outs along the road.

Harper had never suggested a drive in the mountains.

"We're done," Trinity said, because she hated her maudlin thoughts, and she so needed to stop analyzing every adoring look that Connor fastened on Faith. "We'll get the waiter to box up the rest of our bread pudding because I am *not* wasting a bite."

Beside Faith, Connor merely raised his eyes to stare at Trinity beneath his eyelashes.

"I love bread pudding," she said in defense. "Besides, Josie wants half of it."

Josie opened her mouth, then shut it.

"See, I knew you did."

The sooner they were out of the restaurant, the better. She had an extraordinary need to call Scott, and she didn't think she could wait until she got home.

She needed more of that all-powerful *something* he gave her.

8

SCOTT took half an hour picking her up, yet when he arrived, Trinity didn't care. His scent filled the car, making her greedy for more of him.

"Take me for a drive in the mountains." The Santa Cruz Mountains specifically. That's what Trinity found to be the best thing about living in the San Francisco Bay Area. You were never too far from the beach or the mountains or the Golden Gate shrouded in fog. Granted, there was no skiing, but most winters, there was at least one storm in which you could drive up to the top of Skyline for a snowball fight.

Except that Trinity hadn't done so since she was a teenager. Snowball fights were undignified. Yet she badly wanted to throw a snowball right down the back of Scott's neck just for fun.

"Your wish is my command." He took the turnoff for the two-lane highway leading up into the mountains. He drove a European car, not a luxury model, but not inexpensive either. She liked that he didn't have to be overly ostentatious.

"I'm not sure which I like you better in, jeans or a suit and tie." Goodness, he looked yummy in either. Tonight, he'd paired the jeans with a chambray button-down shirt. She wondered if he'd changed at the gym, but didn't ask.

Instead, she itched to unbutton his shirt.

"I like you naked," he said.

Her heart rate spiked. Leaning over, she gave in to her desire, undoing three buttons, then slipping her hand inside to caress his nipple.

He trapped her fingers beneath his palm. "This is a winding road. You don't want me to lose control."

Oh yes, she did. She wanted him to give all his control to her. That's why she'd called from her car and told him to meet her. It wasn't enough on the phone. She wanted to feel how much he wanted her, not merely hear it. Just as she had in the hotel room the other night.

Where are you going with this, Trinity?

She subsided into her own seat, though she did leave his shirt unbuttoned. Leaning back against the door, she curled her feet beneath her. "Why did you meet me tonight?"

He took a steep curve, then glanced at her. "I want you."

Her heart went straight to her throat.

"You make me do crazy things I've never done before." He reached across to stroke from her knee to halfway up her thigh.

She shivered in the short, pleated skirt.

"And I like that." He concentrated once again on the road. "It makes me feel very alive."

"You make me feel alive, too," she whispered. She'd never thought of that before. She'd seen her bizarre behavior with Scott as being hurt over Harper, stress with Inga, and a need for something fresh, sensual, powerful, and exciting, but she'd never considered that he made her feel alive. He made her want to taste new things, not just bread pudding and ice cream, but life.

Trinity had never relished life itself. She'd been too busy pleasing other people—men especially—and making sure everyone liked her. Now she wanted to savor it all. With him.

"Find a place and pull over." She wanted to touch him right this minute.

There were all sorts of little tributaries off the road, old logging tracks that eventually trailed off into nothing.

"Why?"

"Because I want to kiss you." Gazing at his mouth, she licked her lips. "I haven't kissed you yet and I want to." How had she missed doing that? A kiss, a taste, a new exotic flavor.

"That sounds good enough for me." His voice was deeper, huskier.

This thing with Scott was insane, in direct contrast to Miss Trinity Green the debutante who always did everything perfectly. She was tired of being perfect. It hadn't done a damn thing for her anyway. Now, she wanted some secret, crazy, wonderful, scary fun with this man. "You're the unknown," she whispered.

She wanted to be surprised and delighted and swept off her feet. Except that this time, she'd have her eyes wide open. Her relationship with Scott was about lust, yet lust was more emotion than she'd ever experienced.

He found a little lane leading off to the right, up a hill, the car bouncing in the ruts left from the hard rain they'd had three weeks ago. The road became a trail, then was swallowed up entirely by the overgrowth of ferns, bushes, and long grasses visible in the car's headlights.

Scott shut off the engine, plunging them into darkness, with barely a ray of moonlight making its way through the trees. His seat belt unsnapped, and she felt rather than saw the bulk of his shadow turn to her.

"So. What was this about kissing me?"

The scent of soap and the aphrodisiac tang of sizzling male settled over her, yet he didn't lean forward to meet her halfway.

If she wanted his kiss, the act was up to her. As her eyes adjusted, his outline filled the driver's side window, and he lounged,
one arm draped over the steering wheel.

With the windows up, not a sound penetrated. Trinity lowered
her voice to match the quiet of the night. "We need to get in the
backseat."

"Why?"

She tipped her head. "Are you playing hard to get?"

She couldn't see whether he smiled or not, but she was sure she
heard it in his voice. "I want to make sure I know what your intentions are before I let you take me into the backseat. You might be
planning to have your wicked way with me."

"You *hope* I am. Now get in the backseat." Another new and
pleasurable sensation, she liked being the aggressor.

"Yes, ma'am," he murmured. Beside her, the window slid down
as he tapped a button, allowing two inches of night air, spiked with
the sharp zest of greenery, to stream in. The snick of the door set
off the dome light, the sudden illumination gleaming in his eyes before he climbed out.

Oh yeah. He was more than hoping she'd have her wicked way
with him. Trinity shoved open her own door, pushing aside a tena-
cious bush that snagged her skirt. He was already seated, legs
splayed, hands on his thighs, as she crawled in beside him, shutting
off the light when she pulled the door to.

Her eyes needed to adjust all over again, and she reached out,
encountering his cheek. She petted, stroked, loving the feel of
manly whiskers. "You're very handsome, you know."

"Throwing the dog a bone?"

She laughed. "You know you're an extremely good-looking
man. I bet you have women falling all over you."

He didn't say a word.

"Not that I'm fishing to find out about other women that you're dating or anything." But suddenly, she *was* thinking about it. She didn't like the idea of another woman having him.

"There's no one but you." Without proper lighting, the intensity in his voice came across more strongly.

"Good." She'd had enough of competition. She shifted and her knee touched his. Pulling the pleated skirt higher, she was glad she'd worn something that allowed her to move freely. She leaned in close to nuzzle his hair, soft despite the gray in it. "You smell good." Soap, shampoo, man.

"You smell better." A husky note laced his words.

She nosed his ear, then flicked her tongue along the shell. His shiver traveled across the sultry air between them. Power shimmered through her. She liked exciting him, taking his breath away, teasing him. He was a man at her mercy, and Trinity adored the feeling. She wanted to take a long time savoring his mouth. She hadn't kissed for the sake of kissing since high school.

"Do you like that?" She licked again for good measure, enjoying the shudder that once again rolled through his body. His skin was sweet on her tongue.

"Yeah. I like it."

Trailing down, she kissed his neck. Light touches of her lips, a puff of breath against his skin.

Scott itched to grab her, speed her up, pull her on top of him and take, take, take. Yet her slow seduction was so damn pleasurable. She got off on the tease. By the time they finally came together, she'd be as wet as he was hard. So he bided his time, kept his hands to himself, and let her set the pace.

A kiss had never made him ache this way. Her thumb across his lips left a trail of heat.

He'd been home when she called, yet he'd jumped in the car and taken only half an hour to make it back over the hill. That's how damn bad he had it for her.

"*Mm.*" She made little noises the whole time, driving him nuts. She kissed the corner of his mouth, then stroked his lips with the tip of her tongue. Like a cat licking up cream. She smelled of citrus and tasted of brandy, sweet, tangy.

He was rock hard and ready.

Cupping his cheek, she pulled him closer. In the barely there light of the moon, there was simply a gleam in her eye and shadows across her face.

"Wanna kiss me?" she murmured against his lips.

He wanted to fuck her. Now. Screw the preliminaries. His cock ached to be inside her. His hands trembled. The slow steady tease of the last two weeks pounding through his veins, he *wanted*. Everything and anything he could get.

"Yes," he managed, though his voice was little more than a croak.

She kissed him. A little girl peck on the mouth. Then another, and another. Slower, lingering. Her tongue darted out to taste his lips, her kisses all the hotter for their very lack of carnality. Testing, teasing, tasting.

Then she pulled up her skirt, straddled him, and took his face in her hands. His body surged up and he grabbed her hips, pulling her close, closer, losing himself in her heat. She couldn't have made him harder if she'd devoured his cock.

She kissed him with her mouth, her tongue, her lips, her whole body. She turned a kiss into a feast. His cock rode between her thighs, her nipples scorched him through his shirt. A groan rose up from the well of his belly.

She pulled back. "Do you like the way I kiss?"

"Yes," he answered with that same throaty croak.

"Do you like my mouth?" Her eyes shimmered.

"Yes."

"Would you like my lipstick on your dipstick?"

He laughed, groaned. "Your lipstick's already gone." He rubbed against her, let her feel how badly he wanted her.

"Picky-picky." She caressed his nose with hers, Eskimo style. "You'll have to wait until I finish kissing you. Because I'm not done yet."

He'd die before she was done, but he didn't have a chance to utter a word before she took him. Instead of a thrusting, open-mouthed assault, she took him with a bone-melting sensual play of lips and tongues. He cupped her ass cheeks, keeping her close against his cock. Wrapping her arms around his neck, she kissed, licked, tongued, slipped down to nip his throat, then back up again. His arms sneaking around her, he molded her body to his, and angled his head to take her deeper.

She allowed him the luxury of one long, sweet kiss, then pulled back to suck his lip. "I love kissing," she whispered.

"And you make me crazy with it."

She licked his cheek. "I'd like to sit here with you deep inside me, not moving, and kiss you while I can feel you filling me all the way up."

Like the proverbial devil on his shoulder, his cock pulsed with a mind of its own. *Do it, do it. Lift her skirt, take her.*

Yet he wanted to enjoy the thought of it, the idea, the sensual fantasy she created for him. Taking her too fast would rob him of half the pleasure, the build in his balls, riding the ache. Relishing the desire for its own sake.

"I wanna fuck you," he muttered against her mouth, teasing her with words the way she teased with her lips. "I want to put my finger on your clit right now and make you see stars."

She wriggled against him, turning the heat on high. "I think I'm wet." She took his mouth once more, three light kisses, a flick of her tongue, then a deep but brief foray.

"I can determine your wetness for you." He slid his hand beneath her skirt and stroked her bare thigh.

"I'll rephrase." She breathed across his cheek, following up with another lick. "I *know* I'm wet."

"Let me feel it." He didn't mind begging. She had him enthralled, giving him the heat and passion he'd craved. If she gave him half a chance, he could revel in her forever.

Wrapping her fingers around his throat, she tipped his chin with both thumbs. "Let me feel *you*."

Air puffed from his lungs. His pulse raced against her touch.

Before Trinity could think, Scott pulled back, staking inches between their bodies, and folded her fingers around him. He was hard and he was big, filling out the crease of his jeans along his groin.

"God, you feel so fucking good." He laid his head against the back of the seat.

"*You* feel good." She stroked all that hard cock. He was perfect in her hand. So hard, all for her. She'd loved kissing him. But this was so much more daring. Completely powerful. Literally holding him in the palm of her hand.

"I don't think I've ever liked sex this much," she murmured against his lips.

He reeled her in, his arm like a band across her back molding her to his chest. His mouth against her ear, the warmth of his breath, the slide of his tongue before he whispered, "I'm going to make you love it. Make you beg for it. Make you die to have it with me every chance you get."

She wriggled, grabbing a little distance. "Don't get so cocky." Yet she wanted to take everything he offered.

He pulled her hand down on him once more. "Feel how *cocky* you make me."

"All right, so you're cocky." It heated her inside and out that he was so hard, all for her. "Don't let it go to your head."

He trapped her hand with his, gently forcing her to stroke the tip of his erection through his jeans. A bead of moisture seeped through the material. "I'd say that means it's gone to my head," he murmured.

Trinity's mouth watered. Lord, she could taste him again. The salty sweet flavor she'd licked from her fingers the other night. "I want more," she whispered.

Even in the dim light, she saw his eyes widen, then slim down to slits. "How much more?"

She couldn't say she'd loved oral sex. It was merely the thing a man wanted. The power had been fine, but as for the act, she could take it or leave it. She'd certainly never allowed a man to come in her mouth. Yet with Scott, she was compelled to experience everything, his flavor, texture, scent, sound. The pulse of his cock in her mouth.

She trailed a finger along the skin visible through the open buttons of his shirt, then undid the rest, baring him to the waistband of his pants. "I want to taste you."

With his hands under her skirt, he grabbed her butt and snuggled her closer to cradle his cock between her legs. "What do you want to taste?"

"This." She licked his lips. "And this." She parted his shirt and bent to take one nipple in her mouth. Sucking, she drank in the ripple of tension through his body just before he thrust up against her. She laughed, delighted. "You like that."

"It makes me nuts."

She was sure he was harder between her legs, throbbing. She pinched. He pulsed again. Then she bit him, not hard, teasing. His groan vibrated against her belly as it rose up in his throat.

"I think your nipples are more sensitive than mine."

He raised one hand to the outer swell of her breast. "Shall we test it out?" He hovered close, the heat shimmering off him in the dark. "You have the most perfect breasts."

Her breath came a little faster. "They're too small."

He dipped his head to her throat, inhaled deeply. "They're the perfect size. I want to touch them, taste them."

Oh Lord, he couldn't know how badly she needed him to worship her breasts. Yet she pushed him down. "No. I'm not done having fun with you yet."

"You'll make me come if you're not careful."

She grinned. "That's the best part of the fun." Then she stole a kiss. "Or maybe the fun is *not* letting you come."

His teeth flashed in the dark. "So you're a tease?"

She nuzzled his throat and lightly twisted his nipple, eliciting another groan from him. "Maybe. Want me to stop?" She pulled back to gaze at him. The little bit of moonlight through the side window only served to throw his face into shadow. "Tell me to stop or let me tease. Take it or leave it."

She waited a beat, her own feminine power pulsing through her. He could call a halt to their play, or he could let her tease him without mercy. She licked her finger and glided around his nipple. "It's your choice." But she wanted him to give her everything.

With his head against the neck rest, he watched her, the epitome of a relaxed, confident male . . . but for the insistent pressure of his cock between her legs.

Then quick as lightning, he grabbed her face in both big hands and pulled her down to his mouth. "Fuck," he muttered against her lips. "Tease the fuck out of me, I love it."

Then he devoured her with a kiss that made her insides gooey, going on and on until her head spun, and she wanted him inside her so badly, she almost lifted her skirt and tore off her panties. Who on earth was doing the teasing?

She forced a hand between their vacuum-packed bodies and stroked him. She craved his flavor, needed to memorize it.

Shoving back, she dragged in air. He hadn't even let her breathe. Then God, she attacked his belt and the button on his jeans, and finally, finally, his gorgeous cock was right there. She'd never thought a man's penis was beautiful, yet he was magnificent. *I love this.*

Then she slid sideways off his lap. Raising both hands, he let her have at him. She teased the head with her tongue, sliding into the little slit, savoring the droplet of come. Sucking the crown into her mouth, she closed her eyes and moaned. He was so good, so perfect. He made her want, and she'd never wanted before. Not like this.

With his hand on her head, he urged her to take more of him, crooning words, naughty words, dirty words, fuck-me–suck-me–take-me words that made her heart soar.

She wanted so much, she didn't even have a chance to worry if she was doing it right, if he liked it, if he'd need it again.

His hips rose to meet her, and he filled her. So big, so good, her eyes watered. Letting him slide all the way back out, she swallowed the next big beautiful taste of him. Warm, solid, silky steel between her lips. Sweet, salty, pungent, and gorgeously male. He massaged her head in his hands, gently pushing her, tangling his fingers in her hair, wordlessly begging her to take him. Then he held her still and made love to her mouth with short, fast pumps of his body. He filled her mouth, her mind, her body, her heart the way no man ever had before.

Pulsing against her lips and her tongue, he groaned, swore, long and low, then his seed pumped into her mouth. She took every drop, drank it, needed more. Sucking on the tip, she made him give it all until he jerked against her, gulped in a breath and pulled her up. The moment was so amazing. Her eyes teared, and it was more than the insistent pressure of his penis deep in her throat. As she'd taken him, he'd done the same to her.

"Jesus," he swore, "that's so damn good it hurts."

She licked her lips and tried to sit up. Scott tucked her close to his chest.

"Don't move," he whispered. "I need a minute. Just let me hold you."

His heart beat hard as he cradled her tight to him and stroked the hair from her face. Resting back against the seat, he couldn't stop the stream of words flowing through his mind. "That was good, baby, that was so freaking good."

So good that she owned him completely now. He'd do anything to have her again. It was her passion, her flirting, her laughter, her sweetness, her lust for him, for life itself, and how she'd turned wild in his arms. She teased and played her little power games, yet she made him heady, orgasmic. And now, the way she snuggled against him, her arm wrapped across his waist, her breath teasing his nipple, it was too close to heaven.

He wanted everything she'd done to him, and he needed so goddamn much more. He wanted all of her. He didn't give a damn that she was fifteen years younger than him, closer to his daughters' ages than his own. He appreciated the mystery, thrived on it, but if she walked away, he'd die inside. And if she hadn't told the truth about not being married . . . he wouldn't accept that. Besides, there wasn't a mark on her ring finger.

Still, he needed her name.

"NO name, no phone number, no address." She loved the anonymity. No longer bound by self-imposed rules for Little Miss Perfect Trinity Green, she was free to do all the naughty things she'd only imagined. It was wild and crazy to suck a man in the backseat of his car, just that and nothing else. She could never explain how powerful that felt. If he knew her name, she'd lose it all.

Then she'd have to start thinking about how other people would judge her behavior. If she kept her name secret, she could keep Scott himself in a separate compartment of her life where no one could interfere. Not even her own sense of shame.

At a little after ten on a weeknight, the restaurant parking lot where she'd left her car was emptying out. Standing beside the

Mustang beneath an overhead light, she went up on her toes and kissed him, short and sweet, then licked the seam of his lips. "Still wanna play the game anyway?"

"You know I do." Scott trailed his fingers down her arms, leaving shivers in his wake.

She adored his height. He made her feel petite, feminine, special, desired.

He tipped her chin, his gaze mapping her face. "We need one rule."

Her heart skipped a beat. "I don't like rules." Actually, she lived her entire life by a set of rules, yet she didn't want rules between them. Except the one where they didn't talk about his daughters or his marriage or his other women.

"Only one, I swear." He waited.

She had to acquiesce. "What?"

"If you decide not to call again, you need to tell me."

"You mean like at least a see-you-later sayonara, baby?"

"Yeah, *sayonara, baby* will do."

His eyes were dark, he smelled so yummy, and his taste lingered in her mouth. "I can handle that rule." She couldn't imagine giving him the old sayonara. She needed what he did for her. "Ditto?"

Smoothing a finger down her cheek, he played with the corner of her mouth. "Ditto. But I have a feeling I'm not the one who's going to be calling sayonara." Then he kissed her, tracing her lips with his tongue. "You have my number."

Oh yeah. She did.

Retreating to his car, he watched while she climbed in and started her engine. As if he were making sure she was safe before he left.

Glancing at him in her rearview mirror, her heart gave a little jolt. God, he was so perfect. Everything she could have hoped for at this point in her life. He'd asked for her name, yet taken it gracefully when she refused. He tasted better than brandy bread pudding. He held her as if she mattered.

She could live with that one rule. Because she needed it in return. Honestly, she couldn't bear it if one day he suddenly stopped taking her calls or cut off his e-mails to her. The thought gave her palpitations.

How had he come to be so important?

"It's not *him*," she told herself. "It's how he makes you feel. There's plenty of men out there who can give you that when he gets tired." Men always got tired, didn't they? Which was another reason to keep her identity a secret. Men chased what they couldn't have.

When she got home, the street was quiet. Harper's car wasn't in evidence. Hopefully he'd given up trying to get back in her good graces. Inside, she flipped on the hall light, tossing her purse and keys on the entry table.

Then she stopped in complete and total horror. Her reflection in the gilt-edged mirror was atrocious. Mascara and eyeliner had leaked down beneath her eyes, and her cheeks were bare of blusher. Good God, she was lipstickless. And her hair was . . . well . . . askew. Instead of her usual silky smooth blonde tresses, she wore a rat's nest. Trinity clapped her hands over her eyes, shutting out the horrific sight.

What must he think of her? Thank God he hadn't been able to see her clearly.

A bubble of laughter welled up. She'd gone down on him in the backseat of his car. Not to mention swallowing, which every lady knew was terribly undignified, yet *she'd* loved it.

She splayed her fingers and looked through them like a child watching a horror movie.

Scott *had* seen her. Beneath the parking lot lights, he'd lifted her chin and traced her face with his gaze, every last inch of it. Then he'd kissed her anyway. Scott didn't care how she looked. And she loved his hot, sweet taste, his skin beneath her fingers, the soft silk of his hair.

Maybe he thought she looked just ducky with makeup shadows under her eyes and bare lips. "He looked at you, and he wanted you anyway." Perfect or not.

Trinity dropped her hands and stared. Really, she didn't look so bad. Nothing more than a long day at work, which resulted in dark circles under her eyes. As if she hadn't combed her hair all day. But not *so* bad.

"Heh." She laughed, and wow, she looked even better with a smile on her face. She didn't have to be perfect all the time. She scrabbled in her purse for her cell phone because she suddenly experienced a huge need to call Scott.

Instead, her doorbell rang. She almost jumped at the sound, for one very split second, thinking it might be him, and she wanted to let him in, in, *in*!

Until reality hit. Scott didn't know where she lived.

Her heart stopped. Oh God, it had to be Harper. He'd been skulking in the dark, waiting for her.

9

HEART pounding, Trinity put her eye to the peephole. Good Lord, it was her brother Lance.

Swinging the door wide, she threw herself at him. "Where have you been, why haven't you called me? I was so worried!"

Lance pried her arms from around his neck. "You're suffocating me, sweetie pie."

She knew he'd done some scummy things. But he was still her brother, and she loved him. Her mother would have wanted it that way. *Love him no matter what.* Stepping back, she dragged him into the foyer. "You've lost weight." There was something else, too. "Oh my God, you shaved off your mustache and beard."

He stroked his bare chin. "I got tired of it."

Besides, the goatee look was so out, though Trinity would never have said that. "I like it. It makes you look younger."

"Look at you." He leaned in. "Your makeup's all messed up." Her hands clasped in his, he held out her arms and surveyed her body critically. "And are you *gaining* weight, Trin?" He slammed her with a grimace of absolute horror.

She whirled to the mirror. Did her cheeks look fat? She patted one. No, it was her mussed hair that made her face seem rounder. She tried rubbing the mascara streaks under her eyes.

"Long day," she managed to spout. "Rushing around. Just got home." *Been out doing nasty things in Scott's car. It was oh so good, I loved it and need to do it again.*

"I'm sorry about Harper."

She glanced at his reflection behind her. "Who told you?" God, please, not the country-club circuit. She so did not want to be gossip fodder. In fact, she hadn't been to the club since she kicked Harper out.

Lance gave her a *duh* look.

"Verna." She stepped away from the mirror. The mascara wasn't coming off. Who cared at this point? "She never told me she talked to you." Why had Lance called Verna when he hadn't returned one of Trinity's messages in all this time? Six months, for God's sake. She wouldn't think about that. He was back, and that's all that mattered.

"I asked her not to. You'd get into trouble with Dad if he found out I'd talked to you."

Wasn't that sweet of him to worry? That's why he hadn't answered her messages. "You want a drink or something?"

"I'd kill for a margarita."

She wouldn't normally have kept a bottle on hand, but Harper liked a margarita in the evening. Leading the way to the kitchen, she flipped open the cupboard beside the fridge. At least Harper hadn't taken the bottle on his way out.

"So what happened, Trin?"

Running the ice-cube maker and filling a glass for Lance took all her concentration. She poured a smidge for herself. Then a double smidge, because why the heck not? Handing him a tumbler, she finally answered. "I jumped before I looked. We weren't compati-ble." That was all she'd say. "Let's sit down."

In the living room, she folded herself into the corner of the sofa while Lance took the chair. "So where have you been?" she wanted to know.

Until her marriage, she'd lived with her father. The house was huge, and she hardly had to see him if she didn't want to. Lance had moved out of Daddy's house and left the Bay Area a week after the merger announcement.

If Daddy knew Lance was in her living room now, he'd have conniptions. These days, she didn't tell her father everything, and Lance would always be her big brother. Yet between them, she felt pulled apart. How could Lance have ignored her calls for six months, as if *she'd* had something to do with his and Daddy's battles? She had to forget about that. He was here now.

He shrugged. "Aspen. Santa Fe. Around."

Despite losing the income from his vice presidency in the com-pany, Lance had a trust fund from their mother, just as Trinity did. Her father, however, was trustee of hers and had made sure Harper couldn't get his greedy fingers on any of it.

"It sounds like you've been having fun," she said, trying not to think of Harper and his fingers. If she was going to think about anything besides her brother right now, it would be about Scott. How he tasted—so much better than a margarita.

"Right," Lance scoffed, "loads of fun."

Trinity sighed. "I know it hasn't been easy on you. But you've been okay, right?"

He sipped his margarita, the ice cubes chinking. "It's been hard, Trin."

She didn't want to scold him for what he'd done, yet neither could she agree with it. "I'm sorry" was the least innocuous answer she could give without being judgmental.

"I want to come home."

"Then come home," she said. "You can get an apartment."

"I mean *home*."

"But you can't go *home*, Lance." She dropped her voice to a whisper. "Daddy won't even talk about you."

Daddy might never forgive Lance. It wasn't only that Lance lied, but he'd involved her father in the lie. It could have permanently damaged Daddy's relationship with Jarvis Castle, Faith's father, and they'd been friends since their college days.

"That's why I need you, Trin."

"Me?" she mouthed, her hand to her chest.

"Talk to him." He swirled the cubes in his glass rather than looking at her. "Tell him I know what I did was wrong."

"That has to come from you." If she opened her mouth, her father would simply shut her down.

"I've tried. Verna's tried for me. He won't talk to me."

"Send him a letter."

"He'd tear it up." A lock of dark hair fell across his forehead, and he looked quite boyish. Two years older than her, he suddenly seemed several years younger.

"No, he wouldn't. He might not read it right then." She considered exactly what her father would do. "He'd put it in his desk drawer. And every day he'd open the drawer and look at it. Then one day, he'd take it out and read it."

"Trin, I've already waited six months. I don't feel like waiting weeks for him to get around to reading a letter." He grimaced. "Besides, I don't even know what to say."

"Say you're sorry."

"I *have* said I was sorry from day one." Surging forward, he slammed his glass on the coffee table. "He doesn't listen."

She hated that he was so upset. "I wish I could change it, Lance, but I tried, and Daddy won't listen to me, either." Her mother would have been able to bring them back together. Moisture clouded her eyes, and her temples ached. "I swear, he's like one of those little monkeys with its hands over its ears."

"Then talk to Faith."

She pulled her head back. "Faith?"

"She can talk to her father. If Jarvis were to go to Dad and tell him enough's enough . . . ," he trailed off with a sad droop to his lips.

She swore tears gathered at the corner of his eyes, but still. "That's worse than *me* talking to him." Faith didn't like Lance, not one bit. Nor would Trinity use their friendship to get something done that she was nervous about doing herself.

"I miss my family, Trin. I miss *you*." He bit down on the inside of his cheek as if he didn't trust himself to say more.

And she gave in. "I'll try another talk with Daddy." She wagged her finger at him. "But I'm not promising."

"You're a doll." He rose out of his chair, grabbed the back of her neck, and planted a kiss on her forehead. "Look, I gotta run 'cause I know it's late and you need your rest."

She followed him to the front door. "Call me?"

"Sure, hon. And let me know what Dad says."

Ug. Daddy's blood pressure would skyrocket. "I will." Kissing him once more on the cheek, she shoved him out the door and locked up.

Wonderful that he was home, but Lord, what was she supposed to do about Daddy? She'd think about that tomorrow.

In her room, she punched a key on her computer, and the screen popped out of sleep. She'd forgotten to turn it off this morning after checking for any Scott messages.

Logging into e-mail, lo and behold, exactly what she was looking for. Her heart tripped all over itself.

Not one message, but two. She opened the first. "You are like no woman I've ever known before."

She got an incredible thrill. Covering her mouth with her hand, she read the second. "I am madly, deeply head over heels in lust with you."

He didn't use the word *love*. She wouldn't have believed it anyway. Lust was so much better. He wanted *her*. Badly. She'd never been wanted in quite this way. She'd been admired from afar. Men had certainly wanted to have sex with her. But Scott wanted her in the dark when he couldn't see her. He wanted her over the phone. He'd wanted her when she was just a voice.

And he was *madly* in lust with her. It made her problems with Inga, Lance, and Daddy a little easier to take.

"WHY would I want to go to lunch with *you*?" Inga's red lips curled in a sneer.

Trinity held her breath, counting to three. She would not blow up at this woman. She would not give Inga the satisfaction. "It's not just you. I'm inviting all the AP and AR girls so we can get to know each other." It was Friday, her first full week complete. Lunch could actually be called a celebration.

Inga snorted, turning back to her computer. Her cubicle was the antithesis of the woman. Pictures of fairies and mythical creatures dotted the cloth-covered walls, secured with decorative butterfly and bumblebee pinheads. A crystal unicorn reared its forelegs on the hard drive beneath the monitor. Hanging from the arm of a desk lamp, a winged horse readied itself for flight.

She should have had a Valkyrie's battle ax instead of this menagerie of delicate creatures.

Inga glanced over her shoulder with a telling look. *Are you still here?* "I see enough of you all at work." Inga's overly loud voice carried through, up, and over the cubicle walls, dispersing through the entire Accounting bullpen for maximum humiliation. "I don't need to socialize at lunch as well."

Trinity clearly remembered the AP girls, including Inga, going out to lunch on Wednesday. The *all* in "you all" didn't apply. It was Trinity she didn't care to socialize with.

"That's too bad." Trinity gritted her teeth for a moment before easing the tension from her jaw. "Everyone else can make it. We'll miss you." *Not.* Except that the whole point of the lunch was to placate Inga. Then again, Inga was only one of her five employees, and *they* deserved a welcome lunch.

"I'm sure they're dying to have lunch with the boss's daughter." A tick appeared at the corner of Inga's mouth.

The sneer did nothing for her. She'd be pretty if her attitude didn't suck. Trinity was darn glad she hadn't asked Inga first. The others might not have agreed without their de facto leader's consent.

"Now if you'll excuse me—" Inga tipped her head. Animosity shimmered around her like a halo.

Eyes narrowed and lips decidedly pinched, a look she knew was not her best, Trinity exited the cubicle. Just outside, she almost tripped over Boyd. Pity sparkled in his eyes as he leaped out of her way. On the other side of a cube partition, she was sure she heard a snicker. Whispers. Finally a phone rang, then another, and the bullpen returned to its normal din.

God. She craved a mocha in the worst way. Extra chocolate. With a shot of orange. To be the object of pity, well, Trinity couldn't quite fathom it. Inga's rudeness went beyond anger that she hadn't gotten Trinity's job. Inga hated Trinity herself.

In her own cube, Trinity checked her in-basket. The morning's list of received cash transfers and auto deposits still topped off the stack. There must be a binder or a folder to file it in, but she had yet to find it.

But *why* did Inga hate her? Figuring that one out was like trying to find the fix for global warming, but she would not give up. At least she'd figured the system out herself. It *was* like shopping at her favorite online wholesale hair product sites. Right now she couldn't do more than peruse customer and vendor profiles, addresses, phone numbers, and balances. But she was getting the hang of it despite Inga Rice.

Yet she could feel herself getting hot under the collar just thinking about Inga. Maybe she needed a cold water splash on her face. In the restroom mirror, she did seem a little flushed. Her cheeks almost matched her bright fuchsia shift.

Trinity sucked in a breath.

Good Lord. Her stomach had a bulge she hadn't noticed this morning when she stepped into the dress and zipped it.

"I'm fat," she whispered. Just as Lance had said last night. Too many late-evening bowls of ice cream, not to mention that whole piece of bread pudding. How many calories were in the brandy sauce alone? Oh God.

Breathe. The sudden anxiety was all about Inga and nothing to do with her dress. She sucked in her belly, turned sideways, and smoothed a hand down the flat plane of her tummy. All she had to do was hold her breath and everything was fine.

"And look at those breasts." She marveled at how she filled out the dress's darts. Wow. She'd always had to stuff a little extra cotton in there. But not now.

Scott said she had gorgeous breasts. He'd also said he was madly, deeply, head over heels in lust with her. He thought she was perfect. So there. She stuck her tongue out at the mirror, then laughed like a child.

Hmm. Why would he give her that kind of power, though? Perhaps because lust wasn't the same thing as love. A man could turn it off as easily as he turned it on. Unlike love. Yet Harper had said he loved her and it hadn't meant a thing. Yes, being the object of Scott's lust was so much better.

Behind her, the restroom door squeaked on its hinges. Trinity let out her breath in a whoosh.

Christina Lee appeared in the mirror's reflection. Her black hair in a pageboy style, she tucked an absolutely straight lock behind her ear. "You mustn't let it get to you."

How had the girl known about the weight gain?

"She treats everybody like that at first." She spoke perfect English with a hint of foreign diction. "But she'll get warmer the more she knows you."

Oh. Christina meant the *b-i-t-c-h*. Trinity debated how to handle it. Could she trust the girl? After all, Inga might have sent her in here to further tighten the screw.

Since when had she become so suspicious? In the mirror Trinity didn't like what she saw, and it wasn't the extra ice cream, orange mocha, or bread pudding drenched in brandy sauce.

A silly, frightened woman with dark circles under her eyes stared out of the mirror. Her confidence and self-assurance had circled the drain the night she found Harper with his lover. He'd washed it down with the pulse of the showerhead.

She swallowed her emotions and smiled at Christina. "Thanks. I appreciate it." It was noncommittal, devoid of any slam against Inga, yet it acknowledged the girl's kindness.

Christina nodded, and still observing her in the mirror, Trinity realized she wasn't a girl at all but as old as Trinity herself. She was, however, slender as a will-o'-the-wisp and a head shorter than Trinity.

"Have you girls decided where you want to eat?"

"Anything but Chinese food." Then Christina smiled and disappeared inside a stall.

Trinity washed her hands and returned to her desk. On the way, Mr. Ackerman—she still had trouble thinking of him as Mister—waylaid her in the hall. "Can we talk in my office?"

"Certainly." Jeez, what had she done wrong? And wasn't *that* a negative thought?

Mr. Ackerman rubbed the top of his head as she entered the office behind him. In the chair opposite his desk, Trinity sat and crossed her legs. He tapped his upper lip where a bead of sweat sprouted like an ingrown whisker.

"What can I do for you?" she said brightly.

"I wanted to see how your first week with us has gone."

"It's been fine, thanks."

His office walls were covered with an impressive array of certificates. He'd successfully completed a SOX seminar. To do with baseball? On his desk, blobs of fired clay held down stacks of papers. "Is that a turtle?"

Anthony beamed. "My daughter's taking a pottery class." He brought the turtle to eye level, staring cross-eyed at it. "I think it's a frog."

"She's very talented."

Anthony barked out a laugh. "The next Rembrandt, by Jove." He looked so much less harried talking about his daughter.

"Now, why did you really call me in here?"

He grinned, a sheepish sparkle in his blue eyes. "Your father wanted to make sure you were happy here."

Her *father*? "I'm very happy. Are you happy?"

"Oh, infinitely happy."

"Then we can both tell Daddy how happy we are." She smiled, yet it felt brittle on her lips. It was a bit like being in college and still needing your mom to call the teacher for your homework assignment. Trinity didn't need the humiliation.

"Anything else?" She smiled as sweetly as possible and rose to her feet.

"No, no." More moisture gathered on his upper lip. "Keep up the good work."

She hadn't done any real work to date. Christina handled most of the AR calls. The AP girls handled the vendors. Inga did the check run. All Trinity did was review. She didn't even know if there was anything wrong with whatever she reviewed. She'd played incessantly with the computer system, slogged through the AP/AR procedures manual, studied the wire book in preparation for sending a wire transfer, but had yet to do even that task.

"Well, everything is fine and dandy, Mr. Ackerman. You can tell my father that, then we'll *all* be happy."

Why did it feel so demoralizing?

Because no one else in the entire work world had their father checking up on them. Not even Lance. Which *had* been a problem. If Daddy'd checked, he might not have screwed up.

Lord, thinking about Lance reminded her she had to plead his case. She couldn't do that now. Not today.

She backed out of Mr. Ackerman's office with all its certificates and unrecognizable clay animals. "I'm taking the girls to lunch," she said. "I feel we should get to know each other."

He stood. "Good idea. Wonderful."

Rah-rah. Go Trinity. It sounded like a high school cheer. If she screwed up and cost the company a ton of money in late fees on a past-due bill, she had the feeling Anthony Ackerman would still tell her father she was perfect. She wouldn't get fired, because she was the boss's daughter.

She should have gotten a job somewhere else. Where she could make a *real* first impression. Where she wasn't Herman Green's daughter. Or Harper Harrington's cast-off wife.

"Take an extra half hour at lunch, too." Waving a hand in the air, Mr. Ackerman pulled a folder close and opened it.

How was she to show everyone at Green that she could actually do the job and do it well?

Dead center in the hallway outside his office, Trinity put her fingers to her lips. She sounded like a whiner even inside her own head.

This was bad. She'd morphed from normal to whiner within the space of two weeks. Dammit, she *would* get over it. And she'd wow her employees with bread pudding at Vatovola's.

*   *   *

"MEET me."

Damn, he loved her voice over the phone, especially when she was demanding. "When?"

"Now."

It was Friday. He glanced at his watch, a habit, since he already knew it wasn't quite five. "Where?"

"I don't care, you pick." A note he couldn't identify laced her voice. She spoke quietly, as if she were somewhere she could be overheard, but it was more. Defeat? Depression?

Scott didn't like to think of those emotions where Jezebel was concerned. "My house."

"No."

"You said I got to choose. And I want you in my bed."

"How badly do you want to see me?" she asked.

Ah, he understood. She'd had an off day, and she needed an ego boost. "So badly that I've got a ton of paperwork on my desk, and I'm willing to walk away from it this minute."

He had a Monday morning audit committee meeting to prepare for, but he didn't care. Neither of the girls was coming home this weekend, so he'd work through it.

And he'd have his candy now.

"Is that because you're madly in lust with me?"

He laughed. "Hell yes."

She sighed, a light, satisfied sound. Then refused him. "If you want to see me, pick a place besides your house."

"You're a tease." She wanted him just as badly, he knew.

A shadow in his periphery caught his attention. He cocked his head slightly. Grace stood in his doorway. For how long, he didn't know, but she raised her hand and gave him the "come see me" signal. He jutted his chin in acknowledgment.

Jezebel gave a musical laugh, then lowered her voice. "With last night in the back of your car, you can't call me a tease."

"Correct." His cock rose with the memory. He wanted to repeat last night's activities and more. Over and over. In his bed. All night long. He just had to figure out how to get her there. "If it's my choice, then I want dinner with you."

She paused a long moment. "I can do that."

Ah, victory. It was so damn sweet.

"But I don't want to go anywhere near Vatovola's." A slight edge trimmed her voice.

It was a good restaurant, but he had something better in mind anyway. "I know a hole-in-the-wall place with great food." It had the advantage of being close to his office, too.

"Will it be crowded?"

"No." Which is the way he wanted it. Quiet, candlelit, with her almost to himself. He gave her the directions and told her to park in the garage where he kept his car. "Meet me in half an hour." He waited for her to object.

"God, yes, I'll be there. I need to get out of here." Click, and she was gone.

Definitely, she'd had a bad day. It was evident in the slightly sharp edge to her tone. He'd make her forget it all.

He had enough time to deal with Grace's issue before he left to meet Jezebel, but for the first time in memory, he was irritated with the fact that he had to address work first.

It struck him that that had been Katy's complaint. His job came before her and the girls. It wasn't true, but his work had been what supported them. The more *things* he provided, the more time he was away from his family. But hell, he didn't need the depressing thoughts now. It was done, over.

Grabbing his keys out of his desk drawer, he locked his office after him and headed down to Grace's. If she didn't drag out the conversation, he had enough time to make it to the drugstore for something very essential to his evening.

Elton stopped in the hall and gaped, his eyes wide behind his wire rims. "Are you leaving?" He gulped. "Not that I'm saying you shouldn't be leaving. It's, well—" He stopped before a stammer entered his voice.

"You don't have to explain, Elton." And neither did Scott. Yet it was odd for him to leave work on the dot of five.

By her desk, Grace leaned over, her skirt up her thighs as she straightened her pantyhose. He almost backed out, but she saw him, her cheeks a ruddy red as she tugged her skirt down.

"You need something before I leave?" He didn't mention finding her intimately occupied. He didn't think of Grace as a woman, but obviously she was struggling with the aftermath of divorce, something he understood all too well.

"I was curious what gym you go to." If possible, the heat in her face deepened. "I'm interested in joining a good place and wanted a recommendation."

That was the last thing he would have imagined. "My gym?"

Her gaze flashed over him. "You're in such good shape, I just assumed . . . ," she trailed off.

"I do go to a gym, but it's a men-only club." Which avoided the meat-market atmosphere. "Sorry I can't help." He didn't thank her for the compliment, either, since it was obvious she hadn't meant the words in that particular way.

Yet . . . why was she embarrassed? She couldn't have any ideas about him. He was her boss. She'd never jeopardize her job. "If that was it, then," he said, "I'm outta here. I'll be in on the weekend to set up for the audit committee meeting."

"Okay." She smiled, if a bit sheepishly and without meeting his gaze. "Have a nice Friday night."

In the hall, he stopped a moment. Nah. Really. She wasn't the type for an office fling, especially not with the boss.

Now Jezebel? She was a whole different kind of woman. Where she was concerned, he wanted far more than a mere fling.

10

HER stylish hot pink dress accentuated her breasts, and the brevity of its length called attention to her mile-long legs.

Je-sus. Scott was instantly crazy hard.

She stood by the side of her Mustang, five spots down from his car. Beeping his remote, he threw his drugstore package behind his seat, then relocked.

The restaurant was close. "Can you walk in those heels?" he said, salivating over her trim ankles as he approached.

"I'm a woman." She glanced down at the matching pink sandals. "Of course I can walk in heels."

He grinned. She was definitely a woman and her usual sassy self. Damn, he was becoming obsessed. It was a good thing. She made him feel alive.

He grabbed her hand before she could balk and led her to the elevators heading down to street level. Millennium housed its headquarters in downtown San Jose. It made for a long commute home over the mountains, but Scott arrived early and left late, so he missed the traffic. He enjoyed working in the city because he could go home to mountain living, leaving the mad rush behind.

"What kind of food are we eating?"

"Greek." Her hand felt small and dainty in his. He couldn't remember the last time he'd held hands with someone other than his daughters. It was probably pathetic, but he liked the glances Jezebel garnered on the street. More than one well-dressed businessman took an extra long gander at her.

Yet she didn't seem to notice. Instead, she gazed up at him as he guided her through the early evening throng taking up the sidewalk. He adjusted his stride to hers. Despite her gorgeous long legs, she couldn't keep up in those shoes.

"Greek's a lot of lamb, right?" Her eyes were a startling blue in deep twilight.

"It's one of their specialties."

She closed her lids a moment, a pleasure sound rising in her throat as if she were having sex. "I love lamb."

She made him wish he was her next meal. "Then you'll be glad to know they have the best."

She clung to his arm with enthusiasm. For a woman so slender, she definitely loved her food. "I've had an *absolutely* rotten day, and I deserve lamb."

She deserved all the delicacies he'd give her tonight. "This is it."

She stopped, stared. Café Demetrius didn't appear special. Paint flakes left holes in the restaurant's window signage, and the screen door needed a new hinge. Yet inside the miasma of scents, rosemary, garlic, roasting meat, was mouthwatering.

"Don't let looks be deceiving," he whispered in her ear. "I've been in the kitchen, and it's clean as a whistle."

Demetrius himself scuttled forward, his protruding belly covered by a neat, still-white apron. "Mr. Sinclair, we've been wondering when you'd be back. Mama has missed you." Mama was his wife, a stout, rotund woman, and the genius in the kitchen. "And my, your lady is so lovely." He grabbed her hand, bending over it just shy of placing a kiss and revealing the balding spot on the crown of his head. "We have a wonderful special tonight."

"She's going to need lamb."

"I can speak for myself, thank you very much." She cupped both hands over Demetrius's grip on her. "I'm definitely going to need lamb. I'm having a lamb attack, in fact."

"Oh my wife is making the most perfect lamb dish tonight." He kissed his fingers. "Her specialty."

"Then I can't wait."

Demetrius melted under her smile. "This way, please, I've saved my best table for just such guests as you."

Since it was early, three tables of the approximate twenty-five were occupied. Scott had the feeling they were all the "best" tables. The old-fashioned black-and-white checkerboard floor was faded yet spotless. The tables were round and small for intimate conversation, a bud vase of daffodils and a flickering candle in the center of each.

With a flourish, Demetrius swept out a chair at a table in the back corner. Jezebel smiled as she sat. "You're so kind."

Taking the seat next to her rather than opposite, Scott ordered his favorite merlot to start. Demetrius bustled off to the opposite corner of the room and slipped behind a screen.

"The place isn't very full." With her fork, she drew patterns on the tablecloth, again clean but faded with many uses. "It's a wonder they can stay in business."

"This place is a favorite for the traditional Greek community." His leg next to hers, he felt her heat all the way to his gut. "Greeks are a late crowd, Demetrius tells me."

"I like that he knows your name." She smiled.

His heart beat faster. Even the woman's smile set him off. He wondered how deep he was going. He wanted her in his bed, but he envisioned taking her to all his favorite places, restaurants, Point Lobos down in Carmel, the wine country, Hyde Park in the heart of

London, the French countryside, Buenos Aires, a city he'd never been to but somehow found fascinating.

Another couple, both men, entered and proved Demetrius knew everyone's name.

"He's a very friendly guy." Scott had started coming here after Katy left, before he'd forced himself to learn to cook.

After seating the men, Demetrius brought the wine. Pouring a jot, he waited as Scott swirled, sniffed, and tasted.

"Perfect, as usual."

The portly man beamed, then took their orders, the lamb specialty for the lady and Scott's traditional moussaka, a minced meat dish with eggplant and a rich cream sauce. Mama added potatoes to her recipe. He hadn't had a bad meal at the café.

When they were alone once more, he tipped the candle to the side and studied the flame. "So, it wasn't such a good day?"

"It was a fine day." Yet the air between them turned icy.

He took her fingers in his hand, playing with the nails. She had what he'd heard referred to as a French manicure, clear nail, painted white half circles on the tips. Still nice. He was waiting for the naughty red polish to come out. "I'm so glad to hear your day was fine. How was your week?"

"That was fine, too." She pulled her hand away and clasped both in her lap.

"Good." How could he get her to talk to him? Then he wondered why it was important, the reason probably akin to his wanting to take her to his favorite spots.

"All right, it was my first—" She paused, almost as if considering her words. "My first week at this new job."

"Hard fitting in?"

She tipped her head, perusing him through her lashes, the candlelight playing across her face, her skin smooth, flawless. "I've never had trouble fitting in." *Before.*

He was sure he heard the word tacked on. Which didn't clarify about the new job, but it did make several other things clear. Her stress sometimes when she called, like tonight. He suddenly felt like a substitute for what might be missing in her life, and he wasn't at all sure he liked it. "Tell me about it."

She laughed. "What, like tell Daddy everything and he'll make it all better?"

"Not Daddy." He didn't like the age reference.

"Good, because I've already got a daddy, and I'm not in the market for another one." She smiled at the end, but he felt the edge of something in her voice.

It was easier talking sex than talking about her life. At least she wasn't looking for a sugar daddy. Demetrius brought their meals, the service quick since the place wasn't busy. With Mama doing the cooking by herself, it could sometimes take upwards of half an hour, but the food was worth it.

She closed her eyes, leaned close to her plate, and inhaled deeply. "Oh my God, that smells absolutely divine."

Demetrius beamed, a dimple flashing at one side of his mouth. "I'll tell Mama." And he rushed away to do just that.

The familiar hardening of Scott's cock took over. She made everything a sensual experience. He wanted to partake of so much more, though even he had to admit the lamb smelled damn good.

She sliced a small bite, relished it a long moment, then bit her bottom lip and moaned. Just as she did when she touched herself. "You were right about this place."

His mouth watered and not for the food. "Try this." He held out a forkful of moussaka.

Wrapping her fingers around his wrist, she guided his fork to her lips. First, she drew in the scent. "Ooh." Then she tested with the tip of her tongue. As if she were licking at a drop of his come. "Mmm."

She made him hard and his briefs wet. He couldn't take much more.

His wrist still captured in her grip, she slid the fork into her mouth, lids half closed, as if she were taking his cock between her lips. Then she moaned as if the meat were caviar.

"I'm not sure which." Helping herself to another bite right off his plate, she murmured, "I still think the lamb." She carved a piece, glanced at him, then instead of spearing it with her fork, she picked the bit up in her fingers, and motioned him.

He ate from her fingers, her skin smooth, supple, scented with lotion. Taking the lamb in his mouth, he sucked her finger as she pulled away. The lamb was fine, but she was so much more tasty.

Watching him, her eyes deepened to ocean blue.

"That was so fucking good," he murmured, and they both knew he didn't mean the lamb. He'd kill to have her for dessert.

Her pulse fluttered at her throat. Then she put her hand to his shoulder and pushed him back in his seat. "You," she whispered, "need to stay over there." She licked clean the finger he'd sucked. "Or Mr. Demetrius will have us arrested."

"Let's go now." He meant every word.

She arched one brow. "I can't miss my lamb."

Fuck her lamb, he wanted to say. She was a tease. He loved it. He'd let her tease him all night. In the end, she'd be his.

"Okay, here's what's on my mind. I've got this friend."

The abrupt change threw him. He'd been in orgasmic heaven. Yet if he wasn't careful, he'd overload right at the table. "So, you have a friend." He drew in a deep breath, tamping down his excitement for the moment. Everyone had a friend by the same name as their own. "And your friend's in trouble?"

"Not *trouble*, per se." She groaned over a bite of potato. She'd make him nuts before the meal was over. "It's just that she, my friend"—she glanced at him through her lashes—"has family issues going that she doesn't quite know how to handle."

Hence the tense comment about not needing another daddy. "And you want my advice?" Somehow, the fact that she asked his opinion was almost as pleasurable as eating from her fingers.

She speared a grilled cherry tomato, raising it to her lips to lick away the juice before she popped it in her mouth. Did she know how she affected him?

"I want to see if your advice is the same as my advice." She tucked a lock of blond hair behind her ear.

"Why don't you tell me the story?" His heartbeat pulsing in his ears, he added a chaser of wine to his bite of moussaka.

"Well, it's complicated, but her brother did something wrong that reflected badly on her father." She shot another gaze through her lashes. "Professionally speaking, that is."

"Was it something illegal?"

Her sudden nervousness came out in the way she toyed with her food instead of attacking it with her former gusto. "It was more unethical than illegal."

"I'm assuming her father found out and . . ." He raised an eyebrow in query.

"Well." She paused, then rushed on as if afraid he wouldn't understand. "She loves them both and hates seeing them at odds, but her father was so disappointed he won't talk to his son now." Cutting a bit of lamb, she chewed longer than necessary.

"Let me guess the next item on the agenda. The son wants his sister to intercede with their father."

She looked straight at him and gaped slightly. "How'd you know?"

"I figure out the mystery before the end of the movie."

She laughed. "And annoyingly, you reveal it, just so everyone knows you're right."

He liked the smile back on her face, but a slight ache beat against his heart. He hadn't watched a movie since Lexa and Brooke were home for Christmas. On his own, he didn't bother, working instead. "My girls hate that." He quirked his mouth in a half smile. "But I'm always right."

"Remind me *never* to watch a movie with you."

He imagined how good it would feel to have her folded in his arms watching movies on his rarely used big-screen TV. The simple things were as hot as sex. "How about a sexy thriller?"

She eyed him.

"So, your friend's brother," he said to clear away the strange urge, "what did you tell her?"

"I haven't told her anything yet." Instead of playing with her meal, she set her fork down and her hands disappeared beneath the table. "What would you suggest if you were her friend?"

"He did something unethical, if not illegal, and somehow compromised her dad's position." His elbows on the table, he steepled his fingers. "He's obviously made a big mistake, and if he's asking his sister to talk to his father, then I'd say he hasn't learned his lesson yet."

"You don't think so? What if he wrote to their father, who tore the letter up without reading it?"

"Then I'd have to ask if her father told her that or her brother did. Because whatever he says is suspect."

She gazed over his shoulder, studying either the painting of an old Greek sailor or something deep inside her mind. "You're right," she whispered. "You have to learn your own lessons, and you'll make lots of mistakes along the way, but you'll come out better in the end." She tipped her head. "Won't you?"

He wondered what mistakes she'd made. Her marriage? He sure as hell knew about making *that* mistake. Had he learned his lesson out of the dissolution of his own marriage? He was still a workaholic. Sure, right now his little Jezebel came first, but if he actually had a relationship, would it go the way of his marriage? Late nights, broken dates, business before pleasure. He recalled a time or two he'd shortchanged the girls, chosen a business need over a school play or a soccer game.

Yet the girls were still the most important thing in the world. "Yeah. You learn from your mistakes if you recognize they were your mistakes and fix them yourself." He took her hand in his and kissed her knuckles. "Which is a damn sight harder than asking your sister to do it for you."

She blinked, gazing at him with troubled blue eyes, and he couldn't tell a thing about what she saw.

Until her mouth curved in the slightest of smiles. "I think I should tell my friend to let her brother handle it himself."

"I think you should, too."

"Thanks." Then she graced him with a high-wattage smile, and his heart turned over in his chest.

"Problem solved," she whispered.

He had a feeling he was stepping into a whole new problem. In addition to lusting after her, he now admired her family loyalty and caring nature. What the hell was his next emotion about her going to be? And how much would it cost him?

SCOTT was a like a Xanax fix. Not that she'd taken Xanax, but she imagined the semi-euphoric rush in her blood was exactly how Xanax would feel.

His hand clasped around hers as he walked her back to her car was big, solid, protective. He held onto her despite the fact that the street was empty, or maybe because of it. They were much more alone than earlier, at the mercy of a mugger, but San Jose's financial district was clean, well lit, and she'd seen a couple of cop cars cruising. She'd buttoned her sweater against the chilly night, but she could have stayed warm all the way through with the touch of Scott's hand.

It was his advice that gave her the Xanax fix, though. She'd used the "friend" excuse so it wouldn't seem like she was getting *too* personal, and granted, Scott hadn't solved her problems, but it felt good to talk about it. She'd been on edge all day, wondering what to do about Lance, how to approach Daddy, not to mention that horrible lunch with the girls. Except for Christina, they'd chattered amongst themselves as if she weren't there. When she'd tried to engage them, they'd ignored her or talked over her. There were two camps on the AP/AR battlefield, and they'd clearly chosen Inga's.

But that was another matter. For now, she felt satisfied with letting Lance take care of his own issues. She'd advise him on how to make things better, but doing it was up to him.

Steering her to the elevators, Scott punched the button. They'd parked in the underground garage beneath his office building. When the doors closed, he drew in her, sliding an arm across her back. "Come home with me."

Her heart pitter-pattered. "No."

His mouth quirked in his familiar devilish smile. "Yes."

"*No* means no."

Tightening his arm, he rubbed his erection against her. "I promise not to do anything you don't want me to."

She wanted him to do a lot. She imagined she wouldn't even want to get out of bed until morning. Scott was a dangerous man. She could start wanting *more*. She could start feeling the need to don her Trinity debutante mask, acting the perfect little lover so he wouldn't run away.

When he tried to hold her in the elevator, she dragged him out into the car park. "I am not going to your house." It was too . . . intimate. She would see how he lived. She would know more about him. She'd *want* to know more about him.

"You're a hard woman."

She couldn't resist running her hand across the front of his slacks. "You're a hard man."

He groaned. "Tease." He stopped her as they approached his car. "Come home and watch a movie."

"Hah." She clucked her tongue at him. "You'll probably put on something X-rated and get all randy."

"I don't have any X-rated movies." He crossed his heart. It was endearing. "Wouldn't want my daughters to accidentally come across them and think their dad's a perv."

She giggled. "Their dad *is* a perv."

Leaning back against the rear hatch of his car, he reeled her in until she was once again plastered to his body. "Only with you," he murmured, nuzzling her hair.

Despite her heels, she still felt small in his arms. God, she adored his height. He was so, so dangerous to her equilibrium.

"Come home." His voice seduced her, his body melted her.

She wanted to do exactly as he asked. "Why don't you show me your office instead?" That was relatively safe.

"Done," he said, pinning her close for a long second.

His office had possibilities. She could kiss him, maybe do a few naughty things, but they couldn't go too far because, after all, it was his *office*. It *was* only eight. Why, the place might not even be empty, all his little accountant worker bees buzzing about. Or the cleaning people could be making their rounds.

Both hands on her arms, he set her away from him, beeped his remote, opened the back door, retrieved something, then slammed and locked the car again. Gathering her hand in his, he set a pace so fast she almost had to skip to keep up.

Once in the elevator, he swiped his card key access and entered the fifteenth floor before the car would move. Then it shot them sky-high. On his floor, he led her out into a short but well-lit hallway. "We have two more floors," he said. "Reception is on the fourteenth along with Marketing. Plus there's our manufacturing facility down in Morgan Hill." Pride radiated through his voice. He loved his job and the company. Flipping a thumb, he indicated a set of double doors beyond the bank of elevators. "On that side of the hall are the executive offices"—he tipped his head to the other door—"and my bailiwick, Accounting, is behind door number two."

He swiped his key once again outside the unmarked entrance. It was dark inside after the bright light of the hallway, and the alarm beeped as they stepped over the threshold, its green readout flashing. Hitting a few numbers on a keypad, he shut it off.

"With all the proprietary information, we've got separate alarms for each section," he explained. "Which is handy because we know we're alone." He stroked a finger down her cheek. "Everyone's gone." His teeth flashed white with a sexy smile.

Uh-oh. Maybe she'd miscalculated on how safe from temptation she was up here.

The emergency sign overhead provided the only light. Then he flipped a switch and a single row of fluorescents flickered on, highlighting the center bullpen of cubicles. Offices ringed the perimeter, fashioned with movable walls for easy rearranging.

Scott led her to the corner office and unlocked it.

"Ooh, you're Mister Big," she said, glancing around.

His window overlooked other high-rise buildings and bits of the San Jose skyline. He hit the lights, and the sky disappeared in the reflection. The large office was appointed well with solid wood furniture, a small oak conference table, and comfy chairs. His notebook computer sat on the desk with wireless keyboard and mouse. A white board hung on one wall kitty-corner to an elegant painting of a Japanese woman in a stunning kimono.

Feeling him close behind her, she ran a finger along the edge of his desk. "You're very neat."

He liked colored pens and lots of Post-it notes in varying sizes. Piles of folders and papers loaded down several stackable wire inboxes. She needed something like it to separate the papers she hadn't looked at from the ones she'd gone through and the stuff she had no clue what to do with.

"I'm a lot of things." He slid his arms around her waist, fingers gliding up to undo the buttons of her sweater. "And right now, hard is one of them." He punctuated his declaration with a roll of his hips.

She pushed back. "You left your office door open." The slight fear of being caught delighted her.

"I did. That way I can hear if the outer door opens. Wouldn't want the janitors surprising us if they unlocked my office door." Cupping both breasts, he pinched her nipples.

She sucked in a breath and bit down on her lip. So good. A tad painful, but that enhanced the pleasure.

Along her spine, his cock grew. With her hands over his, she guided him down to her abdomen. "Bad boy," she whispered.

He kept on going, down to her hips, her thighs, her pussy. "Very bad," he breathed against her ear. "I want you now."

He inched her dress over her hips. She fought it back down. "There are lights on in that building. We'll be seen."

With one hand, he trapped hers against her tummy, and tugged up her dress. "Yeah, we might be seen." Nuzzling aside her hair, he murmured, "It'll be fucking hot." Then he slid past the elastic of her thong, delving into her pussy. "Feel how wet you are. The idea turns you on as much as it does me."

She tried to wriggle away. "Of course it doesn't." Oh God, it did. He caressed her lightly along her center. She wanted more. His hand. His mouth. His cock.

"A woman executive maybe. Wearing a thong like yours. She'd have to touch herself."

His words seduced her. She'd never been like this with anyone, willing to do naughty things that turned her inside out.

Pushing her forward until her hands rested on his desk, he continued the erotic play, teasing fingers, sensual words.

"Hmm, maybe a CEO." Leaning over her, he brushed her hair with his chin as he nodded. "Over there, top window. He shuts off the lights so he can see us better, then sits in his big chair, takes his cock out, and jerks off while I fuck you."

She shivered, and her breath seemed trapped in her throat. "You're very crude." It was the crassness of his words that got to her. She wanted it.

Reaching between them, the back of his hand stroked her bared butt as he undid his belt. His zipper rasped, and she closed her eyes, a low moan rising in her throat.

"You want to make us both come, don't you? Me inside you, him watching. You have us in the palm of your hand right now, willing to do anything." Bending his knees, he rubbed the head of his cock along the crease of her butt.

She'd never had a man without foreplay. Even *with* foreplay, sex had never been anything like it was with Scott. His *voice* was foreplay. Her heart beat loudly, her breath came fast, and between her legs she was wet and ready.

Leaning over her, he nipped the back of her neck like a tomcat sensing her heat. "Tell me what you want."

She gasped. "I want you."

"How do you want me?"

"Inside me." She pushed back, straining against him.

"Say it. Say what you want me to do."

Tears of need gathered at the corners of her eyes. "Fuck me, please fuck me." It wasn't her word, yet that's exactly how she wanted it, right this minute. Hard, dirty, raw.

He shifted, rustled, noises, the sounds titillating her senses. She closed her eyes, and he rubbed her with the condom. Lightly kicking her legs apart with his foot, he held her hips as he tugged aside her thong. The threads popped, the sounds of tearing material so elemental, her knees would have buckled if he wasn't pinning her to the desk.

Hunkered over her, he breathed her in. "God, you smell good."

Then Scott coated himself in her moisture, groaned, and plunged deep. She went rigid beneath him, her fingers outstretched, then slowly she clenched her fists.

"Tell me how good it is." He needed to know. Wrapped in her heat, he felt close to implosion.

She sucked in a breath, moaned on the exhale, and murmured, "Move. I want to feel you."

He twisted her hair around his hand, pulled her head back, then grabbed her hip and seated himself deeper.

"Oh my God," she whimpered. "It's never felt like that."

He retreated almost to the tip, then slid inside her, slowly, every inch of her warmth pulling him in. She jammed her hands down on the desktop and pushed back. Sliding an arm under her, he hitched her closer, riding her more deeply.

"You make me crazy." He didn't know if she could hear, but her breathy moans, the quaking of her body, and her tight fit around his cock drove him higher than he'd ever been. He took her until she cried his name, then it wasn't even words, just a long, panting wail that cut some deep-seated need loose inside him, pounding harder, faster, deeper. No woman had screamed like that for him. The build in his balls was so intense it hurt, and as her body convulsed around him, he lost his mind, emptying himself inside her.

Nothing had ever been so good.

Long afterwards, she trembled against him. His legs ached, and his back muscles shrieked. He hadn't kissed her, he'd taken her. His hand was still tangled in her hair, and he pulled it all aside to kiss the moisture from the corners of her eyes.

She hiccupped like a child who'd been crying. He rocked with her, still inside her. A contraction rippled over his cock.

He wanted to hold her, stay in her, but bent over her as he was, the desk must have been cutting into her abdomen. Easing back, he pulled out. She mumbled. He quickly dispensed with the condom, burying it in the trash, and flipped out the light. The moon streamed across her hair, setting it aglow.

She hadn't moved, not even to pull down her dress. He covered her, then gathered her into his arms and carried her to his chair, arranging her in his lap.

She immediately hooked an arm around his neck and nuzzled his throat. "What was that?"

Cataclysmic. Earth shattering. "Good sex."

"*Really* good sex." He felt her smile against his skin. Then she rolled her head on his shoulder to gaze up at him. Moonlight sparkled in her eyes. "I shouldn't tell you this. It'll go to your head, but no one's ever done that to me before."

Made *love* to her? His heart kicked. "Taken you on a desk?"

She laughed, that musical sound he adored. "No, silly." She ran a finger across his lips. "I mean I've never had an *orgasm* when I'm doing *that*."

"Then you haven't been with the right man." He wanted to laugh at his joke, but there was nothing funny about it. He was her first. Jesus.

She lay completely still in his arms, then finally, she relaxed. "I don't think anyone ever took enough time."

It hadn't been time. She'd been wet and ready before he even put his hand between her legs. And damn if he didn't want to crow, while at the same time, he needed more from her than an orgasm. Or ten. Even a hundred.

He kissed the top of her head. "Tell me your name."

She leaned back to look at him once more, then she mouthed the one thing he didn't want to hear. "Jezebel."

DON'T spoil it, *don't spoil it*. Trinity willed him to hear her thoughts. She snuggled closer. Sex had *never* been like that. The orgasm had come from deep inside, shattering up and outward, shooting her out of her own body. She'd screamed.

Had she sounded like a braying donkey? Maybe. But so what? He'd gone crazy for her anyway.

Part of what made it so good was that they had *only* sex between them. She was free to do naughty things like have full-blown sex on a desk right in front of the windows. Or to take him in her mouth in the backseat of his car. To make herself come for him, to push him into stroking himself for her. She wanted to do so many more naughty things. With him. For him.

She wanted him to make her come like that over and over.

If he knew her name, he'd find out everything about her, and they'd become just another "relationship" with all the pitfalls, and worse, with the inevitable outcome. She'd proven she wasn't good at relationships. All her inhibitions would come rushing back; she'd start acting a role, drive him away.

Trinity traced her fingers over his lips, then touched her own. "You'll like me better if I'm a mystery."

She could not lose the way he made her feel. Now, more than ever, after that incredible orgasm, she couldn't let Trinity Green scare him away. So much better to remain his mystery woman, Jezebel.

11

"HOLD!"

Ron Rudd squeezed a hand through the elevator doors.

Ah shit. Scott enjoyed his job. He just didn't enjoy his boss. He had to take the guy five days a week, but early on a Saturday morning, Rudd drained last evening's lassitude right out of him.

"Glad you're taking the audit seriously, Sinclair."

"I take my *job* seriously." Ass. Rudd needed supervisor training. His VPs were dropping like flies. Then again, that was a good thing. The company didn't need eight VPs.

"Good. I hope you're seriously considering how to correct the bottom line, too." Rudd tugged on the neck of his polo shirt as if it were strangling him.

"The bottom line isn't the issue, Ron." The value of his stock options were the issue in Rudd's mind. "It's overspending. The *world-class* lobby in our manufacturing facility"—a ridiculous expenditure in Scott's opinion—"doesn't need to be *that* world-class." The design alone was seventy thousand dollars.

"If we want to *be* a world-class company, we have to *look* like a world-class company."

That had been the standard party line all last year, when they put in the new computer system, which Scott had agreed was a necessity. It was the leather lobby chairs, marble floor, and expensive signage on the building he took umbrage with.

"And may I remind you that those are capital expenditures and don't affect the bottom line?"

Where the hell had the man obtained his MBA? "True," Scott drawled, "but cash is king, Ron, and the interest on the credit line plus the invoice factoring is sucking us dry."

"If you negotiate the rate down on the factoring—"

"I've already gotten it down three percentage points." Selling receivables invoice by invoice was a stopgap measure. Why the board of directors signed off on Ron's proposals, Scott hadn't a clue. He'd fought against both capital expenditures.

The elevator dinged, stopping on their floor. Thank God. He wanted a peaceful Saturday with Rudd staying on his side of the hallway. He had enough of the man during the week.

As Scott pulled out his card key, his boss got in his parting shot. "I've discussed the M4 reserve with Johansson, and he agrees it can be reversed."

Johansson was chairman, but accounting was not his strong suit. He didn't know generally accepted accounting principles from his ass. With all the accounting scandals in the last few years, Scott wasn't putting his own butt on the line. "If the analysis bears that out"—he had Grace and her people working on it to satisfy any question in Johansson's mind—"we'll relieve the reserve. But it's still getting disclosed, and it won't help you make projected earnings." The beep of the alarm drowned out Rudd's answer. Scott let the door close on him.

Ah, blessed silence. Since it was early, before eight thirty, if anyone was working on a Saturday, they most likely wouldn't be in until later. He planned on a good two hours, then he'd take care of some garden work. Both Lexa and Brooke were home next weekend, and he wanted to get the chores out of the way so he could spend time with them.

Waiting for his computer to boot up, his mind drifted to Jezebel. Her scent filled the office, sweet, all woman. When he closed his eyes, he could feel her heat taking him. He'd never before crossed the bounds of business and pleasure. Yet in the last two weeks he'd talked explicit sex at least once a day, and last night, he'd broken the no-sex-at-work rule.

His heart beat faster knowing he'd given her the best damn orgasm in a way no man had before. He wasn't sure how much longer he could go on without her name. As long as he was in the dark, she could leave him. All he had was a license plate.

Grace's light knock on his open door broke into his reverie.

"I didn't expect you today." He typed in his password.

She ventured in, took a seat. "There's always a few more schedules to check before the auditors get here."

Her casual clothes consisted of jeans and tight sweater. Conclusion, she was definitely over the divorce and ready to move on. Thus the inquiry about a gym. She didn't look bad, but women always seemed to want to lose another five pounds.

Which made him think of Jezebel and absolute perfection.

"Thanks for your dedication," he answered. With Grace on the other side of the desk and unable to see his computer screen, he felt fine opening up his personal e-mail. He'd checked before leaving for the office, in case Jezebel e-mailed to tell him what an incredible night it had been. She hadn't. Now, his in-box contained only spam.

"If you need help going over the audit committee agenda, just ask." Grace plucked at cat hairs on her sweater.

"Thanks for the offer," he said automatically, his attention caught by an odd subject line on one of his e-mails, "I saw you last night, Scott."

He would have written it off as spam except for the use of his name. He didn't use any identifier in his address. The sender's ID struck him as odd, too, ISAWU followed by a .com from one of the free e-mail Internet sites.

"Are you okay, Scott?"

"Fine." Again, an automatic answer—99 percent of his focus was on the e-mail as he opened it. The JPEG image attachment entitled "Scott and his friend" started a buzz in his gut, his guilty conscience at work.

Grace eyed him, her head tipped like an animal trying to figure out the mysteries of a noise seeping from beneath the family couch.

"Don't let me keep you from your work." He wanted her out, now. "I'll shout if I need anything."

"Fine and dandy." She rose, turned slowly, glanced over her shoulder, then smiled as she disappeared around the door.

At the risk of infecting his computer with a virus, Scott clicked on the attached picture.

Holy shit. He should have known seeing Rudd in the elevator was a bad omen.

The picture had obviously been taken from the doorway, yet he'd never heard the outer door open last night. At that point, he'd heard only sweet moans and cries. Damn. The office lights shone on his hair. He hadn't dropped his pants, simply unzipped, so at least his bare ass wasn't hanging out. All that was visible of his lady was her legs and high-heeled sandals. There was that blessing, yet the act being performed on his desk was clearly intimate.

"I can't fucking believe this," he muttered, and checked the photo's properties. Someone had taken his picture with a goddamn camera phone.

He stared at the e-mail's blank body. Blackmail? If so, why no demand? Without further data, he could only take it as a warning. He debated sending a reply. However, *not* acknowledging was the best approach at this point. It seemed prudent not to let the sender know he'd gotten to Scott.

Yet the questions roiled in his gut. Who the hell had spied on him last night? And why?

OVER the weekend, Trinity took Scott's advice and called her brother to tell him she would not intercede with their father. He needed to deal with the problem himself. Of course, he didn't answer his cell phone. After the fifth call, she left a message, though she hated telling him over voice mail. It seemed like the coward's way out of a confrontation.

Of course, after she'd left the message, she was free to fantasize about Scott for the rest of the weekend. Friday night seemed like her very first time, and she felt all dreamy about it. She couldn't count the number of times she'd picked up the phone to call him. But that wouldn't do. She didn't want to appear totally obsessed, even if she was.

And this morning, getting ready for work, she noticed how she filled out her suit jacket. So there, Ms. Rice!

At work, the coffee room was empty, and Inga wasn't in her cubicle. The cash receipts list was still on the top of the pile in Trinity's in-box. Nothing new. She sighed with relief at both blessings as she pulled out the office supply catalogue to order stackable in-boxes to better manage her influx of paperwork.

She didn't notice the hush throughout the whole department until the thump of footsteps stopped in her cubicle.

"Where is it?"

She thought it might be Daddy, but she couldn't be sure until she turned and actually saw him. She'd never heard quite that note—except the day he told her Lance was fired.

She swallowed. "Where is what?"

"The wire transfer."

"What wire transfer?" She could feel all the ears listening through the cloth partitions.

"The Handle and Harbin wire transfer for the gold purchase." His face was a dangerous shade of red. Explosive red. "I left it on your desk Friday afternoon while you were out to lunch."

"There wasn't anything on my desk when I got back." And the cash receipts listing still topped her in-box. Just as on Friday.

"I put it *here*." Towering over her, he stabbed the desktop.

"Well, I didn't see it, so I didn't do it." And she felt *sick*. Her father *never* yelled at her.

"I know you didn't do it because Handle and Harbin called asking where it was."

"Well, I'll do it right now."

"Do you realize that means we didn't make it into this week's production plan?"

"No," she whispered.

"They had to have the money by Friday to put it in." His nostrils flared, and little red stress lines crisscrossed the whites of his eyes.

"Maybe they'll make an exception if we ask them nicely."

He stared at her. On the other side of the cube, someone stifled a guffaw.

Then her father grabbed her in-basket and started throwing papers on the carpet until he found one he held up to within an inch of her nose. She cross-eyed it, but couldn't read.

"Send it now, and I will beg their forgiveness and promise my second-born child to them as consolation."

"I'm your second-born child."

"I know." Then he stomped out. His footsteps rumbled around the perimeter and out the Accounting Department door.

Trinity couldn't make heads nor tails of it. Then the whispers started. Indistinguishable voices, a snicker, another. She grabbed the wire transfer book and headed to Mr. Ackerman's.

She didn't trust Inga to tell her how to do it correctly. Because *someone* had taken the wire transfer off her desk while she was at lunch on Friday, and *buried* it in her in-box.

LANCE called her back in the afternoon. She took her ringing cell phone out into the hall.

"Trin, I need you to do this for me," he said before she even spoke.

She took a deep breath. "I've given it due consideration, Lance, and I can't."

The upstairs hallway outside Accounting overlooked the lobby and stairs. Glancing up, the receptionist stared. Trinity didn't know *her* name, either. "Let me go outside," she told Lance. On her way by, she read the girl's nameplate, then she smiled, memorizing the name.

Outside, the overcast sky darkened with the threat of rain. January oftentimes could be a good month, sunny, warmish, but by February, the rain was usually back.

"Are you there?" she said.

"Of course, I'm here." Lance snorted. "Where would I go when my whole life is in the balance?"

She huddled beneath the overhang as the first splotches of rain hit the parking lot pavement. "You are so dramatic." Trinity realized she often affected his same drama queen tone.

"This is important, Trin. I want to come home."

She closed her eyes and hugged one arm across her midsection. She should have brought her jacket. "Then ring your father's doorbell and talk to him."

"Why are you being such a bitch?"

Holding the phone away from her ear, she looked at it. A bitch?

First Daddy being angry, now her brother. "Lance, calling me names won't help. I'm doing this for your own good." She was sure her mother would have approved her course of action.

"That is so much bullshit. You're afraid to get on Dad's bad side."

Again, she stared at the phone as Lance railed on. She could still hear every word. Who was this person? Her brother never talked to her like that. But then Daddy had never spoken in such a tone to her before either.

She struggled for calm. The rain started in earnest. "Lance, I am not going to talk to Daddy for you. I'm sorry—"

Then he called her the absolute worst name a man could call a woman. The C word.

No one had ever called *her* that name, most especially not her brother. Just when she was about to scream at him, she realized the phone was dead. He'd hung up on her.

The heavens opened and the rain poured down, beating on the car roofs, streaming off the overhang, and splashing her shoes. Putting out a hand, she caught a piece of the torrent.

The problem with Lance was that he'd always had everything handed to him on the proverbial silver platter. From the day he was born, his place at Green Industries had been secured. He'd always gotten what he wanted right when he wanted it and never questioned how that came to be.

"And you can say the same," she muttered to the rain.

If you were always given everything, you never learned to take care of yourself. All her life, Trinity had painted herself with a different color brush to please, to get what she needed. For Daddy, she was his perfect little girl. For Lance, she was the adoring little sister. And to Harper, she was the silly little wife (spelled *meal ticket*).

She remembered her words to her father this morning. *Maybe they'll make an exception if we ask them nicely.* How pathetic that statement was. She didn't see the transfer so it wasn't her fault, and if she acted like a sweet little girl, she'd work around the boo-boo.

Dammit, this was the *real* world. She'd made a mistake—even if *someone* had helped her make it—then expected Daddy to fix it. Just as she expected Daddy to fix her divorce.

Trinity grabbed the lobby door and yanked it open.

"Wow, it sure started raining out there, didn't it?" the receptionist said.

"Yes, Karen, it did. And I don't think we've met yet." She stuck her hand out. "I'm Trinity Green."

Karen, all of nineteen years old, stared at Trinity with big blue eyes in a round pretty face. "Nice to meet you, too."

Bounding up the stairs as fast as her spike heels could take her, Trinity headed down her father's wing of the building.

"Is he busy?"

Verna glanced up from her computer screen, black-and-white-speckled reading glasses on her nose. "Not for you, sweetie."

Trinity closed the door behind her as her father scooped cigar ashes into his hand and dumped them in his trashcan.

"I apologize for my mistake. I won't let it happen again."

He sniffed. "I realize you're new at this, and I shouldn't have gotten so angry. I can't expect you to read my mind when a wire needs to go out. I should have—"

Trinity held up her hand. "I *will* be more diligent. Mr. Ackerman told me how potentially big this new customer could be for us, and since you handle all the metals stuff, I will always check with you to make sure I've accounted for any wires that need to be sent out."

"Honey . . ."

"If you send me an e-mail reminder when you do leave a wire for me, that would also be great."

He stared at her as if she'd suddenly grown a forked tongue. "Well, thank you, honey. I appreciate the diligence."

"Okay, I have to run, Daddy. I've got a ton of things to do before I go home. Love you."

Actually, she had a ton of things to do before she called Scott at one minute *after* five when she was officially off the clock. After all, she was a working girl.

See, he was a drug. At the end of a bad day, she'd started popping Scott pills.

THE audit committee took almost the whole day. With the meeting afterwards to update his staff on the audit requirements, Scott didn't get to MIS until the end of the day.

He made his way through the maze of cubicles set up in identical style to that in Accounting.

"Hey, Mark. I'd like a printout of the card key accesses to my department over the last couple of weeks. I want to check the overtime my people have been doing on the weekends."

"Sure thing, dude." Instead of the blond surfer type his language imitated, Mark was midtwenties, dark, Latin, and a bit of a dweeb, his shirtfront pocket-protector central. But he knew his network as well as his own body parts. When you needed something, you didn't tackle the head of MIS, you went to Mark.

Punching a few keys, his state-of-the-art laser printer spat out several pages.

The garage elevators and the outside doors required card key access after hours. The inside doors were kept locked even during the day. If you forgot your card key when going to the restroom, you couldn't get back in. Which was good for Scott. Since the alarm had been set, the department was empty. The culprit would have keyed in sometime after he did.

"Here you go."

Scott scanned the list Mark handed him. Hmm, maybe his employees were taking way too many bathroom breaks. Flipping to the last page, he backtracked to his own entry on Friday night, indicated by both his employee and badge number. First, his use on the elevator, then again on the Accounting Department entry.

Beneath it, a few minutes later, there was another double entry, the parking elevator, then Accounting again. Someone had followed him up from the garage. He held it out to Mark. "Why no employee number with this badge?"

Mark gave it a quick glance. "Guest badge."

"Can you see who used it? I don't like guests coming in after hours. We've got proprietary information."

Punching keys, data filled Mark's screen. "See here?" He pointed, but with the angle of the screen, Scott couldn't read it. "This says the badge was issued three months ago to Accounting with no off-hours restrictions." He tipped his head, waiting for Scott's reaction.

Three months ago. "The auditors. We always give them full access." They often came in on weekends or stayed late. It helped keep the term of the audit down, which, when you needed to release profitability numbers, was a must.

But somebody hadn't turned in this badge.

He was back to square one. The auditors turned the badges in to whomever they saw last. It could have been Elton, Grace, or any of the other accountants. Hell, even Ron Rudd had returned two of them directly to Scott.

"Go ahead and deactivate this one. I issued the new set of card keys at the audit committee meeting."

Lesson learned: Keep track of the damn badges. "Print me a list of the guest keys given out this morning. I'll put Grace in charge of making sure they all get turned in or deactivated."

"Sure thing, dude."

He smiled in return. "Thanks, dude."

Lesson learned, yeah, but the damage was done. Someone at Millennium had used an unassigned badge to gain access and take his photo in a compromising position. His gut rumbled. Whoever followed him into Accounting ten minutes after he entered with Jezebel had done so with nefarious intentions.

"Despite the deactivation, will you be able to tell if it gets used again?"

"Sure thing, dude. It'll get recorded as access denied."

He wouldn't know who, but at least he'd know when, and maybe that would narrow it down.

Back in his office, his message light was flashing.

His heart kick-started with the sound of her voice. "Meet me at the movies for a sexy thriller." Instantly, he went hard. She remembered. Tapping into his brief flight of fancy the other night, she named the old-style theater downtown. One of those massive gilded structures with balcony seating, it had recently been renovated as a landmark. Showing an eclectic mixture of old classics from the 1930s and 1940s all the way up to the 1980s, the movies often played to packed houses.

He wondered what his Jezebel had planned for him tonight. He couldn't wait to find out, yet all the while he imagined ways he could get her to come home with him. The tease? *If you want more, we'll have do it in my bed.* Maybe cutting her off? *If you don't want it my way, then you don't get it at all.* Damn, that was too harsh, not only for her, but for him.

Yet however he accomplished it, he wanted to make her so freaking obsessed with him that she'd spend the night, a week, a month, more. He wanted her as obsessed as he was.

12

BEFORE leaving work, Trinity ditched her blouse, bra, thong and pantyhose. All she wore was her red power suit and matching stilettos. She'd freshened her makeup and fluffed her hair. Not that she needed to be perfect for Scott, she just wanted the opportunity to get everything all messed up.

During a slight break in the rain, she dashed to the theater and bought two tickets at the old-fashioned booth. February's playlist included a film noir festival, tonight's contribution being *Body Heat*, a relatively new addition to the genre, made in the early 1980s. She'd never seen it, yet with that title, it couldn't have been more perfect.

The outside pavement was speckled green, gold, and black inlay, and movie posters filled glass-fronted cabinets all around the entry. Bette Davis, Joan Crawford, Burt Lancaster. She remembered him from that old Kevin Costner movie *Field of Dreams*. Goodness, they looked so young. And Burt was, well, totally hot.

Speaking of hot, it started raining again just before Scott arrived, and he shook water droplets off his hair. Oh my God. He was magnificent. Her heart beat faster against her red suit jacket as his eyes roamed her body.

Handing him the tickets, she took his arm. "When I was younger, I used to punish a man for looking at me that way."

He smiled, all devil-may-care white teeth. "And how did you punish them?"

She laughed. "I spanked them." She wouldn't have dreamed of spanking a man. Besides, she adored the way Scott looked at her as if she were a candy he had to unwrap and devour.

He kissed the tip of her nose. "I'd prefer spanking you."

"You wish. No one spanks me, buster." She tugged him inside the lobby. She'd never been spanked. The thought of his hand on her bare bottom set butterflies loose in her tummy.

"We better get in," she quipped to mask his effect on her, "or we won't get a seat at all." Right. There wasn't another moviegoer in the large, lushly decorated lobby.

The carpet was swirls of bright, exotic flowers, the walls covered with murals of jungle scenery, and the floor in front of the candy counter the same green, gold, and black speckles as out front. The scent of fresh buttery popcorn perfumed the air, and the teenage countergirl wore a jaunty burgundy jacket with gold buttons and braided trim.

"Don't you want some candy, little girl? Or shall I eat *you*?" His voice low, the joke for her ears only, yet Trinity blushed as he led her to the glass-fronted counter stocked with assorted boxed and bagged candies.

The pretty brunette took their tickets, ripped them, and returned one half. "If you buy an extra large popcorn and drink, you get free refills all night."

Scott squeezed Trinity's hand. "What would you like, honey?"

She almost laughed at the endearment. "Malted milk balls."

He gave her a look. She leaned in to nip his ear and whispered,

"I want to lick the chocolate off your lips and taste the malt ball when I suck your tongue."

He laughed, choked, and pushed a bill across the glass. "A box of malted milk balls, please."

Doling out his change, the girl slid over the candy. "Thank you, sir." Her voice was as jaunty as her jacket.

"Does that lead up to the balcony?" Scott pointed to a curving, carpeted stairway.

"Yes, and we have new comfy seats, too."

The place must have cost a mint to restore. As they mounted the stairs, Trinity could almost imagine movie stars of old decked out in fine evening dress attending a grand premiere.

With the rainy evening, she would have expected more people, yet few patrons dotted the lower section of the nine-hundred-fifty-seat theater, and the balcony was empty. The movie house was a gorgeous sample from the Hollywood heyday, with faux columns jutting out from the walls painted to look like marble and murals of Greek gods, nymphs, and mythic creatures cavorting about Mount Olympus.

Scott held her hand as they negotiated the steep balcony steps to the top row, then guided her into the corner seat.

"I can't see the screen it's so far away," she murmured.

Tossing his suit jacket next to him, he loosened his tie before taking his seat. "I'll tell you what happens." He placed her hand on his cock. He was already hard.

"Mr. Sinclair, *what* do you have planned for a dark theater?"

He shook the box of malted candy. "I think you should suck one of my balls."

Her mouth watered, yet she couldn't help laughing. "You're a very bad boy."

He spilled two pieces of chocolate onto his palm, his eyes sparkling in the house lights. "But you're a very good girl, and you'll do exactly what I tell you, won't you?"

Her heart skipped, then raced. Just like on the phone when he'd directed her, right down to the moment *he* allowed her to orgasm. She loved his teasing.

"Give me one of your balls." She held out her hand, then popped a chocolate bite in her mouth at the same time he did.

"You like?"

"Mmm." She adored malted milk balls, but she hadn't had one in years. "They're very yummy."

He leaned in, cupped the back of her head, and tasted her. Everything was chocolate and malt, his tongue, his breath, his lips. Light, flavored kisses she wished could go on forever.

Then the house lights dimmed, and the curtain rose. "Shh, the movie's starting." He felt too good. She wanted too much. For a moment, it was terrifying. Trinity tried to pull away.

Instead he held her palm fast to his cock, using her touch to massage himself. "Don't talk, just do whatever I tell you."

The game was too good to spoil with silly emotions. "Yes, sir," she murmured.

"Shh."

She zipped her lips, then shifted to get comfortable as she curled her fingers around him.

The opening credits rolled. He leaned close, his breath against her hair. "You picked a good one, my dear. This is a very hot movie."

"Don't tell me anything. I want to be surprised."

He kissed her openmouthed, hard and fast, to shut her up.

When the sultry Kathleen Turner dropped her shaved ice down her low-cut blouse, Scott unzipped his pants and wrapped her hand around his cock. She smoothed droplets of pre-come over his crown. Turning to him, she slowly raised her fingers and sucked his taste clean.

Scott went up in smoke. "You are so damn nasty."

She simply smiled.

Tugging her close, he devoured her mouth, slipping his hand inside her jacket to pinch her nipple. Christ, she wasn't wearing a damn thing under there. She hissed under his lips, and he pinched harder until she moaned.

Pulling back, he sagged against his seat, fighting for breath. He wanted to come, now, but they hadn't even gotten to the really sexy movie scenes.

"Stroke me." He didn't beg, he demanded.

She closed him inside her fist, caressed him, her gaze on his face, making him wild with the intensity in her dark blue eyes and the heat of her grip.

"What if there was a guy sitting right over there watching you jerk me?" He nodded down the empty aisle, his voice a whisper in the dark.

Keeping her silence the way he'd instructed, she merely smiled, then blinked, slow, lazy, boiling, the movie lights glimmering across her face as the scenes changed. She pumped his cock harder. She held him tight, no limp girlie grip.

"That'd be fucking hot," he went on, wrapping his own hand around hers. "He'd want you. But he'd see you were mine."

She shook her hair out, licked her glossy red lips.

"I'd want you to suck me, show him how fucking good you are, how goddamn perfect." He cupped her chin, stroked her lips with his tongue, then backed off. "I'd want him to see you take my come down your throat." It was primal, the lion fighting all comers for his mate. "Take my cock," he seduced her with his own desire and need.

His Jezebel didn't hesitate. Bending to his lap, she licked away his pre-come, then took him all the way, down her throat. He bucked up against her, almost coming with that first deep swallow. She had him on the edge. Simply being with her made him crazy. Holding her head down, he pumped his hips, begging her to take him. It was so damn fucking good, the heat of her mouth, her hair falling over him, the movie on the screen.

He craved passion, yet somehow she gave him something infinitely better. She'd given him back his youth and aliveness.

"Fuck, fuck, fuck," he whispered, head back, eyes closed.

Until he heard the upstairs door.

An usher trolled the front aisle of the balcony, picking up a few bits of trash. Cupping his hand to her forehead, Scott lifted her, then zipped his pants. He couldn't breathe. He could barely focus his gaze. Yet he leaned into his perfect, gorgeous, sensual Jezebel. "Lift your skirt."

She tugged the sexy red skirt up her thighs, barely revealing her pretty bush. He wanted to taste her.

The usher disappeared out the doors, and on screen, William Hurt picked up Kathleen in a neighborhood bar. The actress was sexy, but Jezebel was more of everything. No woman's mouth had taken him that quickly to orgasm. If not for the interruption, he'd have blown sky-high. And he wasn't ready. He wanted to ride that sweet knife edge awhile longer.

"Touch your clit." He licked the rim of her ear. She shivered with her whole body, sucked in a labored breath, and shoved her hand between her thighs.

Slouching in the seat, she plumbed her depths. Without taking his eyes off the movie screen, Scott pulled her leg up to the armrest, draping her calf over his knee, and stroked her thigh. Her sexy, aroused scent filled his head, and the barely there sound of her slick pussy enthralled him.

Kathleen took William home, and she was wearing the same damn red skirt as Jezebel. He played with her leg, her calf, caressed, dragged his nails along her skin, the soft sounds of pleasure she made driving him nuts.

It was like lying on the other side of the wall that first night, listening to her. His cock ached to slide inside her.

"I want your fingers in my mouth."

Closing his eyes, he sucked her sweet, tangy, delicious juice from them. He opened his lids once more to the crash of breaking glass and good old William tearing at Kathleen's red skirt. Scott turned in his seat and slid a hand along her thigh as he covered her mouth. After one deep kiss, he backed off and whispered, "Watch the movie."

She shuddered as he licked her ear, then blew on her. Her skin was warm, her pussy wet, her clit a hard nub beneath his fingers. He circled and swirled, using her own moisture to tantalize. Biting her earlobe, he worked his way to her cheek and licked, then her throat, mimicking the movements of his fingers with his tongue. She squirmed, her breathing rapid, her nails digging into his shoulder. He could almost hear the beat of her heart. Glancing up, he found her gaze glued to the screen, her bottom lip between her teeth.

"I'm going to make you come." He pushed a finger deep inside her. Her throat worked, and he sucked her skin. He took her clit with his thumb and her pussy with two fingers. Her body undulated with his rhythm. "Don't make a sound," he ordered.

She moved with him, let him fuck her with his hand, her breath harsh, her lips parted. His mind was steeped in her scent, her taste still sweet on his tongue. She slipped her hand inside her jacket, played with her own nipples. The sight of her, the feel of her pussy, made his balls tighten and pre-come dampen his trousers. The music crescendoed, and the couple did the nasty on screen while Jezebel convulsed around his fingers, and when she came, he swallowed her cries in his mouth.

SHE came to herself tucked securely against his shoulder, his arm around her. God, he smelled good. The light scent of laundry detergent on his shirt, soap on his skin, all mingled with the aroma of warm body and come. She could still taste him.

Trinity shivered. She'd never done anything remotely like this in her life. Good Lord, she'd taken him in her mouth, then let him bring her to orgasm in a movie theater. She'd intended some petting and teasing, which was why she'd left her underwear behind. The rest, though, she'd gotten carried away with. But oh God, she loved it. Even the part where he'd talked about a stranger watching, wanting.

Snuggling closer despite the armrest digging into her ribs, Trinity put one hand on his chest and played lightly with a nipple through his shirt. Scott trapped her fingers in his, then raised her hand to his lips, but when he set it back down, she was far from any nipple play.

She rolled her head on his shoulder to meet his gaze. "Am I allowed to talk?" she whispered, referring to his command.

He smiled, mouthed the word *no*, then shook a malt ball into her hand. "Eat it. That should keep you quiet."

She sucked on it, the taste sweet and chocolaty with the slight malted zest, but it eradicated *his* taste. He didn't kiss her, nor did he put her hand on his cock. Yet he hadn't come earlier. Was it all over? Had she done something wrong, come too loudly so that he was afraid of attracting attention?

For the life of her, Trinity couldn't remember how loud she'd been. There was only the feel of his fingers on her, then his mouth, and what he'd said. *He'd want you. But he'd see you were mine.*

She tried to concentrate on the movie, but all the questions kept running through her head. What did it mean that he didn't want her to touch him? If she could figure it out, she could fix it. Her thoughts spiraled down until . . .

Until she realized she was doing the same thing she'd done with every man who'd ever intrigued her. Analyze, then strategize. She had a whole host of tricks in her bag to keep a man interested in her. Let him think he's smarter than you. Let him believe he's the center of your universe. Never ever let him see you without your best face on, figuratively and physically.

Trinity sat up, adjusting her skirt and jacket, then held out a hand. He poured four malt balls into her palm. She ate them before they melted. Then she watched the movie, and after she figured out what she'd missed while she was feeling all insecure and sorry for herself, she enjoyed the spectacular show.

If only she couldn't smell his enticing male scent and the heat of his body so close to hers.

When the movie was over, he rose and tugged on his suit jacket again. "Did you like it?"

"I didn't know those old movies could be that good."

He laughed out loud. "Old?"

"I was a toddler when it came out."

He tipped his head, and she couldn't read his expression despite the fact that the house lights were once again on.

Then he held out his hand. "Let's see if it's raining."

He didn't say a word about how good it had been, not the movie, but the things they'd done in the dark. Trinity chewed on her bottom lip and wondered how badly her lipstick was mussed. She had the strongest urge to check her makeup in the ladies' room mirror, but she beat back the desire.

They made it half a block before the downpour hit, and Scott tugged her beneath the awning of a closed antiques store. "You have an umbrella tucked in that bag of yours?"

She held up her pocket purse. Normally she carried a bag large enough to house the contents of her bedroom vanity—slight exaggeration—but she'd turned over a new leaf. "I barely have room for my keys in here." Plus one lipstick and lip liner. "I'm not going to melt if I get wet, though." She thought of her hair, and the flat, tangled mess it would be.

As if he could read her thoughts, Scott tucked a lock behind her ear. "*I* might melt." Pushing her further into the store's recessed entrance, he pinned her against the wood doorframe.

And she adored his height all over again. "It's my suit I worry about, all those water spots." Shoving her hands beneath his jacket, she clasped them at his back.

"We'll have to stay here until it stops." He nuzzled the flyaway hair at her temple.

He was hard. Everything was okay. With his erection at her belly, she tipped her head back and kissed him. Light nips, a bit of tongue, feathering her mouth over his. "You're a very naughty man doing that to me in the theater."

He licked the corner of her mouth, then her chin, then trailed up to her ear. "That's what I love about you." He nipped her earlobe. "You want to touch and taste everything. Try it all. Take a great big bite out of life. Living it to the fullest." Backing off to capture her gaze, he rubbed against her. "I love that you're a very naughty woman willing to spread your legs in a dark movie theater for me."

That wasn't *her*. Until two weeks ago she hadn't tasted *anything*. He'd created a fantasy woman nothing like the real Trinity. Not that she knew who the *real* Trinity was. She'd been asking *herself* that question for days. Sooner or later, he'd see she was a fraud. Then he'd leave. That's why she needed to keep her secrets, so he'd never figure it out. And jeez, there she went spoiling the game again. She would *not* ruin the night.

"You made me." She sighed dramatically, playing her Jezebel role to the hilt. "I had absolutely no choice in the matter."

He followed every curve of her body down to her butt, tracing the crease. "Right. That's why you're completely naked under this prim little suit."

Pulling back, she jutted her chin. "It's not prim."

"Oh yes it is." He inched the skirt up. "My grandmother would wear this suit."

She loved the banter, and she knew he loved the suit. With his first look tonight, his lids had drifted lower, all dreamy for her. She wanted to see where this particular game went. "I'll have you know this is a power suit."

He rocked his hips against her, then backed off to raise the hem up her thighs. "It's too long, a matron lady's suit."

It wasn't any such thing. In fact, Matty in the movie had worn exactly the same style skirt, and watching Ned tug it up over her butt and slip his fingers in the elastic of her panties had played a role in Trinity's orgasm. And maybe that's what Scott was thinking about. The tips of his fingers caressed below her butt cheeks in slow, sinuous circles.

"So what, you want me to take it off now?" she joked.

His eyes flared, and he smiled. Good Lord, he couldn't mean to have her right here in the alcove, could he? She peeked past his shoulder. The streetlamps gave out a murky light in the downpour, the sidewalks were empty, and cars passed in the roadway, spitting water up from the tires.

Did she dare to let him touch her here? It had been so good in the theater, with the edge of exposure, his fantasy of being watched by a moviegoer in the next aisle. How much of an exhibitionist could she be? With Scott, the possibilities were as limitless as her desire. Trinity wanted to try everything.

"Strip it off," he murmured, slipping a hand between them to the first button on her jacket.

Yes, yes, yes. She pulled in a breath of air and held it. He *said* he was madly in lust with her, yet he wanted her to take the risks. He wanted her exposed. She'd come for him, but he hadn't done the same. He wanted to show she was *his*, but did it work the other way around?

She grabbed his finger, bending it back slightly, enough to get his attention without pain. "I've got a better idea." She reached down to cup him. "Why don't we brave the rain and run to the car to take care of this?" She squeezed, tempting him.

For a moment, the only sound was the patter of rain on the pavement, the shush of wet tires, and his breath. Then he let go of the bit of skirt he'd trapped in his hand, smoothed it down over her thighs, and stepped back.

He idly scratched his chin. "If you want that, you'll need to come home with me."

Her stomach started a slow descent. "Why? You liked it in the car the other night."

"I'm tired." He shrugged. "I don't want to have to drive after I've come. It's a long way home."

"So you want *me* to drive a long way home."

"No. You can stay. I'll drive you back in the morning."

Moments before she had him in the palm of her hand, literally and figuratively. "I don't have fresh work clothes."

"We can leave early so you can get home and change."

He had a reasonable answer for everything. That was the problem. He was so darn reasonable. She wanted him crazy for her. When had he gone from being madly head over heels in lust to *reasonable*? He thrilled her, yet just as suddenly dragged her down. Trinity needed to regain the upper hand, if there was an upper hand to regain.

"No. Not tonight." She'd like to add that she didn't sleep in strange men's beds. *No, you just masturbate for men in strange beds and let them watch you come.*

"Thanks for the movie, I gotta go." She didn't care that it was pouring. It was debilitating trying to figure out how to keep a man pleased.

"You paid for the movie, so thank you."

She pushed past him. "It was *my* pleasure."

"Jezebel." He reached for her arm, and she sidestepped him.

"I'll call you if I have the time this week," she said, then ran out into the rain before she could change her mind and throw herself at him.

She'd thrown herself at Harper, and she couldn't do that again. Not ever.

* * *

HE'D miscalculated big-time. He should have let her do him in the car. But he didn't fucking want it in the backseat.

In the alcove, Scott shot out a harsh breath. Rain pounded the awning. A red Mustang passed, and though he couldn't make out the driver, he knew it was Jezebel running away.

He hadn't wanted to come in the darkened theater. From the moment she went off, he'd wanted hours with her. He needed to give her at least ten orgasms, a whole damn night of pleasure.

He pulled his keys from his pocket. She'd been hot as Hades, he'd been hard as granite. He'd gotten harder sharing that fantasy about an anonymous patron watching her suck him.

He was perv enough to enjoy that along with everything else. Yet it was as an adjunct *to*, not instead *of* something far bigger. Jezebel falling asleep in his arms, waking up beside her, making her toast and coffee in the morning, driving her to work, thinking about her all day, and calling her ten times.

It occurred to him it was pretty pathetic. It sounded like marriage, or at the very least, a relationship. He was out for a relationship with a woman whose real name he didn't know, one he couldn't even call. She was just an e-mail address.

She wanted him for sex, a little kinky play. She hadn't talked about her divorce, but he was sure her marriage played into the reasons she held back.

The rain soaking him, he jogged for his car, beeped the remote, and climbed in, water dripping down the back of his neck. Pulling out of the spot, he headed for the freeway, and the drive home. It would have been better cocooned in the vehicle with her beside him, the deluge pounding on the roof. He could almost smell her rain-soaked hair. Raising his hand to his nose, he scented her like a lion scents his mate's heat. She was all over him, sweet, tangy. He sucked her taste from his fingers.

With that orgasm, he'd thought he had her. She'd have to beg him for more. He might have been better off not letting her come at all, teasing the hell out of her instead. The problem was he didn't have any idea how to bind her to him.

That could be the whole issue. He'd laid his needs bare, told her how fucking obsessed with her he was. Madly in lust. She could lead him around by his cock. She knew he'd be back.

A car skidded in front of him on the freeway, then righted itself, thank God.

The image seared into his mind, and he saw things clearly for the first time in three weeks. He had skidded off course; now he needed to right himself. He needed to take control.

It was a risk, especially after his total defeat in battle tonight. But the woman was too damn sure of him. He needed to shake up *her* course a little, make her doubt that he was a sure thing. He spent the drive over the hill to Santa Cruz composing his next e-mail to her.

13

TRINITY stared at Scott's e-mail and started to shake. She'd thrashed about all last night thinking of him, hot and bothered, nervous and needy, alternately fantasizing, then taking care of the heat her fantasies created. Wouldn't he love that? He'd also crow knowing she'd fallen asleep before dawn, woken up terribly late, and dashed off to work forgetting her underwear.

How did a person forget to put on underwear? She was pretty sure Britney Spears didn't "forget" a pair of panties. Though she was seated at her desk, her knees primly together, Trinity pulled the short suede skirt down a little further.

To think she'd gone commando *intentionally* yesterday. She'd even removed her blouse and bra underneath the jacket. But that was before Scott e-mail ditched her.

"I need yesterday's bank deposits now, Trinity."

She startled at the sound of Mr. Ackerman's voice, then frantically tried shutting down her account. When she succeeded only in opening a very risqué e-mail in which she'd told Scott explicitly what she'd like to do to him, she jumped to her feet, using her body to block the screen.

"Yes, Mr. Ackerman, I'll get that right away." She had the notes on how to complete the task. The system linked directly with the bank, and she could download company bank account activity twice a day. Inga had been doing it, but Mr. Ackerman decided it was a supervisory function. Of course, Trinity didn't do the bank reconciliations or the cash forecast, so between Boyd, who handled the general ledger, Christina, Mr. Ackerman, and herself, there were plenty of checks and balances.

"Thank you so much, Trinity." Pulling at his ear, Mr. Ackerman lowered his voice. "I do usually need the information by eight thirty. Just so you know for the future."

Had he told her that?

Whatever. She shouldn't have been checking personal e-mails. And gee, didn't she wish she hadn't read Scott's message.

I've got a hellaciously busy week. Maybe I can talk to you on Friday.

Maybe he could talk to her on Friday? It sounded like he was blowing her off.

She wouldn't think about that. It sounded like a slur. She finally controlled her jittery fingers and closed her e-mail.

Pulling out her notes, she flipped through until she found the bank's download instructions. Entering the system, she followed the codes, typed in the user name, password, and approval, and her screen filled up with options. Which one, which one? Ah, there it was, *download.*

So Scott was tired already. She could do without. Oh Lord. After last night, *could* she do without the way he made her feel?

Her office phone rang, twice in quick succession, which meant an outside call. Her heart kicked, and she leaped on it before she remembered that Scott didn't have her work number. Or her cell number. Not even her home phone.

"Hello, Accounts Receivable, Trinity Green speaking." How very professional she sounded.

"Your lawyer called me."

Harper. Her lungs went into spasms. She did *not* want to talk to Harper now, not after she'd been fantasizing about another man. She actually felt guilty. What on *earth* was wrong with her? "Yes, he told me he was going to." Daddy's lawyer was working through the settlement agreement in which Harper would have to settle for nothing.

"My lawyer thinks we should meet."

"*Your* lawyer?" She hadn't thought of him getting a lawyer. After all, *she* was the wronged party.

God, she sounded like a total bitch even to herself, and she did *not* want Harper to turn her into a bitch. Not even a harpy.

"I needed advice. What I really want . . ." He paused. She could hear him breathe. "What I *need* is to talk with *you.*"

Her cursor blinked at her. She'd forgotten to enter the date. Clicking keys, she hit Enter, then watched as the data flowed down the screen. God, she'd done something right.

"We talked the other night when you came to *my* house." She tried to sound reasonable, really she did, but that snarky emphasis on *my* sneaked in.

"We didn't talk, sweetheart. I begged, then you slammed the door in my face."

Please don't call me sweetheart. "I don't want to talk. Which is why our lawyers should talk."

He drew in a breath, then exhaled. "I know I hurt you"—it was on the tip of her tongue to deny it, but she let him go on—"but I want a chance to tell you how I feel."

"No." She tried keeping an eye on the download at the same time, but it kept going and going like that battery bunny. Of course, it wasn't just deposits, it was all the cleared checks, too. And she couldn't *bear* hearing how Harper felt. She wasn't responsible for his feelings.

"A weekend up in Napa. Please, Trin."

A weekend in Napa? *Get a grip.* "Don't call me Trin." Only her closest family and friends called her Trin. "Harper, I don't want to sound cruel or vindictive, but I cannot do a weekend with you. I can't even do dinner with you."

She realized in that moment what generated her guilt. She was done with Harper. No second chances. No talks in the wine country. She felt worse over Scott's rejection than she did about finding Harper in the shower.

Good God, she was a shallow, fickle person. But Scott's e-mail *did* hurt worse.

"Please be reasonable—"

And she was unreasonable to boot. "I made a mistake, Harper, let's leave it at that."

"But can't you even let me explain?"

Hunching over the phone, she lowered her voice. "Doing some woman in our shower doesn't require a verbal explanation. Quite frankly, it says it all."

She felt so calm. It was horrible. It hadn't been three weeks, and she no longer cared about Harper or his harpy. She'd already had sex with another man—in a hotel room, his car, a theater, his office, on the phone. God, she'd had more sex in the last two and a half weeks than she'd had with Harper during the marriage. Okay, *big* exaggeration, but that's how it *felt.*

The system beeped. It was done. So was she. "I have to go, Harper, my deposits need tabulating." She gathered a deep breath. "Don't take this the wrong way, but don't call me, call my lawyer." And she hung up.

She stared at the phone for half a minute. *Was* she done? *Will the real Trinity Green please state her true feelings?*

She couldn't remember what Harper looked like, though she *did* recall his lover's expression in the shower. Lord. That seemed so . . . superficial and shallow.

Punching a few more buttons on her keyboard, she saved the download and printed out yesterday's deposits.

She thought about sending Scott a reply e-mail, but a fist closed around her heart, squeezing. Yet her heart was perfectly fine with Harper. Which meant she had a totally fickle heart.

Or she'd never been in love with Harper in the first place.

Her stomach lurched. She had to stop thinking about it all. At least for now. Deposits she'd downloaded in hand, she hurried down the hall to Mr. Ackerman's office.

Plopping the paper on his desk, she tapped the third line item with her nail. "And there's the large receipt from Winterburn Electronics we were waiting for." Last week, she'd gotten the company to agree to pay half their past-due bill.

"Good work, Trinity."

She preened under his praise. Despite her marriage and her love life falling apart, at least she was doing a good job.

The whispering started at nine thirty. A man's higher-than-normal pitch—Boyd?—then someone husky, sultry. Trinity made a face to herself. Definitely Inga. What were those two up to?

Then Boyd passed her cubicle, shoulders hunched, eyes on the carpet, feet shuffling. He reminded her of a frightened animal slinking with its belly low to the ground for self-preservation.

Mr. Ackerman's door latched with a quiet snick.

A few moments later Inga's phone rang, and she answered with her usual Valkyrie hauteur. Then more whispering. Inga wasn't capable of slinking; Trinity heard her coming all the way. Mr. Ackerman's door opened, then closed with a firm snap.

Trinity strained, but with phones ringing and keyboards clacking, she couldn't hear a thing through the closed door.

Then it opened again, disgorging footsteps. *Wham, wham,* followed by *slink, slink.* Looking in her cubicle as he passed, his eyes wide, Boyd almost hit the opposite doorframe before righting himself. Trinity stood as Mr. Ackerman's bald spot traversed the cubicle perimeter to the CFO's office, and moments later, raised voices escaped from beneath the door.

Inga's phone rang again. "Yes, sir, I'll be right in."

Trinity noticed the key clicking stopped and the phones around the bullpen went silent as Inga stomped her way to the CFO's office. This time, the door slammed, reverberating through one office cube after another like an 8.0 earthquake.

Trinity's phone rang. Her heart jumped, and the phone cord shimmied like a snake as she picked up the receiver.

"Miss Green, could you please step into my office a moment?" It wasn't a question even if it was phrased as such.

The CFO. Mr. Wanamaker. Her legs quaking as she circled the cubes, she wished she'd worn her red power suit today instead of yesterday. Especially since it hadn't worked on Scott.

"You are a worthwhile person, you are in control," she muttered to herself, realizing even as she did it that she'd never needed these pep talks when she was just a debutante and Daddy's little girl.

She knocked boldly, then threw open the office door. "Yes, sir, you rang?"

Her chair at an angle, Inga sat in the cushy seat opposite Mr. Wanamaker, her legs crossed, her foot swinging, and a persnickety cat-that-ate-the-cream smile on her face. By the window, Mr. Ackerman plucked at the hair tuft on his head.

Tapping a mechanical pencil on his doodle-covered blotter, Mr. Wanamaker pointed to the chair next to Inga's. "Please, do have a seat." The tone suggested that at any moment, he'd bite the heads off poor unsuspecting kittens.

Trinity was a kitten.

She sat. "Is there a problem, sir?"

"A small one." With a full head of wiry gray hair and lines that bisected his forehead and cut cleanly from his nose to the corners of his mouth, Mr. Wanamaker was still of an indeterminate age. At the

Christmas parties, Trinity knew him as Paul, but she learned he ran a tight ship, and underlings did the Mister thing.

At company functions, he'd never made her quake in her shoes. "I'll help if I can." She slid a glance to Inga. The woman hadn't just lapped the cream, she'd gorged on it, and Trinity knew things were bad.

"It seems the checking account has gone negative."

"Don't you have overdraft protection?"

Three sets of eyes bored into her, whether it was the use of *you* instead of *we* or because she hadn't shown an appropriate reaction, whatever that might be.

"Miss Green, that isn't the point here." His steel gray eyebrows cinched together.

With the look on Inga's face, Trinity knew a slam-down was coming. She wondered idly how many slams she could take and still get back up.

Mr. Wanamaker opened his mouth. There was a flurry outside the door, then it burst open. Boyd stumbled in. "Sir. AR is negative, too." He threw out a deep exhale as if he'd been holding it the whole time he ran from his cube to Mr. W.'s office.

"That's not possible." Mr. W. flopped in his chair, shot himself backwards toward the credenza, whirled around, and started typing furiously on his keyboard. "Why, receipts are posted twice." He pointed as if no one actually believed him. More key tapping. "And checks are posted twice."

Inga licked the kitty cream off her lips. "It sounds like the bank download was duplicated."

"I did it once," Trinity said. She *knew* she'd only done it once. Didn't she? She *had* been talking to Harper.

"*I* did it this morning because you were late." Inga smiled like a viper. "You know it has to be done before eight thirty."

Trinity opened her mouth.

Inga cut her off. "I left you a note, Miss Green."

"I didn't see it." There was no note. "Perhaps it got buried in my in-box." Like the wire transfer request from her father.

Inga actually smirked. "I put it right on your keyboard so you'd be sure to see it."

Trinity wanted to scream, but that was pointless. She'd been bested again. "Well, it does seem like an error has been made. What do we do now to fix it?"

Waves of malicious pleasure rolled off Inga. "We'll have to restore the system back to last night's backup." She waved a hand, smiling first at Mr. Ackerman, then Mr. W. "Unless we have Christina and the girls go back in and manually delete the duplicate checks and AR receipts?"

"We'll do the restore," Mr. Wanamaker commanded. "Ackerman, what does that involve?"

Musing, Mr. Ackerman gave one last tug on his hair tuft. "We'll lose whatever's been entered this morning, then there'll be the work stoppage while the system is down, but that shouldn't be more than half an hour. Boyd"—he pointed a finger—"tell everyone to stop entering data in both the AP and AR modules." And he waved Boyd off to do his bidding.

"Isn't there some sort of safeguard against downloading the bank data twice?" The system hadn't even asked her the question.

"She's got a point, Ackerman." Though Mr. W. seemed slightly awed that Trinity could actually *have* a point.

"This is the first time we've had three people with the access codes. Previously it was myself and Inga."

See! Trinity wanted to blurt out that it wasn't her fault. It was someone *else's* fault. But she was a supervisor, she'd been late, and she had no doubt a note was *somewhere* in her cubicle.

Leaving Mr. Wanamaker's office, Trinity marched back to her cubicle. Where could it be? She sifted through her in-basket. Not there. She ruffled piles of paper. No note. Then she stopped, stared. One crumpled bit of paper lay forlornly at the bottom of her trashcan.

Gritting her teeth, Trinity picked it out, smoothed it on the desktop, and read.

"I've already downloaded the bank data. Don't do it again."

Her blood ran so hot, it scorched her veins. She didn't make scenes. She was better than that. Instead, she entered Inga's cubicle quietly, a smile on her lips and fire in her eyes. Setting the note on Inga's keyboard, Trinity was gratified the way the woman jumped.

"That," Trinity said, her voice low, "was in my trash."

Inga recovered. "You shouldn't have thrown it out."

"That's where you *put* it." She didn't raise her voice.

"I did not." Inga snorted and brushed the note aside.

"I supposed it crumpled itself and *fell* in the trash."

Inga trilled her fingernails on her keypad, then slowly rolled her chair back and rose to her full stiletto-heeled height. "I left it in your cubicle like I said I did." Folding her arms beneath her breasts, she straightened her shoulders. "Everyone can hear you trying to foist the blame off on me." Then she smiled. Like Eve's snake offering the apple.

They both knew she was lying, yet Trinity couldn't prove a thing. She could only make herself look worse.

How did you deal with a woman who lied even when openly confronted?

IN the foothills of the Santa Cruz Mountains where he lived, it didn't rain more days than over the hill in the Bay Area. It simply rained harder, pounding on the roof, dumping it down until the eaves overflowed and created a waterfall out in the atrium. Yet the lush green after the wet season was one of the reasons Scott loved it here, and you had to love the area to justify the trek over the hill every day. In the summer, the fog rolled off the ocean and cooled everything down, while in Silicon Valley, it could be stifling. The view out his floor-to-ceiling living room windows was of the forest, pine, redwood, oak, liquid amber. At night, the coyotes serenaded him to sleep. In the morning, chattering squirrels woke him.

Scott poured himself a finger of scotch and lit a fire to ward off the rain's dampness and the chill of the February evening. He booted up his notebook on the coffee table.

She hadn't left a message at work, nor had he checked his e-mail all day. It felt like the early days of college courtship, who's going to call who, who'll make the first move. He was more than twenty years past that, yet he'd never dealt with a woman who wouldn't give him her name even though she'd fucked him.

Maybe that fact was why he'd needed the scotch. He was man enough to admit he couldn't wait until Friday to check his e-mail. Maybe she'd relented . . .

The back of his neck prickled. One message remained after he'd deleted the spam. It wasn't her. The same address as before, an attachment, the subject line reading, "Caught you again."

This time, there was a message. "You are a very naughty man." Despite himself, he got a chill. Jezebel had called him a naughty man.

Could this all be a blackmail setup orchestrated by her?

Not likely. *He'd* knocked on *her* hotel room door.

The creamy skin of her exposed thigh was the lightest tone in the photo. The dark alcove obscured the rest of her, though there was no doubt his hand explored the mysteries beneath her skirt. Like an ingrained memory, her scent filled his head. His fingers could almost feel the silk of her skin. And he had to stop the obsessive thinking. Everything came back to her.

Mark was a wizard. Could he track the e-mail address and see who originated it? Then again, Scott didn't want to take Mark's work time for a personal matter. Checking on the badge could be accounted for as a security issue: There had been an unclaimed card key out there. Tracking back this e-mail, however, couldn't be justified. The alternative was to admit to Mark the personal nature and ask him to research in off hours.

If Mark could find out who'd sent the JPEGs, he could also get to Jezebel's real identity. The thought spiraled Scott down into a world filled with her scent, her textures, her voice. The detective work was a slippery slope to violating her privacy.

One thing was for sure: Whoever had taken the photo was probably in the theater as well. He was being followed, watched. Threatened? He couldn't be sure, but he did send out a test.

"If this is blackmail, you should know I don't give a damn what you do with those pictures." Then he hit Send.

Hell, there'd be no more public hanky-panky. Hotel rooms were a possibility, but preferably his house.

Maybe the e-mails could actually work in his favor. If he told her about them. Yet, tracking her down, either through her e-mail or her license plate, scaring her with the threat of blackmail, was a shitty path to take.

Jesus. How low would he sink to get what he wanted?

"THANKS for inviting me to dinner, Daddy." Trinity had actually avoided the country club since she'd kicked Harper out.

Her father was already seated, and she bent to kiss the top of his head. He'd ordered a fried calamari appetizer.

"Should you be eating that?"

He shot her a look as he popped one of the morsels into his mouth. Ooh–kay. She'd keep her trap shut about his dining habits. It was just that he'd undo the good habits he'd started.

Trinity primly perched on the seat next to him. "Thanks for ordering me a lemon water."

"You can have some calamari." He stabbed one of the squiggly little things with his fork.

"Thanks, but no thanks." She sipped her water.

Early on a weeknight, the country club's dining room wasn't full. Maybe it was the rain, too, beating against the garden windows. People wanted to get home. Despite the candles against the white tablecloths, the rain made everything seem dark and oppressive. But there were the Plumleys and a few others she knew. Trinity waved and smiled, praying no one came over.

She opened her menu.

"I ordered you spinach salad with no dressing, bacon bits, or egg crumbles."

Which made it a bowl of spinach instead of a salad. How had she managed to eat like that all these years? She flipped a menu page. "Thank you, but I'd like something more substantial."

Daddy touched her forehead. "Are you all right?"

Suddenly she wanted to tell him everything, how her new flame needed a respite from her and her new job was getting old fast. "I'm fine," she said instead. "I just forgot to eat." She'd finally remembered when her temples began to throb with a hunger headache.

Their French waiter arrived, and even his flattering glances didn't make her feel any better. So she ordered the mushroom crepes with a creamy sauce. She'd always wondered how good they'd taste. "You can skip the spinach my father ordered."

He scribbled on his pad, then smiled beatifically. Daddy ordered the salmon. Good. It had lots of omega-3 fish oil. Very healthy.

"How's the job going?" he asked when they were alone.

He didn't call her *sweetie* or *honey* or any endearment at all. "Well, I did have a little issue today," she admitted.

He polished off the last bite of calamari, and Trinity wished she'd shared. His mouth closed, he picked his teeth clean with his tongue, then casually said, "So I heard."

Mr. Wanamaker had probably run straight up to executive row. The reason he didn't have his office up there himself was so he could keep an eye on his harem of accountants.

Gosh, that sounded bitter. She had to stop that brand-new tendency she'd developed. It was very unbecoming.

"I understand," Daddy went on, "that there was a half-day work stoppage."

She cringed. "Everything was back up by eleven so it wasn't a *whole* half day."

He ignored the correction. "All because you were late?"

"Actually it was because I didn't see the note Inga left telling me she'd run everything." Now that wasn't casting blame.

"But if you never saw the note, Trinity, how did it come to be crumpled up in your wastebasket?"

Mr. Ackerman had come looking for it so she'd had to show him, and darn it, Daddy had heard, too. "I don't know how it got there." She would not fall into the trap of complaining to her father about a problem she had to solve on her own.

Her father swirled the ice cubes in his glass of tea. At least she hoped it was tea and not something stronger. "When you asked for this job, I was happy to give it to you."

"I know, and I appreciate that."

"But I thought you'd take it seriously."

Her ribs hurt as if someone had kicked her. "I *am* taking it seriously. I'm doing everything I can to learn the procedures. I even suggested we put in safeguards to ensure a duplicate download can't happen again."

He circled his hand in the air. "Big whoop-de-doo. Plug the hole after you make the mistake."

His words sliced her to ribbons. She didn't even have a comeback. Daddy had *never* talked to her that way, at least not before she started working for him.

The French heartthrob arrived with their meals, bending at the knees to slide her plate in front of her. The crepes were swimming in all that creamy sauce, the air laden with the overpowering scent of garlic. No longer hungry, she pushed the china away with her thumb.

"You don't like?" her waiter asked after setting down Daddy's salmon.

"She just doesn't eat, that's all." His tone denigrating, her father grimaced.

This wasn't her father. This wasn't even her life. It was someone else's life, as if she were playing a part in that *Freaky Friday* movie and switched places with . . . a nincompoop.

"It's a lot of garlic," she tried to explain.

"Would you like the spinach salad instead, no dressing, no bacon bits, no egg crumbles?" The poor man remembered. Probably because he thought she was a total freak.

"Yes, please." She sounded like a child, though not Daddy's perfect little girl.

Will the real Trinity Green please get her head out of her—She didn't finish the thought. Instead, she pulled the crepes right back in front of her. "I've changed my mind. My olfactory senses have gotten used to the garlic, and this is what I want." She'd eat the crepes. She was *not* a child.

When the waiter was gone, she put her hand over her father's, stilling him before he reached for his fork.

"Daddy, you're right. I have improvements to make in my work attitude. If you'll have a little more patience with me, I will not make the same mistake again. I won't be late, either." She'd put the alarm clock across the room so she didn't accidentally push Snooze. "I will be the best Accounts Receivable supervisor Green Industries has ever had."

"We've never had an Accounts Receivable supervisor before."

"See?" She beamed. "I'm already the best, and I'll keep getting better."

She would not let Inga Rice get the better of her. She was, after all, her mother's daughter, and her mom would not have given up without a fight.

14

BY Friday, Trinity was heavy into withdrawal. Her hands shook, her face felt flushed, and her nighttime Scott dreams flashed before her eyes at odd times. Especially in boring meetings. It had been three days, sixteen hours, and thirty-six minutes since she'd seen him, talked to him, touched him, kissed him, and she was going crazy. And it wasn't the sex she missed.

In the break room, she set the coffee brewing for her umpteenth cup of the day, and it was only one thirty. If Scott didn't e-mail today—he'd said Friday, right, and it *was* Friday—she wasn't sure how she'd make it through the weekend.

"Trinity?"

Boyd had sneaked up on her. "What?" It came out far too harsh. "I mean, what can I do for you; I'm making coffee, and you're more than welcome to have a cup when it's done."

"Actually," he said, "I wanted to apologize."

The rich coffee scent in the air made her light-headed. Boyd was a good-looking young man. He was tall—he'd have been taller if he didn't slump—with a full head of hair and a sweet smile. He might be good for Josie. Except that Josie could be a little dominant, and that might not be so good for Boyd. On the other hand, a dominant woman could be exactly what he needed.

"What on earth do you have to apologize for?" Putting her mug near the coffee stream, she switched out the pot for her cup, filling it with the brew. Over the last three days, sixteen hours and change, she'd perfected the maneuver.

"For Tuesday?" Boyd's rising tone made it a question.

Tuesday? Two days, sixteen hours, and—*oh stop?!*—Tuesday was Inga-debacle day. She held up a hand. "You don't need to."

"I have to explain. I should have figured out the issue with the negative cash balance before I went racing over to Inga. I thought it was her fault, and—"

"And you wanted to cover her butt before anyone found out." Oops, had she said that? She almost put her hand over her mouth, but she was tried of watching what she said so no one got pissed off at her. *Pissed off.* It was a new phrase for her lexicon.

"No." While Boyd talked, Trinity expertly replaced the coffeepot and poured flavored creamer—another addiction—into her cup. "I sort of went over there to lord it over her that she'd sent out too many checks with last Friday's run."

Oh. That was a horse of different color. Maybe red, signifying anger. Boyd didn't like Inga. She thought *everyone*, certainly all the males in the vicinity, liked Inga.

Boyd shot a look over his shoulder as if to make sure they were still alone.

"I'll tell you if anyone's coming," she offered.

"Inga was the one who insisted I tell Ackerman. She said she hadn't printed anymore checks than he'd approved, and that maybe someone had given him incorrect cash numbers." He glanced at his shoes sheepishly. "I have to admit I was trying to cover my own ass at that point."

Well, well, well. "And who thought Mr. Wanamaker needed to know?" She held up a hand. "Nope, don't tell me."

"Inga," he mouthed, then used his voice. "If I'd figured out the problem, I would have come to you first, then Ackerman, and it wouldn't have been such a big deal."

So, she'd gotten into the crosshairs of Boyd's little tiff with Inga. Inga had engineered it, though, first the note in the trash instead of on Trinity's desk, then she sicced Ackerman and Wanamaker on her. Oh, how Inga must have beamed when the whole thing got blown out of proportion.

The question was what to do. Trinity hadn't figured that out. Maybe if she wasn't so busy counting the days, hours, and minutes since her last Scott encounter . . . She didn't realize she'd made a horrible face until Boyd's eyes widened.

She patted his arm. "I appreciate the apology. It's not necessary, though. I learned a lot from my mistake." Yes, she'd been instituting checks and balances, writing procedures, etc., yadda yadda, ad nauseam.

"Thanks, Trin."

She cocked her head and let out a gust of air. Trin. It sounded nice, friendly. "You're welcome, Boyd."

When she returned to her desk, there was a Scott mail.

"Happy Valentine's Day. Meet me for dinner."

That was all. She started to hyperventilate and couldn't hear a thing over the thumping of her heart.

FOLLOWING the maitre d' across the restaurant, she stole Scott's breath. Her blonde hair curled softly, cascading over her bare shoulders. The beaded halter neck of her black dress wrapped around her throat like a collar, and the soft material draped her curves. The short length revealed a tempting taste of luscious, stocking-encased thigh. He wanted her. Badly. At his table, in his bed, on his arm, a part of his life.

In the four days since he'd seen her, he'd learned that much about his needs. Perhaps the mystery surrounding her fueled his desires, enhanced the excitement, elevated her to an unobtainable fantasy, making him wish to possess her all the more. This woman wasn't a one-night stand, and he would be doing them both a disservice if he didn't explore the possibility of a longer-lasting relationship between them. Even if he had to force the idea on her at first.

There was truly one way to convince her they deserved a chance at something more. He had to share everything about his life with her. Especially the two most important people.

He rose as she approached the table. The restaurant he'd chosen was elegant, as befitted her, the appointments classy, the waiters attentive, and the tables distanced to allow intimate conversation. He'd requested one in the front corner window overlooking the city lights along the busy street. The wine he'd ordered with her in mind, a sweet white he knew she'd delight in as she had everything else he'd fed her.

"Good evening, my dear." He kissed her cheek before the maitre d' seated her next to him. He was so damn cranked up for having missed her all week. His world seemed crazy without her voice in it.

Once they were alone, he raised her hand to his lips, pressing another kiss to her skin, breathing her in as he might a perfectly scented rose. "Thank you for coming."

She eyed him, a smile flirting with her lips. "If I didn't know better, I'd say you were trying to impress me. I'm sure it took quite some doing to get a reservation on Valentine's Day."

He'd booked the table two weeks in advance, not with her in mind but when he knew Lexa and Brooke would be home. Keeping the info to himself, he stroked her hand. "You're worth it."

She laughed, soft, musical, strumming a chord that reached straight to his cock. "You are pouring it on thick."

"Maybe." He didn't think so.

She was close to fifteen years younger than he was. What had she said in the theater? That she was a toddler when *Body Heat* was made. He'd been graduating high school. When he'd gotten married, she was in grade school. He could get past the age discrepancy, but what of other things that might get in the way? She'd been married, it hadn't ended well, and he had no idea where the fault in that lay. Yet he couldn't cast stones. What he wanted was her sweetness, her teasing, her humor, her loyalty to her friends and family, and her zest for life. He didn't know anything about her, not her name, her job, or where she lived, yet his heart and soul screamed out that she could be so damn right for him.

Convincing her of his feelings seemed beyond possibility.

He leaned close, dropping his voice. "You're too fucking gorgeous for words." He traced the beadwork along the halter of her dress. "Very interesting. I haven't seen anything like it."

She put a hand to her throat. "I'll tell you a secret. I love this dress." She leaned in. "And I'm not wearing panties."

Just like that, he scented her arousal over the faint aroma of the flickering candle in the table's center. He pushed her wineglass in front of her. "Don't turn me on when I can't do anything about it." In more ways than one. "Taste the wine."

"Spoilsport," she murmured, then lifted the glass to her lips. Watching her drink was damn near a religious experience. She breathed in the delicate bouquet first, then took the tiniest of sips. Closing her eyes, she tested the wine on her tongue amidst sexy sounds of pleasure before she finally swallowed.

Maybe the restaurant wasn't such a good idea. He needed to get her alone, make her enjoy him the way she did the wine.

When she opened her blue eyes, he simply fell into them. "That was good," she said, her lips glistening.

She had no idea how damn good.

"So . . ." She twirled the glass stem on the white tablecloth. "How do you intend to make up for teasing me all week?"

"I didn't tease you. Not even one teasing e-mail."

She tapped a red nail on his hand. "Exactly. You're a very naughty man. First you do sexual things to me in a public theater, then you disappear. That sounds like teasing to me. If you were a woman"—she put her lips to his ear—"they'd call you a cock teaser."

"You got an orgasm. I didn't."

"I offered. You made me stop." She smiled. He wanted her lips around him.

"I asked you to come home with me, and you refused."

"Oooooh." She drew the sound out. "You were punishing me."

He took her hand in his. "If anyone was punished, it was me. Do you have any idea how much I missed you?"

Her eyes sparkled. She loved hearing that. Then she blinked, long and slow, and another emotion glittered in her gaze. "I'm not sure what game you're playing. Turn me on, turn me off . . ." Elbows on the table, she raised her arms and spread her hands in a what-gives gesture.

Glancing at his watch, he judged how much time he had left. She'd opened the door for him, and he stepped right through. "I'm not playing a game. I want you. For more than a few titillating episodes."

Her breasts rose with a deep breath. "I'm not sure what you're getting at."

He couldn't help the laugh, but as least he kept it low, between them instead of the whole restaurant. "Let's put it this way. I tell you about myself. You tell me about yourself." He paused to let the idea sink in. "And we have a relationship."

She rolled her lips between her teeth and stared at him.

"I'll start." He didn't know how much of his soul to bare. "You already know where I work and what I do. I was married for twenty-two years, divorced for one, and I have two beautiful daughters. Lexa's almost twenty and Brooke's twenty-one. They're both in college. Brooke wants to be—"

She short-circuited him with her hand over his mouth. He barely restrained himself from licking her fingers.

"I don't think we know each other well enough for all this personal information."

He wanted to howl. How the fuck were they supposed to know each other *without* the personal details? "I want more." The challenge lay on the table between them.

Emotions rioted across her face. Her lips tightened slightly, the smallest movement flared her nostrils, and the arch of her blond brows rose. She sipped her wine without all the ceremony. "I—" She stopped.

Scott waited.

The silence wore on until he checked his watch for the second time. Then he wrapped his hand around her arm, cupping her elbow. "How did it feel when I fucked you in my office?"

She swallowed.

"It was goddamn personal, wasn't it?"

It was beyond anything Trinity had ever felt before in her life. He'd filled her so deeply, she'd wanted to cry. "It was personal," she whispered.

If she told him she didn't want a relationship, she'd lose him. Yet if she gave her name, let him in, eventually, it would all turn out like it had with Harper. Oh, not the cheating, but Scott thought she was some together woman who wanted to take a great big bite out of life. When he figured out she was . . . well, that she had no clue who she was or what she wanted, he'd give her the *sayonara, baby* routine. She wasn't ready to lose him.

So how could she make him stay without giving away too much? "It's only been three weeks. Give me time to work up to it."

"Then at least tell me your name."

His insistence irritated her. "As I recall, when you put your card under my door, you guaranteed my anonymity."

"That was before."

"Before what?" Dammit, she liked it the way it was.

He slid his hand from her elbow to her wrist. Her skin heated, tingled. The breath caught in her throat.

"Before I fell madly head over heels in lust with you."

How did he do that, turn her inside out with a few words? She needed a sip of wine badly, to wet her parched throat. "You need to let me figure this out."

He needed to let her keep her secrets, because she had a terrible feeling she might be a trophy fuck for him. She didn't use that word often, but it was appropriate. She *was* closer in age to his daughters. Maybe this was his midlife crisis, needing a younger woman to make him feel like a younger man.

And hadn't he once mentioned her needing a daddy figure to take care of her? What she needed was a man who wanted her for herself and screw whatever her name was.

He sat back, released her hand. "I'm not a patient man."

She had a feeling that wasn't true at all. Once, when she was a little girl, her daddy's yard got infested with moles. Her cat Bella sat for hours on the edge of those mole holes. And Trinity had watched Bella—not for hours, because she *had* been a child—but she still remembered Bella's fascination. Scott was like Bella. He would wait until he wore her down and she stuck her head out of her little mole hole.

Yet as Bella had, he'd quickly get bored with his trophy once he'd caught her.

"It's just a name," he cajoled.

It was everything. Her name was her only power.

He glanced to the front of the restaurant, then flipped his gaze back to her. "It's not so much to ask. Think about it."

The discussion was over. Which was odd, considering his intensity. Then he started to rise from his seat, tucking his tie close with a hand to his abdomen.

"Hey, Dad."

"Hi, Dad."

Trinity froze. All her muscles seized, even her larynx. No. He wouldn't.

She felt the air shift as if he stepped back from the table.

"Hi, sweetie. Hey, honey." The smack of the kiss, first one, then another, echoed through the restaurant. Or maybe the sound was just inside her head.

He touched her shoulder. "I want you to meet Jessie."

Jessie?

One second, two seconds. Then Trinity sucked it up and beamed at them both. They were almost twins, long, silky brown hair, their father's gorgeous eyes. No fatherly exaggeration, they were beautiful.

A hand on each, he introduced them. "Lexa." He smiled at one, then the other, in turn. "Brooke." He turned that smile on Trinity. "My little girls."

"Oh Dad," Lexa scoffed, "we're not *little* girls." She stuck out her hand. "He'd like to think we'll never grow up."

Trinity shook, and Lexa seemed to glow like the angel on top of the Christmas tree.

"Nice to meet you." Brooke's grip was firm and her smile slightly standoffish.

Scott seated them both, planting a kiss on the forehead of each of his girls. Then he took his own chair. She noted he did not reach for her hand now, but beneath the table, his knee rested against her thigh as if he'd stamped her as his property.

He'd tricked her and foisted his family on her.

And she wasn't wearing underwear. Totally pantiless—and braless—she was seated at a table with his daughters.

It was beyond the pale. She had half a mind to walk out, the other half of her mind being totally stunned. Trinity couldn't remember a time she was speechless. She might not always say the right thing—cases in point, Mr. Wanamaker, Inga Rice, and even her own father on Tuesday night—but she always had *something* to say.

Trinity gathered her wits. "Your daddy's told me so much about you." She beamed, glancing at the offending man. And no, she did not miss Brooke mouthing *daddy* with a great big question mark tattooed on her forehead.

"I'm very proud of them," Scott added.

"I know you are, poopsie." Trinity pinched his cheek. Humor flashed in his gaze. "I had no idea they were so close to my own age." She let her eyes widen with total innocence and turned back to the girls. "I thought you were in middle school."

A look slashed between the girls, and Scott's leg tensed next to hers.

"Oh, but I don't want you to think he's like robbing the cradle or anything." She gasped and thrust her hand out, knocking over her wineglass. "Oops, sorry." She put her fingers to her lips and giggled.

Scott righted her glass and signaled for the waiter. "I didn't realize you'd had so much to drink, *Jessie*." He said the name with a definite emphasis. "Maybe you should slow down."

She shot him a feral grin. "Oh baby, I've barely started. Why don't you pour your little honey-sweetie-girl another glass?" With a little moue, she tapped the stem. "Please, baby? I'm like totally and completely parched." She punctuated with an eyelash flutter.

His daughters exchanged glances.

"And give your girls a glass, too."

"Lexa's not twenty-one yet."

She waved a hand. "Oh, pooh." Patting Lexa's hand, she rolled her eyes. "He like *never*"—she made a horrible face—"bends the rules. Has he *always* been like that?"

"Dad?" Panic laced Lexa's unnaturally high voice.

"Jessie's teasing you, sweetie." He took Trinity's hand, squeezing her fingers. "Right?"

The heat in her glare would have toasted marshmallows. It certainly should have roasted his weenie. "I'm not teasing." She jiggled his cheek again. "I *never* tease. I'm like totally straight up with everything I do and would never *dream* of playing tricks." Then she dropped all trace of ditzy Valley girl. "Have I ever played a trick on you?"

His gaze drifted over face. "No. You haven't."

"Totally up front," she added with emphasis on each word.

The waiter arrived, but the wine had soaked into the tablecloth.

"Can I get you ladies a drink?" His vest extremely white, his hands deferentially behind his back, he waited.

Brooke glanced at her father. "I'll have water, please."

Lexa nodded. "The same, thank you."

When he was gone, Scott refilled Trinity's wineglass. "Don't spill it, honey-sweetie," he imitated her.

She was making the girls uncomfortable. They studied their menus as if they were schoolbooks. She was sure they thought her a total ditz, and as she glanced at Scott, she suddenly had an out-of-body experience. Rising above the restaurant, she saw Harper that very first day at her nail salon.

He'd mixed up his appointment time with hers, yet he'd hung around talking to her, fawning over her, helping her pick out her nail polish. Trinity realized she'd sounded like the same total ditz that she *feigned* for Scott's daughters tonight.

She was not a stupid person, yet she donned a mask she thought men wanted, what made them feel bigger, better. Needed. Even Faith had accused her of "dumbing herself down." For God's sake, she had a college education. She wanted men to accept her for herself, but she'd never even shown a man who she really was. Not even Scott. For him, she'd played the mysterious femme fatale like Matty in *Body Heat*.

Her mind returned to her surroundings, as if she were floating back down into her own body. His head cocked, Scott watched her, perhaps waiting for the next zany remark.

She slipped on the face men wanted, hooked them by playing a role, let them call the shots, and gave them the control. Yet despite all that, she hadn't tried to manipulate Scott. He had no right to trick her. There were rules to their relationship—and yes, they did have a relationship, even if it was odd—and he'd violated them. His insistence on changing things so soon pissed her off even more. Yes. Pissed. Her. Off.

She should have walked out, but his girls didn't deserve the scene. Instead, she stayed, dropped the ditzy Valley girl act, enjoyed the meal, made scintillating conversation, pretended she was in the here and now.

Yet all the while, she plotted ways to show him *she* was in complete control of *this* relationship.

"HOW long have you known Jessie, Dad?" Brooke struggled to keep her tone conversational, even Scott could hear that.

"Three months." The three was correct, the number of months a lie. But when discussing your sex life with your daughters, a few fabrications were in order.

"And how do you feel about her, Dad?" Lexa poured a soda from the fridge. They'd gathered in the kitchen. Since he'd already been over the hill, Brooke had driven the two of them to the restaurant, and he'd followed them home when dinner was over.

"She's great," he said, a noncommittal answer.

He shouldn't have surprised Jezebel, a tactical error on his part. He'd jumped the gun and set her off. Women could be temperamental, and he had to admit, she had a right. He'd stepped over the bounds and tricked her, as she'd pointed out. Was the damage permanent? He hoped not, but he figured he'd have to dig himself out of the hole he'd dug.

Seating herself on one of the stools at the center island, Brooke held out her glass for Lexa to fill. They actually liked each other, at least once they'd both graduated from high school. Before that, the house had often been a war zone when someone borrowed something they shouldn't have touched.

"But Dad, how well do you really know her?" Brooke asked what both girls wanted to know.

He almost laughed, but cut off the sound. "We're getting to know each other."

"Okay, now I don't want you to think we're ganging up or anything." Brooke eyed her sister. "But we talked about it on the way home, and we're worried she might be a gold digger."

This time he did laugh. "A *gold digger*? Where did you hear that old-fashioned term?"

Lexa shrugged. "Gold digger, fortune hunter, money-grubbing blond bimbo, we're trying to make sure she's not after your investments or anything."

It was on the tip of his tongue to say it was his body she wanted, not his money, but . . . they were his little girls. "Thanks for worrying, sweetie, but I'm a big boy, and I'll make sure I keep my assets intact." He knuckled the top of Lexa's head.

She grabbed his hand. "Hey, you're mussing my hair."

"It's not your assets we worry about." Brooke ducked away when he went to knuckle her head. "It's your heart."

"Honey, I promise my heart's not in danger." That wasn't entirely true. He'd claimed over and over that he wanted more than what she was giving him. Just as he'd gotten a taste of her loyalty and vulnerability over a Greek dinner, tonight he'd touched off her ire. She had emotions and feelings, and she could get pissed off and act out just like any other human being. The question was did he value the mystery over the reality.

Even after her antics tonight, the answer was yes. He still wanted a chance to see what could grow between them. "Did you at least like her a little bit?"

Neither of them said a word, Brooke studiously concentrating on the soda glass.

It was a stupid question. *Jessie* had gone out of her way to act the blond bimbo. He had to admit it had been his screwup for tricking her, just as she'd said. But she'd done such a damn good job of appearing like a brainless tart. He'd found himself wanting to laugh even as she made him look like a fool in front of his daughters. That should have pissed him off royally; instead, he'd enjoyed the sparring. Maybe she did make him a little crazy, because most fathers would hold that against the new lady in his life. Yet he'd asked for her little punishment.

Finally, his youngest piped up. "She's a bit of a twit, don't you think?"

"Yeah, Dad," Brooke joined in. "What do you see in her?"

Lexa slapped her elbow. "Duh."

The allusion to sex lay on the island counter between them.

Brooke stuck her fingers in her ears. "Ewwe. I don't want to hear."

"It's not *that*, girls." It was more. She made him feel alive, and he hadn't had that in a long, long time. Were *his* emotions about the woman herself, or more about what was going on with him at this stage of his life? Probably a bit of both.

"Right, Dad," Lexa scoffed. "You might be old, but it's not like you're totally ancient."

"I'm not listening, I'm not listening," Brooke chanted, until Lexa pulled her fingers out of her ears.

"We're wondering"—Lexa smiled as if her question needed softening—"if you're thinking marriage or anything."

"We aren't there, sweetie." Marriage was a giant step beyond a mere relationship. "But she has this view of life that's amazing." He stopped. Telling his daughters how Jezebel affected him was like trying to describe a sunset to a blind man. "I wanted you to meet her. And like her."

Though he'd blown that one. He could only hope he hadn't completely blown the rest of what he wanted, which was more of the way his mystery Jezebel made him feel.

Would he retain this sense of vitality, of truly living life, with another woman? Scott didn't know for sure, but he wasn't willing to let her go until he found out.

15

AT the end of the workday on Monday, Trinity sent him a message. "Happy *After* Valentine's Day. Meet me for drinks."

It was appropriately snarky after the way Scott had tricked her on Friday. If he was smart, he'd expect a trick. She named a time, allowing her to get home after work, change into her night's costume, and arrive half an hour early, this hotel different from the one at which they'd met twice before.

Elevator music played, and candles burned in red vases. Trinity chewed a cashew. The hotel bar wasn't crowded, even for a convention. She'd found a seat at the far end of the counter, and a willing victim. Norman was older, but she liked older men, as evidenced by her attraction to that rat, Scott Sinclair.

"And what do you do?" she asked. Men always found themselves to be the most scintillating topic of conversation.

"Software engineer." He had the slightly soft belly of a desk worker to prove it, though he was handsome, with sandy salt-and-pepper hair, blue eyes, and a nice smile.

"And you're in town for . . . ," Trinity trailed off, raised a brow, and smiled, though Norman didn't appear interested in her smile. He liked her cleavage in the low-cut slut top. The Lycra darn near bonded to her chest. And wow, when she'd stood in front of the mirror, she had breasts.

"The convention here at the hotel," he managed.

Trinity recrossed her legs, and Norman's eyes dropped to the brevity of her tight black micromini skirt, or rather the thigh her skirt revealed.

"You must be so intelligent, charming, and articulate," she murmured, "to talk all day about your software."

He sat straighter on his barstool and smoothed his tie. "Well, not everybody has the technical knowledge."

"I'll bet not. You must have a doctorate." She gave him a little moue. "*Dr. Norman. It has *such* a ring to it.*"

"No, no. I only have a masters degree."

She sighed and gazed at him with wonder. "*Only* a masters? Please, that's such an accomplishment."

Norman preened. "You almost have to have a masters these days to get anywhere."

She nodded sadly. "I wish I'd gone to college. But it seemed so hard." All right, she was donning a mask, but this time it was for a good cause, a little Scott tease. Picking up her margarita, she licked the salt along the rim.

Norman went bug-eyed, and a drop of sweat rolled down his temple. "Here, let me get you another." He waved at the bartender without taking his eyes off her mouth.

"Why, thank you, Norman. I surely do appreciate that. I'm so thirsty, for some reason."

Norman looked positively parched as he ordered another rum and Coke and her margarita refill. The bartender, black-haired, black-eyed, and younger than she was, eyed her with boredom, as if he'd seen the pickup too many times.

When he was gone, she trailed her finger along the back of Norman's hand, a half inch from actually touching him. "Now, back to you and your fascinating job. Are you here all week?"

He gulped. "Yes."

"How wonderful. You should see something of San Francisco," the implication being that she could show it to him.

She and Scott used the expression *cock teaser*, and tonight she deserved the title. Poor Norman. It wasn't nice, she was a total b-i-t-c-h, but Norman was human payback. Twisting a little, she imperceptibly glanced at her watch. Her quarry wouldn't dare be a second late.

"I don't know that I'll have time to make it up there."

"Oh, Norman." She pouted, her lips puckering. "It's a forty-five-minute drive from here. You *must* see the city." She batted her eyelashes. "*I* live up there."

Norman had a small stroke and seemed incapable of speech for a moment. The bartender slid their drinks across the bar, and she was tempted to wrap Norman's fingers around the glass so he'd have something to ground him.

Beyond his shoulder, Scott slipped into a chair at a table in the corner, his dark gaze settling on her.

Trinity swung her foot, the back of her stiletto heel slipping off. In train fantasy parody, she leaned down to slowly slide her hand from her knee along her calf, tipped the shoe back on, then let her fingers glide all the way back up.

She didn't even notice Norman's reaction until he choked, coughed, and finally caught his breath. Deliberately, she put a hand on his arm and squeezed. "Are you all right?"

Norman's gaze seemed riveted to her red nail polish, and she glanced at Scott. Sitting back, his elbows on the chair arms, his fingers steepled, he raised his mouth in a slight smile.

She tipped her lips up in acknowledgment.

The waitress brought him an imported beer. He watched, drank, watched. Unfortunately, Trinity was too far away to see his eyes, and the expression on his face revealed nothing.

But he'd see you were mine.

His very words in the theater. She was not *Scott's*. She was her own woman and did what she pleased. No man *owned* her. Harper had a chance, and he'd blown it. Her anger had grown exponentially over the weekend. Or maybe it was determination not to play the fool for a man ever again.

Except when she *meant* to sound like a bimbo, as she did with Norman. "So, I'm *dying* to hear more about you." She puckered once more and flagged her finger at him. "Where do you live?"

Out of the corner of her eye, she saw Scott stand and head to the bar.

Norman tugged at his collar as if it were suddenly too tight. "Chicago."

"Oh, I've never been to Chicago. The Windy City." She laughed as if she'd made a joke.

"You never said you wanted to go to Chicago, sweetheart." Suddenly right there, almost between them, Scott trailed a hand down her arm, then grabbed her hand. "I'd have taken you."

Eyes wide, terrified, Norman had nowhere to go, trapped on one side by Scott and a wayward barstool on the other.

Scott held up her ringless left hand and stared at it. "Where's your wedding ring, honey-sweetie-girl?"

Norman made a noise. Trinity feared a real stroke.

Yet she smiled oh-so-sweetly for her *husband*. "I thought you told me not to wear it if I went out to a bar by myself. Or men wouldn't want to talk to me."

She was glad their end of the bar was empty. It was one thing toying with Norman, but she didn't want eavesdroppers.

Scott raised her hand, pressing a kiss to her knuckles, then he turned his smoky dark gaze on Norman. "Some men don't care if a woman's married. Right?" He raised a devilish brow. "I didn't catch your name."

"It's Norman," Trinity said, because Norman didn't answer.

"*You* don't mind, do you, Norman?" Scott insisted with a smile. The man's face colored deeper than her father's on his worst conniption-fit day.

"Stop teasing him," she admonished. "The poor man will think you intend to beat him up." She eyed the bartender, who stood next to the house phone in case he needed to make an immediate call.

Scott clapped Norman on the back. "Jessie's right. I'm teasing. Don't worry. I never bust a gentleman's chops when my wife comes on to him."

"I think"—Norman found his voice—"I'll call it a night."

Scott held the man's shoulder, his gaze meeting Trinity's, fire in his eyes. "Tell him we don't want him to leave yet."

What on earth was he up to? Trinity decided to play along. "Please don't leave yet, Norman. I like you."

Easing closer to her side, Scott slipped his arm around her, bending down to nuzzle her temple. Norman now had room to escape, yet he didn't, suddenly fascinated by the scene.

"Yeah, Norman, she likes you."

She stroked Scott's chest. "And he's not the jealous type, Norman. He'd never try to *own* a woman or tell her what to do." She gazed up at Scott fondly. "Or manipulate her or trick her."

He slipped his hand under the fall of her hair, caressing her nape. "No. I give her every freedom her little heart desires." Then he turned to Norman, and blinked, very slowly, as if he were assessing the man's worth in that length of time. "I even let her be with other men when she wants to."

Trinity's heart stopped. She couldn't stop the next words out of her mouth. "You *let* me?"

He lifted her chin and kissed her hard on the lips. "I forgot." He glanced at Norman. "Men don't *let* her do anything. She's woman enough to do whatever she wants." His mouth kicked up in a smile. "Then again," he added, relentlessly holding her gaze, "if she'd rather have another man watch *us*, I'd like that, too." Once more, he slid his gaze toward Norman. "We both like it a lot when someone watches us, don't we, sweetheart?"

The theater wasn't the first time he'd conjured up the image of being watched. She'd participated fully in the role-play. It even made her wet. But he couldn't mean it for real. Could he?

"Would you like to watch, Norman?" Scott turned back to Trinity, kissing her nose. "Unless she doesn't feel like it tonight. I would never trick her, manipulate her, or force her into doing something she didn't want to do." He tipped her head with his thumb beneath her chin. "Because while I think of her as *mine*, I'd never say I *owned* her." Back to Norman he went, as if he were eyeballing a tennis match. "She likes her freedom. I wonder how much freedom she wants to take advantage of?"

He was goading her, banking on her calling a halt to whatever he had in mind. He was *still* trying to manipulate her. Well, she wasn't about to back down from a challenge.

Picking up her melting margarita, she swiped her tongue along the edge, then washed the salt down with a long swallow. "*Do* you want to watch, Norman?"

His eyes were fairly popping out of his head as he nodded.

She leaned closer. "Then here are the rules. You watch. But you don't touch us." She pushed back to snug closer to Scott's chest. "At least not tonight." And finally she smiled. "But you *are* here the whole week."

There. Scott would have to be the one to back down now.

Instead, he slid his hand down her back, along the crease of her butt, and beneath her. She was wet. Her nipples peaked against the Lycra top. Norman couldn't take his eyes off them.

She didn't want this, did she? She *couldn't* want it. It was naughty, nasty, yet tantalizing in a now-that-you've-thought-about-it-you-want-to-try-it kind of way.

But Scott wouldn't let her do it.

"Shall we use your hotel room, Norman?" he asked politely.

Good Lord. He *would* let her do it.

JESUS. He didn't intend to do this, did he?

Hell, yes, he did. She was his. Norman would know it, and more importantly, so would she.

Scott had been damn near close to violence when he'd entered the bar to find her leaning in to give Norman a good long gander at her breasts.

Her nipples beaded so close to the surface, Scott's mouth watered with need. She blew his brain's circuitry with her low-cut top and short skirt. She was dressed to slay, the clothing almost nothing more than bands of material covering her privates. Red lipstick, red fingernails, high heels, long, bare, tanned legs, and a sassy attitude goading him to issue the challenge.

"What do you say, Norman?" He regarded the man with a steady gaze, allowing one corner of his mouth to curl slightly. In a man-to-man contest, if Norman backed down now, he'd never have the confidence to pick up another woman in a bar.

"Umm." Norman fiddled with the bar napkin.

Jezebel held her breath, her body tense under his arm. Oh yeah, she was hoping good old Norman wouldn't have the nerve.

Scott caressed her ear with his tongue. "Don't worry, baby doll, if he doesn't want to watch, we'll find someone else."

She shivered. He held her snug against him, in case she tried to bolt.

He'd never been a jealous man, but she made him crazy. The idea of trashing this guy's face over her had consumed his thoughts for ten minutes.

Until he'd gotten this brainstorm.

And Scott had to have it. He'd never done the like in his life, the extent of his kink being a bit of dirty talk, fantasy role-playing, adult toys, and making her come in a dark theater. This was a whole new level, and it had his blood pumping hard and fast through his veins.

Norman cleared his throat. "All right." He glanced down the length of the bar to the bartender. A towel going round and round the glass in his hand, the guy eyed them with half-closed, speculative lids.

"I'll write my room number on this napkin." Norman double-clicked the pen and wrote. "You can come up in . . ." He cleared his throat. Passing a glance over Jezebel's bare thigh, then her beaded nipples, he looked at Scott. "Ten minutes?"

"Done." Triumph simmered in his blood as she trembled beneath his arm.

Norman yanked out his wallet, threw some bills on the bar for his tab, then slipped off the stool. When he was gone, Scott read the number, folded the napkin, and stuffed it in his pocket. Picking up her drink, he sipped, the tangy taste of margarita, salt, and a hint of her own intoxicating flavor.

Folding himself onto Norman's vacated stool, he never broke contact with her, his thigh tight against her knee.

Something sparked in her eye. "You think I'm going to run out of here now that he's gone."

"I wouldn't hold it against you if you did."

"You think I'm chicken." The spark held an edge of anger.

"Women have different limits than men, that's all."

She climbed off the stool to stand between his legs. "You're the one with limits." Trailing her finger down the center of his chest, she stopped at his belt buckle. "You want me to be the one who balks." She swiped his cheek with her tongue. "But maybe it makes me hot."

He grabbed her hand. "It makes us both hot." His cock filled out his jeans. Her nipples told her story, and her sexy, aroused scent rose in the air. "And I want it bad." He let his breath caress her ear and triumphed in her sharp inhale.

Without even tugging on her, she snugged up against his thighs. "So you can show him that you own me?"

He snaked an arm around her waist. "So I can show you how fucking hot we are together. We'll light him on fire."

Tunneling beneath his hair, she lightly scored his scalp with her fingers. He felt the touch all the way to his cock.

"We do this, you'll be mine," she whispered. "You'll never be able to walk away from me. I'll own *you*."

She already did. "Baby, you're the one who'll be hooked."

"You won't get my name." Her breath at his ear shuddered through his body. He'd take her here if they wouldn't get arrested.

"We'll see." He set her away from him, standing tall over her despite the fuck-me heels. "Ten minutes are up." Raising her hand to his lips, he held her with his eyes. "Last chance."

She tipped her chin, a defiant set to her lusciously red lips. "*Your* last chance," she murmured.

Gotcha. She wouldn't back down anymore than he would. Yet why the hell was he so crazy for this?

She'd come on to Norman, flirted, flaunted her gorgeous nipples and breasts. His cock had gone painfully hard with the idea of showing Norman she couldn't be had by anyone but him. Scott Sinclair. Her lover.

In the lobby, he pressed the elevator Up button and imprisoned her hand in his. Her palm against his raised his temperature another degree. When no one got on the elevator with them, he mashed her up against the wall the moment the doors closed.

It was like the theater, imagining someone watching, knowing she'd do anything for him. He wanted Norman to salivate for her.

Scott wanted her to know she'd never get better than what she could have with him. Not Norman, not her ex, no one.

"Christ." Instead of kissing her and smearing all that red lipstick, he slid down her body. On his knees, he buried his face against
her skirt and drank in her scent.

She moaned and shoved her fingers through his hair, holding
him. "There's probably a camera."

"I don't give a fuck." He gripped her calves, loving the feel of all
that silky smooth skin. She shivered as he traced circles at the back
of her knees.

The lurch of the elevator warned him to stand. His hands shook
he wanted her so badly. He wanted this, the passion, excitement,
and kink, the vitality, the crazy way she made his heart beat a mile
a minute.

When she hesitated, he tugged until they were outside the doors
as they closed. "I'm not going to force you." He didn't drop her
hand. No way was he letting her go until she asked him to. "But I
want this."

He could see the wheels of her mind working, as if she were tabulating all the pros and cons, five for, three against.

"Why?" she asked. Her breasts rose and fell with each breath,
blue eyes deep.

Because in doing it, she'd claim him. And he would claim her.
He knew in his gut, she wouldn't walk away after that. Yet she'd run
now if he told her that. "I don't know your name. When you walk
out of here, no one will ever know you did this."

His gaze tracked the line of her throat as she swallowed.

"When I walk out of here, you'll be sitting at your phone waiting for my next call." She tapped his chest. "Tell me how badly you
want it."

He backed up two steps toward the direction of Norman's room,
their arms stretched between them. "So bad it's like a vise around
my cock. I'm gonna die if I don't have it."

She followed, one step. "Who belongs to who?" she tested.

"I belong to you."

He backed up again, and this time she came with him freely.

"You have the power," he admitted, "because I'm begging."

The first room belonged to Norman. Scott put his hand to the door, but didn't knock. The hallway pulsed with his need. Trinity could scent the tantalizing male aroma radiating off him. His jeans stretched tight over his erection, enticing her.

He offered the world. Her mouth would brand him. All the power would be hers. She could stop in the middle and bring him to his knees begging. Trinity had never known the control coursing through her body. Her skin tingled to the touch. Her breasts felt heavy, her nipples swollen. His eyes were dark, dilated, wild, and his body called to something basic, elemental, and primitive in her.

For once, she would have all the power she'd ever craved right at her fingertips. And she wanted it badly.

Trinity knocked on the door.

Norman had stripped off his suit jacket and tie, and he stepped back to let them in. Scott held onto her hand as if he were afraid she'd come to her senses and run.

Where he was concerned, she hadn't had any sense, since the moment she let him in her hotel room door. And really, how was *this* any more kinky than *that*?

Norman cleared his throat—obviously a nervous habit. "Can I offer you a drink?"

The room was standard hotel fare, two queen beds, tacky paintings, a desk, bureau with drawers and TV, and by the window, a comfy orange chair with table and lamp beside it. Trinity turned a circle and finally let her gaze settle on Norman.

She shoved him lightly in the chest, pushing him down on the side of the bed closest to the window and that chair. "Sit there, Norman, and don't move unless I tell you."

Norman didn't have a doubt as to who was in charge. She wasn't so sure about Scott, but he would learn.

"There." She pointed first at Scott, then the orange chair.

He set it an angle to the bed, but didn't sit yet. Norman would have a bird's-eye view of them. And she'd be able to see him as she . . . performed.

Trinity's heart jumped into her throat, and she thought she might shriek. *Are you crazy?* She was. Panic bubbled like champagne in her veins and made her light-headed.

What would Faith say if she knew all the outrageous things Trinity had taken to doing? Masturbating for a stranger, sex in a car, sex in a theater, sex, sex, sex, and now this, taking Scott in her mouth. Sucking his cock. Making him come for her.

All in front of a stranger.

Good Lord, what would her mother have said? She'd have disowned Trinity.

Scott trailed a finger down her cheek, bringing her back to this time and place instead of the fears of her own mind. Her mother would never have found out. No one would find out. Scott was her secret. Locking eyes, she lost herself in the deep brown. Closer, closer, until his lips touched hers, he took her mouth. She opened, stroked him with her tongue, allowed him deeper, and suddenly she was on the toes of her shoes, flush up against him, lips glued to his, arms around his neck. His kiss went on and on as she rubbed her whole body against him. Her miniscule panties were damp between her legs. Then she slipped back down onto her high heels.

Scott pressed her palm to his pants, rubbed himself. His eyes got darker, hotter.

"Do it," he whispered, and removed his hand.

Trinity stroked him, felt him grow. Norman made a noise, a slight groan choked off in midthroat.

She went to the buttons on Scott's shirt. "I'm not going to make this quick for you. You're going to suffer."

"Make me beg."

"Oh, you'll beg." She gave him a sly smile. "You're going to wish you'd never married such a wild little cat."

His nostrils twitched, flared. "I'm going to be on my knees thanking God I did." He dipped enough to slide a hand under her skirt and squeeze her butt.

She slapped his knuckles. "You don't play, I play."

"Yes, ma'am." Despite his words, he teased her breast before she swatted him again.

Spreading his shirt, she flicked her nail over his nipple. He shuddered. The scent of soap rose off his chest. Licking a nipple, she tasted warm flesh. This time he shivered.

She leaned back to look up at him. "You like that a lot." Tossing her hair, she glanced at Norman. "Are your nipples sensitive, Norman?"

His jaw slack, he nodded his head.

"Undo your shirt and pinch them." Power streaked through her as he did. Two men willing to do her bidding. It was kinky. It was terrifying. It was so damn addicting.

Scott pulled her head back by the hair. "Don't forget me."

"*Don't* tell me what to do," she countered. "Or you won't get anything at all."

A muscle flexed in his cheek.

Trinity pinched his nipple until a groan rose from deep in his belly. "Could I make you come with that?" she whispered.

He hissed in a breath when she did it again. "You might very well be able to. Do it harder."

She pulled on him, adding a slight twist. "Does it hurt?"

"It hurts good."

He was at the right height as she took him with her mouth, sucking hard, then teasing the nipple with her teeth.

His cock pulsed, and he bent slightly at the knees, kneading her shoulders in his hands. "Damn you."

"I like this," she murmured. She loved the power. Taking his belt, she undid the buckle even as she tongued his nipples into hard nubs, harder than she'd ever been herself.

Along with the harsh rasp of Norman's breath, the sound of Scott's zipper filled the room. Slipping into his underwear, she palmed him. Droplets coated her fingers. Pulling out, she leaned back, then put her hand to her mouth and licked his come.

"Fuck." His brown eyes turned jet-black, and he cupped her head, took her mouth, tasted himself.

"How bad do you want it?" she whispered against his lips.

He rocked, holding her hips close with one hand. "So fucking bad I'm close to exploding right now."

She rolled her head on his shoulder and looked at Norman. His cheeks a florid red, beads of sweat gathered along his upper lip. An enormous erection tented his trousers.

She felt powerful, sexy, needy, wanted. "How bad do you want to watch it?"

"I'll beg. On my knees." Norman put his hands together.

Scott kneaded her butt, forcing contact with his cock.

"Take that out." She pointed to the bulge in Norman's pants. "Play with it."

He couldn't act fast enough, fingers fumbling, almost catching himself in the zipper teeth. His head was bulbous, swollen, purple, and wet.

"You're bigger," she whispered to Scott as he filled her hand. She couldn't get enough of him.

Shoving pants and briefs over his hips, she guided him down into the chair. His penis jutted straight up, big, hard. She wanted him inside her so badly, her chest hurt with each breath.

Yet that was going too far.

Scott held out his palm. She gulped air, swallowed hard, then took his hand and went to her knees between his legs.

16

SCOTT had never wanted a woman's mouth on him more than he did now. Her eyes were the blue of a stormy ocean, seething.

"Suck me," he demanded, "or I'll come just watching you."

The scent of her hair rose to fog his mind. Scott buried his fingers in the texture of it as she bent her head to him. Her lips closed over his crown, and he laid his head back, losing himself in the heat of her mouth. His body surged up, pushed deeper. Her teeth raked along the sensitive underside, then her fingers closed around his balls. She rose and fell, sucking him deep, then licking him all the way back up, mouthing his tip, tonguing the slit until she backed off to swallow.

She looked up at him, her mouth barely closing over his crown. Her gaze locked with his, her lips taking him, and his balls filled to the breaking point. With both hands behind her head, he pushed her down slowly until he was as deep as he could go. He thought he'd die with the enormity of her act.

Then she turned slightly to glance at Norman. The sight of the man's fat cock in his hand, beating himself while his eyes bulged, taking in every inch of her, seemed to set her off. She sucked Scott harder. Faster. Mouth and tongue caressing, her hand riding him with each outstroke.

The orgasm built, blinding him to everything but the feel of her lips, the silk of her hair, the animal scent of her sex. She moaned, the sound quivering along his cock.

"Christ, I'm gonna come." His words sounded odd in his head, strangled.

Norman reacted with a furious beat. "She's so fucking hot."

She took him with a last swipe of her tongue along his length, and he lost it in her mouth, hard, heavy. She milked him to the last drop. She owned him, and he needed to own her.

Pulling her up, he fastened his lips on hers, drank the taste of his come off her tongue, and it wasn't enough. He tipped her down on the carpet, followed her, covered her. Wriggling against him, she cupped his cheeks in her hands, pulling his head back and forcing him to meet her gaze. Her eyes dilated, her nostrils flared like a mare's, and the heady perfume of arousal clouded his vision.

He tugged on the tight skirt. "You want this."

She made a sound, a moan, a cry, and bucked beneath him. He crawled down her, spread her legs, shoved the skirt high until he found her damp crotch, the aroma of sweet sex all over her.

"Tell me you want it." He tugged aside her thong, revealing her swollen pussy.

She pushed him, her hips rising. He knew she wanted it.

And his mouth watered with the scent of her. "Tell me."

"Please." Then she yanked the skirt a little higher, pulled her knees wide, and shoved him over the edge with every sense.

He tasted her, drowned in her, played the button of her clit, slid a finger in her depths.

Then Scott used two fingers, pumping lightly inside her, his tongue playing her like an instrument. Her skin heated, and her nipples turned to hard beads.

Trinity pinched them, squeezing as she'd done to him. Heat streaked down to the exact spot his lips tortured. Her body moved in rhythm with his, her breathing hard, all so good she bit down on her lip to trap the scream rising. Pleasure so intense, it almost hurt, she wanted to come, needed to. The climb to orgasm turned her entire body into one pulsing point of need, until it all spiraled down to his fingers in her, his mouth on her. She simply imploded, her cries loud and long, full-throated, strident, and so unlike her she thought it must be another woman screaming. But oh God, nothing had ever . . . never . . .

She opened her eyes to Scott's head between her legs and Norman's fist wrapped around his cock, gaze on her, on Scott, mouth a big round O, tongue hanging out. Norman shouted and a jet of come creamed his hand.

Scott lifted his head and fastened his eyes on her. His mouth glistened with moisture. Meeting her gaze, he licked his lips, slowly, relishing her, showing her how much he loved it. Finally, he blew on her, and Trinity's body quaked beneath him.

Norman lay boneless, arms out, head turned, pupils fixed on her. His tongue was still hanging out. Like a dog.

She was totally exposed, her legs spread. With Scott between them and her way-too-tight skirt hiked up over her hips, she couldn't even pull it down to cover herself.

Scott rose slightly, tugged her panties back in place, then pressed a kiss to her soaked crotch. Her body tensed in anticipation of another mind-blowing orgasm. Norman rolled on his side and started stroking himself again.

Oh my God. Trinity suddenly felt sick. Why couldn't he at least keep his tongue in and his mouth closed? She could not get that image out of her head even when she closed her eyes. And it was horrible. Crass. Sleazy. What would people *think* of her?

She squirmed from beneath Scott. Rolling onto her knees, she yanked her skirt down until her butt was at least covered. "I have to go." Standing awkwardly, her high heel slipped out from under her, and only Scott's hand on her arm saved her.

"I need to get out," she whispered.

Zipped up, shirt buttoned—how did he do that?—Scott held her, his grip unrelenting. "We go together."

Trinity let him come with her because it was the only way to leave. If she didn't get out, she'd expire right on the spot.

"I can't believe I did that," she muttered to herself as she straightened her clothing. "I can't believe it." Teetering on her high heels, she stabbed the elevator button.

"It was hot." Scott's head still swirled, steeped in her scent. It was all over him. When he breathed, her aroma filled his head. He licked his lips, and her flavors shot him to the moon again. She'd tasted so good.

She whirled and stabbed a finger to his chest. Her mouth open, she stopped before she got a word out, as if suddenly she had no clue what she wanted to tell him. Or *how* to tell him.

"It was good," he whispered. "You loved it." She'd come so hard, her legs tight around him, taking all he had to give.

Norman made it all that much hotter.

She closed her eyes.

"Admit it."

"It was good." Then she gulped air as if the words had stolen something from her. "But you shouldn't have touched me."

"You were so fucking ready to come."

"That wasn't the rule."

"We didn't have a rule."

"I *did*."

The elevator dinged, and when the doors opened, she climbed on. He made to follow, but she held out her palm. "No."

"But—"

She pushed him, he stepped back, and the silvered doors closed in his face. His own reflection stared back at him.

It was the absolute hottest, most fucking alive thing he'd ever experienced. The moment he spent himself in her mouth, he'd been as high as he thought sex could take a man, yet he'd needed to taste her to be complete. With another man watching, he wanted her to know she was his, no one else's, ever. He wanted her to *be* in that moment with him.

Not ten minutes later, she'd let the elevator slam in his face. The woman was two steps forward and a giant step back.

He had no idea how to regain the ground he'd lost. Hell, he couldn't even pinpoint when he'd lost it. Friday night with his daughters? Or tonight when he put his mouth to her and made her come in front of a total stranger?

Maybe it was a bit of both. He wanted to pound his fist into something, so instead he punched the elevator button.

Yet it was far too late to chase her down. She was already gone. It was a matter of gone for how long. And if he'd survive until she returned.

TRINITY didn't make it home before she had to pull over. A fast-food lot, its lights far too bright on the hood of her car.

For a moment, she couldn't catch her breath. She couldn't get Norman's face out of her mind. His gaze all bug-eyed, his hand touching himself, his mouth open and his tongue hanging out. It was like all the bad clichés you ever see about horny men addicted to porn on the Internet. Seedy and sleazy.

She'd been fine until Scott pushed her down on the carpet. No, correct that, she'd wanted Scott to throw her down like that, she wanted his mouth, the orgasm . . . everything.

It was the whole morning after thing. You get up, your makeup's a mess, your clothes feel grungy, the guy isn't nearly as good as you thought he was the night before. Everything is plain old sordid, and you realize you slept with him for all the wrong reasons. Because you wanted to punish your boyfriend for an infraction, or you couldn't back down from a challenge.

She'd have felt better if she hadn't ended up naked. That was more than she'd wanted to do. She'd gotten carried away, exhibited no control. She'd exhibited *herself*. What if someone found out? That was the problem with getting carried away. If you weren't careful, someone discovered what you'd been up to.

Trinity climbed out of her car, slammed the door, and leaned against it. The greasy scent of fries drifted on the night air. A posse of teenagers hung about the newspaper racks outside the food chain's door.

She hugged her arms around her middle.

Will the real Trinity Green please stand up?

She'd lost sight of who Trinity Green was *supposed* to be. She'd walked into that hotel room feeling power in the palm of her hand. She'd soared with it when she took Scott in her mouth.

But when she came down off that orgasm, she'd lost it all.

Was it Norman's doggie tongue hanging out? Or what Faith would say or think? Or her *father*? Not to mention her mom looking down from heaven. Trinity closed her eyes.

"Hey, lady, can I bum a smoke?"

She didn't even see the teenager until he was right there. Her heart skipped a couple of beats. "I don't smoke."

His oversized sports jersey hung down to his thighs, yet his pants rode so low, the crotch was at his knees. A pimple reddened the tip of his nose.

"Do you got any change I can bum for a pack of smokes?"

Despite the whiskers on his chin, she was sure he wasn't eighteen. His cohorts hung back by the newspaper stand waiting to see if he scored.

Dragging in a breath, she held it a moment, gazing at him. He wasn't a scary gang kid, just a slightly unkempt normal kid. She didn't feel threatened, as if he and his friends might jump her like a pack of hyenas. But he was too young to smoke.

She, however, didn't have the right to judge what anyone else did. She exhaled in a *whoosh*. "I was going to say that smoking is bad for you." She sighed. "But you look like a smart kid, so I figure you know that." Nodding her head, she indicated his gaggle of friends. "I also figure you want the cigarettes so you can impress your buddies, but I'm pretty sure they all smoke to impress, too, so what's the point? And if I had any cash, I'd keep it instead of giving it to you, because as an adult, I shouldn't be encouraging you to smoke."

"Lady—"

She held up a finger. "I'm not done yet."

He slapped his lips shut.

"As I was saying, I won't give you the money, but I'm not going into the smoking thing either because"—she smiled, because here was her brilliant and profound point—"you're going to have to learn from your own mistakes." She waited for him to see the light, but he merely rolled his eyes, so she went on. "Like when you're hooked on nicotine and coughing with that bad taste in your mouth"—she knew *that* from her one cigarette out back of her middle school's gymnasium—"and you'll hate yourself because it's embarrassing to be asking strangers for money so you can support your habit. Yet, you can't give it up as hard as you try." At least that's what she'd heard. "And going cold turkey?" She blinked. "It'll kill ya."

"Lady—"

"Shh." She waited a second, giving him a chance so she could *shh* him again. "Quit"—she lowered her voice, and he strained closer to hear—"while you're ahead."

He stared at her, the lamp overhead beaming down on his dark hair and turning it midnight blue. Then slowly, one step at a time, he backed up, never taking his eyes off her. As if she were a member of the hyena pack.

"Quit while you're ahead," she repeated.

She couldn't say she was ahead. She'd lost her sense of who she was. For thirty years, she *thought* she'd known, yet she'd lost even that. In searching for the new Trinity, she'd ended up in Norman's hotel room. As exhilarating as some of those moments were, as good as that stupendous orgasm had been, she wasn't gaining power or self-respect with Scott. She was losing that last final ounce of herself.

Tell him your name.

She couldn't. What would it solve anyway? While breaking it off with him would hurt like hell—the thought made her sick—in her heart, she knew it was better to walk away. She'd sacrificed her self-image to men like Harper, men in lust with her body, her looks, or her money.

It wasn't Scott's fault, but he got her to do more than she wanted to do, expose more than she wanted to expose. She had the sinking feeling he would always get her to do more than she could handle. If she gave him her name, she'd have to be Little Miss Perfect again, except that Little Miss Perfect in Scott's case might have a whole new meaning. Whatever, he'd have all the control. There was one lone choice. Scott was an addictive habit she had to quit before anyone found out about him, and going cold turkey was the only way.

Even if it killed her.

THE third day into Operation Cold Turkey, Trinity hit the DTs. Her hands shook, she couldn't concentrate, and she was seeing things that weren't there, like e-mails from Scott that never came. Or maybe it was too much caffeine.

She'd left him a voice mail the "morning after" and told him *sayonara, baby*, though in much nicer words, taking all the blame. Yet a teeny-tiny part of her kept hoping he didn't believe her.

Trinity slid her dollar across the counter. "Here you go."

"Thanks." The countergirl *ka-chinged* on the cash register and snatched up the bill.

The company subsidized the cafeteria, and the bagel and cream cheese was a buck. In addition to her caffeine and Scott addictions, she could now add bagels and cream cheese. Since it was a bit before the normal break hour, the place was relatively empty. Trinity picked a seat by the window. Once again, it was raining, and the lawn was riddled with puddles.

She set her cell phone on the table beside her plate, and oh goodness, the first bite of that bagel was darn near . . . orgasmic. She closed her eyes, and an image of Scott popped into her mind. Scott always popped into her mind, and this time, it was *that* night. With Norman. And Scott between her legs.

She shouldn't have thought the word *orgasm*.

"Your brother is driving me insane."

Trinity startled and opened her eyes. The chair opposite screeched on the floor as Verna yanked it out, then plopped down.

"All right, so what is my brother doing now?" Trinity almost lost the appetite for her bagel.

"He wants me to talk to you about talking to your father."

"I already told him I couldn't talk to Daddy."

Verna raised one eyebrow. "Couldn't?"

Trinity mutinously took a bite of her perfectly scrumptious bagel before answering. She took a long time enjoying the flavors, until Verna tapped her blunt nails on the tabletop.

"Fine. I *won't* do it." Verna was demolishing the joy of her bagel.

"I'm so proud of you, honey." Verna beamed, tiny laugh lines crisscrossing out from her eyes.

"You are?" The last three days, Trinity had turned into a total loser, and Verna was proud of her?

"You always let Lance walk all over you."

Well, that wasn't true. "I blacked his eye when we were teenagers and he called Faith fat."

"You were defending Faith, so of course you gave him a shiner. I'm talking about the little things. 'Trin, could you make sure Rosa gets my shirts cleaned'," Verna mimicked. She was quite good at it.

"That's because he was working, and I was at home."

Verna lowered her head to regard Trinity through her lashes. "That's because he walked all over you."

Trinity dropped her voice as the cafeteria started to fill up for the morning break, though with all the chatter, they wouldn't be overheard anyway. Still . . . "But you love Lance."

"I give him unconditional love, meaning I love him despite the fact that sometimes he can be a real asshole."

Trinity's jaw dropped. "*Unconditional love* means you accept everything a person does because you love them."

Verna imitated a buzzer on a game show. "Honey, it means you know a person's worst traits and love them despite it."

Trinity gulped, and a little voice inside screamed, "Don't do it!" She did it anyway. "What's my worst trait?"

"You think you're Little Miss Perfect. But honey"—Verna patted her hand—"you ain't."

That was nothing new. Trinity had figured it out the day she found Harper in the shower. But it was debilitating that Verna knew about her need to *be* Little Miss Perfect.

"And you want everyone to like you."

"What's wrong with that?"

"Because sometimes making everyone like you means you have to compromise yourself."

Trinity opened her mouth, but what was there to say? If she ever told anyone some of the things she'd done since kicking Harper out, well, let's say they'd have a hard time getting past it. Even Verna.

The older woman waved a hand. "But ragging on you is not the reason I'm slumming." She hooked a finger over her shoulder, indicating the cafeteria, which was nicely outfitted with new tables that didn't wobble and comfy chairs that cushioned a person's bottom.

"So why *are* you slumming?"

Gripping the edges of the table, Verna leaned in and dropped her voice to conspiracy level. "Your father got a letter begging him to forgive Lance. And *you* signed it."

"Why would I send Daddy a letter?" A furrow marred her brow. The lines on her face were multiplying like rabbits.

"*You* didn't send it."

"Duh." How could Lance do that when he knew how she felt about being in the middle between her two closest family members, her *only* family members?

Verna read the frown. "You can love him, but he's *wrong*."

Without allowing herself to think, Trinity speed-dialed his cell phone. It kicked to voice mail. "Call Daddy and tell him you sent the letter, Lance. And don't ever use my name again."

What name? Trinity? Mrs. Harper Harrington the *Third*? Or Jezebel? Even Jessie? Why did everything come back to Scott?

She folded the phone and tucked it away on her lap.

"Your father knows it wasn't you."

"Verna, did you ever think that maybe Daddy's wrong, too?"

"You know what your brother did."

"But unconditional love means you love a person even when they totally screw up." She sighed. "Right?"

"Right."

That said it all. Harper had screwed up—literally and figuratively. Yet Trinity wasn't about to forgive. Had she ever loved him at all? He'd been using her, but she'd used him, too. The question was, what had she been using him to get?

What she'd gotten was Scott, but good God, why did she miss him so when she couldn't even identify what he gave her?

* * *

COMING up on three weeks Scott-free, Trinity was doing quite well with Operation Cold Turkey. She hardly thought about him more than a couple hundred times a day, which was down from a thousand when she first started. A vast improvement overall.

The sleepless nights still bothered her. The fantasies. Waking up overheated, perspiring, her breath rapid, her nipples hard, her body wet. It was so darn lonely masturbating in her bed, yet it was far worse when the shudders melted away. That's when she missed him the most, his breath against her hair, his arms around her. God, even his voice.

But . . . she wasn't going to think about all that. She'd gone cold turkey, and she was doing fine on a Friday morning when the March sun was shining and the air was crisp outside. No rain.

Her computer beeped for a new company e-mail as she slid into her secretarial chair. *IRice* came up on the screen, and Trinity caught the groan a hairy second before it exploded from her lips. Then she clicked and read.

"I cannot deal with this total a-hole anymore. Look at the crap he's written. I have had it. He demands to speak to you. As my supervisor, kindly take care of the matter."

Trinity snorted. Now she had Inga fobbing her work off. Then again, the buck gets passed *up* the command chain. She'd wished for an improvement in the tension between herself and Inga, even a mild step. Maybe having Inga ask for help with a vendor was progress. Trinity began reading the nested back and forth replies to see how Inga had screwed it all up.

After five minutes, Trinity had to admit Inga hadn't screwed up anything. She'd been polite, conciliatory, and accommodating. The vendor was, quite simply, a total a-hole.

She wrote Inga back. Of course, she could have gotten up, walked there, and talked personally, except that Inga's cube had been empty just now when Trinity passed by after making copies.

"You handled the situation with admirable restraint," she

wrote. "I will take over from here. Please provide me with the vendor file."

Inga must have returned, because she shot back an e-mail right away, and Trinity's computer beeped again.

"He's a complete asshole, and he owes me apology."

Trinity sighed. "I will make sure he understands the way he handled the situation was inappropriate." She hit Send.

Beep. She almost growled. How could Inga type that fast?

"But don't you agree he's a complete asshole?" Then in capitals, "THIS GUY IS A COMPLETE ASSHOLE!"

She'd never seen Inga quite so worked up—unless it was directed at Trinity herself. Still, she wrote with sensitivity. "I agree that he has mismanaged the matter. I will make it my utmost priority to rectify the problem."

Trinity sat for a moment after she'd sent her reply. Inga had turned to her for help. It was a huge step, and she couldn't let it go by without acknowledgment.

At Inga's cubicle, she rapped on the metal joining. Inga whirled on her chair, stopping the circle with one foot planted on the carpet. "What?"

Trinity ignored the tone. "I wanted to say you dealt with him very diplomatically."

"I'm always diplomatic."

Jeez, she was giving the woman a compliment. "Of course. But you went beyond the call of duty, and I appreciate it."

She waited for Inga to jump down her throat.

Amazingly, Inga didn't. Instead she shrugged and played with her earlobe. "Thanks."

Wow. Maybe she'd found a way to effect a cease-fire with the woman. Trinity smiled.

From her cubicle, Christina hissed at her as Trinity passed, and waggled a stack of invoices. "If you can look them over, these need to go out this afternoon."

"Sure." Most of what Trinity did as supervisor was check over someone else's work to make sure it was correct. Tipping her head as she walked away, she figured things weren't so bad. Christina came to her with questions, and now Inga had asked her to intercede. True, the other three Accounts Payable clerks went to Inga for everything, but Trinity had succeeded in two out of the five battles. Having won over Inga, it was only a matter of time before the others tumbled like dominoes.

She tossed the sheaf of invoices on her desk, and for a very brief moment, thought of checking for an e-mail from Scott. That, however, would be a losing battle, making her miss him more. After three weeks, he wouldn't suddenly break down and e-mail. They were done. She had to ignore the hitch in her chest.

Instead she ticked off a few things on each invoice. They were system-generated, using the information off the order, plus the ship dates, etc., and all she looked for was if something burped. For herself, Trinity used the invoices to learn the customer base, the big hitters, location, credit status, and so on. As the sales team branched out since the merger with Castle, it was Trinity's job to do credit checks on new customers.

She flipped a checked invoice onto the approved pile. On the next, everything was fine, a new customer buying prototypes, small potatoes, but with potential. She keyed the customer number into the system, and something turned over in her stomach.

Millennium Robotics. She could almost hear the company's recording. *You've reached Millennium Robotics. If you know your party's extension, you can dial it now . . .*

And she would punch in Scott's number.

Dear God, please do not let this be Scott's company.

Data populated her screen. Trinity swallowed. Her guardian angel wasn't listening. She knew the address, the number, the company logo. All off his business card. Millennium Robotics.

She stood, as if that would change all those data fields. Her stomach turned over. What if he found out who she was? What would Daddy say if Scott revealed what she'd been up to?

"What were you thinking?" Trinity whispered, and started to shake in her high heels.

"Did you need something, Trinity?" Christina called through the divider.

Yes, she needed something. A new life. Except that *this* was her new life, and she'd messed it up the same as her old life.

"Just talking to myself." As if she were a crazy person.

Trinity gulped a needed breath of air.

She *had* gone crazy for a couple of minutes. She was a lowly supervisor next to big CFO Scott. How would he *ever* meet her? She was blowing everything out of proportion. That was the problem with Scott. She was too mixed up for a relationship with him. She'd had a major triumph with Inga, things were turning the corner in employee relations. She was becoming a stronger person—until his company's name sent her into a tailspin.

As much as she dreamed about him, wanted him, missed him, he was bad for her. She *would* kick her addiction.

Yet it was like dying a little to think of never hearing his voice again.

THE last three weeks had been worse than anything he suffered after Katy told him she wanted a divorce. Things with his wife had been poor for so long that the divorce had almost been a relief. Yes, he'd tried to talk her out of it, for the sake of twenty-two years of marriage and for the girls. Yet in his heart, he'd known for months, maybe years, that it was over. Katy simply said it aloud.

Jezebel had left him a voice mail saying all was fine, had a great time, thanks for the laughs, not his fault, but she was outta there. He'd never gotten a Dear John voice mail before. He'd hoped she would change her mind. Here it was another Monday morning, three *weeks* later, and his in-box was still empty.

He had to laugh, even if it was pathetic. Dating and romance were no longer done face-to-face. It was an e-mail address and an in-box. How the world had changed. And he was stuck in the middle, not knowing how to find her again.

"Scott, are you ready?"

Grace braced herself on his doorjamb. They had a contract

meeting with the new plating and machining vendor. Plant tour, lunch, the works. If Rudd hadn't insisted he go, Scott would have left it to Grace. She needed more exposure anyway.

But not *that* kind of exposure. Here was a whole new Grace. In his opinion, her dress was too short for a business meeting, its neckline low cut. But God forbid he should say anything, because honestly, it was still respectable.

If Jezebel wore the outfit? He'd be drooling. The woman had him drooling, and he hadn't seen her in twenty-one days. He could not allow himself to believe she was gone for good. Christ, if he thought that . . . hell, it didn't bear thinking about.

He rose, grabbed his keys out of his desk. "Ready. You have the contract folder?"

She waved it. "Right here. Ron said he'll meet us there. He's got another meeting over that way this afternoon."

"What about Engineering?" They were supposed to have a technical guy in on the conference.

"Coming straight from home."

"Fine." He grabbed his suit jacket off the rack. Then he eyed her. "You got something afterwards? Because we can go separately." He wouldn't mind the time by himself to think.

She shook her head. There was something different about her hair, but what? The color? "No, I'm coming straight back, so we might as well go together."

"Okay. I'll drive."

In the parking lot, he politely opened her door. When he climbed into the driver's seat, he noticed the hem of her dress riding too high on her thighs. Damn. Made him a little uncomfortable. She'd be the only woman at the meeting, and he didn't want the Green execs thinking . . . what the hell did it matter? In a work world where damn near every day had become a casual day, at least she wasn't wearing a pair of baggy jeans.

His mind drifted on the short drive. Grace talked, mostly about the few contract changes, and he nodded agreement without focusing on what she said. They'd already gone over it, made the adjustments, had a plan of action, but maybe she was a tad nervous sitting in a silent car.

"I did find a great gym."

Yep, she was definitely feeling strained by the silence. "That's great." He wondered if he was expected to make a comment on her fitness. Whatever he said could be misconstrued, not that he figured Grace was the type to be upset by a harmless comment.

"If you're interested in trying it, they have guest passes."

He smiled his thanks. "I'm fine with the gym I go to."

"I know, you probably think it's such a meat market at those co-ed places. The new pickup joint."

He glanced at her. "The thought hadn't occurred to me."

Thank God the Green facility came up on the right. Poor Grace was obviously uncomfortable alone with him, filling the time with any inane conversation. He hadn't noticed her difficulty with small talk before, probably because their discussions were always business. Except for the time she'd told him about her divorce in the sparest of details.

Ron Rudd was in the lobby when they entered, and Dave Skidman, the engineer, jogged in behind them. The president's secretary arrived shortly thereafter to guide the group up to the boardroom for the meeting. An older woman with a gaze of steel, she handed out badges, then led them from the lobby entrance.

At the end of the procession, Rudd grabbed his arm on the stairs. "I sent you an e-mail."

Holy shit. *Rudd* sent him those damn pictures? He hadn't received one in weeks. He'd thought it was over. Now his heart pounded, and for a second he had the unconscionable urge to beat the man's face in.

"I outlined two scenarios for improving the bottom line."

The red haze faded from his vision. Damn, he had a one-track mind. Jezebel, making love to Jezebel in his office, tasting her on a hotel room floor, watching her give herself the best damn orgasm. And photos someone took of the two of them.

"I haven't seen the e-mail yet," he managed.

"I want profitability up, Sinclair." Unspoken was that Rudd wanted it done at any cost, ethics be damned.

Scott kept his voice low as the others moved ahead up the stairs. "It's the eleventh hour, Ron. The auditors want to sign off the beginning of next week. Nothing changes now." Stepping back, he pulled his arm free. "We know all the reasons why it happened. The sales forecast was overstated, and we put the M4 out too early. The warranty costs screwed us last year." They were still experiencing the fallout, but at least they'd learned the lesson. New product introduction would go more smoothly now, as evidenced by today's meeting and the rigorous qualification they'd put this supplier through. Last year, however, was sunk. "Let's table the rest of the discussion for later." A vendor's office was not the optimum place.

"Our jobs are on the line. You *need* to find something."

Correction. Rudd's job was on the line. He'd pushed for the M4's early release in order to boost sales to meet forecast.

Scott gave the man a last critical look. Would he try blackmail to save his ass? Could he be responsible for those pictures? If he was, then he was taking a damn long time to make his demands. Time was running out. They had only a couple of weeks left to finalize the SEC's 10K reporting.

No. Rudd would have clearly stated his demands already. The man didn't pussyfoot when he wanted something.

Grace waited at the top of the stairs, her glance flicking between them as if assessing the potential impact the secretive conversation might have on her.

To her right, the ladies' room door opened, a blonde stepping out. For a moment, she reminded him of Jezebel. He'd never stop thinking about her, never stop wanting her . . .

The blonde's sharp inhale audible, Grace moved aside.

And the bottom of Scott's world fell away, a chasm yawning at his feet. Jesus. Her blue eyes locked with his, Jezebel backed up against the restroom door. He scented her perfume on the air, a mixture of sweet and citrus. Maybe it was her shampoo, her lotion, her smooth gorgeous skin. Jesus, he had to touch her to see if she was real.

"This way, gentlemen, ma'am." Herman Green's secretary tried to herd the group down the hall.

Only Ron Rudd at his back got Scott's feet moving.

He wanted to make a fucking scene. He wanted to drag her back into the ladies' room, lock the door, find out who the hell she was, why she left him, then shove her up against the door and take her, claim her, fuck her, and show her she was *his*.

Instead, like a lamb, he followed the secretary. At the boardroom door, the last to enter, he stopped her.

"The woman back there, I recognize her from somewhere."

The woman assessed him with sharp gray eyes. "She's Mr. Green's daughter. Perhaps you know her from the country club."

Holy hell. She couldn't be *his* Jezebel. "I don't belong to a country club."

"Then you don't know her," she said, speech clipped, a flare to her nostrils. Like Mama Bear protecting Goldilocks from the Big Bad Wolf—except that he was mixing fairy tales—or as if he weren't good enough to lick the bottom of fair Goldilocks's shoe.

"But she works here," he insisted.

"They're waiting for you, sir."

Yeah. He'd be meeting Herman Green, who *would* reveal his daughter's name if Scott had to use every trick in the book.

"CLOSE your office door."

Scott's voice over the phone made Trinity's knees quake, and she wasn't even standing up. "I'm sorry, sir, do I know you?"

He paused. "I'm the man who went down on you three weeks ago in front of Norman. Isn't that right, Miss Trinity Green?"

She gulped and answered his original question. "I don't have an office." What would he think of her? She was a lowly office worker, a supervisor without even an office of her own.

He didn't seem to care. "I guess you'll just have to listen to me make myself come."

God. She'd known he'd figure out who she was, she just didn't think it would happen so quickly. The meeting in the conference room had gone on until eleven. She'd walked by to check several times. Then Daddy and Connor, who'd come over for the contract finalization, had given the new customers the grand tour. Trinity hid in the file room, ostensibly looking up old invoices. She'd released a sigh of relief when the bigwigs trooped off for lunch.

By two o'clock, he'd found her. She wanted to die with mortification, yet cry with relief because God help her, she'd missed him so.

"Maybe I should call you later to discuss this further." Anything to avoid the confrontation now. She wasn't ready. She hadn't planned her explanation.

She hadn't figured out what to do now that he knew who she was.

"I need it now, sweet Trinity."

The unmistakable rasp of his zipper crackled over the phone, as if he held the cell down to his pants.

"Where *are* you?" she whispered.

"In a very secluded park. In fact, I could fuck you in the backseat and no one would be the wiser. Why don't you meet me?"

He was crass, crude, even insulting, yet he lit her on fire with a combination of fear and sexual combustion. "I can't."

"I want your mouth on my cock right now." He groaned, and she covered the mouthpiece as if someone might hear him.

This was supposed to be over. They'd crossed a line, done things they shouldn't have, and he was starting it all again. And Lord, how she *wanted* it. "What are you doing?"

"You can't help yourself, can you? You need to know if I'm stroking my cock to the sound of your voice, don't you?"

It was like an uncontrollable throb in her chest. "Yes."

He lowered his voice, turned lazy and seductive. "Yeah, I'm stroking. I'm so fucking hard, and my briefs are all wet. I had to stop on the way back to work because I couldn't wait. When I close my eyes, I imagine it's your hand on me."

He made her panties damp, and her heart thumped every time someone walked past her cubicle, yet she couldn't hang up.

"Do you want to suck me?"

"Yes," she whispered.

"Do you want to swallow my come?"

"Yes." Please.

"Christ, I've missed you."

And she'd missed him. She could taste him on her tongue, and his words turned her heart over in her chest. God, how good they were. Frighteningly good. She *needed* him.

"Meet me. Now. I want to come in you or on you, with you."

"I can't." Yet the strength of her desire forced her to her feet right there in her cubicle.

"You have to, you need to. You want my cock so bad you can't resist. It's only ten minutes, Trinity, and you can have me. I'm all yours."

His voice seduced her. She couldn't breathe, and her blood buzzed in her ears as if she'd had a powerful orgasm. Or needed one so badly she'd do anything. She wanted to rush to the women's room and put her hand between her legs. If she'd been on her cell rather than her work phone, she would have.

That's why he was so dangerous. Because she *would* do anything for him. In ways, he was like every other man, making her lose her sense of self. Worse, with him, she craved it.

"I have to work," she whispered, almost pleading for him to stop torturing her.

"I wanna come now, all over you, baby. I want you to stroke me." His voice quaked, his breathing harsh, then he groaned. "Fuck me with your mouth, please, Trinity, Trinity, Trinity."

He came with a sharp, guttural sound she felt right up in her womb, and her name on his lips turned her heart over. She hadn't realized how good it would be, how momentous. How absolutely, utterly frightening. He'd called her *baby*.

The receiver between her breasts, Trinity depressed the hook flash on the phone. He knew her name, held all the cards. She couldn't resist him. She was obsessed. The next time he called, she'd meet him and do anything he wanted.

Even if she lost everything in the process.

HIS car beneath a shady tree at the far end of the park's lot, Scott leaned his head back against the car seat.

Christ. He'd cleaned up, zipped his pants, but he still couldn't move. The orgasm had been hard, heavy, draining him. Simply because she'd been on the other end of the phone.

Wrong. Her name had done it for him. She couldn't hide. She was his. All he had to do was make her see that.

He could be so fucking good for her. She excited him, made him feel aware, all his nerves alive. The next time he called, he'd get her to meet him. He'd almost had her this time, but he figured she hadn't gotten over the shock of losing her anonymity.

Glancing at his watch, he saw the afternoon ticking away. He'd made an excuse, palming Grace off on Dave, getting the engineer to drive her back to the office.

It was time to leave his fantasy world behind and get back to work. Tonight, however, he'd plan his next assault.

He'd given up on Katy, let her walk away. It was a shitty thing to admit, but he'd given up on loving her. She didn't want anything he had to offer, and he'd let her go as if she were a helium balloon floating into the air.

He wasn't going to let go of Trinity Green. He wanted the passion she made him feel.

He would make her feel it, too.

SHE was going to be sick.

"He was *very* interested in you, sweetheart."

Her father had insisted she dine at his house. She wanted to go home and hide. Daddy wouldn't take no for an answer.

The maid set the plate in front of her, and the wafting scent of meat turned Trinity's stomach. So did the conversation, which had been entirely about Mr. Scott Sinclair. When she'd stepped out of the restroom and seen him, she wanted the floor to open up and swallow her whole like that Bible story where the whale swallowed . . . somebody. On the phone, she realized resistance was futile. But good Lord, this was infinitely worse. Her father was trying to set her up with a man she'd had sex with, several times, in various naughty locales, and she wasn't even divorced yet. How could this have happened?

What if Scott told her father how they met?

She could only do one thing. Change the subject. "Daddy, we need to talk about Lance."

"I'm not talking about Lance."

"I want to make sure you know I didn't send that letter."

"I know you didn't." He waved his fork at her. "Now eat your chops."

She picked at the lamb chops. That's what Scott did to her—threw her off her food even as she couldn't stop hearing his groan when he came over the phone. She was so naughty.

"He's CFO of Millennium," Daddy went on as if he were a bulldog with a nice, big fat meaty bone.

With Scott's eyes on her this morning, she felt as if she suddenly had a big red *S* painted on her chest. *S* for slut. "Who's a CFO?" She pretended confusion as she struggled for a way to shift her father offtrack.

"Scott Sinclair. I told you. The new customer." He waggled his eyebrows. "I think he wants to ask you for a date."

Lord. She could not handle her father matchmaking for her. "Daddy, he's got to be in his midforties."

"Ahah!" he crowed, "so you did notice him."

She rolled her eyes. "What did you tell him about me?"

Her father shrugged. "Nothing. He asked who you were, I told him, and that was that."

Trinity pursed her lips. "Daddy. The tips of your ears are getting red, which means you're not telling me the truth."

"My ears do not get red."

"They do. Just like Pinocchio's nose grows."

He laughed, and her heart turned over. He had such a boisterous, wonderful laugh, and she'd missed it terribly in the last few months.

"You're a poet," he quipped, "and you didn't even know it."

"I'm not letting you sidetrack me." She gritted her teeth. "What did you tell him?"

He expelled a gust of air. "He asked who you were. 'Who was that beautiful woman,'" he mimicked. "And I said, 'That lovely lady is my daughter.'"

"And?" she prompted.

He grimaced. "This and that, nothing important."

God. *This and that* could be anything from her name to telling a certain interested stranger she wasn't divorced yet. Men were like that, unable to see the subtle differences between *this* and *that*. She hadn't exactly lied to Scott. She'd just failed to mention the divorce wasn't final. Okay, she failed to mention that she hadn't even started divorce proceedings until *after* she met Scott. Yet from the moment she'd stepped into her bathroom, she knew in her heart she would divorce Harper.

But what did it matter? This thing with Scott *had* to be over. He had the ability to turn her inside out and get her to do things she'd never consider in real life. That said it all. Scott wasn't part of her *real* life. He was a fantasy.

She laid down her knife and fork. "Daddy." She put her hand over his. "I need you to listen very carefully. I just had my marriage end very badly. I do not want you setting me up with another man. Promise?"

Her father shook his head sadly. "I'm sorry Harper did this to you. You deserved so much better." His gaze hardened. "You deserve a man who's going to take care of you."

"I've got a job, Daddy. I'm taking care of myself."

Right. She still had her mother's trust, and if it weren't for that, she wouldn't have the money to cover the cost of her groceries, let alone a mortgage. It was pathetic. She was a spoiled rich bitch. Her father still had to pick out men to take care of her because he didn't trust her judgment in choosing a winner herself.

She'd proven her abysmal judgment by taunting Scott into making that challenge with Norman. And she was weak, because the moment she saw Scott again, all she could think of was how damn good he looked. She wanted to climb his body and take his tongue in her mouth. She'd wanted to run to him this afternoon.

God, she was a slut. Something had gone very, very wrong with her sense of right and wrong the night she let him into her hotel room. If her poor mother had lived . . . she couldn't even think about what her mother would say. Good girls didn't do the things Trinity had done.

Good girls didn't *love* doing them, either.

"Daddy, I'm begging you. Please don't try fixing me up."

She could only pray her father listened to her. Because she cer-

tainly hadn't shown any sense of control or restraint around Scott
up to this point.

SCOTT slumped in front of his office computer, staring blindly.
The entire afternoon, his mind had been all over her. Back at work,
he'd slammed Rudd's idiotic *scenarios* for messing with the bottom
line, snapped at Elton, forgotten a conference call, then holed up in
his office waiting for the end of the day. He'd been alone half an
hour, contemplating *her*. Driving himself crazy.

Outside, the night had turned dark and moonless, and a biting
rain rolled in, slashing at the windows. The fresh storm fit his mood.

He knew he shouldn't have done it, but he researched her on the
Net and came across a wedding announcement not even six months
old. Why the hell hadn't Herman Green come right out and told
him to back off because she was married? Instead, the man had
seemed encouraging. Dammit, this last month had probably been
some lark for her while Harper Harrington the Third was out of
town somewhere. What the hell kind of name was that anyway? It
stank of *rich* and *gaudy*.

Scott knew he sounded petty, like a kid who'd gotten his favorite toy taken away from him for bad behavior.

But fuck, fuck, fuck, he wanted to—

His e-mail beeped. Sure as hell, his pulse rate kicked up hoping
it was her. She needed him, wanted him. Yet, she was married. He
couldn't tear the solid steel block out of his gut.

He maximized the e-mail program only to find it *wasn't* her.

Shit. He sat up. The infamous e-mail address, with another attachment. Why come back after three weeks of silence? He opened
and read, and the steel block rose to choke him.

"Do you really want to throw yourself away on a slut like her?
She could cost you big-time if you're not careful."

For five full seconds, he couldn't move, rage immobilizing his muscles like handcuffs. He ached to punch his fist through the monitor and come out with his hands wrapped around the e-mailer's scrawny throat. She was *not* a slut. She was passionate and mysterious, gorgeous and tantalizing.

And cheating on her husband.

He clicked on the attachment, and a stunning, high-resolution photo filled the screen. Norman was clearly visible, as was Scott, but his profile obscured her face. Still, she made his insides steam up, his cock hard, his mouth water. Sitting on the barstool that night, she'd allowed him to slip his arm around her shoulders as she seduced Norman with a smile on her red lips. A need had boiled in Scott during that moment. He'd wanted to hoist her up on the bar and take her for all to see. His cock had been a raging, painful ache he couldn't slake.

Until he had her in Norman's hotel room. And even then, it wasn't enough, would never be enough. Need and desire etched into the lines of his face just as someone snapped his picture.

Primitive tribes felt that a picture stole one's soul. Whoever took this one had stolen that moment, perverted it.

Flipping back to the e-mail, Scott hit Reply.

"Who the hell are you and what exactly do you want? I'm sick of your fucking games."

Trinity Green had already ripped out his heart, and he was done with this crap. Almost in the blink of an eye, his computer beeped. He opened.

"I know what you did in that hotel."

His heart stopped altogether.

The two people who knew what he'd done in that hotel room were in the photo with him.

Had Trinity Green set him up?

She and Norman had been there when he arrived. She *said* Norman was from out of town, but Scott didn't know for sure. How did he know for sure that Norman was a stranger to her? Until today, he didn't know anything about her.

And look how she'd struggled to keep it that way.

Norman could be the infamous Harper Asshole Harrington the Third. Had they set him up together? A cameraman in the bar, then a hidden camera in the hotel room? Did she have someone following them the whole time, snapping pictures? He'd knocked on her door that first night, and she'd seen an easy mark. She hadn't figured that he'd ever find out who she was.

His whole body screamed in agony, his flesh stretched over his cheekbones, a stabbing pain like a nail driving through his temple into his brain.

Punching the Forward key, he tapped in her address, and his fingers actually shook as he typed his message.

"Are you fucking blackmailing me now? And I understand you're married as well. Maybe Norman is your husband, and you two are out to make a buck. What kind of woman lets another man go down on her in front of her husband?"

He didn't feel one goddamn bit better after he pushed Send. He was overreacting, getting carried away, jumping to unwarranted conclusions, but he felt like a gutted fish with the hook still stuck in his throat.

Even the possibility that she was using him shouldn't fucking hurt like this. She was nothing more than a good lay. And hell, they'd only done that once.

She was a fantasy, a figment of his imagination—the woman he *wanted* her to be rather than what she truly was. Yet it was like watching someone trample your dream into dust. And yeah, it was far worse than the night Katy asked for the divorce. By that time, he'd already lost his expectations and hopes.

With Jezebel, his dreams had only just begun.

18

TRINITY had driven round and round the downtown parking garage beneath Scott's offices, then found his sedan in the same space he'd occupied before. He hadn't left work yet, thank God, because she didn't know where he lived. She hadn't called his office or his cell phone because she'd been afraid he'd hang up.

The night was cold, the downpour incessant since five thirty. She tugged her coat tight as she waited by the side of Scott's car. The things he'd accused her of in his e-mail punched a hole right through her heart. She could not have him think she was a cheat, a liar, a blackmailer, and a whore.

Her tummy trembled. Harper had to be the culprit. He wanted his cut before he got out. But how had he known Scott's e-mail address? Had he been sneaking into the condo, looking at her computer? However it was done, she'd stuck Scott in the middle of it. Involved him. She shivered.

Light spilled out from the elevator as the door opened with a *whoosh*. He was so tall, he ducked automatically as he exited.

A pulse ticked at her temple. He was beautiful. Men could be beautiful, or maybe it was in the eye of the beholder. The dark suit jacket set off the silver streaks in his hair, the white shirt contrasting with the tan he hadn't lost from the summer. His legs ate up the concrete with a determined stride. And she wanted to melt at his feet.

He didn't see her until he beeped the remote, and then he was close enough for her to see the pupils of his eyes dilate.

She wanted to touch him, but though he was feet away physically, he was miles off in emotional distance.

She'd memorized the lines of his e-mail and answered every question. "My name is Trinity Green. I would never blackmail you. Norman isn't my husband. I am married, but I'm getting a divorce. I was at the hotel that first night"—something flared in his eyes and was gone an instant later—"because I found my husband cheating." She gulped in a breath. "I don't know what kind of person . . ." She couldn't say it, not the way he had. "I don't know how I could have done *that* with another man watching." Her mother, rest her soul, would turn over in her grave.

Maybe she was a slut, just as the e-mail had said, but one thing Trinity Green had never been was a coward, and she held her head high waiting for him to speak.

He switched his briefcase to a two-handed grip, car keys dangling from his fingers. "I'm sorry about your husband, but you should have told me."

"You asked to watch me. You didn't ask if I was married."

He closed his eyes for the count of two. "You're right. Still, I wouldn't have gone on if I'd known you weren't divorced."

"I told you in the beginning that I was *recently* divorced," she defended, although there was no defense. "I didn't think any further details were your business."

He closed the distance, towering over her, his eyes deep, dark, rich with anger. "I fucked you. It was my business."

The backs of her eyeballs ached, and her lids stung when she blinked. "You called it lust. It was just for fun. I didn't owe you anything." Yet how could *fun* hurt this badly?

He set down his briefcase, the scent of his body erotic, laced as it was with the aroma of rain and ozone on wet concrete that seeped down from street level. "Again, you're right. I pushed for more than you wanted to give."

This close, he made her head swim. She couldn't think. "That's why I did . . ." Again, she couldn't say it. "I did that thing with you and Norman because I wanted to . . ." Articulating her thoughts would make it worse.

He cupped her jaw, and the touch almost made her fall, it was so sweet, so gentle.

"Because you wanted to put me in my place," he supplied the correct answer.

"Yes," she whispered, then listened to herself. "No. I mean, I didn't do *that* to put you in your place. I wanted to tease you when you arrived." That wasn't sounding better.

"But you got carried away with the whole idea."

She blinked. His eyes were such a deep gorgeous brown, no longer biting with anger. "Yes."

With one last step, his body nearly flush with hers, he dropped his voice to a mesmerizing level. "You were so fucking sexy, I needed it all. Your mouth on me, your juice on my lips." He tipped her chin up with his thumb. "I wanted him to see it, want it, and know he couldn't have it, that you were mine."

Trinity couldn't breathe. It had been so intensely exciting despite her conflicted emotions about it later.

He dipped his head until his lips were so close she could almost taste him. "We were both guilty of getting carried away. And I did trick you on Valentine's Day. I'm sorry for that."

She didn't need the apology. She needed him to kiss her. Instead he trailed his fingers along her jaw, down her throat, the pads a little rough, lighting up every nerve ending. Dipping down inside her coat, blunt fingernails tracing the swell of her breast against the scooped neckline, he shifted her brassiere to find her nipple inside. He flicked, she moaned, unsure if her legs would hold her.

Then there was six inches of air between them, and she was dizzy with the change.

"I screwed up sending you that e-mail. I don't believe you'd blackmail me. You wouldn't intentionally set out to hurt me." His chest rose and fell beneath his shirt, and she detected the rapid beat of his heart against the white material.

She put her hand over the pulse, his heat racing through her palm, up her arm, straight down to her clitoris. "Thank you." She thought of telling him about Harper, her first suspicion that her almost-ex might be capable of blackmail, but Harper had a right to answer the accusation first. Despite what he'd done. "I know it seems silly that I rushed here rather than call." She waved a hand at his car. "You might have already gone home."

He captured her hand. "Come home with me, Trinity Green."

Her heart stopped, stuttered, sparked, and finally beat again. She had all sorts of excuses. It was late, after seven. They both had to work tomorrow. She didn't have any fresh clothing with her. No toothbrush. Or makeup. "Yes."

"I'll drive."

"No, I'll follow you." She told herself this was for tonight. She'd go cold turkey tomorrow. Things she'd been afraid of, that he'd have control, she'd have to wear her mask again, she'd fail to find her identity, they were all still true. But for tonight, she needed to be with him.

He blocked her in. "You'll come with me. I'll take you back tomorrow." He was done letting her run things, of course.

She tried again. "I want you to drive me back tonight."

He held her gaze. "You'll spend the night."

It was all a test. "Scott—"

"Trinity." He seemed to enjoy saying her name, as if it were a victory sign.

He smelled so good, but she could have resisted if it were mere sex he offered. What she couldn't resist was how he'd made her feel all those nights. Free to be anything she wanted, to step outside herself, to experience every tantalizing touch, to savor each new taste. He approved of everything she did to him, all that she begged him to do to her. She needed to feel wanted and accepted one more time. "We'll have to get up very early."

He wound her hair around his finger. "That's not a problem, because we won't be going to sleep."

THE marked contrast between the two women he'd had in the car today exhilarated him. With Jezebel—Trinity—his sense of anticipation and excitement was tangible, physical, a third presence in the car. He could feel his own heartbeat throb in his ears, and his skin tingled as if he stood beneath the sting of a shower. Every touch she bestowed, every breath she took, every move she made enthralled him. It was a damn good thing his subconscious knew the route over the mountain highway.

She wasn't married. The elation that hit him with her revelation almost brought him to his knees, but he'd managed to stand before her appearing unaffected. He'd been an idiot, jealous, angry. Nor could she have engineered the photos. Someone with a guest badge had done that, an auditor badge. It couldn't have been her.

As he turned onto his street, his home a mile away, she curled in her seat, pulling her knees up. "Is your house clean?"

Scott laughed. It was the last thing he expected. "Why?"

He felt her shrug as if he were touching her. "It tells about you as a person. Like if you're the beer-guzzling sports-fan type with empty cans and pizza cartons all over the place."

Damn, she amused him in every incarnation. "I have to admit," he said, negotiating a curve on the hill, "that I'm not the beer-guzzling type." He glanced sideways. "Does that make me less of a man in your eyes?"

"No," she whispered, "it makes you heavenly. No woman likes to compete with beer and football."

That she thought of him in terms beyond sex ratcheted his anticipation higher. She would not be a onetimer, he'd make sure of it. "I sometimes like a good Bordeaux in the evenings, and I'm pretty damn sure I left last night's empty on the living room coffee table." The road curled round a magnificent oak the developers had left, splitting the two lanes down the middle. His car passed under the branches, a natural arbor.

"Naughty, naughty," she said.

"The sheets are clean. I have a woman in once a week." He wasn't a neat freak, but he did have limits.

"I'm glad you're not a total slob."

He wondered if he should share the story of once finding the vibrator from the side table drawer directly in the center of the freshly made bed. He'd let that lady go, of course, but he'd always wondered what the message had been. Disgust or a desire to test it out? Whatever, he couldn't allow someone in his house who went through his drawers. The vibrator had been something he'd hoped to use on a female friend, but she'd preferred her own, and shortly after, the relationship ended. Pulling into the driveway, he pondered the possibilities in the untried toy.

His breath stilled in his chest, and his cock shouted. Christ, he'd love to use it on her, Trinity. He hadn't gotten used to her name yet, but he would after tonight.

"Nice house."

"Thanks." He was proud of the place, which he'd purchased after the divorce. It would never have been Katy's style, but hell, he admitted to loving the life out here, even with the heavy rains. "And I did make my bed this morning."

"Good boy," she murmured as she popped her door handle.

The husky pitch of her voice strummed his nerve endings, and he could almost feel her fingers on his skin as she trailed them along the bushes.

A low-slung bungalow, the entryway an atrium surrounded on three sides by the U-shape of the house. In the spring, the blooming bushes were a riot of color. The previous owner had been a master gardener. Scott merely maintained. The house itself had been plunked down on a hill in the middle of the forest, though the trees had been thinned and the so-called garden populated with camellias, azaleas, and rhododendrons.

As he set his keys in the lock, she pondered his choice. "I would have imagined you more as the condo type with all the amenities, pool, hot tub, gym."

"I don't like sharing walls with my neighbors."

The door opened into the large entry hall, separated from the living room by the open fireplace.

She took the two steps down to his favorite area. "Wow."

Sure enough, he'd left the empty wineglass on the coffee table, yet he liked that she was impressed by the wall of windows looking out over the ravine and the rise of the Santa Cruz Mountains. The houses on either side were hidden by the growth of redwood, dogwood, oak, and pine, yet there was room for the deer to forage and form their trails.

"The view is better in the daytime." Right now, without a full moon to paint the picture, the scene was just a dark shadow.

"I bet it's cool during a thunderstorm."

He hadn't thought about it, but yes, it was "cool" with the hard beat of the rain on the roof and lightning setting the sky ablaze above the mountains.

Yet she was more fascinating than any storm. "Take your clothes off."

Her eyes darkened to the deep blue of a storm-tossed ocean, and she didn't move a single muscle to do as he bid. Yet a pulse beat fast at her throat. He wanted her now, in his house, at his mercy, willing to let him do the things he'd fantasized about.

There was no witness this time, and he wanted to push her farther, deeper, make her as crazy as she made him when all the power lay in her palm. She loved having the control, but he knew he could make her love giving it all up to him even more. From almost the first moment he'd seen her, this was what he'd wanted, to touch her, excite her, push her limits and surpass his own.

Scott sat in a gold wing chair facing the TV, but kept his gaze on her. Watching. Waiting. Anticipating how she'd react.

Trinity saw all that and more in his eyes. And she couldn't move. "You don't have blinds over the windows."

"There's no one out there to see."

She tingled to imagine that there was. A college freshman home for the week. Somewhere along the way with Scott, she'd given up nice for naughty, and Trinity wanted to preen. His gaze like a physical touch caressing her breasts, he made her feel beautiful despite the fact that her stomach was no longer perfectly flat and she'd become conscious of how her hips filled out her dress.

"Don't I get a glass of Bordeaux?" She'd never had Bordeaux because it sounded so fantastically rich and fattening.

Scott rose, doing a slow pace around her, his breath stirring her hair. "Lose the shoes," he murmured.

Kicking them off, she watched in the window's reflection as he leaned close to inhale her scent. His lids drifted shut a moment, he swallowed, then a low sound rose from his belly. Distanced by the reflection yet feeling his heat, his breath, scenting his skin, it was all so incredibly erotic, as if she were a participant and a voyeur all at the same time.

The full length of his body caressing her from behind, he slid his hands round her middle to the tie of her coat and pulled it loose. "Your wish is my command," he murmured, "but first let's get rid of this."

Dragging it down her arms halfway, he held her trapped, the sleeves binding her hands behind her. She felt a moment of helplessness, vulnerability, and yet it was tantalizing. Then he tugged her free and threw the coat across the sofa. His chin resting on the top of her head, he gazed at their images in the window. "Don't move."

Was it pathetic to like to feel dominated? So taken by him? Giving up control could open her to the same kind of devastation she'd experienced with Harper. And yet . . . this was different in a way she couldn't explain even to herself. Her eyes followed as he passed through an arch into the dining area, then disappeared beyond the wall. She couldn't have moved even if she'd had a mind to.

Waiting by his car for him, she'd had things to apologize for. The omission about Harper, the fear that her lies would cause Scott trouble she never intended. She'd let him gather her into his car and bring her here, and she'd never even considered that not another soul on the planet knew where she was.

His footsteps on the hardwood dining room floor heralded his return. In the kitchen, he'd removed his suit jacket. A deep purple wine filled the goblet he handed her. He could have doctored it, dropped in a drug, arsenic, anything.

"Taste it," he whispered as if he were offering beluga caviar or lobster dripping with butter. Or a drop of his come.

Trinity put the glass to her lips, raised the stem, and let the warm, woody wine slip over her tongue. Spicy, a taste fruity, a hint of bitterness that enhanced rather than detracted.

Angled to her side, he pulled her hair back, tracing the rim of her ear as he tucked the locks away. "Good?"

"Yes." She wasn't a wine connoisseur nor knowledgeable about poisons, but wasn't arsenic bitter?

"It's a Syrah. I thought you might like it."

"I thought you were going to give me Bordeaux." Maybe Syrah masked a drug taste more easily.

"Another sip." He tapped the bottom of the glass.

His heat all around her, his male scent calling to her, Trinity lifted the goblet to her lips again and drank more deeply, swirling the wine around her tongue. It went down like ambrosia or the best champagne cocktail she'd ever had, and yet it tantalized her mind, tingled in her toes.

Maybe she should have worried. A normal woman would. But Trinity drank because she trusted him. It hadn't been something she even thought about in the car. She trusted that he would give her pleasure, that he would take her home in the morning, that he would take care of her spirit as well as her body.

If she were to find him in the shower with a woman, it would be because they'd agreed that a third in the mix would be fun.

Not that Trinity would share him with another woman.

God, what was happening to her? She'd never had these thoughts before.

He gathered the glass from her suddenly numb fingers. "Now take your clothes off like I told you to." He punctuated the command with his fingers, trailing down her arm, his nails brushing her breast, his cock hard at her hip, and his lips at her ear turning her body to jelly.

Then he was gone, once again seated in the gold chair, the wine goblet to his mouth. Trinity ached to lick the flavors from his lips. What he offered wasn't sex—it was a journey she couldn't resist.

Hands trembling, she undid the back zip of her dress. With her arms up, the hem rose to the tops of her thighs, and Scott's eyes tracked every movement. A brazen shade of teal, the dress turned her eyes turquoise. With a high waist, the bodice nipped in below her breasts, emphasizing them. She lowered her arms and took the zipper all the way, the lining sliding down to caress her hips as she let the top fall. Then the dress pooled on the gold carpet at her feet, and she stood in bra, thong, and thigh-high stockings.

"Very nice." Scott deliberately stroked himself through his pants. "Pull down your bra and pinch your nipples for me."

Trinity did, pleasure-pain streaking down her legs, then back up. Following a man's command had never felt so good, so exhilarating. But then, no man had bothered to command her. They didn't need to, she was always so willing to anticipate what they wanted. Little Miss Perfect, the perfect date.

"Tell me what else—"

He held a finger to his lips. "Don't speak until I say."

Like in the theater. A full-body flush raced over her skin. She loved what he did to her with words and his heated gaze, and who cared why. Trinity gave herself over to his game.

"Bra, off." He pointed his finger.

She popped the front closure and wriggled the straps down her arms. His eyes traced the progress, the brown irises darkening to rich cocoa. Trinity's nipples peaked. He licked his lips.

Elbows on the arms of his chair, he laced his fingers. "Panties." He indicated, up, down, with a flick of his index fingers.

Her thong was already damp. Deep, sexy, his voice set her body on a high simmer. Hooking her thumbs in the elastic, she slipped the scrap of material down and stepped out of it.

"Give it to me." He held out his hand.

Trinity tossed. He caught the lace confection, then held it to his nose, his eyes on her. His action should have felt perverted, but another flush suffused her body. He was earthy. She'd never known anyone like him.

Crumpling the panty in his hands before clasping them in the same position, he tipped his head. "You're wet, aren't you?"

She opened her mouth, then remembered she wasn't supposed to speak. Instead she nodded.

"Come here."

It was four steps, but a rush of moisture turned her plump and needy between the legs.

"I love that you're so willing. That you get off on each new thing I ask you to do." He passed his palm over her curls, barely touching her mound. "Such passion," he murmured, "and a lust for everything. I want that."

"That's not me," she whispered, despite his earlier order for silence.

He mesmerized her with his deep gaze. "Oh yes it is. Maybe you've been denying it to yourself, but it's your true nature."

Trinity loved how he saw her. He'd wanted her with her hair a mess, her lipstick smudged. He'd wanted her even after she'd played the ditz for his daughters. He'd actually apologized for accusing her of blackmail when she'd been the one to withhold the complete truth from him. He accepted her, it was that simple. And he made her want to do anything for him, to *be* the woman he thought she was. Not a mask she donned, but releasing the real woman inside her. To him, she was special, not just a face or a body, but a woman.

"Spread your feet apart."

Clad in only her thigh highs, she was naked, fully exposed. Scott slipped a finger along her, grazing her clitoris, wetting his skin. Eyes on her, he sucked her juice from his fingers.

Her nostrils flared, her eyes turning a midnight blue. Trinity swallowed, and he knew if he touched her again, he'd find her warm and even creamier.

His cock screamed to push her to her knees and take her over the coffee table right in front of him, yet they had so many more things to do. "Now you do it."

Spreading her legs, she slowly trailed down her abdomen to the trimmed blond curls, and dropped her gaze.

"Look at me while you do it."

Her nipples pearled. He wanted to suck them. But he thought

he'd die when she tunneled two fingers between her legs, stroked herself, then lifted her hand to her lips and sucked her flesh clean.

Holy hell. Scott rubbed his cock, damn close to explosion. He meant for her to let *him* lick her fingers, yet her error set him on fire. "I want to taste it on your lips."

Bracing herself on the arm of his chair, she leaned over, her hair caressing his face. Touching his tongue to hers, he tasted her sweet musk while her heady scent clouded his mind.

Fuck her, fuck her, his mind and body shouted in unison. But he was stronger than that.

When she rose to her full height again, he demanded in a low, husky voice that barely sounded like his own, "Turn around."

She did, revealing her gorgeous ass. Skimming a finger down the crevice, he touched her lightly, testing. She shivered.

"Bend over and spread your legs again."

She complied, wrapping her hands around her calves for balance. Scott nibbled one butt cheek, then slipped down further, past the sensitive flesh of her ass to her wet pussy. Her clit was a hard nub begging for his mouth.

"I want you to stay like that." Behind her, he rose. A tremble coursed down her spine. He knew what she thought. He'd take her now, thrust inside her, but again, that would be too quick, over in minutes, when he had all night to play with her.

Scott rounded the chair and took the two steps up from the living room, leaving Trinity with her butt in the air.

He disappeared through a door on the left.

She was wet and quivering on the inside, nipples hard, aching. Her own taste mixed with his lingered on her tongue. For the first time in her life, Trinity thought about getting herself off right here and now because the need in her was so great. It was beyond mere masturbation—which of course she'd done—moving into the realm of near pain.

Trinity wanted him to fuck her. Yes, *fuck* her. *Please, please,*

please. Where had he gone? She squeezed her knees together, not sure how much longer she could stand up.

"In here." In the hall, he stood by the door through which he'd vanished a couple of minutes earlier. Tie gone, his shirt was still buttoned, shoes on his feet, but visible from across the room, his cock strained against his zipper.

Climbing the steps, she wanted to crawl up his body, cling to him, have her way, every way.

She wanted to talk.

Sliding a hand down her back to her naked butt, squeezing, he turned her, guiding her into the room.

It was masculine, the bed covered by a cushy wine-colored comforter, a couple of matching pillows, books on the low cabinet behind the mattress. The bureau and tallboy were of a dark wood. No blinds or curtains in here either, the sliding glass door opened onto the deck, the view of the dark forest beyond. In the center of the bed, he'd laid a plain, no-frills vibrator.

"You want me to use that on myself?" She'd already played herself for him. She wanted something new, something different. God, she was losing it.

Especially when he put his finger to her lips to shut her up. "No speaking. I want to hear you moan for me."

That's how he'd first known her, her moans through the wall. And she wanted to play whatever game he needed. She nodded.

Her hands in his, he wrapped her fingers around his belt buckle. "Take it off for me."

She undid the metal, then pulled the leather from the loops. When she was about to drop it, he curled his fist around her wrist. "Fold it in four."

Though the leather was stiff, she did, then held it in the palm of her hand. He didn't take it.

Sitting on the bed, he patted his lap. "Here."

He turned her and forced her facedown over his knees, her abdomen to his thighs and her butt once again in the air. Then he took the belt. "Put it in your mouth and bite down."

He was crazy, yet she wanted to do as he asked. Sinking her teeth into the leather to anchor it, she rested her elbows on the bed beside him, her knees bent, one foot on the floor.

She squeaked at the first whack of his hand, then laughed around the belt in her mouth. It didn't hurt, especially when he caressed her cheek afterwards.

"You've been a bad girl for lying to me about your husband, so I have to spank you." Then he rolled down over her body and whispered, "Don't laugh, or I'll have to hurt you."

He slapped her with the flat of his hand, a slight sting radiating out, and this time he slipped his fingers down to caress her pussy. By spreading her legs slightly and bracing herself higher with her one foot on the floor, she gave him better access. And oh she was wet. Moaning around the leather in her mouth, she gave him what he wanted.

He whacked her again. With her butt higher and more of her flesh exposed, the sting shimmied out to her pussy. Trinity moaned for real, pushing back against his hand, begging for more.

Beneath her belly, his cock pulsed, and she rubbed herself against him. He spanked again, then immediately entered her creamy depths with a finger. Oh God. Trinity bit hard and panted. The pleasure, mixed with a hint of pain, was sweet. She wanted more.

Again and again, he swatted her, and each time, he slid deeper, rubbing her clitoris, the sensitive skin between her pussy and her rear. She writhed and moaned.

"Christ, I love the sounds you make."

It wasn't enough, the touches too quick, teasing. She rode the edge, never quite able to bring herself over.

Which was exactly what he wanted. "You're very wet. I think you like this."

She moaned and nodded, wiggled her butt, begging. With each

slap, the pain was a tad more intense, yet the pleasure soared. Her bottom tingled, burned slightly, her flesh sensitive, needy. She tried to rub herself, even put her hand between her legs, but he chastised her.

"I'll stop if you don't behave."

She groaned in answer. His hand took her once again, and this time he played her clitoris until she felt the building implosion. *Almost there, please, please.*

And he was gone. "Your ass is red and delicious." He bent to kiss one cheek, then licked her.

She wanted to scream. Reaching between them, she palmed his cock, caressed him. He pulsed in her grip, yet he didn't give her what she wanted.

Beneath her, he shifted. When he straightened, he came at her again, this time probing her with the hard plastic vibrator. He slid it inside, filling her, then left it deep.

"Do you like that?"

She nodded, moaned, bucked a little trying to get the thing to move inside her.

"Remove the belt and tell me how much you like it."

Spitting out the leather, her mouth dry, her senses reeling, she rocked against him. "It's so good. I don't know why, but it is." Her throat clogged, her eyes teared. "Please."

"Tell me what you want."

Oh God. She wanted so much. "Please do it. Do me."

"You want me to fuck you? Say it." He encouraged her with a sharp swat that made her groan and writhe against him.

Lord. "Yes. Please fuck me."

The vibrator buzzed inside her, and she spread her legs as wide as she could without falling, pushing back on it, on him.

And he fucked her with it. It was a feeling like no other, the intense buzz inside, her body sensitive and aching, her nipples rasping against the coverlet.

"Tell me what you want."

"I want to come, please, make me come. I want it so bad." She didn't know exactly what she said or how long she pleaded.

Then he reached beneath her and stroked her clitoris at the same time, and Trinity screamed as an orgasm rolled her under like an ocean wave.

When she came to, he was buried inside her. She couldn't quite remember how he got there. Her back flush against the carpet, he braced himself above her, his gaze a deep, dark pool.

Then he started to move. Trinity closed her eyes. Withdrawing almost to the tip, he held, flexed, took her with small pumps of his hips.

"Look at me," he demanded.

She did, and Scott lost himself in the blue depths. Her body sucked him deeper, and he held a moment, savoring the sensation. Watching her fall over the edge, he'd barely managed to don the condom before he had to get inside her or die. As it was, his pants were around his knees.

"Fuck me," she whispered, her eyes all pupil now.

Genteel, fastidious, he loved the dirty talk on her lips. "How do you want me to fuck you?"

"Hard and deep and fast."

He flexed inside, short, fast pumps until she gasped.

"Is that how you want it?"

"Fuck me deeper," she begged.

He thrust high and hard until she dug her fingernails into his biceps. Rolling her head, she moaned for him, then panted.

"Is that what you want?"

"You forgot the fast part." She wrapped her legs around his waist and locked her feet over his bare butt. Then she bit his shoulder. "Fuck me, fuck me, fuck me," she chanted.

And he couldn't hold back. She drove him over the edge with the scent of her arousal, the heat of her body, her chant in his ear, and that sweet, heated voice made him insane. He fucked her hard, fast, deep, until the muscles of his arms shook. Then he didn't know his name, or where he was, only that she was everything he needed, the woman he wanted to love, to cherish, and he lost himself inside her.

TRINITY had never woken flush against a man. She'd always remained separate. That way she could slip out of the bed without waking him and transform herself back into the perfect Trinity again.

Water, merely droplets off the trees, pattered on the roof. Scott shifted, flexed, and his cock rode the crease of her butt. He'd woken her twice in the night to have her do naughty things to his body and do even naughtier things to hers.

"You're insatiable." She whispered, in case he was asleep and this was a morning woody, as she'd heard it called.

"I haven't actually slept with a woman in so long that I had a hankering for a little wakeup nookie." He plied her nipple, then slowly rolled her over to face him.

It was dark still, and she felt her way along his jaw with fingertips alone. Slightly rough, stubbled, then the smooth, warm feel of his lips. She hadn't even brushed her teeth, yet she wanted to kiss him. And she did.

It was good, perfect. So perfect that in fact it was a little scary. She could get used to this, used to him. She could actually love waking up next to him all the time.

"No nookie," she murmured against his mouth. "You have to drive me back to my car so I can go home and get ready for work."

"Take the day off."

God, she was tempted.

Last night, he'd ruined her for all time. More important, though, she realized she could still have it all. The naughty phone calls, the kinky trysts. No one had to know. All her dirty little secrets didn't have to be aired. She and Scott could go on as they had before.

"I've missed this so much," she admitted freely. Then she tipped her head back and smiled up at him. "I don't know why I was worried about telling you my name. It hasn't changed a thing. In fact, it's better." She licked his nipple, loving the delicious, heady taste of his skin. "We can be naughty like this, then go off to our regular lives knowing we've got this hot little secret." She kissed the corner of his mouth. "Maybe you should tie me up next time." The possibilities were endless.

NICE by day in her vanilla world, naughty by night with him.

Scott wanted to howl as he watched her drive off in her sporty red Mustang. Her scent still filled the car, and the taste of her goodbye kiss lingered on his lips. He'd gotten her name, but nothing else. While he'd fallen off the deep end for her, she was still wading in the shallows. Knots tied up his gut. The possibility hung out there that he would always be the one more committed.

She'd missed *this*. Not him. *This*. Hot sex. Nothing more.

Love wasn't supposed to be this fucking hard.

19

"HELLO?" Harper's voice crackled as he answered his cell.

"Meet me at noon outside Vatovola's," Trinity said.

"Why?"

She didn't owe him an explanation. "Just be there, Harper." If he was blackmailing Scott to get to her, she'd pull the plug. Last night with Scott had been so perfect, and she would *not* let Harper hurt him. Ever.

A couple of hours later, close to noon, it was raining as Trinity dashed from her car to the green-striped awning of Vatovola's. For the winter, the outside tables had been moved, but there stood Harper, his gray suit tailored and pressed, his blond hair recently cut, not a lock out of place.

Looking the other way, he tapped his umbrella impatiently on the concrete, then glanced in her direction. And smiled.

The smile ticked her off. As if he believed that because *she'd* done the calling, all was forgiven.

"I asked, but they didn't have a reservation," he said.

"That's because I didn't make one. What I have to say isn't going to take long, then *I'm* going to grab a bite at the bar."

"Oh." He shot her a hurt little moue.

Which irritated her, too. God, why was everything making her see red around him? She was over Harper and what he'd done. She'd admitted to herself that she'd married in haste and made a mistake. So why did seeing him turn her raw on the inside?

Because everything was so perfect with Scott after last night, but what if he was another bad judgment? She'd jumped quickly into marriage with Harper so no one else, not her father, not Faith, would have the chance to disapprove. What if that were the reason for Scott to be a secret? Because someone might disapprove, and she wouldn't be able to stand firm against it. That's why Harper rubbed her raw, because he made her *think*.

"I'll make this quick," she said, biting down on her anger. "If you've taken pictures in order to blackmail me into giving you a settlement, you can forget it. I don't care what you do with those pictures." Unless they hurt Scott.

"What pictures?"

She stepped closer. His blue eyes were like cracked crystal, a peculiarity she'd once found attractive, and he'd always worn the most delicious aftershave. That was just the outer shell. "I'm not falling for it. You know what pictures."

Something shimmered on his cheeks, a slight sheen of sweat or raindrops that hadn't dried. "My car." He pointed his umbrella. "Can we talk there?" He glanced over his shoulder.

Trinity realized they were silhouetted against the front windows of Vatovola's for all to see and speculate, yet she was still loathe to get in his car.

Which felt like a sign of weakness. "I only have a few minutes."

Harper beeped his remote, and she climbed into the passenger side of his late-model luxury car. At least he hadn't bought that with her money while they were married. He'd come with it.

Light raindrops pattered on the windshield, and their breath steamed up the inside glass.

"I don't know what pictures you're talking about, Trinity. I'm not blackmailing you. I would never blackmail you. Believe it or not, I actually care about you."

He was such a liar. "I won't let you get away with it. Daddy's lawyers will—" She cut herself off midthought. She wouldn't use Daddy's lawyers. She'd handle this herself. She wasn't a weakling who needed to turn to *Daddy* whenever something went wrong. "I want you to back off, Harper."

Leaning back against the door, he hooked a leg up onto the seat. "I messed up our marriage, Trinity."

He sure did.

"I never meant to hurt you. It wasn't my idea in the first place, but I needed the money." He blinked. "I thought I could do it all without hurting you. Because I liked you."

"But you didn't love me."

"No."

Trinity digested that a moment, surprised to find it didn't hurt. "I didn't love you either."

Once the words were out, she realized how dreadful they sounded said aloud. She'd married a man for her own selfish purposes. No matter how it ended, she was also a guilty party.

"I knew you didn't," he said softly.

"You couldn't have known."

"You never lost control with me, Trinity. You always made sure your makeup didn't run or your hair get out of place." He put out a hand to touch, withdrawing when she flinched. "You were never passionate about me, Trinity."

That stabbed her through the heart, because it was true. She felt so much passion with Scott from the beginning, even when he was just a physical obsession. You didn't have to feel passion to feel love, but the awful truth was she'd never felt anything for Harper. "You were passionate about me?"

"No, I wasn't. You see . . ." He tipped his head, his gaze tracing her features. "I was always in love with someone else."

All the air seemed to be sucked right out of the car. She'd *never* been Harper's perfect little wife. She'd been his perfect little patsy. "The woman in the shower?"

"We needed the money to get out of some financial problems."

"What about the money that *disappeared* from your last business deal?" Daddy had checked on him.

Harper blinked, toyed with the cuff of his pants where he'd put his leg up on the seat. "I was never very good at business, and I lost everything for my investors." He finally looked at her. "I didn't steal it."

It explained one thing, but not everything. "But she *knew* you were marrying me for my money?"

"It was her idea to find a rich woman."

Trinity couldn't wrap her mind around the idea, let alone have an emotion about it. "She didn't care that you were going to have to *fuck* me?"

He yanked back, flush up against the door. "You've *never* used that word."

"It's a perfectly good word." She said it again for good measure. "Fuck, fuck, fuck." Then she beamed him a malicious little smile. "There, see how easy it is?"

It struck her that she'd loved saying it for Scott. It had an entirely different meaning with Harper.

"I'm sorry, Trinity. Honestly, I didn't want you to find us like that." He seemed so sincere, his eyes a pale blue, pleading for forgiveness.

"Apologizing isn't going to get you any money."

"I know that."

"So it was all for nothing."

"Actually, my . . ." He glanced at her, weighed his words. "She found someone that'll work out the way we need it to."

"You mean, *she* married some poor slob for his money?"

"It's not like that."

Trinity put the tip of her index finger on Harper's knee. "Doesn't it bother you that she's letting another man touch her?"

Harper shrugged. "He's old. He can't get it up anyway."

So that made it fine with him? "Doesn't it bother you that she didn't care that I *wasn't* old and you had sex with *me*?"

His Adam's apple slid slowly up and down.

"I wish I could feel sorry for you, but I can't." She wondered, though, if she could forgive him. Yet in the next moment, the answer seemed so obvious. The person she needed to forgive was herself. Harper wasn't the only one who told lies. She'd been lying to herself all along. "I didn't marry you for the right reasons, Harper. I'm as guilty of making mistakes." She flashed him a look. "Yours are a lot worse than mine, but I screwed up, too." She wasn't going to learn a damn thing from this if she didn't at least face that.

She'd been searching for the elusive things that Faith had found—unconditional love and acceptance. Maybe she hadn't found it because she truly wasn't able to give it in return. She wasn't sure she could give it even to Scott.

"Harper, we did a quickie marriage in Nevada. Why don't we agree to a quickie divorce there, too? Then we both walk away with what we had before we started."

She could walk away with what she'd had, but she couldn't ever be the same person. It was time to move back into the master bedroom and stop letting it haunt her. She'd made a mistake. Now she had to forgive herself and move on.

"That's fine with me, Trinity." Harper stuck out his hand. "Let's shake on it."

It was the oddest thing to seal a divorce agreement with a hand-shake. Yet, by letting go of the anger, she felt as if she'd finally done something right.

THE Saturday evening dinner party Herman Green hosted was in celebration of the new contract between Millennium and Green In-dustries. Scott swirled the ice cubes in his glass and observed the gathering in Herman's living room.

All business in an office atmosphere, Connor Kingston now played the fawning husband over his very pregnant wife as she sat on the elegantly appointed gold brocade couch. It was like tearing open an envelope to find something altogether unexpected on the inside.

All the major players from Monday's contract signing were in at-tendance, including Rudd, his wife, and Grace. Jarvis Castle had ar-rived late. The soon-to-be-retiring chairman of Castle Heavy Mining, he was also Kingston's father-in-law, and he doted on his daughter, Faith. He handed her a crystal flute filled with sparkling cider.

Faith Kingston was a pretty woman, not so much the cut of her face, but her smile, the loving look when she gazed at her father, and most especially the heat in her eyes when she held Kingston's hand to her belly as the baby kicked. More than awe at the tiny life growing inside her, it was something profound she shared with her child's father. It was *their* baby, *their* love, *them* all the way.

Katy hadn't wanted to have sex with him when she was preg-nant. Between Kingston and his wife, Scott figured they couldn't get enough of each other even at eight months.

For the first time, he wondered if he'd ever had that kind of pas-sion with Katy. He remembered attributing passion to youth and newness, something you grew out of without intending to. Perhaps he'd never truly known it in the first place.

Until Jezebel.

In a black evening dress, pearls at her throat, she made an entrance through the double living room doors. Her stiletto heels sank in the expensive patterned carpet, and the flare of the dress's skirt showcased her legs. Rounding the glass table central to the large room, she kissed her father's cheek. He introduced her to Rudd and his wife. Glad-handing, smiling, she didn't even turn in Scott's direction.

He hadn't seen her since Tuesday morning, and she'd had a logical excuse every time. The beginnings of their relationship had been spent trying to get her to reveal who she was. Now he'd simply switched from one goal to another, revealing their secret affair to the world. He had the feeling he'd use up every ounce of energy he possessed trying to get her to love him in return.

"She's a bit showy, isn't she?" Grace had chosen a flowered dress, one that was too short and too tight for the event.

He felt mean-spirited making the comparison to Trinity, who couldn't wear anything too tight or too short for his desires. He wanted to run his fingers beneath the flared dress to see if she wore thigh highs or pantyhose.

"She's Herman Green's daughter, so I'm sure that's expected." He hoped the comment came across as innocuous.

While Trinity was beautiful, she was more than a face and body. She had layers he wanted to peel away: exhibitionist, voyeur, and a bit of a submissive, yet she liked her control. One minute she could be sassy and snarky, the next, she was apologizing for omitting the truth about her divorce. Gorgeous, she was still insecure. He'd seen that as she'd stripped down for him in his living room. She'd needed his approval. She hadn't figured out she already had it.

Grace sipped her mimosa. "I'll bet she's a cold fish."

Moving just his eyes, he glanced at her, but she focused solely on Trinity. That was an odd comment. He'd never heard Grace remark on anything so personal, but then he'd never attended a dinner party with her either.

And Grace was wrong. In his few weeks with Trinity, he'd discovered a level of kinky desire he didn't know he had. And she met every challenge head-on. There wasn't a thing cold about her. She'd damn near cried with pleasure when he spanked her and went crazy when he fed her pussy the vibrator. It had been so fucking hot, he'd never go back to vanilla sex. He'd never go back to sex with anyone but her.

The woman made him feel vital, aware, on edge. She kept his skin jumping, his thoughts whirling. Yet his gut had started to grumble that she was avoiding him.

Not that he'd mention his thoughts to his controller. "Grace, I simply don't know what to say to that."

She saluted him with her glass. "Sorry, I was thinking out loud." Then she tipped her champagne toward Herman Green. "Oh, look, here they come, it's our turn." She leaned in slightly to Scott's shoulder. "Watch out, she's giving you the eye."

Backing off enough to look down at Grace, he stared for a moment. Could it be possible she was jealous? She'd come off a bad divorce and was trying to rebuild her fragile ego, so yeah, it was a possibility. He didn't want to see Grace as a woman, but he couldn't help it when she made comments like that.

Thus he could understand why she was envious of a gorgeous woman younger by more than fifteen years. What he didn't understand was why she suddenly felt like sharing her inner thoughts with him.

Herman Green grabbed his arm, and the moment for pondering Grace was over.

"Here you are, Scott, I wanted to introduce you to my daughter, Trinity."

She held out her hand. "So nice to meet you, Scott. I didn't catch the last name."

Despite her high heels, he found her finely petite. "Sinclair. And it's so nice to finally meet you."

Her hand in his warmed, sparked. He held seconds longer than appropriate, until she tugged away.

"And this is my associate, Grace Bunnell."

Trinity smiled. "Nice to meet you." Scott could swear there was a moment when she winced as if Grace squeezed too hard.

He'd never been aware of women's rivalries before. He would have been completely fascinated if he could take his eyes off his mystery woman for longer than a second.

She left him, moved on, threw herself down on the sofa beside Faith Kingston and hugged her so hard the woman could have popped right then. Another facet of the Trinity diamond.

Yeah, she'd brought him back to life. Now, no other woman would do. Before the night was out, he'd show her no other man would ever do for her.

DINNER was interminable. With Scott's gaze on her, Trinity could do nothing more than move the salmon around her plate. The chilled wine, served in Daddy's best crystal glasses, tasted sour. He'd added the two leaves to the dining table, allowing spacious elbow room, yet Trinity had gotten Faith to switch spots with Scott under the guise of allowing the men to talk business. Now that she'd told her father Harper had agreed to a no-contest quickie divorce, he'd played matchmaker, seating her next to Scott. Trinity, however, didn't fall for it.

Things had been great the whole week. Scott called every night, and they'd done all manner of naughty phone things. But he was going to blow their cover with the way he kept staring at her. Daddy and everyone else would figure out something was up—pun intended—between them.

"He is *h-o-t hot* for you," Faith whispered beneath laughter from Daddy's end of the table.

See! Even Faith noticed Scott's focus.

Her father was talking with Grace, Scott's controller. *His* controller, as Grace managed to say several times in conversation before Daddy's majordomo called everyone in for dinner. Had the woman been trying to intimate there was something more than professional between her and Scott? There *couldn't* be.

Trinity cringed at her own jealousy. Where once she was envious of what Faith had with Connor, now she was suspicious of Scott's business relationships. Here was another reason she needed to keep *everything* with Scott separate from her real life. "Connor's talking about you again," she tried deflecting Faith, "that's why he and Mr. Sinclair are looking over here." She was afraid, however, her friend would see right through the lie.

"*Mr.* Sinclair?"

He laughed at something Connor said, and Trinity's tummy turned over. His sexy voice touched her inside, like a stroke straight down from her breasts to her pussy.

"I don't know him well enough to call him by his first name." She knew him oh so well. She wondered why she didn't tell Faith about it. Of course, she couldn't talk *here*, but another time over mochas and a shared bear claw? Still no. She was keeping a lot from Faith. She hadn't even told her about that talk with Harper.

But Scott was her secret. She didn't want any judgments about her activities. Not that *Faith* would judge her, but . . . she didn't want the fear of discovery getting in the way. She wasn't ready for outside scrutiny of their relationship.

"He sure wants to know you. He's got *hot* eyes for you."

She glanced at Faith and grimaced. "What are *hot* eyes?"

Faith smiled, and Trinity noticed how beautiful she'd become. It was more than the baby. Connor was good for her. Trinity had made the perfect choice in getting them together.

"*Hot* eyes means he's doing deliciously nasty things to you in his mind."

Trinity pulled back and frowned at her very best friend in the whole world. Faith didn't generally talk about *nasty*. Had Trinity given herself away? No, she found Faith staring at Connor, and there was definitely some hot eyes going on there.

While Connor was devilishly handsome, the silver in Scott's hair and the few lines on his face were so much more appealing.

Or maybe it was all the things he'd done to her. They could only indulge if she kept Scott her naughty secret. Otherwise, her every action would be analyzed like a blood drop under her father's microscope. She would lose the freedom to indulge, and that's what she loved so much about being with Scott.

"Stop that," she admonished Faith. "Someone will hear." Such as Mrs. Rudd, who sat next to Faith. They'd been ignoring her— bad socialites. Trinity brought her into the conversation with the topic of Nordstrom's half-yearly sale.

She didn't give a fig about Nordstrom's half-yearly sale, no matter how big it was. All she cared about was making sure Daddy didn't notice Scott's "hot" eyes.

"ASSORTED liqueurs in the living room," her father called out jovially, bringing dessert and coffee to an end. With all his laughter tonight, he did seem like his old self.

"Save me a seat on the sofa," Trinity murmured to Faith. "I'm hitting the powder room." If she sat next to Faith, Scott couldn't corner her, something she was afraid he'd try to do.

Climbing the wide spiral staircase, she returned to the upstairs bathroom she'd used to get ready. She'd left all her makeup there. The main bath was at the end, past the long row of Green ancestors. She sometimes wondered if her grandfather had purchased all the paintings at the same time and palmed them off as relatives. They seemed to be of a similar artistic style, yet not one of them looked like a Green. Then again, Grandpa had been pretentious, claiming his family came over on the *Mayflower* when she knew darn well he was a greengrocer in England before World War I. Heh, *greengro-cer*, get it?

She fixed her lipstick first. The door opened, and Trinity startled, leaving a light smudge about her mouth.

Scott leaned back against the wood.

"What are you doing in here?" She knew exactly what he'd do, and her heart *ratta-tat-tatted* against her breast.

"I have to take a leak." His hand went to his zipper.

"You can't go to the bathroom while I'm here." She never shared the bathroom with a man. Even Harper closed the door.

"Then I guess I'm going to have to fuck you instead."

Her blood thrumming, she turned back to her reflection, leaning over the counter to concentrate on her lipstick. "You're very crude." God, she'd started to adore crude.

She also loved it when a man said, *I want you now, fuck every-thing else.* There was such power in that. She craved power. She craved *him.* Which is why, despite the danger of being discovered in her father's house, she didn't throw Scott out.

Standing behind her, he bent at the knees to slide both hands up her dress, propping the hem on the curve of her butt.

His breath eased through his clenched teeth. "I knew it. Thigh highs and a bare ass." He stroked down her center to the top of one stocking, then raised his gaze to hers in the mirror. "All night you thought about me fucking you, didn't you?"

"No." She'd been thinking about it for five days straight.

"Liar," he whispered. Curling his body over hers, he swept aside her makeup and purse, grabbed the lipstick out of her hand and tossed it, then cupped her breasts in his big palms.

"Feel those nipples," he whispered. "They're fucking hard." He pinched. She instinctively pushed back against his erection.

"Oh yeah, baby." He pumped lightly against her. Unzipping the back of the dress, he pushed the sleeves down her arms.

She tried to cover herself. "What are you doing?"

"I want to see your nipples in the mirror as I feel them."

"Just once." She let the material pool on the counter.

"As much as I want," he murmured. Then he gazed at the reflection as he brought her nipples to full peak.

She moaned for him because he loved her sounds. Because she couldn't help herself.

Gliding down her breasts to her abdomen, he held her hard against him. "Your skin is so soft." Then he buried his face at her nape. "And the scent of your hair makes me crazy."

He made *her* crazy. Totally, completely. "You can't do me now. Someone will hear." Yet she'd do whatever he wanted.

The dress bunched at her waist, he skimmed the fabric's edge until he held both her hips and rocked against her. "They won't hear if you don't scream." He bit her neck. "But you can't help screaming, can you? You need this. You need *me*."

Oh God, yes, she did need him. The things he did to her made her forget where she was and who she was. She would always be this way, losing herself in him.

He went to his knees behind her.

"Don't you dare," she whispered, knowing he wouldn't stop, that she didn't want him to.

He pushed the dress high. "Oh, I dare."

Then he licked the crease of her bottom. She moaned. Forcing her to spread her legs wide, he came at her pussy from behind. The most erotic of sensations, his tongue on her, his hair brushing her butt, yet all she could see in the mirror was herself.

A smudge of lipstick by her mouth, her pupils so wide she couldn't see the blue, her skin tinged with the flush of arousal. She leaned on her elbows, closed her eyes, then knew she had to watch every second. He licked her pussy, then her clitoris. Breath panted from her lips. Her nostrils flared as he hit an acute spot. Putting her head forward, her hair fell across her face, sticking to her lipstick. She groaned for him.

Then the woman in the reflection reached up to pinch both nipples. Pain shot down to the point his tongue caressed, and nothing had ever felt so good. She angled higher, giving him better access, and he rewarded her with a finger inside.

Her nipples a dusky rose, diamond-tipped, she palmed both breasts and held them out. So wanton, eyes a little glazed, lips parted, the reflection begged her to pinch harder.

She almost came. "Stop. Wait. Don't make me come yet." She sucked in a breath, moaned, as he strummed her pussy with tongue, teeth, and lips.

"Please don't, please don't," she chanted, trying to stave off orgasm. "Please, I want you inside me."

He rose, and she almost collapsed on the counter. His lips glistened, his cheeks moist with her juice. Leaning forward, he grabbed her chin, and kissed her hard, making her taste herself, and it was too much. "You need me," he whispered.

"Please fuck me, please fuck me." She would always beg.

Unzipping, he donned the condom he had in his pocket, then lifted his shirt and dipped back to watch as he slid inside her. She wanted to turn, look at him, but more, she wanted to watch everything in the mirror.

Her lipstick was crushed on her mouth. Tears had leaked from the corners of her eyes, and her mascara smudged circles beneath her eyes. She looked wanton, used, and loving it.

Just like Harper's lover. For the first time, maybe because she'd come to terms with Harper, Trinity could finally admit that she'd been jealous of the woman's abandon, how she'd given herself up to the sensations. Trinity did the same.

And oh, it was horribly, terribly good. To be turned-on and out of control, to want a man so badly she'd let him mess her all up. Gulping, she pushed back, taking him as deep as he could go.

"You make me fucking crazy," he whispered, his eyes on hers in the mirror.

It wasn't romantic or sensual. It was raw heat, and Trinity reveled in it. She savored the huskiness of her voice as she called out to him. "Fuck me, fuck me, harder, faster."

He filled her, and it was like no other sex act, the pleasure doubled in the mirror. Bracing against the tile beneath the glass, she met his thrusts, strained, groaned, became an animal.

It was beautiful.

Squeezing her eyes shut, she felt the heat build, rise to her nipples, streak along her arms, cascade down her legs.

And Trinity soared off into orgasmic outer space.

HE'D come when she cried out, her body sucking him deeper, shooting him higher. Then he crumpled to the floor, taking her with him. The scent of her come mesmerized him. She filled his head, and he licked his lips to gather the sweet taste of her.

What they'd done wasn't kinky, except if you considered they were watching themselves in the upstairs bathroom of her father's home. It transcended mere fucking. It was, however, idiotic considering that Rudd, a potential blackmailer, was downstairs. Yet Scott hadn't been able to stop himself from following her. She'd been so damn standoffish all night, it made him nuts.

And when he'd tried to force her to tell him how much she needed him, she kept her mouth firmly closed. Even as he pushed her over the edge into orgasm. He loved the word *fuck* on her lips, yet it wasn't enough. He wanted the word *love*.

He feared he'd never get enough to satisfy him.

20

"OH my God," Trinity whispered, her hand on the knob. "You forgot to lock the door."

Scott cursed. Then he smoothed a finger down her cheek. "Does it worry you?"

She'd fixed her makeup, and now he'd messed with it again. She loved that he liked to mess with her. It was truly frightening, the number of things she loved that he did to her or made her feel. "It would have been hot," she admitted, leaning against the door, "if someone saw us."

Except that it was her father's house. She'd gotten carried away. Again. If she wasn't careful, her secret would be exposed. What if someone *had* walked in on them? God forbid, what if her *father* had? This kind of risky behavior just wouldn't do.

One hand by her head, Scott nuzzled her hair. "So that's how I can make you crazy for me, be sure someone is watching."

So tall, so deliciously scented, his nearness did wild things to her. She was weak where he was concerned. Her mismatched jumble of emotions put her off balance. One minute she let him do anything he wanted any*where* he wanted, the next, the consequences terrified her.

Tucking her evening bag beneath her arm, she pushed him away. "We have to get back downstairs before someone notices we're missing *together*." Opening the door, she slipped out alone, leaving him behind. For now. But like an addict, she knew she'd be back for another hit.

Her legs were wobbly as she skated on air down the hall. Could a girl get drunk on sex? Hell yes. Her father's house, however, was *not* the place to be naughty with Scott.

Bouncing down the staircase, she stumbled on her high heels. Daddy stood in the middle of the marble entry hall. Waiting. Her heart stuttered.

Voices, then a burst of laughter drifted from the double doors to the living room. She took the last steps, her eyes glued to the set of her father's lips and his deadpan expression.

"I wondered where you'd gotten to." He glanced past her, up the stairs to the landing above. As if he *knew*—or at least had an inkling.

Trinity couldn't help herself, her own gaze followed, horrified that Scott would be there in plain sight.

The upstairs hall was empty, and she could breathe again. "Just using the ladies' room, Daddy."

He smiled then. "Actually, I was looking for Mr. Sinclair. He seems to have disappeared. I wanted to make sure he hadn't gotten lost." Then he winked. "And a little bird told me you might be together."

Good Lord. *What* little bird? And how much had this little bird chirped in her father's ear? Lord. Mr. Wanamaker? *Yes, Herman, I do believe I just saw Scott Sinclair boffing your daughter in the upstairs restroom. Quite an exciting sight, if I do say so myself. Won't be able to look at her with a straight face on Monday.* Chill bumps pebbled Trinity's skin. If her father had come looking five minutes earlier . . . the bathroom door hadn't even been locked, for God's sake. Stupid, stupid, stupid. Okay, she had to believe Daddy's "little bird" hadn't walked in on them, otherwise her father wouldn't have *winked.*

She went for haughty—"I'm sure Mr. Sinclair will eventually find his way back. He doesn't look like a stupid man"—but was afraid she came off sounding just plain mean.

Scott wasn't a stupid man, but he did want what he wanted exactly right when he wanted it. And he dragged her along, too. Willingly, yes, but this was the *last* time she'd let him corner her. She lost all sense of propriety around him.

"Honey, he's perfect for you."

"Daddy," she shushed him, her eyes darting to the open living room doors, then just as quickly back up the stairs. "Why don't we get back to your guests?"

He didn't let her go. Instead, he squeezed her arm, lightly but inexorably. "I want him for you, honey. He's such a good match. He's older, settled, he can take care of you."

The faint stirrings of ire simmered in her veins. This was Scott's fault. If he hadn't shown his interest to her father . . . "Daddy, I don't need to be taken care of."

But Daddy would not let it go. "I worry about you. I'm not getting any younger. What if something happens to me?" All his earlier joviality slid down his face, and he looked like the haggard man he'd been since he and Lance had their falling out. "Don't mess this up, honey," he murmured. "With Lance gone, I'm counting on you. Now go find Mr. Sinclair and make nice."

Her father's words trapped her neatly between making him happy and taking control of her own life. He waved his hand at her, shooing her away as he backed toward the living room, then turned and disappeared once again.

She was left with only the slightly false tones of dinner party laughter.

That is not fair. The words hovered on her lips. She didn't need a man to take care of her. She didn't *want* a man to take care of her.

"Dare I ask what that little tête-à-tête was about?"

She hadn't even heard Scott on the stairs.

Trinity turned slowly. "My father thinks I need a settled, old man like you to take care of me." God. What a bitch. She hated the sound of it, but the man brought out the best yet also the worst in her.

Scott's jaw tensed. "I don't consider myself old."

With her chin down, Trinity looked up through her lashes, and her eyes sparked. "I don't need a man to take care of me."

"I'd say you needed me badly a few minutes ago."

"That was sex." The words hissed off her tongue.

"Fucking good sex," Scott murmured, well aware of the open doors behind her.

She'd been hot, bothered, and pliable for him upstairs. All his. Yet in the space of five minutes, that woman was gone. As always, she was one step forward, two steps back. Dammit. He should never have shown his interest to Herman Green. Thinking himself a matchmaker, the gentleman only complicated the matter.

"You're worried you'll have to give up your sense of control." He thought it to be a reasonable comment. Control of the situation had been her issue right from the beginning.

Her nostrils flared, her lips pinching. "It isn't about control. It's about the fundamental basis of this relationship."

That pissed him off, yet he kept his voice low. "We don't have a relationship. You meet me, you fuck me. That's it."

"You didn't seem to mind it up in the bathroom just now."

Her spite hit him in the chest. "That was the best. I loved it." And damn her for denigrating it. "But I want more."

"Well, that's all you're going to get," she shot back. "Because I don't need you to take care of me."

"I don't fucking want to take care of you."

With one step, she got right up in his face, her scent all woman, all sex. "Then what's wrong with the way we had it?"

His temples started to ache. "Because it's not *all* I need, dammit." He feared the sharp edge of his tone carried in the high ceiling. Any moment, someone could exit the living room and catch them arguing.

Her answering whisper was just as harsh. "It's all I'm offering. It's all I *ever* offered."

Shit. She had a way of throwing a punch that knocked him in the heart, the head, and the balls all at once. "You just don't like giving up control of what, when, how and where."

He expected her to deny it. "So what?" she countered instead. "You knew when we started that's how I wanted it." She punctuated with a glare. "But you want what you want, and my feelings about it be damned."

"That's crap. I have always considered your feelings."

The tendons of her throat worked as she swallowed, her nostrils flaring as she took a breath, let it out, then finally . . . the words. "Take it or leave it."

"What the hell is that supposed to mean?"

"It means that we keep our affair a secret, the way it was before. And we have fun without all the messiness that goes with *more*."

"No. No fucking secrets."

She stepped away, her eyes unreadable. He could back down, he knew it. But he wanted more than to meet her in hotels, the backseat of his car, or even his bedroom if it meant she'd sneak away when the sun came up so she could change at her own place.

He flexed his fingers. There could be no compromise on this one. "No secrets." Then, in barely more than a murmur, he added, "take it or leave it."

She closed her eyes for a couple of a seconds longer than it took to blink. His heart stuttered in his chest like a gambler's just before

his bluff gets called. In those two seconds, he let his chance to re-
tract slip away.

"Then I leave it," she whispered.

OH God, oh God. Outside on the stone stoop, Trinity covered her
mouth in case a scream tried to escape. *You idiot.* It was her father's
voice. No, Lance's. Harper's. Scott. God, it was *all* the men in her
life telling her what to do.

Her cheeks were flushed yet her hands were cold as ice. She'd
left her wrap inside, and the cool March night pebbled her skin. Or
maybe it was the thought of never seeing him again.

Cold turkey. She shuddered. She couldn't handle the withdrawal
all over again. Staring at the door, she willed it to open, willed it to
be him changing his mind. She didn't want him to beg or grovel.
She simply wanted to go back to the way it had been Tuesday
morning when she'd woken in his arms.

The door didn't open. Scott didn't follow. Trinity knew she'd
lost. She'd gotten angry and reacted on the spur of the moment. Yet
that didn't make what she'd said any less true. She would never
stand securely on her own two feet if she didn't . . . stand.

Why did all the men in her life have to push–push–push? As if
she was a twit without a brain in her head? Because she allowed
them to, that's why. Men did what you *allowed* them to do.

As much as she wanted Scott, she couldn't let him push her into
a relationship she wasn't ready for.

BY Monday morning, Scott realized he was as stubborn as Trinity.
He hadn't told her he loved her. And all Sunday, instead of picking up
the phone, he'd checked his e-mail constantly, waiting for her capitu-
lation. He was unwilling to make the first move because, he told himself, he wanted a helluva lot more than to be her secret "boy toy."

Thank God Monday morning arrived with work to occupy his mind. He signed off on the final version of the 10K report for the SEC. It was now ready for Rudd's and the auditors' approval.

Despite Ron's grumbling over the bottom line, Scott hadn't given in. Ten minutes after he sent off the file, his company e-mail beeped, and he knew damn well who it was.

"We need to discuss," the e-mail read, "now. You do realize your job is on the line here."

Je–sus. Was that a threat? Scott cocked his head, staring at the computer screen. Could Rudd have sent the photos, finally making his demands today? *Change the bottom line or your job and your life are toast.*

Before he had time to analyze, Grace knocked on his jamb. "I need to talk to you." She closed the door, her lips thin, and her face more on the pale side than usual. Something was up.

Instead of taking a seat as she usually did, she leaned back against the doorframe. Sighing, she perused her stylish pumps, then focused on something out the window behind him. He put off his confrontation with Rudd for a few minutes. Scott felt like making the man sweat a little longer, because he sure as hell wasn't giving into any blackmail. Dealing with Grace gave him time to formulate a plan.

"What can I do for you, Grace?" He pushed back from his desk, crossing a foot over his knee and clasping his hands, affording her a relaxed demeanor.

"I don't know quite how to say this."

"Say it plainly then."

Finally, she raised her eyes. "I saw you Saturday night."

The back of his neck prickled.

"I went to use the powder room, and the door wasn't locked." She met his gaze steadily now, not flinching.

Fuck. He'd exposed Trinity. The things she'd said on Saturday might be true. He wanted what he wanted, her feelings and all else be damned. He lost his head around her every time.

"I apologize, Grace, for making you uncomfortable."

She shifted her weight from foot to foot, pushing straighter against the door. "It's an ethical issue. We've got the new contract with Green, and this presents a conflict of interest."

He tapped his fingers together. "There's no conflict. One thing has nothing to do with the other. I know how to separate business from pleasure." Trinity wanted "separate," yet he was too obsessed to actually accomplish it her way. The things she'd said that night were starting to make a lot of sense.

"You wouldn't do anything improper, but it's the *appearance*"— Grace stressed the word with a grimace—"of impropriety."

In her position, he'd be saying the same thing. Scott rose, looked out the window over the high-rises. The sky was dark, the clouds painted on like splotches of gray. Then he turned. "I understand your point. But there is no business impropriety."

Her jaw worked, then she flung herself across the room, grabbed the back of the chair, and her thoughts burst out in words. "How could you do that to yourself? Compromise your ethics? And with someone like her. She's a floozy, an airhead."

"Let's not get personal." Grace was overwrought. He couldn't allow himself to get angry. "The contract was signed and negotiated before I knew the woman's name," he reminded her. He hadn't compromised his ethics, but he had hurt Trinity.

Grace's fingers whitened on the chair. "She's made you lose your mind." She gulped air, catching her breath, and he was shocked at the vitriol rolling across her face. "How can you throw your career away on that *slut*?"

Everything inside him stilled. "Watch what you're saying. You're free to criticize my actions, but don't cross the line and pass judgment on her."

She worried her lip, then did a quick back and forth pace by the side of the chair. "But it's the ethics," she repeated, though she'd already revealed her envy.

An e-mail line echoed in his mind. *Do you really want to throw yourself away on a slut like her?* Grace's question was eerily similar. He studied her. "How many times have you seen me with Miss Green?" he queried.

Her gaze dropped to her shoe's pointed toe. "Saturday."

"That's bullshit."

If it wasn't, she would have looked at him. Instead, her shoe remained particularly interesting. "It's true."

"You've been following me and taking pictures." He was a moron. He'd thought she was acting oddly, but he'd written it off as the divorce. "You even used a visitor badge to do it."

Pressing her lips together, she didn't say a word.

Elton held a hand up in the side window by the door, and Scott waved him away. It was a closed door. When would they understand that meant to stay the fuck out?

"Grace. Don't you have anything to say for yourself?"

She gave him a mutinous scowl she reserved for recalcitrant staff. "What about you? On company property. I *saw* you."

"It wasn't on company time." He didn't feel an ounce of guilt about it. "Nor do I need to explain myself to you."

"But why *her*?"

He recognized the stark pain in her eyes. "Because." That was the thing about need and want, even love. There was no good reason it should be one person over another, yet it was.

"But I've been letting you know how I feel for months."

Shit. He knew that was coming. "We work together."

"That's the point. We work *so* well together." She rubbed her temples. "I thought you were done with her after the picture I sent of you outside the movies." Reaching back, she squeezed her neck muscles as if they ached. "Then you saw her the day of the contract meeting, and I knew it would start all over."

"So you began sending those e-mails again."

She blinked rapidly. "I can be what you want," she whispered. "If you like kinky, I can do that. I've seen you around her. I know what you want. I can give it to you. If you need a threesome, I'd be willing to try."

He took a step back. "That isn't what I'm looking for."

The thought of doing *anything* with Grace was horrific. There was only Trinity. She set him on fire, no one else. It wasn't the mystery or the excitement, her age, his time of life. It was Trinity herself, her voice, her laugh, her zeal for new experiences, her ability to savor every taste, sight, or sound.

"Scott."

The whole scene was like something out of an old *Twilight Zone* episode. He'd been zapped into another reality. "No. A personal relationship between us is out of the question."

She stared at him, two spots of color blooming on her cheeks. Tension rippled along her jaw as she clenched her teeth. "I'm not so sure Mr. Rudd would find it *fine* if he knew what you were doing in that hotel room with Herman Green's daughter."

Sonovabitch. Now she was pissed and out for revenge. He'd never have thought it of Grace, but giving her the upper hand in any way was a big fucking mistake. He nipped it in the bud. "Let's find out what he has to say together." Striding to the door, he yanked it open, then crooked his finger. "Follow me."

She hesitated, until she saw by the look in his eye that he'd drag her if she didn't come on her own. She followed like a lamb. He wanted to smack the walls as he passed, not sure whether he was angrier with himself or her. In Rudd's office, he held off slamming the door with his last modicum of control.

Ron stared. "What's *she* doing here?"

In normal practice, Scott would have castigated the man for the nasty tone used about one of his staff, but he felt the same animosity. "Grace may have something to add to the discussion."

Printed pages of the 10K lay scattered across Rudd's desk. Scott leaned in, jabbing them with his index finger. "These numbers are solid. There's nothing we can do to make them any better. So don't threaten me with my fucking job."

Ron again stared at Grace. "I don't think this is an appropriate conversation to have with your employee present."

Scott glanced over his shoulder. She clasped her hands, fingers laced. "Oh, it's appropriate." A stab of anger pierced his temple. Fuck what *he'd* done, she didn't have the right to try coercion on him. "Grace might have some light to shed on the subject." He waited. She shifted her weight from one foot to the other. "Well, Grace, cat got your tongue?"

He wanted to tear the words out of her. If Grace screwed him over now, so be it. There was nothing in the photos that would lead back to Trinity. He wouldn't let Grace's threat hang over him. Yet he had a feeling . . .

"Scott's correct." She concentrated on the papers spackling Rudd's desk. "I've analyzed the reserves. There isn't a penny to use. If we touch the M4 warranty reserve, the auditors and the SEC will be down our throats. We could get slapped not only with negligence, but fraud." She swallowed, then exhaled in a rush.

She didn't have the guts, or maybe she'd never meant the threat in the first place. He figured it was the latter.

Rudd gave only a one-word reply—"Fuck"—then subsided into his chair. "My ass is grass," he finally said.

"Last year is in the toilet, Ron, but this year is looking pretty damn good." Scott wondered why he was offering the man a bone. The company would be better off without Rudd's leadership, yet anything else felt like grinding the man into the dirt.

"Yeah." Ron sighed, then grabbed a pen and signed the document. A superfluous act since it got filed electronically, the signature was nevertheless a surrender.

Rather than belabor the victory, Scott exited, Grace in tow. The main hall between Accounting and the executives was empty. Scott stopped as the door closed, and they were alone.

"How did you know what went on in the hotel room?"

She sighed. "I didn't. I was hiding behind a potted plant"—the ubiquitous potted plant, he almost laughed—"and I saw the guy scribble something on a napkin. You picked it up after he was gone, then you both followed him to the elevators. I thought if I pushed your buttons a little, made you think I knew, I'd trick you into telling me what happened. I was so upset that you couldn't seem to leave her alone." She grabbed a great breath of air, then lowered her voice to a whisper. "And *I* couldn't seem to leave it alone. I just needed . . . something." The last word was merely a puff of air.

He almost understood. He felt the same about Trinity. He needed something she couldn't give, and it made him fucking crazy, too. But Grace had crossed the line. "So you thought you could blackmail me into"—he spread his hands—"what?"

She shook her head. "I wasn't going to do anything with the pictures. I didn't think about telling Mr. Rudd until . . . well, in your office. You were so immovable. I wanted to hurt you." The tears welled up in her voice, trembled on her lips, but she controlled them before they reached her eyes. "I lost my mind a little," she murmured. "The divorce." She swayed slightly, as if her footing wasn't sure. "You were so understanding."

He'd never been *that* understanding.

"I've screwed it all up." She swallowed again, hard.

Their working relationship was in the dumper. Anything else was never a possibility. "I want your resignation."

She clipped her badge off her jacket and laid it across his palm. "It'll be effective today."

That would put him in a bind with the year-end wrap-up. Scott didn't care. "And the visitor badge."

She blinked, looked at him a long moment, then reached into

her pocket and laid it on top of her personal badge. Damn, she'd been carrying it with her. At his suspicious glance, she shook her head. "I didn't plan it. I was leaving that night, and I saw you down in the garage with her. You went upstairs, and . . ." She blinked. "The way the two of you were, it wasn't business. Then I remembered the badge."

"How convenient." It sounded pretty damn premeditated.

She dipped her head. "I admit I didn't want you to find out I'd followed you. And I was always remembering that damn badge at the end of the day after I'd already locked up, but I kept forgetting to return it." He could almost hear her swallow. "I didn't use it again," she added.

He knew that. Mark had confirmed the ID never came up. Scott went on with his other demands. "The photos, Grace. Trash them." There were no guarantees, but he sensed she was done with her threats. "And lose my personal e-mail address." From time to time, he'd sent her files when he was working from home, just as he'd done with Elton, even Rudd. He'd get a new address and stick with work on company e-mail only. Live and learn.

"I will," she said, adding softly, "I think I need to take some time off." She bent her head and wiped her eyes. "I'm sorry. I don't know what happened to me."

Then she entered the Accounting Department. Holding the door open, he watched her disappear around a cubicle corner.

She went a little crazy, that's what happened. You said and did things you didn't mean because you couldn't get what you wanted, and you were suddenly willing to do anything without even realizing how completely *off* it was.

He was no better than Grace. As Trinity had accused, he'd put his own needs above hers. He wouldn't accept her terms, unwilling even to consider a compromise. And like a child who didn't get the Christmas gift he'd asked for, Scott tossed aside what she offered as if it were the crumpled wrapping paper.

Yet he would never be satisfied with less than her total commitment. He would always be wanting more from her than she could give. In a way, love and passion with Trinity would end up being as big a struggle as they had been with Katy.

He wasn't sure he had the guts to go through all that again.

21

" 'DON'T worry about him, he's an asshole'?" After reading aloud, Mr. Wanamaker looked at her over the rim of his glasses. "You haven't been in the work world for long, Miss Green, but I would have thought you understood that you don't CC vendors on e-mails where you refer to them as assholes. It's just not done."

Trinity gripped the armrests of the chair in Mr. W.'s office. Anthony Ackerman stood by the window, eerily like that scene weeks ago when she'd downloaded the bank data twice.

It's just not done. Mr. W. sounded like her mother.

Her Sunday had been miserable, Scott filling her mind. She wanted to beg him to forget everything she'd said, yet nothing had changed. They were at a stalemate. He couldn't be satisfied with what they had; she couldn't give *more* and maintain her own sense of self. Or hell, at least *define* that for herself. Then there was Daddy. He'd been miffed she'd left the dinner party right after he'd told her not to mess things up with Scott. Yet despite sleeping badly

Sunday night, she wasn't a second late Monday morning. Her job was all she had now.

Yet little more than half a day into the workweek, Mr. Wanamaker had called her on the carpet. "I didn't refer to him as an asshole, sir."

Wanamaker turned the paper toward her and stabbed. "It says right here. From Trinity Green to Inga Rice, CC *our vendor*." His voice rose with the last two words, and the sheet jiggled so much she couldn't make out a single line item.

Trinity gritted her teeth. "I'm afraid there's been some mistake, because I didn't send that e-mail."

With an exaggerated sigh, Mr. Wanamaker raised an eyebrow at Anthony as if to say, "What the heck are you going to do when on top of being an idiot, she's a liar *and* the boss's daughter?"

Well, she wasn't a liar, she was a victim once again. "Somehow an error has been made."

Anthony jumped in, cutting her off. "Inga assures me it was an honest mistake, that you accidentally hit Reply All when you didn't mean to. Happens to the best of us."

Well, it didn't *happen* to her. *Someone* had done it deliberately, obviously after Trinity had talked to the man at the beginning of last week and straightened out the issue he'd created with Inga. For now, though, she had Mr. Wanamaker to pacify. "I did *not* send that e-mail, accidental or otherwise"—she gave Mr. W. her best quelling look when he opened his mouth—"however, I realize that *our* vendor needs reassurance and that's the most important thing right now. I'll take care of it immediately."

Mr. Wanamaker couldn't resist tacking on his own two cents. "It's going to be a tricky tap dance. He's angry enough to cancel the order."

Trinity smiled. "Leave it to me, Mr. Wanamaker, I'll handle the situation with the necessary tact."

Her CFO, who on Saturday had been *Paul* instead of *Mr. Wana-maker*, slid his glasses all the way to the end of his nose, and something flickered in his eyes. A little bit of respect? "Thank you, Miss Green. I appreciate you putting your utmost attention to the matter."

She thought of telling him that Inga had sent the e-mail to make Trinity look bad. First, however, she couldn't prove it, and second, you didn't blame your subordinates because the buck stops with you. It was better that she'd refuted his charge without impugning anyone else. She'd take care of Inga herself.

"I assure you I take this job very seriously." She went on, "In fact, I have a list of improvements I'd like to implement with Mr. Ackerman's permission." Then she gave Wanamaker the nod. "And yours." She'd worked on the list all morning. It kept her from thinking about Scott, from missing him, from aching inside, but primarily because she *wanted* to do a good job no matter what anyone else thought of her.

She turned to Anthony. "May I use your office to make the phone call?"

Wanamaker made the decision. "You can use my office, Miss Green. Take all the time you need." On Saturday, she'd been *Trinity*. Then again, the use of *Miss Green* seemed deferential, as if he believed she might be able to pacify their vendor, and, in fact, do it well. He crooked his finger. "Ackerman, follow me."

Alone, Trinity sat at Mr. W.'s desk and picked up the phone. Her plan was simple. She explained the incident was a practical joke gone awry, one she'd deal with in her own way, assured her vendor no one at Green would refer to him as an asshole, nor even think it, least of all her as they'd worked so well together, and she hoped to continue with the excellent working relationship.

In the end, she had *him* apologizing for making an issue.

She didn't take blame, didn't grovel, and the man still came around to her way of thinking. Wow. All her life she'd *groveled* to make sure people liked her. That's why keeping Scott a secret had been so important, because for once she didn't have to grovel. She didn't get judged. She got to be naughty without being bad. She'd never had to compromise herself with Scott. For him, she'd been real, asked for what she wanted. Loved it.

The only thing he'd ever asked for was *more*. She'd assumed *more* meant giving away pieces of herself to satisfy him.

Yet Scott hadn't been the one she'd compromised herself with. That she'd done for Inga, practically begging the woman to like her. The harsh reality was that some people were *never* going to like you. Inga was one of them. Trinity either had to put up with it. Or quit.

"I will *not* let her take this job away from me," she whispered through clenched teeth.

She was not going to sit still for being a victim or an idiot one minute longer.

Stabbing the hook flash with her finger, she then dialed Inga's number. "Wanamaker's office. In here. Now," she said without giving Inga a chance to say more than hello.

"I'm in the middle of—"

Trinity cut her off. "I said *now*." Then she jabbed the hook flash one more time and put the phone down.

The door opened. Inga smiled and sauntered over to the chair. Seating herself, she crossed her legs. "What can I do for you, Trinity?"

Smarmy little *b-i-t-c-h*. "You doctored that e-mail and somehow sent it from my address."

Inga raised one blonde eyebrow. "I did not."

Trinity couldn't remember what happened that day. They'd e-mailed, she'd gone to Inga's cube, then . . . to the restroom? Could Inga have hightailed it over to Trinity's cube? Then again, she could have done the deed on any day in between. How she'd accomplished it didn't matter. "You realize we're going to make each other miserable until one of us either quits or dies."

Inga smirked. "I've got staying power."

Trinity plucked a pen from the holder and twirled it on the blotter. "Even if I'm gone, you're not going to get the job."

"I can do it better than you." Inga glowered.

Trinity merely smiled in return. "No, you can't. Because you turn the department into armed camps where people tiptoe around each other depending upon who's pissed you off that day."

"They *love* me."

"They tolerate you." Christina was afraid of her, Boyd wouldn't touch her with a ten-foot pole even if she was a tall, blonde goddess with stupendous breasts, and the AP girls were sweet as pie so they didn't accidentally incur the wrath of Inga.

Inga's eye twitched. "Anthony wouldn't know what to do without me."

"You're right." Trinity leaned forward. "But *Anthony* will never make you supervisor because you're too divisive." She tipped her chin up. "How long was the job posted?"

Inga didn't so much as open her mouth.

Trinity answered for her. "Three weeks. And you applied right away, didn't you?" The former, she knew for a fact, the latter she guessed at.

"I did not." Inga toyed with the arm of the chair as if she couldn't sustain the lie and full eye contact at the same time.

"I got the job," Trinity whispered, "because I know how to get people to work together."

Inga's jaw tensed.

"I had our little vendor eating out of my hand by the time I hung up," Trinity continued. "I will be here long after you're a faded memory. And until you go, I will be your worst nightmare. You'll hate getting up in the mornings because you'll have to see me"—she tapped her chest—"every day."

Inga licked her lips, and Trinity noticed a smear of lipstick on her teeth.

"Or," Trinity beamed, "we can start working together. The

choice is yours. War"—she flipped out one palm, then the other—
"or a cease-fire. Which do you prefer?"

Inga dragged in a big breath through flared nostrils. "I'm not
ever going to like you."

"I don't need you to like me." Trinity was proud she actually
meant that from the pit of her stomach. "I just need you to start
working *with* me instead of against me."

Inga tipped her head and regarded Trinity for a long pause.
"Why don't you just fire me instead?"

"Because you know your stuff, you're a good worker, and the
company needs you." Inga would have been supervisor if she had a
better temperament. "Why don't we give it six months? If the
cease-fire works, we can make it a permanent truce."

"Life," Inga muttered, "could be easier than it is right now, I
suppose."

"We could both like coming to work every day."

"Maybe." Inga rose. They didn't shake on the deal. Trinity
wasn't sure if they'd ever make it to a total cessation of hostilities.

Then Inga turned with her hand on the doorknob. "Why didn't
you tell them I'd sent the e-mail? They would have had to believe
the boss's daughter."

Trinity popped the pen she'd been playing with back in Mr.
Wanamaker's pencil holder. "Because it's *our* battle, not theirs."

Lips pressed together, Inga considered that a brief moment.
"You're right." She threw open the door, her usual heavy footing
rattling the dividers as she returned to her cubicle.

Trinity felt good, powerful. With a shock, she realized that she
felt powerful without Scott feeding it to her. She'd taken charge.
Inga didn't like her. Inga would *never* like her, and that was okay. In
the past, her actions were based on what other people would think.
The real Trinity Green had been just a reflection of what everyone
else believed about her. For the first time, she'd done what needed to
be done rather than what she hoped would make someone like her.

She'd wanted to be just like her mother, a lady everyone adored. The problem was, in trying to emulate her mother, she'd never learned to be her own person. Just as she'd let Inga dictate her actions, she'd also let fear of her father's harsh judgment direct her. Until Harper, she'd never dated a man her daddy hadn't approved. She'd put on a face so that men would think she was perfect, adorable, wonderful. She'd actually married Harper not merely because of Faith, but as a first step in trusting her own judgment. Of course, when her marriage turned into a disaster, she'd fallen back on old habits, trying to please Daddy. She'd kept Scott a secret so that no one, not her father, nor Faith, not Josie, not Verna, could tell her what she was doing was wrong.

Needing other people's approval had to end now. She'd made a great start with Inga, but it had to continue with her father.

Upstairs in his outer office, Verna's hand hovered over the phone just as she caught sight of Trinity.

"Is he alone?" Trinity asked.

"He's alone," Verna confirmed, "but I'm not sure he's in a good mood."

Trinity put up her hand. "His mood doesn't matter. I can handle it." She couldn't be Daddy's little girl forever. She had to grow up. And her father had to listen to some things he simply didn't want to hear.

In the inner sanctum, cigar smoke choked the room. "Daddy, you're not supposed to smoke in here. It's illegal."

He rose and opened the window, then held the cigar just outside. "There, now I'm legal." He saluted her, blowing out a stream of smoke. "To what do I owe the pleasure?" Yet he didn't sound terribly pleased. He obviously hadn't gotten over his annoyance that she'd left the party early.

Trinity plunged ahead anyway. She was done trying to find the right time to tell Daddy something so that he wouldn't get mad at her. "I haven't been completely honest about Scott."

Her father cocked his head, and a glimmer of disappointment grew in his eyes. "If it's something I don't want to hear, don't tell me."

"I knew him before he came to the plant that day."

"*Knew* him?" He blew out a stream of smoke and stared at her through it.

"We've been dating for a few weeks." She didn't say what they'd really been doing. That wasn't her father's business.

"While you were married?" His voice rose a note.

"While I was proceeding with the *divorce*."

He grumbled something she couldn't make out.

"I didn't hear that, Daddy."

He grumbled once more, then raised his voice. "Why all these secrets? I don't understand." He snorted. "It reminds me of your brother and all *his* secrets."

That stung. She *wasn't* like Lance. "I didn't feel that I needed to tell you. We met after I found out about Harper." And suddenly she felt like she was overexplaining, begging for approval. "My relationship with Scott is my own, Daddy."

He rubbed out the butt on the sill and shut the window. "You could have told *me*." He patted his chest. "I'm your father. I care about you."

"And you think I need someone older and wiser to take care of me. I don't. I have a job, I'm taking care of myself. I want to be independent, not waiting around for my *daddy* to approve of the men I date." She held up her finger when her father opened his mouth. "Yes, I made a mistake with Harper, but I've learned from that mistake. I'm not going to do the same thing with Scott." But then Scott wasn't the same kind of man at all. "And speaking of mistakes, that brings me to Lance."

He blew out the last vestige of smoke through his nostrils. "I don't want to talk about Lance."

"Well, we're going to talk about Lance."

He reached for another cigar. "Don't dictate to me in my own office, young lady."

Last Saturday, earlier this morning, even an hour ago, his tone would have made her tremble. But she *was* a new woman with a new attitude. "Lance made a mistake. I've made mistakes. But you can't throw us away because we messed up. I wouldn't throw you away."

"I never make mistakes." He punctuated by clipping the tip off his cigar.

"Yes, you do make mistakes, but I love you anyway. I'll love you no matter what." She took a deep inhale and exhale. "And I want the same from you. Forgive me for screwing up with Harper, for being less than truthful about Scott, and love me anyway."

He stared at her for the longest time without a word. Then finally he tossed the cigar down unlit and leaned both fists on his desk. Moisture shimmered in his eyes. "I do love you, sweetie," he whispered. "How could you think otherwise?"

Because she'd always had to be Daddy's perfect little girl. In her own eyes as much as in his. She knew it was a battle she would have to fight with herself, and him, for a long time to come. In the scheme of things, this was a tiny step, but it was a step between them, and that's what counted.

He would, however, like the rest of what she had to say even less. "Now you need to do the same thing for Lance."

He was so still, so silent.

But she had to push this issue with him, not for Lance, but for her father. "If something happens to him or to you"—God forbid—"you'll lament all these wasted months. Don't let them become years."

"You know what he did. How can you ask me to forgive him?"

"I'm only asking you to talk to him. Say whatever needs to be said, and *then* see if you can forgive him. Give him a chance."

Her father wagged his head and plopped down in his chair. "It won't make any difference. He's never going to change."

"He might not." She perched on the edge of the desk and reached for his hand. "But *you* need to make a change so *you* don't regret it. That's what I worry about."

Turning his hand palm up, he held onto her. "He severely disappointed me."

What he meant was that Lance had *hurt* him deeply. Trinity empathized. "Maybe somewhere along the way, you disappointed him, too. Maybe I did. Who knows? But he's your son and my brother, and cutting him out completely hurts *us*, not just him."

He closed his fingers around hers. "I'll do it for you."

She pulled back. "No. *Not* for me. For *yourself*."

Closing his eyes, he rubbed his temples until finally he looked at her again. "You're right. It's been wearing on me. But things can never be the same."

"We don't want them to be the same." She sat in the chair opposite. "We want them to be better."

He wagged his head. "I think your hopes are too high."

"All I care about is that you try. The rest is up to Lance. I love you." She was ever hopeful Lance would see the light.

Just as she needed to see the light—about Scott. He'd never asked her to be anyone other than she was. He'd simply asked her to give more of herself to him. Was that such a bad thing? Did it compromise her ability to be her own person?

Only if *she* let it. Scott had never been the problem. Her need to please other people had been.

Will the real Trinity Green stand up? Trinity stood. "And now, Daddy, I have to see a man about an apology."

That man would be Scott. Running out on him Saturday night had been the biggest mistake of her life.

THE envelope arrived at the office by courier, hand delivered near four o'clock Monday afternoon. Scott signed for it. No sender was listed, yet turning it over, his sixth sense screamed it was from her. Closing his office door, he leaned back, pulling the tab. As he shook the envelope, a train ticket slid out, his name blazing on it.

A ridiculous, giddy smile rose to his lips. He thought he'd fucked up too badly to be forgiven, yet she was giving him his train fantasy. Then the meaning of it dawned on him.

Trinity wanted their relationship to return to its original footing. Fantasy sex. Games. Emotional distance. He had to laugh even as he ached inside. The man traditionally wanted the hot sex and emotional distance. They'd reversed roles.

He could never ride the surface of a relationship with her. He'd done it for too many years with Katy.

He made it to the depot in San Jose by 6:05, a few minutes prior to departure. Traffic had been hell, but thank God most commuters took either the light rail or Caltrain so he didn't need to fight for a parking spot. The southbound train rumbled on the track, the platform deserted except for a mother bustling two children and a collapsible stroller through the middle door of the second car. Diesel fuel laced with the scent of damp concrete faintly perfumed the night air. Since he didn't have luggage, he boarded with a minimum of fuss.

Seating was unassigned, a free-for-all, but the compartments were sparsely filled. Starting at the front, he worked his way back through the aisles and the double-decker dining area.

He found her in the last car, huddled in a companion row of four seats facing each other. Her blonde hair piled in a knot on her crown, she buried her nose in a book. In the otherwise deserted train car, he took the window seat facing her and waited for her to drop the book. She didn't.

The cover displayed a torrid clinch of naked body parts. There might have been scarves twined about a pair of hands, but he couldn't determine without closer perusal. Crossing her legs, calling attention to the slit in her skirt, she flipped a page.

And ignored him. The train belched, shuddered, jerked lightly, then rolled out of the station. Scott absorbed himself in her every detail as the night began to race by.

The three open buttons of her emerald green blouse revealed a significant amount of cleavage. The calf-length skirt was circumspect, but the black stockings were a promise, and her left high heel swung back and forth on her toes. Keeping her nose in the book, she leaned forward to slide a hand slowly down her leg, propped the shoe back on her heel, then slid all the way back up, lifting the hem of her skirt enough to make his cock jump.

She would always do *that* to him. He didn't know how to convince her they could be so much more. The fantasy would never be enough. No matter how badly he wanted her, he needed more.

Lifting her eyes to his over the top of her book for a brief glimpse, she then returned to the pages. Two, three times, she glanced up, each a little longer, her gaze gliding over his body. Finally, she dropped the book to her lap and began to play with a button as she read, tracing one finger idly down her chest to disappear in the V of her blouse. He wanted to follow with his tongue. Up, up, up again, to the hollow of her throat, his gaze tracked every move until his breath came faster and his blood pressure rose. His pants got tighter. She leaned forward, slipping her hand from her knee to the bottom of the skirt's slit, where she stopped to caress her ankle. Her blouse fell open, giving him an eyeful of her breasts and the lacy bra that barely covered her nipples.

She began to straighten, shifted her body slightly, and the book fell from her lap. She met his gaze with an *ooh* of dismay.

Scott bent to pick it up, snapping it shut, then slid into the seat next to her. Raising the armrest so it no longer separated them, he let his thigh come to rest against her. The train rocked, and she swayed toward him.

Handing her the book, his fingers lingered on hers. "I'm afraid you lost your place." He needed her to find *him*.

"And it was such a good place, too." She sighed. "They were about to . . . ," she trailed off, then smiled, her lashes lowered seductively. "Well, it was something naughty, so I really shouldn't say."

"Show me the spot, and I'll read it myself." He would write them a fucking new story with the ending he wanted.

She hugged the racy novel to her breasts. "I *couldn't* do that. I don't even know you."

"Oh, but I do believe we've met somewhere before."

"I don't think so," she murmured, her voice low, husky, tempting. "I'd have remembered you."

"Let me introduce myself." *Let me start over with you and make everything right.*

She put her hand over his mouth, and his brain misfired at the light scent of her fruity lotion, her soft touch, and her gorgeous eyes.

"Let *me* introduce myself." All her seductive flirtiness vanished. "I'm Trinity Green. My husband cheated on me two months ago, and I knew in that moment that I'd divorce him." She lifted one corner of her mouth in what he could only hope was a smile. "I used to want men to tell me how pretty I was, what a perfect little girl I was, the dream wife, the dream girlfriend."

"You are." And so much more.

She shushed him with a finger to her own lips. "When my husband left me . . ." She fanned the pages of her book as if looking for an answer in its words. "When he left, I decided I was going to indulge in all the things I'd missed. Good food, good wine." She saluted him with an imaginary glass. "But most of all I was going to enjoy good sex." She captured his gaze. "I met you that same night."

Scott forgot to breathe.

"And ever since, I've been trying to get you to tell me how perfect sex with me is, that I'm the best you've ever had."

"You're that and more—" He cut himself off at her look.

She tipped her head, regarding him a long moment that stretched his nerves. "But," she said, "I finally realized that I was doing exactly the same thing with you as I'd done with my husband. Looking for my perfect reflection in your eyes."

She *was* perfect for him. In every way, not just sex. But she was trying to tell him something, or maybe she was trying to tell herself.

She curled her feet beneath her and shifted back into the corner of her seat. "It isn't true that beauty is in the eye of the beholder. My own beauty is in *here*." She rubbed her temple. "What counts is how *I* feel about myself. I'm the one I have to try the hardest to please, not everyone else." Reaching for his hand, she lifted it to her lips and placed a sweet kiss on his knuckles. "I wanted to keep you a secret so that no one could say I was wrong for the things I did with you. So that no one could make me feel ashamed."

His chest hurt, and he closed his eyes. The one thing he couldn't handle was her shame, when everything they'd done together was so right. Then he felt her touch along his jaw.

"But I figured out I was seeing it all wrong," she murmured. "The shame was in letting other people's opinions matter when what we had between us was so hot and so beautiful. Even Norman." Her breath whispered across his cheek.

Something started to melt inside him.

"The only thing wrong about what happened with Norman was *why* I did it—to punish you. Two people who care shouldn't resort to punishing each other."

He opened his eyes. She beamed him a gorgeous smile that kickstarted his adrenalin. "Forgive me?" she asked.

"There is nothing you've done that needs forgiving."

The blue of her eyes softened. "I am ready for a relationship, Scott."

"What kind of relationship?" Scott put his fingers to her lips before she could answer him. "Wait. Don't say a word."

Her eyes widened.

"My name's Scott Sinclair. I'm forty-five, I have two beautiful daughters in college, and a couple of years ago, after twenty-two years of marriage, my wife walked out because I put my job and my career above my family and my home." Removing his touch from her mouth, Scott leaned close, inhaling as if he needed to gather her scent deep inside. "I'm not perfect at relationships, and I've made a lot of mistakes."

Trinity knew all that about him, but just as he'd let her say everything she needed to, she had to allow him the same, when God, all she wanted was to throw herself on him.

He touched her chin and tipped her head to meet his gaze. "I bulldozed over your feelings, always demanding more." Stroking a lock of hair, he tucked it behind her ear, his caress so sweet and gentle. "It's hard admitting aloud that I was a total jerk Saturday night, but I wanted you to walk into the living room and make some sort of open declaration to your father. Tell him you were mine. It felt like shit that you wanted to keep what we had a secret."

She parted her lips, but he wouldn't let her say it, stopping her with a tilt of his chin. "Don't apologize for that either. I never gave you the chance to deal with your divorce, your father, me. I rushed everything. I rushed what happened with Norman."

She leaned in to nuzzle his ear. "It's nice to have a guy take all the blame." No one had ever done that for her before. Scott had given her so many firsts. "But it does take two to screw things up, you know. I've made mistakes, treated you badly, and I'm not perfect. I won't *ever* be perfect."

He cupped her jaw and brought her gaze back to his. "I don't want a perfect dream girl. I don't need a dream. I need a real woman, imperfections and all."

It was just what her heart needed to hear.

He tipped his head back, closing his eyes, then finally stroked with the lightest touch down her cheek to the corner of her mouth. "But I can't be your hot little secret anymore."

Her heart stopped, then thumped hard, fast. "I don't want a secret."

"And I don't want *just* a relationship."

This time her heart beat its way into her throat. "What do you want then?" *Please don't leave, not now, not when I've figured out I can do this right with you.*

"I'm in love with you. Are you prepared to deal with that?"

Oh God, she could breathe again. She wanted to laugh and cry at the same time. Instead, she held his hand to her cheek. "Don't scare me like that. I thought you'd *sayonara, baby* me."

He laughed but it had the slightest edge to it, as if he were remembering her *sayonara, baby* voice mail. "I told you I'd never be the one to end this," he said.

"Yeah, I know, but I'm struggling to find myself, and for a second there I didn't think you'd put up with that."

Turning, he kissed her palm. "Trust me, I'm a helluva lot older than you, and I'm still struggling."

The train swayed on the track, the iron wheels a steady shush outside the window. The heating was on a little too high, but Trinity still wanted to burrow into him.

"I've never been in love before," she whispered. "I'm not sure what it feels like." Was it the ache in her chest when she'd left him the other night? Or the way she wanted to e-mail him a thousand times a day? Or how his scent, man, soap, aftershave, made her feel safe yet hot all over?

"Sometimes it feels like you're dying," he said.

Like the three weeks she'd gone cold turkey and kept telling herself she was fine even though the fear of never hearing his voice again was . . . like dying. "I've been afraid of *thinking* I'm in love and finding out—" She cut herself off before she even finished the thought and sat up straight next to him. "I've been afraid of *every-*

thing. What other people think of me. Upsetting my father. Doing a bad job. Being a bad friend. Afraid you're going to ask too much of me." She took his hand in hers. "But you make me want to stop being afraid and give you everything."

With a hand at her nape, he pulled her close for a lingering kiss. "I will always ask for too much. Because I want so much."

His smile felt so good, her heart actually ached with it. "You make me love you, Scott. I don't have a choice."

"Good, because neither do I. With you, I feel more alive than I have in years, and it makes me a little crazy wanting to get inside you." He glanced down. "In a metaphorical sense."

She laughed, slightly giddy with his closeness. "You didn't mean that metaphorically." But he did bring up the age thing earlier, and really, it wasn't something they could ignore forever. Especially after the nasty thing she'd said in her father's foyer. "I apologize for calling you old. I was angry with something my father said, and I took it out on you." He nodded his acceptance, and she went on. "But does it bother you that I'm closer to your daughters' ages than I am to yours?"

"I love my daughters, but I'm *in* love with you. Age doesn't make a difference." Then he leaned his forehead against hers to whisper, "Now, about how fucking kinky you are. *That* makes a definite difference."

Her heart turned over at his words. He loved her. It was incredibly scary yet amazingly wonderful. "You turn everything back to sex," she teased.

"And I always will because you make me crazy enough to want to try every new thing I can think of."

"See?" She smiled. "You're all about sex." She put a finger to the tip of his nose. "But will your daughters get over me being a ditz that night at the restaurant? I mean, first impressions." She pursed her lips. "Not that I'd give you up even if they hated me."

With a hand on her hip, he hitched her closer to his body heat.

"I'll never let you give me up. Once was enough. I couldn't take it again." He pecked her mouth. "But my girls love me, they want me to be happy, and you make me happy, so they'll come around."

His words cocooned her like a fleece blanket. "You make me happy," she whispered, then poked him in the chest. "But don't think you're going to get out of doing naughty things with me wherever and whenever I choose"—she dropped her voice seductively— "even with *whomever* watching us." Craning over the top of the seat, she glanced through the rest of the car. Empty. "So"—she nuzzled his neck—"do you think anyone would notice if we got a little kinky back here?"

"I'm not passing up my train fantasy, baby."

"I can give you that." She licked the seam of his lips, loving his taste. "And a whole lot more." Whatever he wanted. She wanted it, too.

Jasmine Haynes has been penning stories for as long as she's been able to write. Storytelling has always been her passion. With a bachelor's degree in accounting from Cal Poly San Luis Obispo, she has worked in the high-tech Silicon Valley for the last twenty years and hasn't met a boring accountant yet! Well, maybe a few. She and her husband live with their cat Eddie (short for Eddie Munster, get the picture) and Star, the mighty moose-hunting dog (if she weren't afraid of her own shadow). Jasmine's pastimes, when not writing her heart out, are hiking in the Redwoods and taking long walks on the beach.

Jasmine also writes as Jennifer Skully and JB Skully. She loves to hear from readers. Please e-mail her at skully@skullybuzz.com or visit her website www.skullybuzz.com. Her newsletter subscription is skullybuzz-subscribe@yahoogroups.com.